W9-BQT-013

To Michael
Thanks for all your help. It's
great to work with you
Jack Partridge
6/17/08

Straight Pool

By

J·J·Partridge

A CHUKAR BOOK

A Chukar Book
Published by Chukar Books, a division of Gryphon Corporation
First Printing, May, 2008
10 9 8 7 6 5 4 3 2 1

® REGISTERED TRADEMARK – MARCA REGISTRADA
Library of Congress Control Number 2008904252
ISBN – 0977307814
Printed in the United States of America by Meridian Printing
Book design by Don Paulhus Design

PUBLISHER'S NOTE

This is a work of fiction. Names, characters, places, and incidents either are the product of the author's imagination or are used fictitiously, and any resemblance to actual persons, living or dead, business establishments, events, or locales is entirely coincidental.

BOOKS ARE AVAILABLE AT QUANTITY DISCOUNTS WHEN USED TO PROMOTE PRODUCTS OR SERVICES. FOR MORE INFORMATION, PLEASE E-MAIL CHUKAR BOOKS, A DIVISION OF GRYPHON CORPORATION AT INFO@CHUKARBOOKS.COM

Praise for *Carom Shot* by J J Partridge

"Algy Temple is the kind of fictional friend you'd want watching your back, whether in a dark alley, a boardroom, or a courthouse. *Carom Shot* is a terrific debut that brings old Providence alive from the church steeples to the cracks between the cobblestones."

— MARK ARSENAULT, author of *Gravewriter*

"Mystery-aficionados are always searching for a new detective: we gobble up stories faster than writers can write them. Algy Temple is a wonderful addition to the ranks of sleuths."

— *Prime Time Magazine*

"*Carom Shot* is a good old fashioned crime novel, set in a familiar location, but with an imaginary character to the city."

— *Providence Monthly*

"A unifying factor for all the novel's characters is what Partridge calls the 'old world murkiness' of the city of Providence, which he captures so well in descriptions of both the physical setting... and the emotional atmosphere."

— *East Side Monthly*

"*Carom Shot*... is a good read."

— BILL REYNOLDS, *The Providence Journal*

"*Carom Shot* is a solidly plotted traditional mystery with enough twists -and- reversals to appeal to puzzle-lovers. An engaging protagonist."

— ROBERT KNIGHTLY, editor of *Queens Noir* and contributor to *Brooklyn Noir* and *Best American Mystery Stories of 2007*

Someone once wrote that if you
believe that man is at the mercy of Fate,
then life is tragedy, with the end of the story
inevitable — and maybe predictable —
from the beginning.

I prefer to believe that the bad among us
will inevitably be unhappy, the good will be
rewarded, and most of us, with mixed fortunes,
will survive the confusion.

PROLOGUE

Along Block Island Sound, a mackerel sky is a washed-out blue sky screened by scattered, greenish-gray clouds imitating the markings of the most common of coastal fish.

On September 21, 1938, Westerly, Rhode Island awoke to the familiar cloud pattern masking a warming, silvery sun. The air was sea-tanged, bringing the prospect of relief from a dreariness that dogged the coast since Labor Day. For residents with the luxury of time or the where-with-all to ignore the grind of the lingering Depression, the day offered a welcomed opportunity for postponed gardening, a last picnic on the sandy spit of Napatree Point, or a round of golf at the town's new attraction, Windmere Country Club.

Not everyone along the Sound shared the buoyancy of that luminous dawn. Tradition held that a mackerel sky at daybreak is a harbinger of abrupt weather change. To grizzled fishermen in rubberized waders heading out from Little Narragansett Bay, to farmers on belching Ford tractors haying in fields that ran to salt ponds, and among self-described 'old timers' on worn benches at the docks of Avondale and Stonington, the cloud formation and the yellowish tinge to the horizon 'weren't right.'

And what happened to the gulls?

By early afternoon, the temperature was near eighty and cumulus clouds rolled in from the southeast. A freshening breeze tossed the shrubs, willows, and silver maples that rimmed salt ponds and flattened dune grasses on barrier beaches. In the rough at Windmere Country Club, blooming goldenrod swayed, thistles released silky parachutes, and red sumac and scarlet poison ivy leaves rustled with the scratchiness of autumn; on the clubhouse veranda, globe light fixtures caught the wind and began to spin in slow, ever-widening orbits.

Not surprisingly for a weekday after season, few members arrived at the golf course during the morning hours and only a handful more ventured out after lunch when the wind became squally. By late afternoon, with the sky crowded by ranks of rapidly moving clouds, the clamshell surfaced parking lot in front of the clubhouse's canopied pier was empty. Inside the twin-turreted, shingled building, the staff was thinking it might stay that way: the Twilight Golf League, the Club's midweek mainstay of activity, had been cancelled because many members would be attending tonight's Masonic Lodge annual dinner at the Ocean House in Watch Hill. A hand-lettered card tacked to the clubhouse's entrance doors informed prospective diners that only 'light fare' would be available that evening. When intermittent sprinkles became a misty rain and then a hard downpour, the cook, the two waitresses, the busboy, even the club manager, considered the possibility of an early night. Maybe, they'd be home in time for *Amos 'n Andy*.

Meanwhile, despite the beating wind and waves splashing noisily against yellow oak pilings that anchored the clubhouse in the shallow waters of Wynomet Pond, they tended to the ordinary. Joey McAndrew, a gangly, tow-headed twelve year old, in his busboy's uniform of starched white jacket, white shirt, black bow tie, and black trousers, and the waitresses, Mrs. Babcock and Mrs. Gavitt, solidly built women in white blouses, aprons over black skirts, and starched lace caps, busied themselves in the commodious dining room, setting tables and folding linen napkins into 'bishop hats.' In the kitchen, Mrs. Kenyon continued her preparations of the promised 'light fare'—New England quahog chowder, choice of cold baked ham or sliced chicken plates garnished with side dishes of green beans, last-of-the-summer tomatoes, and potato salad—while water boiled on the new Garland gas range for a rice pudding dessert. Behind the service bar, the manager, thought by the staff to be officious—Mrs. Gavitt told her husband that the manager's 'arse could crack walnuts'—wiped stemware and beer glasses, seemingly miffed that with the regular bartender being called to the Ocean House event, it had been left to him to mix cocktails and serve drinks.

By five-thirty, with no reservations called in and the weather laying siege to the coast, the manager reluctantly agreed to Mrs. Kenyon's request to tune the Philco console radio at the bar to WJAR in Providence. As dance music resonated in the dining room, Mrs. Babcock, finished with preparations, found her place in her lending library copy of *Rebecca*, while Mrs. Gavitt flipped through *The Saturday Evening Post* and Joey McAndrew started on his homework. Despite screeches and moans from the swirling wind and the crash of waves that sent barely felt vibrations to the floor above, the staff remained unconcerned. The clubhouse had been constructed fifteen feet—the exact number was in the Club's brochure—above the high water level of the pond, and they were all, except the manager, Westerly natives accustomed to autumn's gales. They were confident that the clubhouse, the only sizeable structure built on the shoreline from Watch Hill to Narragansett Pier since Roosevelt's inauguration, would rebuff any storm. As for Joey, well, who was he to complain? After caddying at the Club all summer—his freckled face retained its tan—he had the coveted after-school job of dining room busboy, with a guaranteed take home of five dollars a week!

After the six o'clock news, Mrs. Kenyon, always the most independent of the staff, left the kitchen to cajole the manager into an early closing. Nobody would be coming out, she complained; the newsreader on the radio said the weather would likely worsen. The manager was unmoved. Suppose members arrived and found their clubhouse shuttered. That would not 'do.' It was Windmere Country Club's first full season and members had been promised the availability of evening dining through September and weekends through Columbus Day. A stern 'we'll wait and see' quieted Mrs. Kenyon's objections.

Moments later, after a blast of wind tattooed rain against the windows separating the dining room from the veranda, the lights flickered, the radio became static, both went off, and resumed. Mrs. Babcock muttered that hadn't happened before, not once all summer, and despite the lights back on and music, now a Dorsey tune, filling the dining room, an itchy anxiety grew. Joey left his school books and accompanied by a cannonade of thunder, walked across the dining room to the rattling, rain spattered windows. He could hear, could almost feel, the 'boomers' pounding the barrier beach that protected Wynomet Pond from the boiling ocean. He used a handkerchief to wipe condensation from a pane and saw a mass of low, sullen clouds over the peaked roof of the Club's bathing pavilion across the pond on the barrier beach and a horizon that was a rumpled sheet of gun metal gray, as though angry sky and turbulent sea had been fused into one.

Except, he noticed, out to the southeast, where the clay cliffs of Block Island were visible on any clear day, a slash of ominous black-green seemed to separate from the grimness of sky and sea.

Mrs. Kenyon left the kitchen to share whispered complaints with Mrs. Babcock while Mrs. Gavitt joined Joey at the windows. The rain drummed on the veranda roof and they had to raise their voices to be understood. Joey rubbed away more condensation so that Mrs. Gavitt could see the peculiar dark band becoming more distinct as it expanded rapidly from east to west. Maybe, he said to Mrs. Gavitt, it was heavy fog fading into a low cloud, but in this wind, and what a strange color, and look how quickly it was gaining the shore. Mrs. Gavitt murmured agreement, and turning to call the others, her voice was lost in an explosion of glass as a fixture from the veranda escaped its tether and smashed against a window, sending a shower of razor edged shards on to dining tables and the oak plank floor. The shrieking wind entered the gap in the clubhouse's protection and scooped up tablecloths, sending water goblets and place settings to the floor and 'bishop hats' swirling like a flock of birds.

Mrs. Gavitt threw her arms around Joey who, despite the danger of another shattered window, was transfixed by a swath of black water, flecked with green and topped by a spume of gray, closing on the barrier beach. Slack jawed, his hands grasping a window sill, he watched the rental cottages on the dunes disappear in the churning blackness, followed moments later by the pavilion. As he gave into Mrs. Gavitt's efforts to tear him away, Joey realized that he was witnessing something he had read about in school, something that occurred in exotic places, but not in Westerly, Rhode Island. He shouted over the howls of wind: "Tidal wave!"

The clubhouse, in a violent tremor, yawed on its pilings as though attempting an escape to the protection of land only thirty feet away. The women, screaming, discarding their aprons, their carefully pinned hair falling on their necks and shoulders, giving no thought to coats or handbags or to the glowing rings of gas burners, ran to the narrow entrance hall. Joey followed, aware that despite the tumult, the electricity remained on and Bing Crosby was crooning *South of the Border*. The manager, out from behind the bar, waved his arms and shouted for calm as they gained the hallway to the outer doors where too many hands fought to grasp knobs. With a click, the doors flew open and they crammed on to the swaying pier.

Fragments of canopy flailed them as they staggered forward, barely conscious of pond water sloshing over the pier's planks and the eerie, echoing, all encompassing, roar surrounding them.

Breaths were sucked away by the furious wind, their shoulders beat against the canopy's frame, the women's skirts billowed and wrapped around them. Mrs. Gavitt stumbled, Mrs. Kenyon toppled over her into Mrs. Babcock and Joey. Joey braced himself against a railing and tried to pull Mrs. Gavitt to her feet as the manager struggled to close the clubhouse doors; somehow, he got one door in place when the handle of the other was ripped from his hands, the wind slammed the loose door into him, and Joey saw him thrown inside.

Behind the tottering clubhouse, the ocean and pond had become a surging mass. Wave upon wave climbed higher and higher into a mountain of froth and black water. Confined by the pond's shallows, a single monster wave rose, relentless, towering, hurtling forward, reaching the point where gravity demanded obedience.

Tons of water crashed downward.

They were like rag dolls. Pieces of flotsam.

The wind and water carried away their cries.

CHAPTER ONE

"He's in another goddamn mess!"

At a few minutes before nine on Saturday morning, Jimmy's Billiard Club was as quiet as a high school classroom after four. Cones of light illuminated a new Olhausen pool table where I faced Tony Tramonti unzipping a black nylon Providence Police jacket with his last name stitched in white above 'C'mish'. He had the vinegary look of someone who had drunk too much coffee and had not enough breakfast. Moments ago, he said he'd spotted my Mini Cooper in the parking lot that serves both the Billiard Club and Jimmy's Restaurant one floor below and that he *really* needed to talk to me.

The cause of his agitation? So far, all I knew was that it involved Charlie Fessenden, his feckless brother-in-law.

Despite Tramonti's obvious impatience to let me know more about the 'goddamn mess,' I was determined to continue my pool drills, exercises designed to enforce muscle memory of shot fundamentals. But my concentration lost out to Tramonti's presence when his large hands grasped the opposite rail with enough force to whiten his knuckles.

"Hands…?"

"Sorry." He stuffed them in his chinos.

The drill I had reached was a series of carom shots, with the cue ball about two inches from the rail. I set up, shot too quickly, and the cue ball hit the one ball which kissed the nine ball and blew by the pocket.

"You need practice. Aren't you defending…?"

I ignored him, chalked the cue stick's tip, aimed, drew back, and saw his hands back on the rail. I straightened up, my scowl eliminating the necessity of words, and his hands dropped to his sides. I aimed and shot; the cue ball smacked the two ball into the ten and spun across the table toward a corner pocket where it rattled around without falling in.

"Am I distracting you?" he said not very apologetically.

Ugh! Pool requires self-discipline and concentration and I would have neither while he hovered at the table. There's an old pool hall saying that 'bad practice is prelude to bad play,' so, sparing him a snide answer, I slipped my Vulcan cue stick into its place in one of the mirror-backed wall racks reserved for members and headed into the lounge area and its mahogany, twenty foot long bar. A sign reminding members that 'Pool is a sport—not a game' was above a gleaming Mignatti espresso machine behind the bar. I filled a brewing pot with ground beans from Pastiche on Federal Hill and placed two white ceramic cups under its spigots. A red light blinked as I hit the 'on' switch and turned to Tramonti who was slumped on a stool. As the machine burped and gurgled, with his elbows on the bar and palms together at eye level, he began.

"What a screw off! First, he gets canned at Hospital Trust for speculating with that old lady's trust fund." I knew about that escapade. "Then, he and his Newport buddies set up the hedge fund and bet the wrong way on interest rates and currencies. What did that cost to keep him out of the clutches of the SEC and settle with the investors!" My former law firm, Champlin & Burrill, defended Charlie in that fiasco. "So, he and Dani"—Charlie's wife and Tramonti's sister—"move into his family's place in Westerly and he starts selling houses to people buying into Watch Hill and Weekapaug." Charm and a rising market go a long way in selling expensive second homes because the Tramontis had thought Charlie was prospering. "Now, this …!"

'This,' it turned out, related to Charlie Fessenden being the Club Secretary of Haversham Golf Club, a very expensive, new golf course in Westerly that in common knowledge had been plagued by permitting delays and costly construction overruns. To add insult to injury, a week ago, a fire gutted its spanking new clubhouse the night before the club's grand opening. As I recalled it, the *Journal* reported that the wind driven blaze set off fireworks in storage for the following night's celebration, creating a spectacular, explosion packed, conflagration that took hours to control. Arson was suspected and an unidentified body had been discovered in the debris.

I handed Tramonti a cup of espresso and took my own to the end of the bar. "I need a cigarette," he said, his black eyes lifting to mine and then to the shelf under the bar.

Jimmy's Billiard Club is 'members only' so it was legal to smoke, notwithstanding Providence's 'no smoking in public places' ordinance and despite the disapproval of Young Jimmy Hannigan, the proprietor, after his wife's bout with breast cancer led him to give up thirty years of Marlboro Lights. All of the ashtrays, except for one kept under the bar, had disappeared. Despite my own objections to smoking, I reached down and slid it toward him.

A pack of Salems and a lighter came from underneath Tramonti's jacket to the bar. He lit his cigarette and inhaled deeply leaving me to thoughts of Dani Fessenden, née Tramonti, the youngest by eight years of the four Tramonti children, the surprise *bambina* for whom her mother had made repeated novenas to St. Anthony of Padua. Maybe because the Tramontis treated me like another son, I didn't much notice the string bean kid sister while I finished college and law school, did my stint in the Marines, and suffered through two years in the Manhattan District Attorney's office and a short lived marriage. Coming back to Providence and finding her grown up, vivacious, and drop-dead gorgeous, with long legs, a sexy body, and a cloud of curly black hair that fell to her shoulders, it was something out of *Sabrina*. Too bad for me, because by then, she had eyes only for Charlie Fessenden. With his sun-bleached hair, clear blue eyes, bold chin, red Mustang convertible, and dazzling tennis form, Charlie reeked of style, money, and pedigree. For Dani, fresh out of Salve Regina University and ready for love and marriage, it was a summer crush that ripened into Rhode Island's biggest wedding the following June. I attended The Dunes Club bash, more than a little jealous, wondering what I had missed, and not for the first time, what she saw in her empty-headed dink.

"Yesterday morning, early, he phones me at the Department. 'A bit of bother,' he says. A 'bother' means he's got himself in trouble! He's in town, at the Club's lawyer's office, needs to see me. So I agree and he's off the call before I can tell him to meet me someplace else and five minutes later, he sashays into the Public Safety Building in a blazer with a floppy silk handkerchief in the jacket's pocket. The eyes gotta be *rollin'* at the front desk when he asks for me! He gets an escort upstairs by telling everybody he's my brother-in-law, jabbering, asking what's it like to work for me. O'Neill, one of McCarthy's guys, brought him up, could barely contain himself, the way I hear it. You know the way Charlie talks, that nasal, whiny, Waspy voice…." Tramonti took an angry suck at his cigarette, looked up to the slow turning ceiling fan over the bar, and let the smoke exit his nostrils.

I let the 'Waspy' pass. Nothing personal, and I knew it. Always have. Tony Tramonti is my closest friend so some things go unchallenged. Education at Moses Brown Academy, Harvard College, and Harvard Law School, years as the in-house lawyer for his family's international construction management company, and his nascent political career hadn't softened his edge when it comes to Rhode Island's class consciousness. Besides, Charlie Fessenden, priggish, elitist, with a business IQ matching his shoe size, would give any lineage a bad name.

" 'Fra-n-k-l-y,' " Tramonti stretched out the word to imitate Charlie's lock-jawed intonation, "he says, he needs my help. The first thing I think of is that somehow he was involved with the storage of the fireworks. But he says 'no'." Tramonti flicked an ash into the tray in disgust. "You understand I've been hearing about this goddamn club for years! You would think they need another golf course down there like they need another middle name. Anyway, Charlie got hired early on as their real estate broker, then as Club Secretary, because he's *supposed* to know his way around Westerly and he lives there year round." Again, a deep inhalation of nicotine and fifty other bad-for-you chemical combinations. "And he looks and sounds right. Right?"

Did he expect at least a nod? I knew what 'right' was since I own some of that 'right' as a fiftyish, white, Anglo-Saxon heritage, male with a voice vaguely East Coast that doesn't throw away vowels.

"The Club's almost four years in the making! Disney built Disney World in less time! Two hundred fifty members, at a hundred and fifty a pop initiation fee, fifteen more a year in dues, ready to party ..., and there goes the clubhouse!"

I said, "You know, Nick joined early on...." My brother is the family's golfer.

"Yeah, too bad. Charlie told me. But your brother collects golf courses, doesn't he?"

True, Winged Foot, Augusta National, Congressional, Ballybunion....

"The Club Secretary is a part-time coordinator for all the committees that keep members involved and happy, an administrator until they get things up and running and hire professional management. Charlie tells me nearly all of the Club's financial records were destroyed in the fire. Even with backup records at the accountants, to put together a real set of books for the insurance claim, they need the few that were salvaged by the State Police. This is where I come in. Could I get copies from the State Police?"

Charlie, or the Club's lawyer, was right to think that Police Commissioner Tony Tramonti could get copies of whatever the State Police had recovered. It was just a small favor, in a state where favors and connections are synonymous with governance.

"I told him I'd call somebody. Then, he complains about a rumor…."

"Rumor?"

"… that he cut a side deal when the Club was pulling together the real estate. Before anyone thought of a golf course, Charlie gave an option on a few acres north of his home to the seller …," his voice caught in a smoker's cough, "… that became part of what the Club bought. Supposedly, Charlie got something more than he was entitled to from the seller when the option was exercised and the entire parcel was bought by the Club."

"Did he?" Charlie's response would be that he was 'appalled' at the suggestion, so loudly defensive as to give rise to a suspicion of the opposite conclusion. And, suspicion comes easily to the Tramonti brothers, Aldo, the oldest, who runs the family's business, Fausto, the middle brother, a bluff lawyer-politician with little patience for his ne'er-do-well brother-in-law, and, of course, Tony who despised Charlie Fessenden for the pain he had caused Dani.

"If he did, he loses his real estate broker's license and maybe it's fraud." In the hedge fund fiasco, Charlie's vehement denial of any knowledge of certain currency transactions turned out to be less than truthful. "I called the Colonel's adjutant at the State Police. No problem with copies of the records. They always grab records in an arson case. He said that they had identified the body as a guy from Westerly by the name of Oliver Randall who used to work at the Club. I spoke the name aloud and thought Charlie was going to have a conniption! The Staties think Randall sets the fire, it spreads too quickly, and he gets caught …, except for one problem. His skull was cracked. From before or during? They dunno." He shook his head vigorously, stubbed out his cigarette, and put the package and lighter away.

"After I hung up, I asked about Randall. Charlie had recovered by then and said he'd known Randall for years, that Randall lived close by the Club, and the Club had hired him at Charlie's suggestion as a general handyman-watchman. Now, get this," he added rolling his eyes, "Charlie had him axed a week before the fire for showing up drunk."

O-h-h, *that* wasn't going to go down well with the Club's members.

"The Club's Board of Governors has scheduled a membership meeting. With your brother a member, that gave me an idea."

Too obviously, his 'idea' had something to do with my brother being a partner at the Brown Brothers investment firm, an international financier, and our family's *Forbes 400* face. His name would have resonance with a club membership from Manhattan, Philadelphia, and Palm Beach.

"The members may have more money than God but now they gotta be wondering what happened to their dough, what's left, and can the place be rebuilt without digging into their pockets. They'll pepper Charlie with questions. He'll act like he knows everything when he doesn't, then like a deer in the headlights if it gets personal or complex. His only hope to survive is that you can shape him up….

" '*You?*' "

"… for the meeting, and …,"—this came out a little more

slowly—"… if you go with him. As Nick's proxy, I mean. Having Nick Temple's brother walk in there—"

"Wait a second. You want me to be a …, a shill?"

He realized belatedly that he had not set me up for the ask. "Not a shill, more like a …," he struggled for the word, "… a mentor. Algy, you prep him, maybe even serve up a couple of easy questions that he can answer, and he might get through. Meanwhile, the auditors get the numbers together and Fausto and I kill the rumor. If we can." An emphatic 'no' was forming in my throat when he added, "It's for Dani. She couldn't take another disgrace. After Newport, she was with the shrinks for years. She's got her legs back under her now, but …."

Low blow. I tested Tramonti's face for sincerity and it was there; it told me that he realized he was reaching for a touchstone beyond friendship. I guess you can do that, even to a best friend, if you've always been a big brother to your much loved baby sister.

I finished my espresso and turned to the sink to wash out my cup and tap the coffee grounds from the brewing pot into the trash container under the bar. I took my time and waited for more from Tramonti. Because, there would be. After a few moments, he cleared his throat. "I hired a freelance investigator to keep us in the loop. Was a State Police detective for years. Benno Bacigalupi. A little different but competent, with loads of contacts. The Westerly cops and the State Police will cooperate with Benno."

With my back to him, Tramonti couldn't see my reaction to that familiar, comical name. Benno Bacigalupi and I had crossed paths once before and Tramonti, despite being my best friend, didn't know. Benno Bacigalupi was more than 'a little different.'

"When's the membership meeting?" I asked.

"Next Sunday morning. We have a week—."

"This is Commencement Week…!"

"Yeah," he replied sheepishly, "I know."

"... and I've got Sonny to deal with!" Carter University and its nemesis, Providence's Mayor Angelo 'Sonny' Russo, were in a highly public battle over a police incursion at the Arts Quad dormitory complex, a foray that our mendacious mayor had purposefully turned into a full blown 'town and gown' media brouhaha.

Ugh!

I put my hands on the edge of the bar and stretched back, taking time to get my bearings. The Tramonti brothers are all about family pride and loyalty and both had been sorely tried by Charlie Fessenden. They could accept, barely, a dumb brother-in-law so long as he was their sister's choice and he stayed out of the limelight, but not a sticky-fingered brother-in-law of a rising politician promoting a reform agenda. Because of our relationship, the brothers would expect that I should, if I could, try to ameliorate a family embarrassment. Dani's well-being was at issue as well; she is so ... *nice*, and had put up with so much already....

"Okay," I said, my voice showing all the reluctance I could muster, "when and where do we interview Charlie?"

Tramonti's troubled face opened for the first time. He actually let his lips work into a slight smile. "Tomorrow afternoon ...."

"What...!"

"... in Westerly with Benno and a local lawyer, Tom Flanaghan. Good guy, knows everyone in town, can help with the prep and keep an eye on Charlie."

The truth was, I had no excuse; until late Sunday afternoon, my time was my own. Over this morning's espresso, a moody Nadie Winokur abruptly announced that she would be cooped up today and tomorrow in Ralston Hall, the Department of Psychology's building off Brook Street, with student grades and an overdue book review for a psychology journal. To add to my disappointment, tonight being the last Saturday night before

Commencement, when counseling needs would inevitably rise, she was the volunteer 'on duty' psychologist at the Women's Center. Thanks for the notice, I had thought, and so long until Sunday!

I shook my head. "What time?"

His fist pounded the bar in satisfaction. "Great!" he bellowed and stood to leave. "I'll pick you up at noon. You'll be back by four-thirty at the latest. Promise!" He zipped up his jacket and took car keys from a pocket. "Don't expect much from Charlie, by the way. Can't imagine that the 'boys' would really go after him. It's all a 'cock up,' he says." His eyes closed to a squint. "Can you imagine that, a *'cock up?'* "

After he left, I went back to pool drills and was absolutely lousy, distracted by the thought that Charlie Fessenden was already dead meat. For the members of the Club's Board of Governors, individuals with status in their insular, image conscious, summer community, the cachet of Board membership would have soured with the first snicker by a second guesser. Their collective reflex would be finger pointing, especially when they learned they had been put in harm's way by one of their own. Charlie's limited business acuity, gossip about a kick-back during the land acquisition, and his involvement in the hiring and firing of the suspected arsonist, would set him up neatly as the fall guy.

Charlie Fessenden wouldn't know what hit him.

CHAPTER TWO

Sunday morning, a cold front moved in, bringing fog to upper Narragansett Bay. Sluggishness, induced by an evening without Nadie and an empty bed, made it easy to forgo Nordic Track exercise and pool drills. Instead, I lay in bed, staring at the ceiling, my hands clasped under my head, uneasy, peevish in my solitude, imagining her at the computer in her spartan second floor office, pounding out her book review or finishing grades, not giving me a second thought. Lately, and too often, there were these times, usually after a spate of very good days, when she was like a tennis player that took a mighty swing to keep what we had in play, and then went to the sidelines.

My ruminations stopped when the newspapers *thunked* against the front door. I went downstairs, made a double espresso that energized me to get through the *Sunday Journal* and the 'Week in Review' of the *New York Times*, then I showered, shaved, donned casual clothes, and started the *Times* crossword. At noon, I waited in the central hall, watching drops of rain collect and spill down the windows by the front door, until Tramonti's GMC Envoy pulled to the curb. I put on a windbreaker and an old brown fedora that is my favorite hat, locked up, and got inside the SUV that smelled of a full ashtray. Immediately, I was ambushed by the slobbering muzzle of Oboe, Tramonti's chocolate Labrador Retriever. Tramonti gruffly ordered Oboe to retreat from my ear, explaining that Sunday was his 'Oboe day.' I adjusted my fedora, and we were on our way.

Route 95 was a glistening wet as we drove south in the comfortable silence of old friends. The SUV's wipers and defrost didn't quite mute the hiss of highway water meeting tires. Shortly after the Route 4 split, Tramonti reached into the console between our seats. "Club propaganda," he said. "Charlie gave it to me last year."

The brochure was glossy and thick, its cover a full color depiction of a shingle style clubhouse with a fieldstone chimney, green framed dormers jutting out of the roofline, large windows with red sashes, a second floor wrap-around porch, and an elaborate, pillared entrance. I took off my glasses and opened to thick, creamy pages separated by opaque sheets that gave the brochure heft and formality. Eventually, I got to text.

'Welcome,' it read, 'to Haversham Golf Club. Haversham Golf Club combines a great golf experience for all levels of players with the ambience of facilities that will set a new standard for New England golf clubs. Enjoy the company of your friends on the clubhouse's classic wraparound porch overlooking a spectacular golf course, acres of unspoiled landscape, and Block Island Sound. Indulge yourself with gracious dining and other amenities you would expect at only the finest private clubs. No detail of design or functionality has been missed.'

I turned a page. 'Your course will test every golfer's skill with both links-type play on the Scottish Nine as well as traditional northeast golf on the treelined fairways and challenging greens of the South County Nine. With multiple tees on each hole, two practice ranges, superb putting and chipping facilities, and an experienced PGA staff at your service, you'll enjoy your golf more at Haversham Golf Club.'

Next was a rendering of what looked like an upscale spa but was labeled 'Locker Room' and the following page was an illustration of the 'Players Grille Room,' richly paneled with a bar where all offerings would be from the top shelf, card tables, and a billiard table. The text continued, 'The most demanding of tastes will be satisfied at Haversham Golf Club.'

I flipped through more pages depicting a spacious dining room and assurances as to the Club's commitment to gastronomic pleasures; biographies of the Club's world renown course designer, the clubhouse architect, and professional golf staff; and a self-congratulatory piece as to the Club's commitment to environmental sensitivity. The last few pages consisted of schematics of the course layout, a mark-up of a score card, a puff piece on historic Westerly—founded 1669, once named Haversham, thirty square miles of shoreline beauty—and location maps demonstrating travel ease by air, rail, and car from Washington, Philadelphia, New York City, and Boston to a golf course only 'ten minutes from Westerly's airport and Amtrak station.' Tucked into the brochure's back cover was a membership application asking for two pages of personal information, required references, and a request for a fifty thousand dollar deposit upon submission to the Membership Committee.

A rather impressive piece, I remarked—I almost said pretentious—as I returned the brochure to the console. But, not the kind of club my brother, a dedicated scratch golfer, would join for its local amenities. He said as much yesterday when I telephoned him at his Manhattan apartment and explained my request to act as his proxy at the membership meeting. All he seemed to care about was whether the course itself, which he said had received initial rave reviews in golf magazines, would be open for play during his sporadic visits to Rhode Island.

The sun was attempting to pierce gray clouds that looked like dusty bags of cement when we drove past Westerly's Spanish Renaissance style Amtrak station as an Acela Express roared through. Tramonti made the sweeping turn into Canal Street where granite faced office buildings and brick store fronts were elegant reminders of a prosperity once brought by the town's numerous quarries, textile mills, and machine tool plants. Tramonti gave me the street address for Flanaghan's office, but too late as we had already driven past it, requiring us to circle around the town's elegant and rightly renowned Wilcox Park. We parked in a puddled asphalt lot facing the Pawcatuck River; Oboe took his owner on a tour of a grassy plot where Tramonti lit a cigarette while I waited for them at the embankment. Pretty spot, I thought, as I surveyed riverside brick buildings obviously converted to condos or apartments, their colorful awnings and flower pots brightening iron railed balconies, and in the distance, past the deck bridge to Connecticut, the imposing headquarters of The Washington Trust Company mimicking a Florentine palace in its granite block exterior, maroon tiled roof, and Palladian windows.

Oboe, finished with his duty and smell detection, and eager for affection, pulled Tramonti toward me. I knelt and rubbed behind Oboe's ears as Tramonti flicked his cigarette into the inky, quietly flowing water. "You'll like Tom," he said. "Lived in Westerly all his life. Used to be the town solicitor." We entered a two-story, freshly painted clapboard building with a discrete sign on the door reading 'Thomas A. Flanaghan, Esq. and Associates.' Tramonti whispered, "His kids are his 'associates.' "

A pleasant faced, full figured woman in her fifties, with short white hair, wearing a loose green blouse and black pants, rose from behind a desk and greeted us warmly. She took my hat and our jackets, and gestured toward a doorway filled by a middle-aged man, big in body, head, nose, and smile. His hair was black and unruly and looked like nothing could make it stay in place. A brown belt held up trousers and enclosed a billowing white shirt; a green tie was loose at his collar. "Tony," he called loudly, "Good to see ya. C'mon in here. This must be Alger Temple." I moved forward, my hand extended, and it disappeared into Tom Flanaghan's meaty, two-handed grip.

"Jean," Flanaghan called over my shoulder to the front desk and took Oboe's leash from Tramonti. "My wife, Jean," he said, and we exchanged 'hellos.' "Came down to straighten out a few things which we always appreciate," he said fondly and handed her the leash. She stooped to scratch under the dog's ears and Oboe fell in love as he was led away.

"Meet Benno Bacigalupi," Flanaghan said as he led us inside a conference room, gesturing toward a slender man in a gray suit, starched white shirt, and monochrome tie. Below a shaved scalp, a hook nose dominated a narrow face with tight, thin lips. I wasn't sure what to expect since our first encounter hadn't worked out well for anyone involved, including Benno, but he nodded, meeting my eyes with a hard stare that bared the chilly personality of a naturally suspicious man. I knew when he spoke, it would be rapidly and out of the corner of his mouth and be full of Rhode Island's floating 'r's' and 'ah's' instead of 'o's'.

Breaking the silence, Charlie Fessenden stood and said quickly, "Tony," which got a mumbled response from his brother-in-law. Then, he grabbed my hand. He remained trim and good-looking in a boyish way, although time was beginning to work its way into the skin at his eyes and the flesh under his chin; longish blond hair strayed over his shirt collar and his face had the smirky grin that had been tolerable in a twenty year old. "Algy, so good to *see* you! *Good* to have you on my side. How's Nick? *Great* of him to join the Club. Can't *wait* to get him on the course!"

His genial greeting was not unexpected since Charlie is, after all, first, last and always, a salesman. But he couldn't quite disguise his anxiety since superficiality only goes so far. And what a contrast to drab-on-purpose Benno: Charlie wore an open collar Madras plaid shirt, brown slacks, black belt with a cell phone holder, and I didn't have to look to know he wore sockless Dock Siders.

Tramonti and I were directed to seats facing Benno and

Charlie, and Flanaghan squeezed by us to the head of the table. "Okay," Tramonti said abruptly, "what can we do with this mess."

Charlie made his first miscue by protesting fussily, "Could we avoid calling the situation a 'mess.' It sets the wrong tone. Really, it's straightening things out...."

"It *is* a goddamn mess! That's why we're here," Tramonti snarled back. Charlie's jaw muscles bunched up at the rebuke.

Flanaghan, now wearing half lens reading glasses that seemed too small for his large, round face, apparently sensed, as did I, that the meeting needed a facilitator. "Let me go through where I think we are and how we got here," he said as he unrolled what appeared to be a tax assessor's map of a portion of Westerly and spread it on the table. An area south of Route 1 near the Charlestown line marked 'Haversham Golf Club' was highlighted in yellow and divided by various colored hatch marks. A crooked black line ran north-south through the Club land with the left side—the west side—marked 'owned' and the right side marked 'leased.' "The Club's land was assembled," he began, "over the past ten years by—"

Charlie, unable to contain himself, interrupted. "You see where my land is?" He reached across the table and tapped the map on a parcel shaded red between the golf course and Wynomet Pond.

Flanaghan ignored Charlie. "This large parcel," he pointed to an area set off by purple hatch marks within the Club's land, "a hundred and fifty or so acres, was part of the estate of Admiral Horatio Duffie, a stretch leading north from Charlie's land up to Route 1. The Admiral purchased the land from Charlie's grandfather back in the late forties." Flanaghan fingered a second parcel in green hatch marks within the Club's boundaries, partly within the 'owned' portion of the Club's land and all of the leased portion. "This land here, mostly contiguous to Admiral Duffie's, was part of the land owned by the Randall family until Darius Randall died about five years ago and his estate sold it to ...."

I said, "Randall. Any relation to the guy in the ashes?"

"Yeah, same family," Flanaghan replied, "and it gets better. The Randalls are old swamp yankees. At one time, they owned everything south of Route 1 but gradually lost it or sold it off. What was left was a couple of hundred acres, a lot of it wet, crisscrossed with streams and creeks, except where they farmed or took out gravel. As you can see, part of the Randall land is now owned by the Club, part is under long-term lease to the Club, and the rest of what the Randall's owned is choice development real estate that borders the golf course with access to Wynomet Pond and the barrier beach." Flanaghan's long index finger moved down the map parallel to the Club's leased land to the Pond and over to the barrier beach. "So, the Club consists mostly of the Duffie parcel on the west and the Randall parcel on the east, some owned and some leased, bordering Charlie's land on the north. Now, important to why we are here, Charlie owned this finger of land, about six acres"—he pointed to a slender parcel hatch marked blue within the Club owned land—"between the Duffie and the Randall parcels, a remnant from...."

Charlie, who apparently couldn't help himself, leaned forward. "My grandfather originally picked up his land through a couple of foreclosures, including one against the Randalls back in the Depression. Built his summer home—now my house—and sold some of his land to the north to Admiral Duffie. Now, this was before regulations on subdivisions and town planning and the deed to Admiral Duffie had one of those descriptions like 'to the apple tree and down to the stone wall' kind of things they used back then. Later, when the Admiral had his parcel surveyed, he found that he didn't have title to about six acres between his land and Randall's remaining property. The Admiral sued my grandfather for the land but my grandfather was a tough old character and he won." Charlie put his finger on the blue hatch marks. "Six acres on the ridge line where the clubhouse was built…."

Flanaghan murmured, watching Charlie carefully, "Highest point in the area…."

"But worthless!" Another interruption from Charlie, anxious to put his spin on Flanaghan's facts. "Landlocked by a sliver of Randall's land. We couldn't get to it! Since the Admiral was angry with my grandfather over losing the lawsuit, he refused us access through his property and, of course, so did the Randalls who despised us. Without access, the six acres weren't worth a dime. You had to own either the Duffie land or the Randall property, or get an easement, to link up."

Charlie looked at each of us to make sure we were following and excitedly continued. "To make things worse, Dani and I had just moved back to Westerly when the goddamn Quonnies claimed that parcel and…."

"Who?" I said but Charlie was charging ahead.

"My dad had gotten crank letters for years from those rag-tags before he died, all nonsense, but they included the parcel in their land claims when they tried for federal recognition as a tribe. Outrageous! Everyone knows the Quonnies have been up in the Indian Swamp in Greenwick for generations! And now, they wanted our land?" He was waving his hands excitedly in front of his face. "It was more of the Randalls' spite! Somehow or other, they're part Quonnie. Old man Randall, and then Ollie, let them through their land to trespass on our six acres to set bonfires! Said it was a 'signal' hill or some such nonsense. We'd call the Westerly cops to chase them out but since they had to go through Duffie's or Randall's land to get there, the police didn't do anything but cite them for open fires without a permit. Less than useless. It was dangerous to have those fires up there…."

I had a vague recollection of stories or legends about the Quonnies but also had become impatient with Charlie's sidebars and so had everyone else. Flanaghan recognized the mood and said, "Now, you'll want to know how all this land became the golf course. That brings us to Ugo Calibrese."

My breath caught. "Did you say *Ugo Calibrese?*" I turned to Tramonti whose expression told me he already knew.

But hadn't told me!

CHAPTER THREE

Every small city on the East Coast has one or more Ugo Calibreses. They come out of nowhere to own half of the downtown, the half that is decaying, dirty, and desolate, the Class C office space, the crumbling buildings with yellowed 'for rent' signs in fly-spattered windows and the remains of last night's wino party in entrances. Then, they go a little upscale, in Calibrese's case, picking up real estate on Federal Hill, buying into upper-scale restaurants and the club scene by the harbor, slowly emerging from the shadows. When he purchased Greenwick Downs, a rundown dog track in Greenwick, about ten miles to the north from where we sat, he took it out of bankruptcy by getting the state to grant him a license for video slots, bingo, and simulcast horse racing. That's when he became a person of interest to the *Journal*. It didn't take the newspaper long to dredge up his background as a slumlord in Olneyville and the West Side and his connections to various unsavory characters, including members of the Marfeo crime family. He also showed up as one of Sonny Russo's biggest financial supporters which was no surprise since the Mayor 'owned' the members of the city's License Board, political hacks who for fifty thousand a year, approved liquor licenses, closing hours, and security requirements at all Providence restaurants, bars, and clubs. Ugo Calibrese, in other words, had become a Providence 'somebody.'

Flanaghan, who hadn't noticed my reaction, was into Calibrese's background. "Born in Westerly, in the North End. Moved up to Providence, made his money … howsoever … and bought the Watson mansion in Watch Hill when prices were in the pits during the early eighties. Sometime later, on the quiet, using various front companies, what we call 'straws,' he started buying any available land south of Route 1 between Dunn's Corner and Charlestown...."

Again, Charlie interrupted. "But I never dealt with him! Not once! I was approached by a ...," a slur formed on his lips but he managed to stop, "... a Jewish fellow from Providence. I figured he had a deal with either the Duffies or the Randalls for some of their land so I agreed I'd give him an option to buy the 'finger,' as you call it, at what I thought was an absurdly high price. I was paid a good price for the option, too." He checked our faces for level of belief. "Told him about the Quonnies' claim but he said he didn't care. I even tied up the option parcel with restrictions so that if the option was exercised, the land couldn't be developed to adversely affect my home. He never once mentioned Ugo Calibrese!" He turned to me. "Algy, that was at least a year before anyone was talking about a golf course! My option deal was in place before I was hired to represent the Club and I disclosed it to the Board when we focused on the land! It was the best available property for a new golf course anywhere along the shore! I swear!"

Flanaghan stopped Charlie's search for my affirmation by spreading his hands out over the map. "The town was already on edge about the Quonnies' claim for a piece of Westerly when word got out that Calibrese was buying nearby land. We put two and two together that, maybe, the Quonnies and Calibrese were going to build a casino right here in Westerly...."

Charlie cleared his throat noisily. "When I found out who was holding the option, I was extremely upset. If I had known it was a thug like Calibrese ...."

Flanaghan took off his glasses and stared at Charlie. Clearly, he had evaluated Charlie and found him to be wanting in character and, as I already knew, a class conscious twit. Then, he surveyed our tense faces and decided we needed a break. "Anybody want coffee? Soft drink? Water?"

We all responded 'no' except for Charlie, whose forehead glistened with a film of sweat, who thought water would be 'grand.'

Flanaghan left us in an uncomfortable silence. A quick glance to Tramonti saw him staring past Flanaghan's vacant chair and through the window to spring green maples dipping branches into the river. Benno, who hadn't uttered a word as yet, was focused on a large multi-colored map of Westerly from pre-1900, seemingly bored with all the local history. Charlie stared at his hands as his fingers played with a Yale class ring. Me? I hope I maintained a neutral, 'I'm here as a friend' demeanor.

Flanaghan returned with two bottles of AquaFina, one for himself and passed the other to Charlie who opened it and took a gulp. Flanaghan, with his glasses back on, said, "Everything down here is complicated, isn't it?" His comment was clearly designed to give Charlie a modicum of support and his easy manner evoked confidence and familiarity. "About then, some Watch Hill summer people began to investigate the possibility of a golf club and hired Charlie as their real estate agent. Charlie says he suggested approaching Calibrese because Calibrese's land had more than enough acreage for a golf course, was convenient off Route 1, had ocean views, plenty of groundwater, and very importantly, was in the hands of a single owner. Charlie thought the town fathers might cooperate with the Club on permitting if the purchase would get rid of Calibrese and the threat of a Quonnie casino."

"What about the Quonnies' land claim?" Tramonti asked.

"A condition of the deal with Calibrese," replied Flanaghan, "was that the Quonnies give up their Westerly claim. It took awhile, but Calibrese did the 'magic,' as they say. Not a huge surprise since he's got a lot of the Quonnies on the payroll at his dog track. Their tribal council voted to take the Westerly claim out of their application and recorded a release in favor of Calibrese's entities." Flanaghan began to roll up the map. "That's the story...."

"A lot of people in Westerly told me then I had rescued the town from the Quonnies and Calibrese," Charlie proclaimed with more than a little sanctimony. "I was a blinkin' hero! The Club never would have been put together without my efforts." And then under his breath, "How easily they forget!"

Flanaghan's response was to loudly snap an elastic band around the rolled-up plan. "Which leads us to the rumor that's going around. Essentially, the rumor is that in addition to getting the agreed upon sales price for his property when Calibrese exercised the option for the six acres, Charlie got something 'extra.' "

"Poppycock. Mean, despicable, poppycock," Charlie responded, his voice unexpectedly loud and strident, repeating a word that was odd but reflective of Charlie's persona. "I didn't get a nickel more than what I bargained for. It was a fixed price option! I disclosed it! I worked hard to get the Calibrese deal closed because my clients wanted a golf course. Tom, when I find out who started the rumor, I'll sue!"

The room hushed. Collectively, we sensed a soft spot in his story that matched the soft spot in his backbone. People with a history of behaving badly rarely behave better.

Flanaghan took a sip of water, then said, "Next, insurance. Charlie is the Club Secretary. Which means he sat on the Building Committee that bought most everything for the clubhouse, and among other things, was responsible for purchasing insurance. The issues are whether the Club was adequately insured and can it prove its loss."

Charlie, after drawing a deep breath to give us a sense of his burden, began his defense. "Insurance was one of the last things we got to when we accepted the clubhouse as finished from the contractor.

With everything else going on, hiring a club manager, inspections, preparations for the opening of the course, furnishings coming in, it was a confusing time. I don't claim to know a lot about insurance. I just paid the bills the Building Committee approved. The insurance broker basically took care of it. We got a binder from him for insurance that was supposed to include *everything* to protect the Club as far as the Building Committee was concerned. The policy was to come later." He looked around the table, a victim of circumstance, focusing on me. "We're not insurance experts! That's why the broker got his commission! What do you think, Algy?"

Why did he ask *me*? Because, Charlie would wrongly assume my sympathy because he looked for class affinity. I would, he would think, understand the interlocking relationships, institutions, education paths, and financial affluence of Club members; I would appreciate how the Haversham Golf Club's committee system operated, the chummy atmosphere of Building Committee meetings, and a reliance on an insurance broker who likely was somebody's friend if not a member himself!

I deflected Charlie's plea by playing lawyer. "The insurance company is going to investigate, wait for all the numbers to come in, and decide how much it is going to pay, and when. Arson isn't a defense under the typical fire insurance policy, unless the fire was set to get the proceeds, which didn't happen. At the membership meeting, you should be prepared to answer questions that you can answer, about the purchasing process, the Building Committee, and the insurance broker, and don't try to answer any questions on coverage. Leave that to the lawyers or the broker. Short, simple answers. And, blaming others isn't going to help!"

"But...."

Tramonti's right hand banged the table, jolting Charlie into silence, pulverizing what was left of Charlie's poise. "Who's representing the Club?" I interjected.

"Gordon Ackley," Tramonti replied. Of Brinkley & Alley, an archetypical 'white shoe' law firm that specialized in real estate development. Ackley, a contemporary of mine, is a stiff, full of preening superiority, the kind of lawyer whom other lawyers instinctively dislike. But smart.

"Finally," Flanaghan said, "Least we forget, Oliver Randall." With that, Bacigalupi, whose aquiline features had thus far shown no interest in Charlie's plight, raised his eyes to stare at Charlie who was patting a damp forehead with a pocket handkerchief. The professional observer had come to life.

"Ollie Randall," Charlie said in a disparaging voice, his eyes avoiding everyone at the table, "lived in a beat-up trailer, next to the family's crappy house and barn on the property Calibrese bought from his father's estate. One of a miserable lot of drunks and lay-abouts. I was concerned he'd cause trouble during construction so when the land was being grubbed out for the golf holes, I got the Club to hire him, despite our misgivings, as a handyman working with the maintenance people on the fencing, keeping out the riffraff. But he was incorrigible. Despite being warned several times, the week before the fire, he shows up drunk at work, a surly insulting drunk. I was there with our new club manager who took one look at Randall and fired Randall on the spot. He had to call the Westerly cops to get him off the property. How could we have known that he would take revenge…?"

"The point is...," Flanaghan began.

"It's just not fair!" Charlie lamented, his hands raised to make his point. "Why should I take the blame because the fire destroyed our records, that we don't have an insurance policy in hand, or have any responsibility for Randall burning down the clubhouse? And this rumor? It's not fair!"

Haversham Golf Club had its scapegoat.

CHAPTER FOUR

Despite Tramonti's objection that it would take too long, I insisted that we inspect the fire scene. We followed Route 1 toward Charlestown and left the highway at stone pillars incised 'Haversham Golf Club' and 'Private.' We drove up an incline bounded by cedars to find Benno Bacigalupi getting out a gray Malibu parked in front of a gazebo-like structure marked 'Valet and Bag Drop.' Two hundred feet away, on the crest of a knoll circled by bales of hay, a blackened fieldstone chimney was a lonely remnant of what had been the elegant clubhouse of the brochure. The acrid smell of burnt wood and wet ash lay heavily despite a brisk wind off the Sound.

We left Oboe complaining in the SUV with the windows half open as Benno rolled out a set of plans on the hood of his car. "I got these from the architects." He picked through the plans until he found one that laid out the site. "From what I can figure, the clubhouse fire started here," Benno said, pointing to a spot in the main structure, "under this porch. It was used for temporary storage for paper goods, everything from toilet paper to menus, for the opening weekend. The way the drafts would have run, the flames would shoot up this stairwell like a flue into the locker rooms and from there, the kitchen and dining rooms." He turned to the knoll and we did as well. Against the background of a misted-over sun, the foundation's fieldstone walls folded into the rise and formed a catch basin for debris; on the side of the knoll, what had been landscaped beds of flowers and decorative grasses, were burnt out or ground into mush.

"This is where they found Randall," he said returning to the plan, indicating a smaller building marked 'maintenance.' "He started the fire in the clubhouse, using gasoline as the accelerant. That shows it was planned if it was brought up here, although Charlie tells me they got their own gas tanks at the golf cart garage on the other side of the clubhouse. So maybe not. Then, down to the maintenance building where they kept supplies and greens mowers and other small equipment"—his fingers went left to right on the plan—"and he set off the fireworks stored there for their opening night party. Forty-five minutes worth of starbursts, roman candles, rockets, the most spectacular, newest, and loudest New Jersey could supply. Caused multiple explosions including one that blew the roof off!" He shook his head at the thought. "Can't imagine bein' so dumb as to store fireworks on site! The Westerly fire marshal told me they couldn't use their pumpers with the explosions going off. Randall was so crisp, he got identified by a back brace."

Benno rolled up the plans and stacked them in the back seat of his car. Tramonti said, "Let's take a look," and led us up a cart path carved into the knoll and lined by blue stone walls to a strand of yellow police tape that blocked our way; behind it, a Westerly cop was in a bantering conversation with two men in green overalls taking videos of the debris. After a show of Tramonti's I.D., the cop loosened the tape and let us pass. To our left, two front-loaders blowing blue exhaust, with treads evidencing clods of chewed up landscaping, were heaving the carbonized remains of a porch into huge mobile dumpsters; to the right, down the cart path a hundred feet or so, was a tee box seemingly untouched by the fire. We gained the crest and peered over a foundation wall into an odious cavern of charred wood, gray ash, and muck. Tramonti lit a cigarette as he and Benno identified lockers, spa equipment, a stove, upended refrigerators flashing a metallic brilliance in the jumble, an elevator slot—where was the car—and a stairway against an inside wall going nowhere. The girders that had supported the building's post and beam construction had been transformed into blackened pick-up-sticks.

While they ruminated, I looked up from the overpowering stench to the prospect of emerald fairways to the north bordered by cedars, oaks, and pines, outcroppings of ledge, and a string of silvery ponds. "That must be the ninth or eighteenth," I said half aloud, indicating a well-bunkered, undulating green nestled in a hollow of the ridge, and imagined golfers lining up putts as their friends, with long, cool drinks in their hands, watched from the wraparound porch. A lot of very expensive enjoyment had crashed and burned.

A dog's bark distracted us from the wreckage. A border collie raced up the knoll and joined us, an ungainly, friendly animal with big paws, white bristled muzzle, and groomed coat, his tail beating against our legs. Benno ignored the dog but both Tramonti and I stroked its head and I found a Westerly tag with a number and the name 'Shadrach.' Apparently happy for companionship, Shadrach followed us to what had been the front entrance to the clubhouse, now an intact, pillared entryway to nowhere. From there, we looked south toward Wynomet Pond at rolling, narrow fairways bordered by swaths of swaying grasses, pot bunkers, hummocks, and gorse, obviously, the 'Scottish Nine' links from the Club's brochure. In the distance, a house capped by a silo or large cupola stood at the pond's edge. 'Charlie's,' I thought, and remembered that I was standing on Charlie's 'finger' of land, the Quonnies' 'signal hill.'

With the collie trailing us, we continued around the carnage past a burnt-out pro shop identified by a heap of ruined golf equipment and racks of spoiled clothing and took a wider cart path down the knoll through scorched trees toward what remained of the maintenance building. Blackened masonry walls, standing like ruins in an archeological dig, held a pile of rubble; what might have been a garage door and a crumpled metal roof lay nearby. "The fireworks crew got here late from Jersey and had a problem setting up so they decided to leave the stuff in here overnight," Benno said with scorn. "Stu – pid!"

With nothing more to see, we retraced our steps up the knoll. "Security?" I asked Benno.

"They did, and they didn't. Keyless entry with security codes plus locks, all kinds of burglar detection devices, with audible alarms on all doors and windows in the clubhouse. Not sure about here, but I'd think they would have audible alarms on the doors and windows, and a tie-in to a central control box within the clubhouse. I'll get that information from the alarm company. A security patrol checked the clubhouse every couple of hours starting at eight, did a quick look around, and went off to their next stop. The Club kept a guard until eight at the main gate, and it planned to have a night watchman on site beginning with the grand opening." He shook his head warily. "Makes you wonder, right? Whoever set the fire gotta have known that. Came in either from a back trail or from the highway after the guard left, did the job, and got out the same way, … or didn't, if it was Randall, which it probably was. There's a maintenance trail that goes out toward where he lived. Almost too easy, because under the porch, where they stored the paper goods, just lattice work behind a cheap lock, easy to bust through, and no alarm. Open a few boxes of paper goods, spread a little gas, and…."

"Sprinklers?" I asked.

"Inside the clubhouse to meet building codes. But not under the porches. The place went up too quickly for sprinklers to be of much use, anyway. When the sprinklers started spraying, the security system—that was in a room in the basement—sent out the alarm, and then was burnt out. Dunn's Corner Fire District sent the first truck, a pumper, at ..."—he checked a flip-up moleskin notebook—"... nine fifty-six, got here ten minutes after the alarm went off. Took one look and called in Westerly and Charlestown, which took another twenty to roll in. Something as big as this gets started our here in the boonies and there's no chance for the locals. Makes them 'chimney savers.' "

At the parking lot, the collie, attracting Oboe's barks, ambled off to a paved trail that disappeared into the woods. Tramonti soon had a fretful Oboe pulling on a leash, leaving marks on nearby bushes and rocks. I heard Tramonti say to Benno, "You gotta stay up on this. It's important we know...."

"Everybody thinks it's straight forward, so maybe it is," Benno replied. "Except, how does Randall get stuck inside after he sets off the fireworks?" Benno opened the door to his car and slid inside. "With a cracked skull? And why set the fire only a week after he made his threats against the Club? Was he that drunk or crazy? And they tell me he was a little guy, scrawny, with a limp. How does he get up here? Walk? With a gasoline can maybe? I don't know."

○ ◯ ○

A short time later, we were heading north on the South County Trail, a three hundred year old road that links the shoreline to metropolitan Providence, in a parade of slow moving traffic led by a Charlestown police cruiser enforcing the twenty-five mile per hour speed limit near Town Hall and the Narragansett Tribe's health center, smoke lodge, and headquarters. Tramonti, who drives as though speed limits are suggestions, was frustrated by our pace but didn't dare to plug in the dashboard flasher and defy a local cop. It was time to ask why he hadn't told me about Ugo Calibrese's involvement in the development of Haversham Golf Club.

"I was going to," he demurred. Then, louder, "Look at that

guy!" as he braked as the Ford Focus in front of us yanked into a dirt trail without the benefit of a turn signal. 'What, give you a clue…?'

"You should have."

"Okay, I know. I was afraid you wouldn't do it if you thought this was about politics. But, it isn't. This is about Dani." His voice left me no doubt as to his sincerity. "Charlie embarrasses her again, and she's back to the shrinks. If Charlie had a conflict while representing the Club, Fausto thinks Sonny will turn it into a public spectacle, maybe at the Real Estate Commission, on his broker license. What's that gonna do to Dani?" I was about to point out that such a gambit would implicate Calibrese in something unsavory when he complained, "Just to embarrass me!"

A reforming Police Commissioner could have a dunce or a business failure for a brother-in-law, but not one caught in blatant illegality or a conflict-of-interest scandal. It would be manna from heaven for Sonny Russo, a payback for his embarrassment when Tramonti, appointed by Sonny through Fausto's influence, shut down Sonny's patronage operation run by Chief Daniel Patrick McCarthy, and began to push for change in the famously inefficient, ill-trained, and politically gutted department. Over the past two years, Tony Tramonti, through his choice of enemies and with the *Journal* backing his reforms, had gained traction as someone willing to take on the seemingly unbeatable mayor. Meanwhile, Sonny bleated to his intimates that Tramonti was a 'traitor pissing in my soup,' and that he, Sonny, was going to 'kick his ass across Kennedy Plaza' when Tramonti announced his candidacy for mayor.

We drove a few miles in silence, picking up speed after we left Charlestown. He touched a button on the console and a Junior Brown song began, 'I got a star on my car and one on my chest.' My face was to my window as the rolling meadows of farms blurred; rows of vegetables were already leafy and where the dark earth had been harrowed, corn had been planted. "Let me tell you about Benno," he said, lowering the volume on the trooper's hymn. "Ran into promotion problems with the State Police a few years ago. Did a lot of organized crime, Mafia stuff. After twenty-five years, eighty percent pension, there wasn't much use in his hanging on. Now he mostly freelances for insurance companies, and on the side, the Staties let him do cold case files. The rap on him is that he couldn't get use to unit policing. Too much a loner, the kind who keeps his own files. A bachelor. Whole life is catching bad guys. His house in Mount Pleasant is supposedly chock-full of clippings and boxes of stuff he's collected on people he'd like to get, crimes that didn't get resolved to his satisfaction. He's also the kind of guy I wouldn't want to have on my case. Never gives up."

I recognized the character as described. In fact, I'd been to Benno's modest raised ranch near Rhode Island College. Even its living room floor had cardboard boxes and plastic crates full of files, photographs, faded manila folders, and notebooks with tiny writing on musty, clammy pages. "What do you expect him to do?" I asked, thinking of his parting remarks to Benno.

Tramonti waited a beat before responding, as though forming an answer that didn't come readily. "It's Fausto's idea," he said, almost plaintively because it was Fausto who would be looking at every angle in what might become a political crisis. "Keep in touch with the insurance adjusters so we know if the Club is going to have a problem with Charlie in the middle. Put Charlie through a grind with Flanaghan to find out about the kickback." I noticed he didn't say 'alleged kickback.' "Come up with his own angles on Randall and the fire and see where that takes us."

His response seemed to me, hesitant, maybe shallow or incomplete. But I had to agree the whole episode could use tidying up.

We were now in South Kingstown passing through its famous turf farms, hundreds of acres of carefully tended grass on either side of the highway, the color and flatness reminding me of pool table cloth. Rain streaks began to line my window even as toward the west, shafts of light pierced dark clouds, creating luminous yellow-green patches on the turf, in what my family referred to as 'Jacob's ladders.'

"I appreciate this," he said, sounding more like the Tony Tramonti of pre-political days. "I can take the heat from Sonny but I don't want Dani sick again. How's she gonna hold up her head unless somehow Charlie comes out of this with some reputation left? Her life's down there now. All I ask is that you be tight with him until he gets through the membership meeting." He coughed and then continued. "I can't deal with him without wanting to puke!" He banged his fists in anger on the steering wheel. "He's pathetic!"

"I can't do much to improve his brain power, let alone his reputation."

He replied sourly, "You can't shine sneakers."

CHAPTER FIVE

Nadie, in jeans and a striped short sleeve shirt, was in the loft, a functional work area and bedroom that takes up most of the second floor of my Greek Revival house on Congdon Street. The cool-blue slats of the window blinds were closed against the bright late afternoon sun, leaving barely enough light for her to be at our shared worktable. Hunched over her laptop, her ears covered by Bose earphones, she didn't hear me enter. I knew I shouldn't do it, but I did: I touched her left shoulder.

If I had poked her with a cattle prod, I couldn't have gotten a more severe reaction. She ripped off the headphones, jumped up, wide-eyed and indignant. "*Why* do you do things like that?" Her fists pounded my chest, not especially playfully. How does someone so waif-like pack such a punch!

"You were too tempting a target." I smiled. Winningly? Apparently, not enough.

"Don't do it! Just don't do it! I hate it!"

"Okay, okay," and with palms raised in mock surrender, I left her for the bathroom, stripped for a quick shower and for a moment had a mirrored glance of a body that was holding up despite fifty plus years. I decided against shaving, smiled largely at myself, and ran my fingers through white flecked, wiry hair which didn't change course one whit. As the hot water scoured my body, my thoughts focused on Nadie, her recent mood swings, attempts to be compatible and happy, followed by periods of fussiness and irritability. It seemed to begin in January, after she had requested to teach a course in 'positive psychology.' What I took from her enthusiastic description was that it was a newish slant on the human psyche focusing on individual strengths and virtues as the point of departure of analysis, in stark contrast to clinical, more traditional, behaviorist psychology. The Department chair gave quick approval for second semester next year, and Nadie, with great excitement and purpose began to prepare. In March, at a curriculum meeting, came belated reactions from a few colleagues that Nadie, the Department's *wunderkind*, found insulting and dismissive—'it's all happy faces and happy talk,' 'where's the clinical evidence,' 'it's philosophy, not psychology,' 'it smacks of religion'—being some I could remember. Although bothered, she managed to suffer those comments, only to be angered when in April, she received a list of 'suggestions' to her course syllabus authored by two senior professors. She responded aggressively, informing the Department chair that she would not be 'intimidated,' making pointed comments about finding a more 'open' venue, using as leverage what amounted to invitations to her from Wellesley and Penn. What about us, I had asked, when she told me of her threat. She retreated into an 'off limits' mode that made discussion short, me anxious, and her—maybe 'troubled' best describes it. Our first crisis? Did our relationship depend ultimately upon a college course?

I shook off my thoughts as I toweled and dressed. Get on with it, Algy.

I went back into the loft and loudly announced that I was making martinis. We had been on a kick where I mix popular cocktails of the fifties and sixties featured in the weekend edition of *The Wall Street Journal*, luscious, often sweet concoctions like Old Fashions, Side Cars, Rob Roys, and Ward 8's—the last, a mix of bourbon, lemon and orange juices, and grenadine, being our favorite—so, this was a return to our standby of Gordon's gin, a drop of dry vermouth, very well shaken. I brought the frosted shaker out to the den with two straight up glasses and a dish of assorted nuts and olives because I expected she would join me; it was getting close to our usual time for a cocktail or glass of wine in the comfortable, over-furnished room with a striking prospect of the downtown. I poured my drink and stood at the floor to ceiling windows, admiring an early summer sunset that turned the horizon's clouds pale purple with peach tones, and bleached the patina of the mansard roofs of office buildings and apartment towers in Capitol Center; a blaze of gold reflected on chimneys and gables and flashed in windows. The skeletons of new condo towers at WaterPlace Park were gaining height and would soon replace my distant view of the Westin Hotel and brick-faced, neon lit, mass that is Providence Place Mall. I took a sip of my martini, remembering that it wasn't that long ago when Providence was a smudge on the map from New York to Cape Cod! And now…!

"Okay, I overreacted," Nadie said as she sat on the salmon colored divan and plumped up two pillows as an invitation which I accepted. I poured her martini, touched her glass to mine, and asked her about her plans for tonight. She tossed her long, silky, black hair around her elegant neck, her intelligent green eyes alert and playful, and said with the verve of the Nadie I love, "So long as you don't sneak up on me again!" Then, she was on to her book review and whether she felt comfortable as a reviewer because she had met and did not like the author, while I concentrated on the freckles on her elegant nose, a Mediterranean complexion that seemed never to need makeup, and lips with a natural pink some women might seek from cosmetologists. Her fingers, without any rings, found an errant lock and I caught up to her during a giggly story about a colleague's affair with a middle-aged internist we both knew at the Carter Medical School. Nadie was mildly disapproving because she said he was a 'putz'—her word—and making me wonder why she seemed so confident in her assessment.

I replenished my glass, she declined, as she sampled the olives purchased from Venda's on Federal Hill, and I told her about Tramonti's request, today's meeting in Tom Flanaghan's office, and the visit to the clubhouse ruins.

She surprised me, since I knew she didn't like Charlie Fessenden, by her focus on the plight of Dani Fessenden whom she had met at parties at Tony Tramonti's home off Elmgrove Avenue and at the family's compound on Ocean Drive in Narragansett. A distinct although polite iciness on Nadie's part had been evident on those occasions. Afterwards, when she wondered aloud why Dani married such a wimp, I also caught an unexplained, discernibly sniffy, attitude toward Dani.

I finished my cocktail and suggested that I cook a Providence 'Saturday night suppa'—what I would have prepared last night if not stood up—of Saugy hotdogs, B&M beans, and cole slaw for me and a chicken breast scaloppini and salsa salad in respect of her mostly vegetarian diet. She said 'fine' and asked if there was any more of the Eden Valley Chardonnay we had pleasantly consumed on Friday night. She soon had a glass of the straw colored wine, along with an ice cube, served with a bowl of cold shrimp with a dollop of my homemade hot sauce. With a CD of Puccini arias softly filling the den and her wine, the shrimp, and a *New Yorker*, she seemed content and I went to the kitchen, glad to avoid further discussion of the Fessendens.

My kitchen—large enough according to Nadie for a small bistro—is functional, a focal point of our day-to-day living, and laid out to accommodate a Jenn-Aire grill in a center granite topped island, a Viking oven, a Sub-Zero refrigerator, rows of gadgets and machines, lots of cabinets and two double sinks, all designed for efficient cutting, slicing, chopping, smashing, mixing, and tasting. Quickly, I marshaled the chicken and hot dogs, vegetables, pots and pans, herbs, condiments, and wine, and went to work. A cabbage was quartered and shredded within the Cuisinart; vinegar, mayonnaise, two teaspoons of sugar, and a generous amount of celery seed went into a mixing bowl with the cabbage, and after a vigorous toss, the cole slaw went into the Sub-Zero to cool. Barbecue sauce, chili powder, chopped onions, and molasses were added to the beans on the stove's gas burner at low heat. A chicken breast was malleted flat, tossed in white wine and herbs, and prepared for the grill. I was happy in the cooking, the savory smells of Rhode Island's favorite hot dogs and the grilling chicken, a glass of sparkling San Pellegrino and a bowl of Goldfish crackers at hand, when Nadie climbed the three stairs from the den and sat on a stool at the breakfast bar. She picked at the few Goldfish left in the bowl and licked the tips of her fingers. Two little creases appeared between her brows. "How close *were* you and Dani?"

Whoa! *That* surprised me. And didn't. We have an unspoken rule to avoid any mention of old relationships, and this one was positively ancient, but Nadie, sometimes, crossed the line. My marriage and divorce long ago, in particular, seemed to come up recently, always obliquely, although how we both lived and with whom before we met each other, and the twenty years between us were usually respected. I replied, "When she was growing up, she was Tony's little sister. I never paid attention. When I came back, she was engaged to Charlie."

"Oh," she said as though considering my response clinically, and used a wet finger to get the last of the Goldfish crumbs. "And after that…?"

I paused. She made me feel transparent. But experience told me to be boldfaced honest with Nadie. "Once, a long time ago, when Dani was having problems with Charlie because he was drinking and had trouble at his bank job, we talked on the phone and had dinner once or twice. That's as far as it ever went. She's always been crazy about that guy. Always thought of me as a brother."

"Then you're involved in this only because Tony asked you?" Her voice made that a question.

Her premise bothered me. I was going to ask 'What's this all about?' when she said, "I know what you're going to do. You're going to get yourself involved defending Charlie and…." A pause with a sulky breath. "It's okay," she muttered and finished her wine.

I couldn't let that go. "Tony's got a real concern that Dani will be back to the …," I almost said 'shrinks', "… therapy if Charlie has another problem. And Charlie may be an ass but he probably doesn't deserve being the blamed for everything that's gone wrong with the Club. Besides, with this Arts Quad mess and Commencement Week, I can only do so much…." I let that hang.

My references to the Arts Quad controversy was on purpose. As an undergraduate, Nadie lived there junior and senior years and had sharp, predictable opinions as to its continued viability as a campus institution. "How's that going to work out?" she asked. "We can't have the cops thinking they can burst in there any time they want. There's still a Fourth Amendment!"

"Ask me after my meeting with Puppy Dog tomorrow." Leon 'Puppy Dog' Goldbloom, the Providence City Solicitor, is Sonny Russo's *cucciolo*, his lap dog, a sly, treacherous, amoral lacky whose idea of the rule of law is whatever Sonny Russo needed. And at tomorrow's meeting, he held all the good cards.

Nadie brought the wine to the breakfast bar while I flipped the cap on a bottle of Narragansett lager. She put out trivets, place mats and utensils, as well as mustard, piccalilli and pickle relish for me, and we sat across from each other after I delivered our meals.

"I don't really see what you're supposed to do," she said after she tasted, appreciatively, the salsa salad. She was back to Charlie. "He has a lawyer, Tony has hired this detective…."

"I'm a cosmetic, a shill. I give Charlie respectability at the meeting. Beforehand, I help out by preparing him with some Q and A. Tony thinks Charlie will pay attention to me."

"I can't see you as a shill. That's not like you. You don't front for people." She cut into her chicken. "How do you get into situations like this? What kind of friends do you have?"

"Real people, real problems," I replied. Sometimes, her conversation reminded me of a law school professor's use of the Socratic method—always questions, very few answers.

Her fork clattered on her plate. It was unintended but served to get my attention. "No, you positively enjoy it!" she said, sitting back, her fork now pointed at me. A strand of hair had fallen over her forehead and she whisked it away.

"Seems like the thing to do." How can I explain this 'honor your commitments with integrity' ideal that is my parents' lasting gift to their sons.

"Don't you think *maybe* you could be taken advantage of? Even by Tony?"

"No," I replied. As she well knew, at various times in my life, Tony Tramonti has been a protector, coach, good or bad for my morals and maturity, and above all, steady friend. While his battles with Sonny Russo had made him self-absorbed, nothing had changed the basics of our relationship. I took a long pull on the beer. "He's doing what a friend should do. Ask for help. What's wrong with that? I'd do the same."

"Sure. When do you ask for help? You never need help. Your family...."

"Please, let's not go there...."

She backed off but said severely, "And do not, I repeat, do not, let anything keep you off the plane to Milan. I don't care what stage your soap opera might be in...."

We were to be leaving in ten days for two weeks in Northern

Italy, our second trip to Italy and my anniversary present to her in April, celebrating our initial conversation at a faculty cocktail party years earlier. The prospect of Italy was the one thing that seemed to perk her up when whatever had been 'troubling' her manifested.

"Not to worry," I said as I finished the first Saugy. And I meant it.

CHAPTER SIX

City Hall, according to tourist brochures, is 'designed in the fashion of Second Empire Baroque.' Think of it as four floors and a grand staircase in search of a building.

During Providence's golden age of innovation and economic expansion in the 1870's, the impressively squat pile of gray granite, tiered columns, recessed windows, multiple balconies, mansard slate roof, and stone balustrade was a projection of the city's prosperity. That was the era of Rhode Island's great industrial enterprises like Corliss Engine Works, American Locomotive Company, American Woolen Company, Gorham Silversmiths, and Brown & Sharpe Manufacturing. All world class companies …, and all gone.

Maintenance within City Hall is a flit and a wipe, a reminder that sleaze prevails within these precincts. Still, that is better than when City Hall was *really* a dump, before the Preservation Society turned its wrath on the Mayor's Office. Trash piled up in its hallways, blown light bulbs could go weeks without being replaced, water from urinals in the men's rooms gushed in sluices across the floor. 'Lunch' was available in a dingy, airless coffee shop where any day, you could order the special 'meat' sandwich with cold French fries in a watery gravy from unfriendly people—all relatives of a political somebody—behind the counter and there was any kind of soft drink so long as it was Diet Pepsi which arrived fizzless. Ice? Fahgettaboutit!

I entered from Fulton Street and inhaled the dry smell of disinfectant and ancient coffee that is an effluvium in Providence municipal buildings. The morning's brilliant sun, diminished by a layer of grime on the enormous skylight sixty feet above me, provided a meager light to the cavernous interior. A half dozen city workers in casual clothes—it is always 'casual day' at City Hall—clutching Styrofoam coffee cups were in conversation in front of the pokey, still manned, often out-of-service, elevator so I decided to climb the worn marble staircase adorned with brass stanchions holding rarely illuminated globes to Puppy Dog's third floor office.

At the second floor landing, I adjusted my shoulder valise in front of the Mayor's Office. Interior lights penetrated the frosted glass in the doors to his suite and I wondered if Sonny Russo was in residence this early in the morning 'workin' for the City!' Not to worry, Providence, his staff always knew where 'hiz honor' was schmoozing or politicking or if he was in the cozy confines of his hideaway suite at the Hilton across Route 95 from Federal Hill. A columnist for the *East Side Monthly* recently wrote that Sonny's message to his constituents was 'I'm doin' the best I can and it's not as bad as you think,' unless you had business with the City in which case 'but for you, it could be worse.' The writer's real estate tax assessment will be carefully examined!

One more flight through motes of old dust and a turn to the right brought me to an oak double door marked 'Solicitor' in gold *Olde English* script, with an aperture at eye level for someone five foot five. I knocked. The aperture opened, closed, a buzzer sounded, and the door opened to a high ceilinged room with worn red carpeting. Puppy Dog's long-time secretary, Paula Ciccone, whose raspy voice I had heard innumerable times announcing 'Mr. Goldbloom is on the line,' had her face two inches from a computer screen, ignoring a flashing telephone console on her desk. The lummox who admitted me, a City Hall 'guy' for sure as evidenced by his brush cut, squinty, black eyes, round face with a double chin, and greenish haspel suit a size too small, didn't let me pass until Paula said without more than a second's glance, "Hi, Mr. Temple, Mr. Goldbloom has the Chief with him."

Great!

Unbidden, I took a chair under a studio photograph of the smiling Mayor that captured Sonny in a moment when he could have passed for Joe Pesci planning a mob hit. Paula seemed unusually grumpy, sweeping away her version of a Hollywood version of Cleopatra's hairstyle: jet black, parted down the middle, bangs cut sharply above her dark eyes, and not a strand out of place. Her lummox, apparently no longer considering me an immediate threat to the peace, awaited instructions which came as she swung away from the computer in a frustrated squeal for a latte from the Starbucks in the Biltmore and a PowerBall ticket from the newsstand on the first floor.

With Paula now answering the telephone in a flat voice indicating that *all* incoming calls came at a moment of high inconvenience, I considered the University's positions, likely to be assailed at the meeting. From my valise, I took a dog-eared copy of the now ten year old *Protocol For Security and Law Enforcement between the Providence Police Department and the Carter University Security Office*, and the 'incident' report on the Arts Quad confrontation prepared by Bill Tuttle, Carter University's Chief of Security, a retired major of the Providence police and no favorite of Chief McCarthy.

I didn't have to review the Protocol since I had negotiated its provisions when I was the University's outside counsel, and had revisited it many times since. In a few succinct paragraphs, it outlined the authorities and obligations of the Security Office in relationship to those of the Providence police when it came to security and crime on the campus. 'Concurrent jurisdiction' is the key phrase which means that except in an emergency, the Security Office provided basic security for the campus and its residents, controlled noise, parties, etc., and Providence cops took care of traffic and general crime. Nothing in the Protocol gave any additional right of entry to Providence cops on University property; nothing indicated that they couldn't investigate crime or arrest when appropriate. Rapid, accurate communication, and robust cooperation were the keys to making it work …, and it did when there was the 'peace.'

I then skimmed Tuttle's report. Two weekends earlier, at the close of the reading period before examinations, a Saturday night party attracted, in addition to Arts Quad residents and other Carter students, party goers from other venues, including downtown clubs, because every utility pole on Thayer Street had been stapled with colored flyers advertising an end of the semester 'debauchery.' It was a warm May night and by midnight, the crowd spilled out onto Orchard Street from the music echoing courtyard. That coincided with the arrival of three Providence patrol cars, sirens on full blast and strobe lights spewing a psychedelic dazzle. The half-clothed drunks milling around reacted with rowdiness, the cops forced their way into the courtyard, the kids scattered, and the cops found themselves braced up against a couple of our security officers who didn't appreciate being pushed around on University property. Then, surprise, surprise, enter stage left, Chief McCarthy and Mayor Russo from a patrol car, along with a video van from Channel 11. Supposedly, the Mayor and the Chief were doing a documentary on Saturday night patrols in the city and had been 'called to the scene.'

It looked, smelled, and was a set up.

With video camera lights blinking, the Mayor, the Chief, and the handpicked cops went nose to nose, belly to belly, and almost baton to baton with the harried security officers. Only Tuttle's quick arrival kept things under control. In minutes, the diminutive, paunchy Sonny and girdle-strapped McCarthy were on

Orchard Street strutting for the cameras, giving us a course in politics by media, decrying the 'riot' and the Arts Quad's well-earned reputation as the 'campus drugstore.' Over the next several days, video and sound bites aired on local stations and the citizens of Providence saw and heard their mayor and chief of police, righteously cloaked in law and order, decry the 'druggies,' 'trust fund kids' and 'Keystone Kops' of Carter University.

I remember Tuttle saying, "It's only a movie."

It could have ended then, but it didn't. The Carter *Crier*, our student daily newspaper, proclaimed Russo and McCarthy 'Buffoons of the Year' and a group of Arts Quad residents picketed the Mayor's home in Elmhurst, allegedly scaring the rarely visible Mrs. Russo to death, and got arrested for breach of the peace. We got them out on bail which led to an 'extra' from the *Crier* that was over the top: *Nazi* became shorthand for city officials and cops. That gave some of McCarthy's minions in the FOP license to picket the Arts Quad which brought out tired security officers, the tipped-off media, and Arts Quad residents who were, how to put it, none too gracious in their reception. The local television news reveled in the standoff and we barely kept the ugliness from becoming more physical and permanent.

Unlike prior confrontations, Sonny didn't overplay his hand. In the days that followed, he used friendly media interviews and talk radio hosts to stress that Police Commissioner Tony Tramonti didn't back his 'men' whenever Carter University was involved because he was too 'chummy' with those 'snobs' up on the Hill. For Sonny, it was a public relations coup, something to chortle about with his cronies at watering holes where political people appreciate a 'win.'

Ugh!

I put Tuttle's report and Protocol back in my valise and considered the clear injunction of the Provost at this morning's senior staff meeting: "We need a truce, Algy, we need cooperation." The University was most vulnerable to retribution during Commencement Week. Streets have to be closed, traffic rerouted, VIP's escorted, the ban on parking overnight not enforced, and a general tolerance of minor offenses, like walking on public streets with 'open receptacles of alcoholic beverages,' has to prevail. Otherwise, chaos. With almost two thousand seniors graduating, and two to three times as many parents, relatives, friends and other visitors soon to converge on a ten block circle around The Green, Puppy Dog knew that I had to 'make the peace.'

What would he try to extract from me?

At ten-twenty, Puppy Dog's office door opened and Chief Daniel Patrick McCarthy, his map of Ireland face looking none too happy, burst into the reception area. In a dress, dark blue uniform replete with golden shoulder boards and brass buttons, his growing bulk was only somewhat disguised. He had to know I had been kept waiting and that would have pleased him. Curtly, he said, "Gettin' ready for Commencement?"

Right on target. I acknowledged we were.

"Hope the weather holds." His blue eyes drilled mine; he was close enough for me to get a whiff of Aqua Velva as I focused on his bulbous, roseate nose that operates like a thermometer: the angrier he gets, the deeper the red.

"It never rains on a Carter commencement," I smiled. "The President doesn't permit it." Ha. Ha.

No reaction. His steely stare and lips remained set; then he took a service hat with a scrambled eggs brim from under his arm and put it firmly on his square head. The color of his nose seemed darker as he sputtered a 'see ya' to all and marched out.

Puppy Dog had observed the pleasantries. His seersucker suit looked slept in, his faded white shirt and his trademark dark blue tie were rumpled and none too clean. A strand of dyed black hair was slipping from his balding pate. But, in lieu of his usual dour expression, his rodent face was awash in a superior amusement. "Come right in, Alger, come right in," his thin, oily voice instructed, and I passed by him into a room with red and black flock wallpaper once found in seventies' cocktail lounges and a framed poster of Sonny from his first mayoral campaign. A massive desk and credenza were piled with files, folders and message slips that probably hadn't moved since my last visit; a high back, black leather executive chair was behind the desk. Dusty looking drapes framed a slice of grimy window with an exceptional view of the scaling concrete of the parking garage behind the Biltmore. Across the room was a door, perhaps to the rumored back stairway to Sonny's office one flight below.

Puppy Dog gestured toward a metal chair in front of the desk which I took as he eased into position across from me. With his rat catcher eyes burning bright, he began in the middle of a cackle. "The Chief really has it in for your security people. He doesn't appreciate the lampoons, the disgusting antics, ..."

I knew that but that's why God gave cops like McCarthy tough skins.

"If it was South Providence, out come the wagons and everybody gets brought in. So why are Carter students any different...?"

Vulnerable at that jibe, I ignored him by pulling out the Protocol and saying it was clear what was supposed to happen when city cops met campus cops: communication, deference to the force on site, etc. It could use an update, I said, especially on communications, but the basics were there. Puppy Dog, his eyes impatiently wandering around the office, began to wave his hands at me which I took as a signal to halt my defense. "Despite the Chief's ... reluctance, we could all use a breather," he intoned. "I'm willin' to look at the Protocol this summer, get past this outrage at that drug house you call a 'quad.' The Mayor's willing to keep the rhetoric down, if we can move on."

Huh? Did I have too many espressos this morning?

"Leon, what's up?"

One of Puppy Dog's many irritating traits is that his face twists into an altar boy's piousness immediately prior to his message. "It's gettin' outta hand! You know that. There are a coupla things I could mention that could … *maybe* … get us on track." His snake-like tongue slowly wet his thin lips. "For one, you heard the Mayor created a 'sister city' relationship with Verona …, Verona, Italy? Ever been there?" I had heard and had been there, although Puppy Dog, his face glowing with the transcendence of Sonny's brilliance, didn't care. "Wonderful place, arcades, squares, old buildings …, like they have in Italy."

Really?

"Went there for the signing. They loved Sonny!" I bet. "We agreed to sponsor a Verona festival here during the first two weeks in November. Next year, it's in Verona, with Providence going there! Going to be big, very big, Alger. Lotsa artisans coming over, goldsmiths, silk weavers, painters, great chefs from their restaurants will cook at ours, you name it. They're gonna make jewelry, sell cheese, the local vino, cook, it will be fantastic! Tourists will love it! The hotels are dizzy with the possibility. So, we've been asking ourselves, where can we show 'em off? Someplace big enough for the crowds?"

Rhetorical questions? Hardly.

"The Civic Center isn't the right venue. Got Bruins hockey, PC basketball by then, it's too far from the river, and anyway, it's a shit box these days. Forget the Convention Center, that's the State's, not ours, and Sonny's not going to give up jurisdiction. Nothing on Federal Hill's big enough. We need space downtown…."

I suggested, half in jest, "WaterPlace Park? Tents?"

"Tents! Are you shittin' me?" he shouted, amazed that I still had no appreciation of the magnitude of Sonny's event. "For maybe the President of Italy?" His arms spread wide. "This is big! We gotta have proper space. And on the river!" His hands went over his head to stretch behind his scrawny neck and his voice lowered to a suggestive tone. "Like those three buildings you just got on South Water. Perfect, I told the Mayor, they'd be perfect! Cleaned up and made available for a couple of weeks, a month, what a goodwill gesture to the City! Of course, they gotta be really cleaned up …."

He was referring to a recent donation to the University, three brick faced buildings on the RiverWalk at the Providence River between Verrazzano Park and the Point Street Bridge, most recently a warehouse, an ill-maintained office building, and a furniture store, all parts of a long defunct costume jewelry factory. And would you believe it, they were built in the 1860's in an Italianate design, including a connecting colonnade! Cleaned up, they would be perfect for exhibition space for events. But since Puppy Dog suggested it, I shrugged. "Sonny dumped all over us when the gift was announced. 'More real estate off the tax rolls,' …."

"Oh, c'mon, you probably don't know what to do with them"—he happened to be right; the Planning Office was thinking sale rather than reuse by us—" and if the City could use 'em for awhile after you clean'em up, that takes away some of the beef. Right?"

That meant a tiny concession in our battle with Sonny, so I denigrated the possibility. "I hear they're in terrible shape. Not up to code. Probably a lot of other issues we …."

"Not a problem. We can have the fire marshal and the building inspector down there any day."

"I could check with the President's Office…."

"Do that, Alger, do that."

"And the Protocol?" That was my way of asking, 'do we have a truce?'

"We'll work on it over the summer."

"And Commencement Week…?"

"I don't see a problem. Want all your folks to have a great time. I spoke to the Chief. All set there, although he's none too happy. And we can talk some more about a coupla things …." He let that last comment hang but my mind was on how much more could I wangle.

"The streets around the campus could use a clean up…."

He didn't hesitate. "Okay, streets get swept, potholes fixed, sidewalks patched…."

"How about the city arborist takes down some of the dead trees and plants some new ones…."

"Hey!" Puppy Dog replied sharply, warning that I was ungrateful for his largess, "don't push it! Commencement is a breeze. We work on the goddamn Protocol this summer, if you can keep your druggies off the street that long. You clean up the buildings as a contribution to the Verona event and we use 'em for a couple of weeks. Maybe we work out something permanent? Sonny might say something nice about ya for a change."

"I'll do my best to get a quick answer."

"Good. Why not enjoy your Commencement? Do your thing and we do our thing."

Providence politicians are one in their appreciation of 'things.' This 'thing,' that 'thing I told ya about,' the 'thing that was taken care of?" And deals. I got 'dis,' you got 'dat,' I want 'dis,' so make a deal. All Puppy Dog and I needed to conclude our arrangement was the 'hand.' But I couldn't make myself do it. No handshake. Puppy Dog stood as I did. He waited long seconds but I kept my fingers on my valise. My hesitation brought out his need to give me a jibe. "I hear our Commissioner's got family stuff going on."

" 'Stuff?' "

"His brother-in-law down in Westerly," he replied snidely and I thought of Ugo Calibrese's connection to Sonny Russo.

What to do? I had the deal I needed on Commencement Week, but no 'hand' was going to be clasped. Instead, I smiled the widest smile I could manage and heard myself falling into that Bertie Wooster tone of rarified East Side Waspishness that irritated Puppy Dog. I began to prattle about this year's chances for the Red Sox, right out into the outer office, and past a surprised Ms. Ciccone. I never stopped talking until the door closed behind me. Puppy Dog never got the 'hand.'

CHAPTER SEVEN

Artemus Vose looks like a Provost: a mane of silver hair, reading glasses affixed to the forehead of a craggy face, a white shirt with bow tie, colorful suspenders and creased dark trousers. He exudes confidence and competence with a kind of world weary, seen-it-all demeanor fitting a former big business executive. All of which he needs as the University's chief administrator, the iron hand in President Charles Danby's silk glove. I rapped on the open door to his office and his glasses flipped up as he swung away from his Mac.

"Good news," I said brightly. "The truce is on."

He blinked in surprise. "What happened?" I summarized the meeting with Puppy Dog and watched suspicion grow in his gray eyes. "I don't get it," he responded, a frown crossing his face. "There's got to be more to it."

"Not that I can see."

The Provost rubbed his chin thoughtfully. "I don't see a problem with the buildings for his Italian event. But hold off on a response until after Commencement. Keep Puppy Dog dangling during the week. Okay?"

"Sure"

He clasped boney fingers behind his head and turned in his chair toward a window overlooking The Green. "Why," he intoned, "after beating us up, would Sonny opt for peace?"

"Must need the buildings," I said as I remembered Puppy Dog's 'coupla things.'

◦ ○ ◦

University Counsel occupies a tiny suite in College Hall a floor above and down the hall from the Provost's office. As I entered, I waved at my paralegal Marcie Barrett in her office and seeing the empty desk facing the entryway, was reminded that the formidable Maria Lopes, our shared secretary and receptionist, our pipeline for all University gossip, had Commencement Week off. Inopportune but she had a grandson graduating from Providence College and relatives were coming in from all over, including two sisters from the Azores. Marcie and I would have to survive a week of direct phone calls, mail sorting, calendar juggling, and the like. And importantly, no 'inside info' from within College Hall.

I slipped off my jacket and hung it behind my office door, emptied the Protocol, Arts Quad file, the *Journal*, and the *Crier* from my valise onto my desk, plugged my BlackBerry into a charger, and pulled out my desk chair. Although the Provost's evident doubts had spiked my glow of accomplishment, I remained ready to accept Marcie's accolades as she entered my office holding two coffee mugs. Dressed for work, even when College Hall is on a casual wear kick as it is during Commencement Week, she wore a muted red shirt dress accented by a matching belt and buttoned pockets, with modest jewelry. I took an offered mug and she sat in her usual chair across from my desk. "Well, how was Mr. Goldbloom this morning?"

I took a polite sip, then as I rolled up my shirt sleeves, I recounted my meeting, stressing the truce, the street repairs, and promised negotiations. Could be I embellished my role a tiny bit. Typical of her, her response didn't mince words. "Something's going on. You breeze in there and ten minutes later you have cooperation during Commencement Week, negotiations on the Protocol…?"

"Sonny needs those buildings and made the offer," I complained, chagrined at her reaction and even more aware of the nagging 'coupla things.' I was boorish enough to add, "I'm good enough to know when I've got a deal."

Marcie shifted her gaze to the office's lone window and its view toward Shea Library and downtown, her thin, handsome face registering surprise at my defensiveness. Recovering quickly and meaning to make amends, I suggested we skip our Monday morning review of pending matters in the office, with the comment that most of the student disciplinary cases had been resolved, except those that had been kicked over to September in the hope that the miscreants would find another school. "After all," I said, magnanimously, "it's Commencement Week!"

Her response, given stiffly, was to ignore my peace offering. "Steve Winter's memorandum on the Arts Quad Fourth Amendment issues will be e-mailed later today." Marcie, ACLU to the bone, and Steve Winter, a senior litigation partner at Champlin & Burrill, were salivating at the opportunity to brandish the University's constitutional rights against Sonny's media driven invasion of our campus. I said smoothly that we would use it if the situation heated up again or as a background piece during the summer's negotiations on the Protocol. She responded coolly, "Don't hold your breath."

∘ ○ ∘

Bill Tuttle can get salty when it comes to Sonny, Puppy Dog, and Chief McCarthy but he restrained himself when I explained I had Puppy Dog's promise of police cooperation during Commencement Week and negotiations to update the Protocol. Still, he was justifiably wary of reliance on Puppy Dog's promises. I asked him to insure his staff was instructed that there were to be no—I stressed 'no'—confrontations with the cops during the week unless in dire conditions. Tuttle affirmed he would get the 'word' out in the unsettled voice of someone who acknowledged rank and took orders, but wanted to make the point that the likely outcome of my directions would not be as predicted.

So far, the three recipients of my news from City Hall hadn't reacted according to expectation. Not a word of praise, no 'good job!,' only disbelief in the efficacy of my negotiation, if that's what it was. I glanced at a photograph of a radiantly happy Nadie under a red umbrella on the patio of Osteria Panzano in Chianti from our first trip to Italy. What would be her take?

Undaunted, I considered what I would suggest for a revised Protocol. Better communications? Team investigations? Reasonable notice? With whom, I wondered, would we negotiate? Puppy Dog, for sure, and who else? McCarthy wouldn't deign to be there….

And that's when being snookered hit me. My colleagues had grasped that Puppy Dog is as good as his word—and his word is no good. And I hadn't even mentioned the bothersome 'coupla things.' There wasn't going to be any negotiations! The University would agree the City could use the buildings. We'd begin to fix them up. Then, I would be calling Puppy Dog, asking when we would meet about the Protocol, and he would explain how busy he was and put me off. Then I'd call again and I'd be put off again, and pretty soon, he'd have his cleaned-up buildings ready for the festival, and I would have only a cooperative Commencement Week and, maybe, some minor street repairs. Eventually, I'd hear from Puppy Dog about a 'coupla things' which I wouldn't like and could say truthfully were not promised. Puppy Dog would say he had been double-crossed and we'd be back throwing punches again. 'I told you so' would be whispered in the corridors of College Hall.

"Ugh!"

○ ◯ ○

I worked without interruption into the afternoon until the sun found my window and changed the room's colors, making the sheets of paper on my desk starkly white. Marcie had remained uncommunicative and left the office at four-thirty without a good-bye. An hour later, I walked across a deserted Green, its buildings gray and bronze and angled by streaks of shadow, through College Arch and out to Waterman Street to the commercial hodgepodge of Thayer Street.

While there was a diminished level of commerce coincident with a rapidly emptying campus, Thayer Street was hardly in hibernation. Students wired to iPods or with cell phones glued to their ears flowed toward me, bicycles whisked by, and the familiar sounds of sidewalk laughter and street noises echoed. Starbucks' window couches were occupied by kids with laptops, pizza joints and kabob shops had customers, skateboarding high school kids were 'hangin' in front of the CVS, and the owners of a line of shiny motorcycles parked in double rows across from the Book Store had to be ensconced in one of the many bars. Further along, at Paragon and Andrea's, tables had been set for sidewalk dining, push carts selling hot dogs and Del's Lemonade competed for curb space, and a familiar, forlorn saxophonist, his instrument case open and strewn with coins and currency, blew screechy notes that competed with the rumbles of car engines.

My destination was a recently renovated Victorian ark near the corner of Thayer and Lloyd Avenue, home to a senior administrator in finance who was throwing one of many end-of-the-academic year cocktail parties. Not that I'd make every list but I could have been in more than a few East Side living rooms over the past month as administrators and senior faculty belatedly crammed their neglected social obligations into the weeks before

Commencement. In five minutes or less, I greeted my host and his partner, said hello or nodded across the double parlor to several colleagues and acquaintances, had a tepid, unshaken martini in hand, and sampled the offerings of canapé and excellent bruschetta from Creative Cuisine. To be honest, only not wanting to appear standoffish drove me to some of these soirees; too often after crowd scanning, a faculty member would discover me in a discrete corner and rush to instruct me as to the 'appropriate' course of action for whatever the Administration was about to get wrong. But not tonight. My expectation was that Nadie would be my shield; she would save me from irritation and enforced dullness.

Nadie was holding court on a rear porch. I threaded my way through the crowd to a circle of casually dressed, thirtyish males. They looked toothy to me, with the smell of the hunt. Shamelessly, I brushed a possessive kiss by her ear as she introduced me to two assistant professors from Psychology and one each from Earth Science and English. I took their reactions to my explicit claim in stride.

Unfortunately, my timing was poor. Their conversation was centered on the Arts Quad. Words like 'crisis,' 'thuggery,' 'cretins,' and 'Gestapo,' were thrown around to the nodding agreement of all. The Earth Scientist, with his oily ponytail and soulful brown eyes, was the most agitated and goading. I smiled back, nodded occasionally, was vague and sympathetic, and explained the Protocol, even as I sensed Nadie was waiting for me to respond with a brilliant, righteous defense of the University's right to be free of unlawful, bellicose incursions. Her questioning glance and, eventually, eyeful of challenge led me to excuse myself for a refill of my glass, and circulate. After finding myself accosted by a professor of English—all reason and quotations and of a type we once called a 'tweed brain'—for whom waiting to express his opinion was the same as listening, I found pleasant company in a professor of Italian literature and his beguiling wife who let me practice my ill-used, academic Italian; they gently suggested some conversational practice would be beneficial if I wished to order veal and not insult the waiter's family.

Nadie and I circled back together around seven-thirty, thanked our hosts, and walked up the incline of Lloyd Avenue, crossing over Prospect Street and down to Congdon Street. She wore a green silk blouse and dark slacks that gave her trim figure a youthful profile; her hair was tied back, giving prominence to ears that were adorned with tiny silver hoops. All together, stunningly beautiful. She seemed to have left her edginess at the party—maybe her coterie of admirers helped—and the wine exaggerated her natural conversational whirl-a-gig as she recited suggestions from other party guests as to restaurants and points of interest at Lake Como and Verona. I nodded often; another of the weak martinis, a glass of Gavi, two plates of bruschetta, followed by pink petit fours, espresso, and a not very smooth grappa, had made me very solicitous.

When we arrived home, she went directly into the kitchen for a glass of San Pellegrino while I checked the pile of mail in the salver on the central hall table. Ms. Pina, my wonderfully efficient day lady, had been in today and the hall retained the heavy botanical scent of Garden Fresh Glade. Alcohol had rejuvenated my ego so that when I joined Nadie in the den, I was full of my success with Puppy Dog: peace during Commencement Week, campus environs cleaned and repaired, a commitment to review the Protocol, and aid for the city's Verona exhibition. Progress on all counts!

Nadie's definition of 'progress,' however, was complete and abject surrender by the City, apologies all around, severe punishment for the cops involved, and a pledge that the Arts Quad was forever inviolate. She said to get my 'deal,' I was playing in Sonny and Puppy Dog's sandbox. " 'Truce?' With these cretins? If you don't go after them, they'll think the University is pulling its punches...."

Ugh. I didn't answer—I was disappointed—and opened the screens to the breezes which lapped the Hill and brought the buzz of traffic from a distant I-95. Building lights silhouetted office and apartment towers that lined the rivers of downtown; the State Capitol dome was brilliantly uplit. Then, suddenly and surprisingly, her hands were kneading my shoulders, consoling me. Another one of those rapid changes in mood?

"Easy for me to say, right?"

"Right."

She asked me when I was going to meet Charlie Fessenden and it was then I remembered that I hadn't mentioned one aspect of the Charlie Fessenden saga.

" 'Quonnies?' " she said.

"Actually, the Quonochontaugs. I can say it but can't spell it." How dumb was that! And I continued to relate what I had learned at the Sunday meeting.

"Why did they release their claim to Charlie's land?"

I repeated what Flanaghan had said, that the Quonnies wanted federal recognition and a casino and didn't want to cloud it up with a fight about the land claim in Westerly. Offhandedly, I continued, "Every tribe seems to think it has an inalienable right to go into the casino business."

I never saw it coming. She was all over me! Of course, 'every' or 'all' was a mistake, a slip of the tongue; 'every' or 'all' didn't 'think' anything. "And," she said, her emerald eyes sparking, "why not? Europeans destroyed their cultures, smothered their traditions, spoiled their forests, took their land, ..."

"Okay, you're right, you're right," I protested, but unwilling to leave the field without honor, I said "but why casinos? Lots of other opportunities, I would think."

"*You* would think…? It's not up to *you*. It's their land. They need the money. Rhode Island's hooked on gambling anyway."

"That's right!" I snapped back. The martinis made me do it! "That's the problem. So, we should make it easier to throw away money? I don't mind casinos someplace you have to get to, a resort like Las Vegas or Atlantic City, even forty miles away in Connecticut. But we've got too many people ready to spend their lunch breaks in a casino or Social Security checks or welfare money at any slot machine they can get to by car or bus. We already have slot machines in Greenwick. Face it, Rhode Island doesn't need another casino."

Her eyes widened in her attack. "You can be such a snob! And a nimby! The same people you always complain about. Native Americans are within their rights to have a casino if they are sovereign nations, as, I believe, the courts have ruled. They can do pretty much what they want, where they want to. If the 'white man'," she mugged, "likes to gamble, and gives them back some of what was stolen, why not? It's not up to you. In fact, you ought to be sympathetic since it was probably your ancestors who …."

She stopped and I'm glad she did. We can get into heated discussions over our different backgrounds and notions of class which can end in long silences. She says I listen to minorities with a tin ear, despite personal good will, and maybe I do get my back up whenever she presses her causes. Nadie, on the other hand, easily slips into self-identification with those who fit within her vast universe of downtrodden. Her saving grace is that she hates cruelty, and fiercely believes that the scales of justice require periodic balance. I no longer ask 'by whom.'

So, how is it we've managed to be lovers for three years? Because we respect each other … and sometimes learn.

I announced I was going to the loft to watch the Red Sox. On my way, I stopped at the drinks cabinet in the dining room and poured two fingers of Macallan. I'm not even sure that I wanted the Scotch but somehow I thought it was going to be a good idea. Upstairs, Mrs. Pina's ministrations were further evident in the shipshape neatness, shiny woodwork, and lemony smell she brought to our principal living space. I turned on the fifty-two inch plasma screen television and became engrossed in the game against the Blue Jays. Curt Schilling was getting knocked around and then a David Ortiz homer tied it up. I barely noticed when Nadie came upstairs and sat a few feet away at the HP computer on our work table, although every few minutes, there was an 'I thought so' or 'shoot' or other expletive. Ortiz was up again in the top of the seventh with a man on first and two out when a sheet of paper was thrust into my line of vision. I grabbed it; it was a two page printout from the *Rhode Island Almanac of History* concerning the death of Metacom or King Philip, chief and visionary leader of the Wampanoags, in 1676.

It was a particularly gruesome story. Philip, after reverses in his war against the colonists, his allies seeking peace, his son and wife captured, enslaved, and sent to certain death in the West Indies, took refuge at his encampment at Mount Hope in Bristol, Rhode Island with a few of his most loyal warriors. Colonists and their native allies attacked at dawn and Philip, brought down by a musket ball from a native, died in agony. The militia captain, one Benjamin Church, ordered Philip's body drawn and quartered as a traitor and hung on four trees; one hand was chopped off and given to the marksman, and his head was taken to Plymouth where it remained on a stockade pole for twenty years. There was a listing of militia officers present at his death and his body's mistreatment, and underlined, were the names Issac and Nathaniel Temple.

"Any relations?" she said unctuously.

"I have no idea."

"That's why I think if they want a casino, they can have a casino!"

"I have nothing to do with the Quonochontaugs," I said defensively. "That's Charlie Fessenden."

"You can't escape history!"

Her argument was one I couldn't win. She always had righteous indignation on her side.

I used the remote and turned off the game. I said, "I know this isn't particularly timely or romantic but would you like to go to bed?"

Her eyes softened. She said, "Well, why not."

And we did.

CHAPTER EIGHT

A sulky mist dulled the shapes of RISD buildings and drained the grass of color as I walked to College Hall. Even the hum from the distant highways was muted until buses and cars on Angell Street and a four-wheel boom box spewing rap music brought me perspective. Then, through College Arch, and into The Green, soon to be a focus of Commencement Week activities and virtually deserted as though no one wanted to be responsible for the dramatic change about to occur on our campus. Despite the evocative buildings, green lawns, and ancient trees, there was a sense of vulnerability as graduation approached. Our brightest and best were poised to move on, and Carter University soon would be diminishing in the rear view mirror of their memories.

Marcie ignored my entrance to our suite and, immediately, I apologized for my defensive attitude of yesterday, admitting that my victory over City Hall was pyrrhic. She reacted with an appreciative smile, and then, as certainly planned, got even.

"Guess who's on the invitation list for tonight's bash," she said with a mischievous glint in her eyes and answered her own question. Ugh! The 'bash' she referred to was a cocktail party at President's House before tonight's prestigious Commencement Week kick-off, the Carter Forum. Her self-identified 'who' was a big donor impatiently awaiting my letter on significant income tax issues relating to a proposed gift, a project that was currently dead last on my 'to do' list. I left her with a drawn out 'thanks.'

° O °

The next several hours were spent in our library/conference alcove punching up IRS rulings concerning donations of real estate to charities on our computerized legal research system. God, I hate tax research, particularly the jargon used by the IRS to give 'advice' on arcane tax issues. It was defeating me when the Quonnies came back to mind. For a break, I googled in a few spelling variations before hitting on 'Quonochontaug Tribe.'

A lot of two finger exercises brought up hundreds of newspaper articles from the Westerly *Star* on the Quonnies application for recognition from the federal Bureau of Indian Affairs, followed by a denial which sounded almost apologetic. If only the Quonnies could demonstrate this or that, the Great White Father would happily bestow its blessing, laying out a virtual road map for a subsequent submission. Included in the application was a list of financial backers, including Greenwick Dog Track Association, a/k/a Greenwick Downs, which meant Ugo Calibrese. Under 'Consultants,' I stopped at the reference to Carter University's Department of Anthropology and Professor Derek Kirk.

Derek Kirk is a Scot who landed at Carter a decade ago, one of the bright lights of the younger faculty, despite his scathing humor and 'I take no prisoners' attitude toward the pretentious. Soon after I arrived as University Counsel, his department became immersed in a controversy over the return of two totem poles to an indigenous group in British Columbia. Emotion, proprietary instincts, and hubris clashed as to their return, with Derek championing the position of the claimants. Eventually, Derek prevailed, impressing College Hall with his reasoned approach to an ugliness ignored for too long, that some of the Department's most unique and valuable objects might rightly be deemed stolen property.

"Leaving tomorrow for home for three weeks, laddie," he said when I telephoned to get his ear for a few minutes. "So-o, has to be today." I said I had some questions about the Quonochontaug Tribe. "Yew mean Quon-o-chon-taug *Band*." Sometimes, he laid on that burr so thickly, it had to be in self-mockery or play.

" 'Band' "?

"We use the word 'tribe' in a way native peoples of New England ne'er would have. Their basic organization was a wee more like our concept of 'clan'—'people' as a family, by tradition, and language, but loosely organized. In any credible list, yew'd find many designated in English as 'bands.' How much time do yew have?"

"Enough to be educated."

"C'mon down. Bring an inquisitive mind."

∘ ○ ∘

The Department of Anthropology is housed in a renovated factory building near our boathouse on the Seekonk River, a ten minute walk from College Hall. Pleasantly surprised that the sky had cleared to a cloudless Easter egg blue, I left the office at noon, my steps quickened by relief from numbing tax law. Through to Governor Street, my walk was shaded by canopies of oaks, maples, elms, and plane trees; traditional spring flowers brightened gardens and window boxes of Georgian Revivals, gabled Queen Annes, and filigreed Victorians. East of Governor Street, carefully preserved period housing gave way to vinyl siding and aluminum over-hangs, American and Portuguese flags, satellite dishes sprouting from three story tenements, tiny cottages on postage stamp lots, and more exotic flowers like zinnias, delphiniums, and sunflowers. National Grid was ripping up Ives Street in front of the neighborhood's delis, bakeries and taverns so I detoured to Transit Street, past triple-deckers with backyard arbors, cinder block garages with climbing crepe myrtle, and artificial flowers adorning

Holy Mary 'bathtub' shrines. With students vacating this popular apartment area, overfilled barrels, bursting trash bags, and dilapidated furniture lined the curbs.

At Gano Street, I cut through a small park, unaware that it memorialized the arrival of Roger Williams, the heroic founder of Rhode Island, by dug-out canoe on the nearby Seekonk, until I read a bronze plaque on a granite pillar. Narragansetts greeted his party with 'What cheer, Netop' or 'What news, friend.' Reading that inscription, I realized that I knew diddlysquat about the native people who then populated Rhode Island, other than they left familiar place and river names like Pawtucket, Woonsocket, Narragansett, Pawcatuck, Seekonk, Matunick and Pawtuxet. I became annoyed; if I didn't know, who did?

Derek Kirk, sandy haired, red-faced and lean as a reed, was in the parking lot of a two story brick building at the Seekonk's edge, enjoying a fat, black cigar. Smoking is not permitted within fifty feet of any University doorway but Derek, being a Scot and a nicotine addict, didn't pay much attention to 'foolishness': he once regaled me with other 'naturals' he had inhaled in his treks around the world and compared to those, tobacco is benign. Khakis are his year round uniform—he changed from trousers to shorts when it was warm enough to do so—and today he displayed knobby knees, tanned legs, and high white socks in beat-up hiking shoes. He greeted me warmly as he rubbed out the cigar in an empty flower urn which I suspect was there for that sole purpose, and pointed to two motionless blue herons fishing where the river became brackish with Bay water. He then ushered me up a flight of stairs into a small office furnished with a beat-up wooden desk, an equally ancient wooden swivel chair, shelves of books and manuscripts, and a file laden table with a computer; weavings adorned one wall, a white board another, and the flag of St. Andrew was the backdrop of his desk. Despite the clutter, there was something about the office that seemed ordered. Ironically, for an explorer and anthropology professor, over the pile of books perched precariously on a sill, his view was of the Dunkin' Donuts across the street.

"So, 'tis the Quonochontaugs, the 'Quonnies' that interest yew." His eyes were bemused. "Canno' imagine why our University Counsel needs a history lesson?"

I told him. As I finished, he shifted in his chair and stretched his hands out in front of him, cracking all his knuckles. "Tis my belief that Quonnies deserve to be recognized as much as any eastern, so-called, 'tribe.' But unless yew are a reader of the Westerly *Star,* yew likely know little if anything about them." The blue of his eyes became more piercing as he warmed up to his subject. "Ready? The ten minute course?"

"Yes," I said and he began a well practiced narrative.

"When the colonists arrived in Rhode Island, from Plymouth mainly, it was a fairly chaotic place. Most of the Indians were of the Algonquin linguistic group...."

"You said 'Indians....' "

"I say 'Indians' because 'native peoples' and 'indigenous people' and 'native American' are awkward and wrong. And they refer to themselves that way. Yew know, the 'American Indian College Fund?' If they kin, so kin I."

I was reminded that Derek was very non 'pc' for an anthropologist, maybe eccentrically so.

"The native population was down by the time Plymouth was settled, decimated by white man's diseases like typhoid, syphilis, various pests and germs for which they had no immunity. Around here, the Narragansetts held the west side of the Bay, the Wampanoags the east, and Pequots were pressing in from Connecticut. Lots of smaller groups like the Niantics, Nipmucs,

Sakonnets, and others under sway of still others, all goin' back and forth over what is now Rhode Island and southeastern Massachusetts. Now, we are talking about sophisticated people. Not only were they warriors, farmers, and fishermen, their sachems were consummate politicians, always ready to change sides. Could have been pupils of Machiavelli."

I smiled at how his accent turned the Italian philosopher into a Scot.

"Despite commonalities among them, they warred on one another, sometimes for the hell of it, sometimes for food or captives, or real or imagined violations of traditions. They made and broke alliances among themselves as fast as they did with the colonists in Boston, Plymouth, and Providence, but for fifty years, they mostly got along with the whites. Eventually, it got dicey as more colonists arrived and squeezed them into smaller territories. Which leads us to King Philip." From a shelf behind him, he took a large book, thumbed pages, pressed the book open on the desk to a full color painting of a handsome, full faced man of perhaps thirty, with piercing eyes and a hook nose, long black hair pulled back and tied in ribbons and feathers, dressed in scarlet robes and adorned by bead and bone necklaces and shell bracelets. "Not really him, of course, but the jewelry and garments are close to authentic."

"Now, this is where legend and fact may diverge," he said as the book was closed and reshelved. "Legend has Philip as the acknowledged leader of most tribes in Massachusetts and Rhode Island, a hero, intelligent, charismatic. But contemporaneous writings say he was often beset by doubt, sometimes surprised in battle, and egotistical enough to lose support of important allies. In any event, he conceived a united effort by all New England tribes against the predatory whites, and began what became an epic battle for survival that history calls 'King Philip's War.'

Derek took a boxed display of arrow heads off his desk and handed it to me. "These were collected by a settler from what was left of his farm house in Lincoln, Massachusetts after a raid in 1677." There must have been twenty or so, including one that was a glossy obsidian.

I handed it back and he continued. "Neither side gave quarter in their raids and pillaging during the summer and fall of 1675. That winter, the Narragansetts, Philip's sometimes allies, withdrew into a fort in the middle of The Great Swamp down in Kingston. Now, this was during the mini-ice age of the middle of the seventeenth century, colder than a witches teat, if yew get my drift, and the Narragansetts probably thought the place would be impregnable because it was fifteen miles from the Bay and there were no trails into the swamp. They may have let their guard down because in December, about a thousand colonists from Plymouth, Providence, and Connecticut, dragged themselves there through miles of frozen, swamp, guided by native allies."

He hunched forward for emphasis. "Now, remember, about half of the natives supported the settlers! Some for loot, others were paid, others because of old scores to be settled. Imagine that!" he said as he smacked the desk with an open hand.

"It was a fierce battle and the defenders eventually gave way where a palisade wasn't high enough, and a fire, probably from an arrow, destroyed the refuge in the center of the fort where the aged, the women, and children huddled. A bloody slaughter, with only a few escaping capture. Devastating to Philip's cause." The regret in Derek's voice was obvious. "Still, the war continued for two more murderous years, with towns and settlements and native camps destroyed, more abandoned. All of Providence west of the river was burned in 1676 and the east side would have been razed except that Roger Williams, at the age of seventy-six, addressed the raiding party and out of respect for him, they left that part of the settlement alone."

He paused in his narrative and his face became somber. "So, the tides of war turned against Philip, forcing him back to his camp at Mount Hope in Bristol where a native sharpshooter brought him down. Do yew want to know what they did to his body?"

"Not particularly."

"Well, it was nasty. After that, whatever was left of native unity fell apart and one-sided treaties were signed which brought the loss of most tribal lands. Maybe half of the already reduced native population had died or had been sold into slavery to the West Indies for the goin' price of thirty shillings a head! Kin yew believe it? Our God-fearing Pilgrims did that ...? And in less than two decades, most had abandoned their tribal organizations, except the Narragansetts who endured in Charlestown."

"You still haven't mentioned the Quonnies."

"I'm gettin' there. Be patient!" He was getting agitated as he described the disintegration and desolation of the tribes and his burr was becoming as pronounced as a bagpiper's wail. "A few survivors, refusing to be reconciled or to acknowledge their losses, found refuge in an almost impenetrable swamp in Greenwick that the whites didn't covet. Privation and disease quickly dwindled their numbers but a few survivors eked out a bare existence trapping and fishing. Eventually, escaped slaves joined them—Rhode Island was a slave state then—along with outcasts of one kind or other. So long as they laid low in what became known as 'Indian Swamp,' the whites left them alone. Eventually, the whites called them 'Quonnies' from 'Quonochontaug,' a salt pond south of the swamp. They didn't care what the whites called them, and it stuck."

His description of the South County swamp brought to mind a Cub Scouts overnight camping trip at age nine or ten. For a city boy, the dense woodlands, ponds, swamps, and mosquitoes and, why remember this, holly trees, made a lasting impression. Our camp site was near Worden Pond, and that night around our fire, our pack leader frightened us with a creepy legend about a lost tribe, the Quonnies, whose ghosts roamed the swamp nearby. Our imaginations ran wild that night as we huddled in our tents, with the ghosts outside waiting for anyone who foolishly slipped past the fire's light.

I mentioned my camp experience and Kirk smiled at my naivety. "Good stories to frighten the whites, don't yew guess," he responded.

"They practically disappeared from history until 1726 when some Greenwick farm boys got drunk and decided to get rid of these swamp dwellers, whom they blamed for any local mischief, once and for all. They got about as far into Indian Swamp as where the band has its headquarters now, when a young Quonnie leader called Magua, with a handful of followers, started picking off the invaders as they were strung out single file on a trail between swamps. After the whites took a half dozen casualties, they ran away. The militia was called out and got about as far as the ambush site when some wiser heads called it quits." Derek obviously thought 'good on you, Quonnies.' "After that, Indian Swamp was, effectively, off limits for whites. The colony put out a reward for Magua but it was ne'er claimed. Supposedly, he lived a Robin Hood life raiding farms for cattle, sheep, and chickens, and escaping into the depths of the swamp. One night, according to their legends, Magua went into the most uninhabitable part of the swamp and after building a huge fire, walked into the flames and disappeared, becoming a ghost who still haunts Indian Swamp. Years went by, memories dulled, a few Quonnies survived, and Indian Swamp became a kind of reservation without being a reservation."

Magua, I thought. The name was so damn familiar. Got to remember to google.

"Now," he said, "we get to the nub of the problem for the Quonnies and federal recognition. The Narragansetts retained tradition and organization, even after Rhode Island mindlessly declared the tribe extinct in 1881 and gave each of them about fifteen dollars for their land claims. *Ipso facto*, they were supposed to disappear! But they didn't. They kept their sachems, their medicine men, crafts, a church, burial grounds, pow-wows, corn festivals...."

"The Quonnies...?"

"None of the above. Remember, they were isolated in a swamp nobody wanted. As swamp dwellers, they didn't keep records, not even births and deaths, barely had an oral tradition, and because of their origins as remnants of different bands and non-Indian groups, there wasn't much of an organizational structure during the eighteenth and nineteenth centuries, despite clear evidence of differentiation from the Narragansetts, whom they warmly hated. All they had were the legends about Magua, some family alliances, a few customs and fire rituals near the solstices. As time went on, with a lot of prodding from the state after it bought or condemned a good part of the swamp, most Quonnies eventually left the area, got educated, intermarried with others, integrated in the community. Then, in the nineteen seventies, one family in Greenwick, the Gardiners, identified all who they thought were Quonnies, about forty of them, and organized a council composed of Gardiners mostly, along with some Jones' and Booth's and Ballou's. One of our faculty members heard about them, collected their few legends, and weaved them into something coherent."

Derek pushed his chair back, stood up, raised his hands far above his head in a stretch, took a step around his desk and opened a door to a closet containing a file cabinet. "My Quonnie library.

I study those still in or around the swamp, called by themselves, and others, 'swamp Quonnies.' Their meager oral history is in being outsiders, over three hundred years of not giving in to white man rules or standards, retaining the independence they achieved in their swamp, holding grudges against the Narragansetts, a few antagonistic to whites. Some fight Oaky Gardiner, their elected sachem, on everything that comes before their council, claiming he is too 'white.' One or two even claim not to be bound by 'white man' laws. Reminds me of the stories of wild Highland boys I heard as a boy."

He closed the closet door and sat on the edge of his desk. "Now, quickly, to the present. In the early seventies, the Narragansetts filed a land claim—*a lis pendens*, it's called—against all the real estate in southern Rhode Island. Claimed the land had been taken from them illegally by the state in violation of a federal law, the Non-Intercourse Act of 1792." He chuckled. "Love the title. Anyway, the suit scared every property owner in South County and knocked the hell out of the real estate market so Rhode Island offered a compromise: the Narragansetts would get a state reservation in Charlestown, about eighteen hundred acres on the condition they had to agree to be subject to all Rhode Island laws. That was the trade off: they got a reservation of undeveloped land and state recognition, and gave up their claims. Federal recognition came a couple of years later. This settlement, of course, didn't include the Quonnies who were not Narragansetts." He studied my face. "Are yew getting all of this? Too much?"

I responded that I was and it wasn't.

"When my colleague retired, I took over about when they applied for federal recognition. That was denied because the Quonnies failed to document their organizational history or prove they were a separate band before the United States was formed.

Another petition is being prepared to meet the objections of the Bureau of Indian Affairs. The land claim has been narrowed to most of Indian Swamp which is largely owned by the state, worthless enough to persuade the bureaucrats and assuage the fear mongers."

"How many Quonnies are there?"

"Ah, that is a good question. Remember, for over two centuries, they rarely recorded births and deaths so membership standards have tended to be loose. According to the 'official' band records, about a hundred. Only about twenty or thirty, mostly from the Jones family, live on or near the swamp. Oaky Gardiner, for instance, lives in Richmond now."

"A casino? Is that what they want?"

"Some, like Oaky Gardiner, more than others. A few, mostly the swamp Quonnies like the Jones family, are set against it or want to control it exclusively because they claim to be 'authentic' Quonnies. Quite divisive in the tribal council."

"Did you ever hear of a place called 'signal hill?' "

"Aye," he said, surprised by my question, "*Mouwneit*. How did you come on that? South of Indian Swamp in Westerly, wrapped up in the Magua legend. That's where Magua gathered his kinsmen before they ambushed the whites. Later, they used it for fire rituals through part of the nineteenth century and started again after Oaky Gardiner got them organized. But, without a dig there, nobody will be able to prove anything helpful to the application, and that's not bloody likely, since its been bulldozed…?"

"You mean, the golf club…?"

Derek shrugged and said in a conclusion, "Alger, I know a lot about the eastern tribes and bands, but the swamp Quonnies are like no other group. They remain secretive, independent, and some have their own ethical slant on things which you might not approve. They don't even want me to know everything, and I'm on their side!"

I said, "I hope this isn't out of bounds, but how do you get away with saying things like that?"

"High-minded blunders are worse than outright lies," he responded. "They are humans after all, some good and some not so good, in our eyes." He smiled. "Glad that yew asked?"

I couldn't help it. "Aye, laddie!"

● ○ ●

I thanked Derek for his time and exposition and left shortly after, but not before asking him why Rhode Island had forgotten the Quonnies and their struggles. "Because it had to," he said.

CHAPTER NINE

Flanaghan laughed when I telephoned him from my office to confirm arrangements for Charlie's vetting and mentioned I'd gotten an education on the Quonnies.

"How'd you get into that?"

I told him about Nadie's challenge and he listened, chuckling discretely.

"Up there in Greenwick, in the Indian Swamp area, the Quonnies own a few acres, the state owns most everything else in a land management reserve. There's still some camp sites in there, fishing shacks, trapper's trailers, back from when nobody cared who did what there. If you go in, get into the maze of trails that peter out into swamp, you can't find your way out. Every year or so, somebody goes missing and the DEM rangers and emergency people have to rescue them. Even ATV's don't go in because of the tales about quicksand."

"Sounds like what Kirk described."

"And Oaky Gardiner? He runs a tavern near Low Town. That's in a corner of Greenwick at the edge of the swamp where it borders Richmond, Westerly and Charlestown, next to the tribal headquarters he set up. Oaky's been pretty much getting a wink and a nod from the three towns' cops for years for whatever he gets into, gambling, after-hours drinking, you name it, because he keeps the petty vices out of their nice neighborhoods. I don't mean to say his customers are only Quonnies; they're some other lowlifes we got down here, too. Anyway, by the time a Greenwick police cruiser could get to Oaky's, it'd be as quiet as church."

Could this hellhole be run by the sachem of the Quonochontaug Band? I asked and his voice cooled to a 'let me tell you, I've had experience' tone. "The Quonnies I know are mostly regular, law-abiding folks except a few that call themselves 'swamp Quonnies,' or 'real' Quonnies. When I was solicitor, I prosecuted a couple of them. They never cooperate, are always defensive, and got more issues than National Geographic. Oaky, because he's the Quonnie leader, raises bail when one of them gets arrested, hires the lawyers, and most of the time, Oaky, backed up by his son Peter—now, that's a piece of work—keeps these characters under control. While Oaky's pretty smooth, Peter is about as smart as a sack of rocks. And mean! He's a security guard at Calibrese's track when he's not enforcing whatever his old man wants."

"Still sounds bizarre to me."

He paused as though considering my motive for inquiry. "Oaky wants no trouble in Westerly, in case this is where you're headed. I can't see Ollie Randall, even drunk, going against Oaky to prove a point about rights some Quonnies think they lost. Not with Peter around. This had to be personal…."

Flanaghan had picked up a vague thought I had on my walk back to my office. Smart guy. End of thought.

∘ ○ ∘

Commencement Week at Carter University includes colloquia and public forums featuring renowned political leaders, scholars, and occasionally, celebrity parents of graduates. Full of big ideas, these luminaries come to promote themselves and their causes before appreciative and supportive audiences of alumni, graduating students, their families and friends, buoyed by the tactile sense of 'being there' and finding agreeable affirmation for positions they likely already hold.

Events run from tonight's Carter Forum through Saturday's graduation. Our distinguished guest for the Forum, a 'DG' in the jargon of senior staff, was our nation's most recent President, not an alumnus but a 'close personal' friend of several influential alumni and Trustees, on the speakers' circuit raising money worldwide to support AIDS research. Sharing the stage would be the popular Dean of the Carter University Medical School, the chairman of an international AIDS research foundation, and a billionaire financier whose private foundation supported AIDS research. The Development Office drooled at the panel's prestige which would drive positive media attention to our small Ivy, almost matching the hype when Bono was the DG the year his daughter graduated. Perhaps, their presence would put to bed forever the notoriety we suffered when Danby's predecessor invited a 'gangsta' rapper who arrived with his posse in armor-plated SUV's for a Forum on rap music as an art form. Within minutes, the audience was chewing on their seats.

Prior to the Forum, the University's VIP list, scoured and reduced to seventy-five 'necessary' people, would enjoy cocktails and a light buffet at President's House. As Marcie had warned, included among the invitees was a prominent alumnus, very rich, very prickly, very much used to getting his way, and remembered by me for his sneers at legal niceties. At his twenty-fifth reunion, he had offered, with appropriate publicity, to donate an upscale apartment complex in downtown Philadelphia to the University. His plan seemed simple enough, an annual donation of a portion of the partnership that owned the complex, until the University owned the whole thing and could sell it. On its face, it should be 'thank you very much!' The problem was that, according to the Development Office, he was seeking an aggressive valuation for his gifts, high enough so that our benefactor could quickly meet his longstanding, multi-million dollar pledge to the University's capital fund drive at a discount. My task, not atypical of what I do when not scrapping with Puppy Dog, was a letter replete with citations warning of federal income tax perils if his claimed tax deductions didn't match appraisals which the University would require with his annual gift. And, more delicately, that the University would credit his incremental partnership gifts toward his pledge at its own appraised value. It was a *Mission Impossible* moment and I fully expected to be cornered at the cocktail party.

At the last decent moment, I walked down Carter Street past the Old Quad through swirls of dogwood and mock cherry petals to President's House, then waited to gain entrance to the brick-faced mansion through a phalanx of our security people and Secret Service officers. Eventually admitted, I maneuvered through the crowded, familiar rooms of the first floor and outside to a sculpture garden where a throng of Trustees, big contributors, important alumni, a sprinkling of administrators and faculty, and of course, our DG, were enjoying drinks and hors d'oeuvres. I accepted an offered San Pellegrino and found a spot nearly hidden by the girth of an oak tree facing a Calder sculpture, a set of rotating, interwoven plates shimmering in the light evening breeze. I scanned the crowd and spotted the apartment baron in a cluster of gushing admirers surrounding the DG who was patiently posing for cameras and signing autographs. The financier had attracted a smaller group, including our aggressive Vice President for Development.

Charles Danby approached me. "Artemus told me that you arranged a 'truce'?" His questioning face reflected the same wariness of all to whom I had declared victory.

"I should have never used that term."

"If it keeps things peaceful this week, it will be more than a truce as far as I am concerned. And if longer, the better." He motioned toward the DG, now with his arm around the stooped shoulders of the billionaire. "Getting them in and out of here, controlling the picketers and protesters, the parking, all the security issues, Commencement Day. Could be chaos if Sonny gives us trouble."

"It will cost some money to ready those buildings …."

"Peanuts in the larger picture. Even a good idea. Shows how we could work with the city. In any event, we've got to figure out what we want to do with them. I'm thinking maybe we should offer them to RISD. That's really their part of town."

"Artemus thinks I should let Puppy Dog hang until after Commencement. But thinking about it, maybe, I should give him a hint of acceptance, a teaser…."

"Check with Artemus, but I like your idea. With Sonny, you never know…."

Danby left me and returned to his guests. Smart, determined to succeed, witty, and sincere, this first African-American president of an Ivy League university is perceived by his College Hall colleagues as a rare, innovative leader in the highest echelons of academia. After tamping down campus cultural warfare with its policy-killing, interminable debates, and surviving national bad publicity caused by a serial rapist on campus, he had gained sufficient stature in his third year of office to embark on a dynamic plan of future growth for the University. Important to me, he recognized my role as a trusted advisor and delegated legal affairs willingly, giving me wide latitude to make decisions. For that, I was appreciative and had become a downright admirer.

∘ ○ ∘

I finished my dutiful stay at the cocktail party, having skillfully avoided the donor who, despite an occasional wandering eye, was enthralled by his proximity to the DG and the financier. By seven, I was in my kitchen, a bottle of *vinho verde* uncorked, a spaghetti, tomato, onion and garlic frittata in the frying pan. I envisioned a quiet night, perhaps watching the second game of the series between the Red Sox and Blue Jays, with the prospect that Nadie would appear after the Forum likely on fire with the cause! God, why can't I get that way! Why is it I balance everything and then craft a response? Somehow, I can't, could never, just jump into things!

As I flipped the frittata for the final few minutes of cooking, the kitchen phone rang. Dani Fessenden's voice was tremulous. I had half expected, maybe hoped for, a 'thank-you-for-helping-Charlie' call, but this wasn't one. She choked back emotion when she said that after insistent prodding, Charlie had described our Sunday meeting in Flanaghan's office and she realized that he hadn't been totally candid. "*Why* does he do things like this?" she said. "I know this is an embarrassment, and he's had such trouble, but he has to be totally open with you. He says he didn't think it was relevant."

What she was talking about? My reply was to ask her to start again.

"He thought he was protecting me." She sniffled into something and took a deep breath. "Ollie Randall was fired not just because he was drunk—and I'm sure he must have been—but because I had an ... incident ... with Ollie that same morning. I know he doesn't show it but Charlie is over-protective. Beyond bounds, sometimes."

Charlie's violent jealousy was one of the 'issues' from years before, along with drinking and some abusive behavior, maybe booze related, that her brothers didn't know about, would rip him into pieces if they did.

"I've known Ollie for years and he's never done anything to me, but he's kind of creepy because he doesn't shave and he's not ... clean. And he drinks. He had some disease or accident that put him in a back brace so he limped. The morning he was fired, I was out for a ride. My dog was with me. Ollie was crossing from his property ..., I mean, the property his family sold ..., and I probably wouldn't have stopped but he waved and it seemed like the polite thing to do. Came over to me, and then I could see he was red-eyed and he slurred his words. My dog growled at Ollie, and Fancy, my horse, got skittish and started pawing and snorting and got a forelock up pretty close to him. He grabbed for the reins—which is about the worst thing you can do when a horse is skittish—and started yelling and swearing and slapped Fancy on the flank! She reared, took off, and I barely held on. I managed to get her back to the barn. I was on the verge of hysteria when I told Charlie what happened. He stormed out after Ollie but he was gone. Later, when Ollie showed up at the Club, and they got into it, Charlie told the manager Ollie was drunk and insulting and Ollie got fired. When he wouldn't leave, they called the Westerly police to remove him."

That stupid, silly bastard! Why didn't he tell us?

"I thought if the Board knew there was something personal...."

Dani, I wanted to say, wishful thinking. The Board would heap blame higher on Charlie because Ollie Randall's revenge against the Club might have been triggered by that 'something personal.'

"I told Tony and Fausto, but Charlie should have told you and ...."

"You told your brothers? When?"

"After Charlie heard that evil rumor. I ...." Her voice lowered. "Charlie's coming in. Please don't say I told you," and quickly ended the call.

Goddamn! Nasty thoughts flooded my mind as I returned to the stove top. The brothers had been purposeful in not telling me of the Calibrese connection *and* Charlie's personal motive for the firing of Ollie Randall. Was anything else being kept from me? Why?

∘ ○ ∘

The frittata was overcooked but edible and, fortunately, the young wine was fruity and delicious. I ate and drank in the company of the 'down' clues of last Sunday's *Times* crossword, noting that the caption clue was appropriate: 'Two-Time Loser.'

I took a last glass of wine upstairs to the Red Sox game. In the sixth inning, Tim Wakefield's knuckleball stopped fluttering and he was replaced by Mike Timlin who promptly gave up two homers which blew open the game. I was about to call it a night when Nadie telephoned. She was still captivated by the DG's message, augmented by a one-on-one discussion at a post-Forum event where the DG no doubt enjoyed the attention of an intelligent, beautiful, and impassioned proponent of his cause. After listening to her ardent endorsement of the DG's politics, I told her of my meeting with Derek Kirk. She seemed pleased that I had consulted Kirk but before I got into his exposition, she said, "If someone like Derek Kirk is in their corner, the Quonnies have legitimacy. He's not going to support a spurious claim."

"I never said that they had a 'spurious' claim. For all I know, there are five other groups out there with similar claims so we can have casinos on every street corner."

A hiss of disagreement followed. Nadie is ever alert to a challenge. "Well, I wouldn't worry about it. I don't see a casino on Congdon Street." And, she was back again to the AIDS epidemic in the Third World, that there seemed to be some hope for a cure despite an uncaring world order prejudiced against poor people, particularly poor people with AIDS, and that she was heartened by the passion of the DG and the other speakers. Then, we discussed schedules, mine wrapped up in the last days of Commencement Week while she, through with exams and grades, would finish her book review tomorrow and, as long planned, take the Acela to visit with her mother, up from Miami and staying with Aunt Ida in Brooklyn, until sometime Saturday. Then, she was back to the Quonnies.

"Okay," I said, "I have been educated about Rhode Island's native people. Interesting and thank you."

Her voice told me she wasn't satisfied that I felt enough ancestral guilt but said, "Good."

I said, "I love you and miss you already."

She replied, "By Saturday, you will. Be a good boy. Visit your mother, watch a DVD, and if Dani Fessenden calls and is a little vulnerable, don't get too sympathetic."

How did she know?

CHAPTER TEN

Responding whistles and trills of cardinals from the trees of Prospect Park and down the Hill on Pratt Street woke me from a confused dream—a lot of sex and some vertigo—before the alarm went off at six-twenty. I donned shorts and went to the basement where I put in a half hour on the treadmill watching the murderous Matt Damon as *The Talented Mr. Ripley* morph into Jude Law's character in the classic thriller. I lingered until Mr. Ripley crushed his former friend's skull with an oar while in a rowboat off San Remo on the Italian Riviera. Ouch! Then, I played a game of single-handed eight ball and followed that with an espresso, a toasted croissant sliced in half and spread with Rose's lime marmalade, and a perusal of the morning *Journal*. After that, it was a long, hot shower, ablutions and off to College Hall by eight o'clock.

To my surprise, Human Resources had dispatched a temp to our office, a fragile looking, bespectacled graduate student in English, who upon arrival declared that she was our receptionist-secretary for the rest of the week. Marcie patiently gave her some instructions on filing, how to answer and use the telephone console, and our computer system. The temp immediately pegged us as an undemanding duo, set up *Snood* on her computer, and informed Marcie, without embarrassment, that she wasn't adept at 'multi-tasking.'

In the next hours, I worked conscientiously, e-mailing my letter to the apartment baron, marking-up a proposed contract with ESPN for coverage of Cats football and Ivy League basketball games for next season, and outlined a legal strategy for a continuing fight between the University and a sports marketing firm who claimed ownership to the 'Carter Cat' logo. Nice, traditional law. After a lunch at the Faculty Club with Marcie who was at her indignant best after having digested Steve Winter's legal memorandum on the Arts Quad intrusion, we returned to the office. As I began to read Winter's memorandum, the temp appeared at my office door. "There's a Mr. Goldbloom here."

Puppy Dog? Here? No way!

"Said he was taking a chance you might be in the office."

Ugh!

He wore the same seersucker suit as Monday and a much battered straw fedora with a wide, red, and soiled band. His narrow face was flushed after a climb of three flights of stairs. "Just passing by, Alger. Thought I'd see where you spend all of your time."

Ordinarily, the rare unexpected visitor to our suite would have me ushering him or her into our mini-conference room/library, apologizing for its apparent disarray, asking about coffee or water or juice, clearing away files from the conference table. But, I couldn't make myself do that for Puppy Dog. Instead, I waved him into my office where he took in the piles of redweld files and folders on my sofa and desk before sitting in Marcie's chair by the open window. His hat rudely remained in place as he craned his neck to survey the room's photographs and paintings, focusing on a monoprint of the chalky hills of the Tuscan Crete. "Italian?" I managed a 'yes' and there was silence as I expected another dismissive question or comment. I found myself staring at his hands hanging out of frayed cuffs, his small fingers with nails bitten to the quick. Eventually, he sucked in a breath and exhaled loudly. "I try my best, Alger, I really do, but you guys put your heads in it up to your keesters every time."

"Not every time, surely," I said, barely thinking of my words, intent on his hands. The right one showed a number of liver spots and made me wonder as to Puppy Dog's age. Sixty? More? Was Puppy Dog really that old? That black sweep of hair over his pate didn't disguise much—was there another liver spot on his scalp—and there was his prominent Adam's apple almost lost in the folds of a turkey neck.

"By the way," he said, "are we set for the buildings?"

I replied, feigning disinterest, "The President hasn't gotten back to me yet with Commencement Week being so hectic. I expect so but I'll call you on Monday." The bobbing and weaving was beginning.

"Don't wait too long, Alger. McCarthy is offended! *Pissed off!* I've got all I can do to keep him from bringing charges against your security people." He leaned toward me to deliver his confidential advice. "Gotta get Tuttle on the team, Alger. He's going to blow it for you. Has these chats with his old buddies on the force and word gets out. We have the jurisdiction to decide what we are going to do and Tuttle's gotta remember that. Otherwise, …." His voice drifted away as he twisted his head toward the open window. He likely could see the blooming mock cherry trees and dogwoods out to Prospect Street.

I didn't comment.

"Beautiful place here. I can see why kids want to get in. Like the Mayor's niece. His sister's girl. At Bay View Academy. Ya know Bay View? Over in East Providence? Has her heart on gettin' in here. Parents too…."

Ugh.

"… and smart as a whip. Did very well on the PSAT. Should be right up there."

So, there it was. A typical Puppy Dog farrago. The first of Puppy Dog's 'coupla things'? He was like a Portuguese man of war, a gas bag with poisonous tentacles.

"I'm sure if she applies, has the grades, the extra curricula, and SAT's, she'd receive every appropriate consideration."

Puppy Dog smiled back at me, as though my neutral words contained a hidden promise. He took out a stained handkerchief, blew his carrot-like nose, and assumed a 'that didn't hurt too much, did it' pose.

"I'll send you a note with her name and particulars."

Silence for at least thirty seconds. The message had been delivered.

"And I'll speak to the Chief. Maybe he and Tuttle can straighten some of this crap between themselves so we don't waste a lotta time." He got up to leave and my eyes were drawn again to his hands. Somehow, I didn't want to look at his face. He said, "I suppose it quiets down here in the summer."

That was meant to be insulting. "A-c-c-tually, it's a very busy time," I lied in that super-Wasp tone he found so irritating.

His mouth pursed in disbelief. "Well, enjoy your Commencement. But, I gotta hear on the buildings. Monday," he said and got up to leave.

I smiled the widest smile I could, and surprised him by taking his elbow and ushering him out of the office, all the while chattering about my planned trip to Italy, which I said without thinking about it, included Verona.

"Small world isn't it," he said, with a snort of latent suspicion at any coincidence involving me.

I smiled at his back.

∘ ○ ∘

At four-thirty, I left College Hall and walked past the undergraduate dorms of the Old Quad on Carter Street where U-Haul vans, SUVs, and cars were being packed by kids in tee shirts and shorts in the shade of plane and dinko trees. At President's House,

I turned on to the cobblestones of Boone Lane, and quickly arrived at the high brownstone walls of Mary Street where the iron driveway gates to Temple House were closed. I unlocked a side gate and went up a sweeping gravel drive banked with flowering azaleas and lilacs into a courtyard with a porte-cochere where I punched in the required five numbers into the alarm system's key pad, wiped my feet on a cocoa mat, and unlocked the rear door to the mansion.

The Wednesday before graduation—today—until a few years ago, would have found Temple House bustling with graduating seniors, their guests, faculty, and members of the administration, for what had been known for over a hundred years as the 'Senior Picnic.' The enormous greenhouse and the two acres of landscaped grounds and formal gardens would be toured by hundreds; live chamber music would serenade those enjoying the shade of ancient copper beeches, elms, and chestnuts; tables would be laid with catered drink and food. But changes in the predilections of students and the University's administration eventually took its toll, attendance lessened, and the event was 'deinstitutionalized' by Charles Danby's predecessor as not germane to the serious business of a Carter graduation—this, by the same 'reformer' who invited the rap star as a DG! My mother, gracious as always, conceded. However, the decision had to have been costly to the University; she called the lawyer handling her estate plan the very next day.

Because my mother and Sylvia Odum, her companion, were in Beauford, South Carolina attending the funeral of a girlhood friend of my mother, the house was dark and silent and unwelcoming. My steps echoed on the tile floors of the pantry and kitchen and in the central hall where a pile of mail was strewn on its oak floor by the front door. For a moment, sorting the mail on a salver under a seascape of the surf at Beavertail by William Trost

Richards, feeling a world away from everyday concerns, I almost forgot my mission. But, of course, it was Nadie's challenge. Were colonial captains Issac and Nathaniel Temple ancestors? I was in a unique position to satisfy my curiosity because my grandfather had commissioned a family history, a dry-as-dust account by a Carter history professor of the rise to affluence and influence of the Temple family within and without Rhode Island.

My father's study is a seriously formal room with a Wedgewood blue ceiling, a granite fireplace, walnut floor to ceiling shelving, bookcases behind glass doors, beige draperies that were usually closed, and illuminated portraits and overhead light fixtures that went on as the door opened. As I entered, memories were stimulated by the scents of old paper, leather, and glue. As a child, the study was a place to hide, or to make a path of books like flagstones in the garden, or to lay out a board game where it could be left to come back to undisturbed, or to pester my father at his writing desk. Especially on hot summer days, because it remained cool no matter what the outside temperature.

The leather bound book was in a glass fronted cabinet under sepia photographs of Temple Bank in downtown Providence and the Temple wharves along the Providence River. I lay it on my father's marble, Italianate desk, turned on a green shaded banker's lamp, took off my glasses, and went to the volume's index. 'Issac Temple-Nathaniel Temple. Pages 38-40.'

"Ugh!"

Issac and Nathaniel Temple were the sons of Pardon Temple and Priscilla Atwood, second generation colonists. The brothers were born on their parents' farm, a large tract of land in Swansea, Massachusetts. Issac married and left Swansea for Aquidneck Island in the 1660's where he farmed in what would now be Portsmouth, Rhode Island. In 1675, King Philip and his followers torched most of Swansea, killing men, women and children, including Pardon and Priscilla, and Nathaniel's wife and daughter; Nathaniel, with the militia in Plymouth, rushed home too late to defend his family. The following winter, Nathaniel joined Issac and the colonists and their native allies who converged on the Narragansett's fort in The Great Swamp. After the savage battle, they made their way back to Portsmouth where Nathaniel remained with Issac. As men of property and natural leaders, they formed a company of militia that was part of the troop under Captain Benjamin Church that found and killed King Philip at Mount Hope. Nathaniel married again, raised a family of seven sons and two daughters, moved up the Bay to the new settlement of Warren, and eventually to Providence where he turned to coastal trading. He died in 1697 in Providence.

I turned to the front of the book where the family tree was contained on a fold-out section on vellum. With it spread before me, I easily traced the hereditary line that showed I was a direct descendant of Nathaniel Temple, 1636-1697.

My fingers went to the circle of light on the shiny desk top. Was I supposed to feel something? Anything? Those were ferocious times, I mused, both sides were in a fight to the death, barbaric in their cruelties. Could it have been avoided? Is it really so different today? Terrorism and trauma are everywhere, with revenge and sadism melded too often with religion, ethnic fears, and tribal hatreds. Maybe Nadie's militant passion about people and the avoidance of cruelty is really all that matters.

Anyway, it was over three hundred years ago. I'm not responsible for those tragic events.

Right?

CHAPTER ELEVEN

Charlie Fessenden was to be prepared by the 'team'—the accountants, Flanaghan, and me—at various times on Thursday, a scheduled day off for the Office of University Counsel. According to our play book, I was the designated mentor. Flanaghan would work with Charlie and the accountants in the morning, developing questions and answers that Charlie would, not to put too fine a point on it, memorize. I would arrive before noon, encourage Charlie's diligence to the task at hand, and pick a few softball questions to toss at Charlie when and if appropriate. He had requested that our session be held in the privacy of his home rather than in his real estate office or downtown at Flanaghan's; I could appreciate his desire for privacy.

Flanaghan told me that Benno Bacigalupi was still 'investigating'—exactly what was unclear—and would contact us if there was anything we had to know. So far, the enigmatic Benno had remained so.

With a high seventies temperature under a bright sky, it was a Carter 'Cats' baseball cap, RayBans, 'top down' day and I soon had my Mini Cooper convertible in the sparse mid-morning traffic on Route 95 south. I figured on forty-five minutes to Westerly by way of the South County Trail and was soon clicking along, thinking I'd be there in forty, when a turf farmer's lumbering eighteen wheeler brought me to a crawl at the URI exit. Damn!

Coming in from Charlestown on Route 1, the first left past Haversham Golf Club was posted 'Private,' more of a blacktopped country lane than a private way. Bordered by walls that spoke of tedious field clearing, of stones hauled, wedged, and wrestled into place by colonial farmers, it was shaded by mature trees appropriately spaced among rhododendrons in bloom and mountain laurels bursting with blossoms. Occasional gaps showed glimpses of verdant fairways and the grasses of the Club's Scottish Links. At the lane's end, marked by an oversized mailbox reading 'Pond House,' was a pea stone driveway leading to an oversized cape with salt-silvered shingles, chimneys at either end, dormers on the second floor, and an awkward looking glassed-in, octagon-shaped tower over one wing. At the rear of the house was a three stall garage and behind that, a freshly painted, dark red barn. I left my car in the driveway and walked by a modest clapboard boathouse on Wynomet Pond which guarded a dock where a gleaming sports fisherman with powerful looking Yamaha engines was secured by lines and protected by blue and white buffers. A horse whinnied in the distance and the gulls patrolling the pond sounded their angry hunger; to the north, there was a space that in my mind's eye was filled by Haversham Golf Club's clubhouse. Maybe I could barely make out its forlorn chimney.

Dani Fessenden greeted me on a front lawn dimpled by lumps of rounded ledge; to my surprise, she was accompanied by the friendly border collie who chummed with us at the ruined clubhouse on Sunday. In a pink shirt and designer jeans, Dani was as slim and comely as ever. Her curly hair, a glistening black, was tied back with a silver barrette. I received a polite kiss on the cheek and noticed that her makeup didn't disguise her tired brown eyes. The collie wanted my attention and Dani pulled the dog from me by its collar as she said that the accountants had left and 'Mr. Flanaghan' was working with Charlie in his second floor office. Keeping the dog outside, she led me inside to a generously-sized tile foyer where I had a glimpse of rooms that had the airy freshness, colors, and furnishings of a Crate and Barrel summer catalogue, then I followed her up a flight of curving stairs through a gallery and into a room with beadboard wainscoting, comfortably furnished, and full of sunlight. Charlie, in casual clothes, his head propped up by his palms under his chin, faced Tom Flanaghan in white shirt, loosened red tie, and suspenders at a long table covered by neat piles of manila folders. Charlie, with obvious relief, greeted me with, "Algy! Great! Now we can have lunch."

Dani's expression slipped to one of dismay, either because of the dismissiveness in Charlie's manner or because I was earlier than planned. She murmured, "Another twenty minutes or so," and excused herself.

I could see Flanaghan was on the brink of exasperation. "We could use a break," he said. "Maybe I can stretch my legs with Alger if he'd like. Meanwhile, go through the purchase orders one more time. Concentrate on the Grille Room...."

Charlie, whose face drooped at the prospect, reluctantly agreed and we left him at the table. Flanaghan straightened his tie, put on a suit jacket, and followed me down the stairs and out the front door. I headed for my car and retrieved my cap and sunglasses for some protection from the sun's glare. "The accountants put him through the ringer. Had to," he said, squinting in the bright light. But, he added, they seemed confident, given enough time and expensive effort, and in spite of the 'informality' of some purchases and invoicing, they could build a solid insurance claim. "This committee, the Building Committee, had the ultimate say on the purchases, but the invoices didn't get booked on a current basis. That administrative duty was squarely on Charlie's shoulders and he relied on a part-time bookkeeper who didn't keep up. Not that Charlie would know. The accountants say it should take another week to get numbers together from the general contractor, the architect, the interior designer, all the suppliers, and check on what got delivered, but they should come up in the ninety-five percent range, maybe better. Charlie, and the Building Committee, are goddamn lucky, if you ask me."

While that was good news, I said that I presumed there would still be plenty to negotiate with the insurance company, particularly issues relating to what the insurance binder actually covered. Flanaghan agreed. "The broker should be sweating since it's his binder and he's connected to board members. He says he's committed to a fair shake for the Club. He better be!"

We had a number of choices for our walk since Charlie's land stretched a good way around the pond's boulder-strewn shoreline. However, Flanaghan turned away from the sun and led me by the barn where open carriage-sized doors emitted the damp smells of hay and animal. Behind the barn, a corral with a rickety split rail fence, its posts riddled by woodpeckers and rot, encircled a smallish sorrel horse. It looked up from its grazing, flicked its tail, and resumed its solitary occupation. Like old country boys, we each put a shoe on the bottom rail and spread our elbows over the top rail facing the horse.

"I've also learned a lot more from Charlie," he began, "about the negotiations between the Board and Calibrese. Brutal! After months of haggling, with Calibrese not budging on his price, getting a free membership and other concessions, at the last minute, he takes two hundred acres or so off the table!" He snapped his fingers. "Just like that. Claimed he needed to protect himself in case the golf course didn't move forward." Flanaghan shook his head, either in disgust or as a comment on Calibrese's negotiation skills. "They must have been apoplectic but they wanted his land so they compromised with a deal under which the Club would lease the two hundred acres for twenty years from the closing date, with an option to buy at a reasonable price after ten. Then, the day before the closing, Calibrese demanded that if the course isn't up and running in four years from the date of the agreement—that would be July third of this year by the way—the Club has to buy the leased land for a couple of million, or pay an enormous increase in rent for the balance of the term, or the lease terminates and Calibrese gets the land back. That demand almost croaked the deal, the Board members all say, but Charlie convinced them to close because they might need the land for expansion, the annual rental on the leased land was relatively cheap, and four years would be plenty of time to be up and running. That last concession is referred to by the Board, and everyone else familiar with the negotiation, as 'Charlie's deal.' "

He found a handkerchief in his jacket pocket and unfolded it to wipe his face, then shook it at a swarm of midges sensing our presence, which led us to walk up a narrow dirt trail with deep tire ruts. High above us, a pair of red-tailed hawks wheeled on vigil for anything that might make a meal; the breeze off the water brought the dank smell of woods. Two foraging rabbits scampered into the briars as we approached a new cedar fence which marked the boundary of Charlie's land with the golf course. I assumed we would turn back but Flanaghan took off his jacket and put it over his arm, his thumbs went under his suspenders, and with his back against the fence, his eyes closed.

"Did you ever hear of Windmere Country Club or American Golf Company?" Flanaghan asked.

I hadn't and realized he was about to tell me a Westerly story.

His right arm swept toward the golf course. "In the early twenties, some Masonic lodges from New York City acquired four hundred acres back there, mostly pasture and hay fields, rocky as hell, along with a patch of barrier beach across Wynomet Pond. The idea was to build a shoreline retreat for lodge members, a golf course, along with a bathing beach across the Pond, lots of open space for hiking and outdoor activities, a boy's camp, too. They were going to drive up here or take the train, tramp around the trails, swim, sail, hit the golf course. There was a ramshackle inn off Route 1 that they renovated into forty guest rooms and a dining room, and had the premier golf architect of the day, Donald Ross, who designed Misquamicut and Winnapaug, design their course. Had flower gardens next to the inn that were so elaborate, tourists made it a regular stop between New York and Boston. They built a dock at the Pond, used a little steam launch to ferry folks across to their private beach on the Sound. In 1929 or so, in addition to the golf course, they began construction of a new clubhouse about where Charlie's boathouse is now."

He opened his eyes. "Love the sun but my wife says that skin cancer will get me. Keeps giving me tubes of sun block which I always forget to put on. Better head back." He flung his suit coat over his shoulder and we left the fence for the trail, with the raconteur still into his story. "Well, good things come to an end, don't they. The Depression came on, and for the Masons, even handshakes couldn't stave off disaster. They had a friendly bank mortgage loan but the friendly bank went under. They couldn't afford to keep it going and, eventually, the place was virtually abandoned. Their clubhouse never got much beyond the exterior structure and roof."

I was a half step behind Flanaghan, and he turned to check if I was listening, which I was. "A fellow by the name of Mayo, an Irish guy from Philly, started buying up bankrupt private golf clubs for pennies on the dollar. Had one outside of New Haven, one near Bridgeport, and another on Long Island, and he bought the Mason's retreat. His idea was to have a string of golf courses, all close to the water, a highway, and a railroad, from New England down to Florida. Join one, you join them all, private but not too exclusive or too expensive, more like family resorts than fancy golf clubs. So, like here, a guy could drive down from Providence, in those days maybe ninety minutes, and put mom and the kids on the shuttle boat to the beach, while he and his friends played golf. Add a few attractions that people liked in those days, a clambake shed, picnic grove, shuffleboard, tennis, croquet, miniature golf, horseshoes, …, give 'em a decent, plain restaurant, and you get the idea. He named this course the 'Windmere Country Club.' But there was a kicker. If you joined, you also had to buy stock in his company, American Golf Company. 'Golf for Americans' was the slogan. Floated stock everywhere he had a course, including here. He was a great salesman, and people liked his idea."

Flanaghan stopped, wiped his face with his handkerchief, and continued. "It took a year or so to clean up the golf course and then another year to finish the clubhouse—a huge thing from the photos I've seen—and build a beach pavilion. By the summer of '38, his idea took off. Waiting lists for membership. New courses in Florida and Virginia. American Golf ran a tour where you went from course to course by train all summer and into the fall, then down to Florida for the winter. The stock kept going up when nothing else was. People flocked here that summer, filling the hotels in Misquamicut and Watch Hill, and for the first time in years, things looked a little brighter."

We had now reached the corral. Flanaghan stopped, put his hands on the top rail of the fence. He was winded and when he continued, his voice lowered in a coolness I didn't expect.

"The Great Hurricane of '38 did him in. One afternoon, he had a successful business. In Westerly, a beautiful new clubhouse over Wynomet Pond, a beach pavilion, a golf course with a waiting list, and two hours later, he was finished. Caught the head of a massive tidal wave, smashing the clubhouse, wrenching it off its pilings into the Pond where it broke up. The pavilion was smashed. The golf course was ruined, scorched by salt water." He shook his head. "You probably never heard how terrible it was in Westerly. Over a hundred people died. All the houses on Napatree

Point were destroyed, most of the big ones in Watch Hill and Weekapaug were damaged, and cottages all along the beach here were gone. Three employees at the clubhouse, including ... a kid, drowned. The manager, who barely survived, got nailed later for manslaughter because he kept them at the clubhouse until it was too late."

We were now at the barn and I couldn't help but notice the perspiration on Flanaghan's face, the spot of dampness on the back of his shirt. "That was the end of Windmere Country Club and American Golf. Mayo's other places were also damaged or destroyed. And guess what?"

"Not enough insurance to rebuild...?"

"That too, but much worse. Mayo had cooked the books, robbing Peter to pay Paul. The cash was gone. Couldn't reopen. Faced with disaster, Mayo takes off, eventually gets arrested in Florida for stock fraud as he's leaving for Cuba, and that put him away for a good long time. Windmere Country Club gets foreclosed on and that's when Charlie's grandfather bought the land and built his house. After a few years, the way things grow down here, you never would have known that the land back there was once fairways and greens and sand traps. But I've heard every once in awhile at very low tide, a few pilings from the original clubhouse stick out of the Pond."

We continued past the house to the rocky shoreline not far from the boathouse. The sparkling length of Wynomet Pond was marked with boat moorings and lobster pots, and beyond the grass and brush of barrier beach, Block Island was a sliver of green on the horizon. A set of bobbing orange cones seem to warn boaters of something to avoid, maybe those errant pilings. A light breeze ruffled its waters as a Boston Whaler skimmed by, scattering a flock of cormorants drying feathers on a jumble of rocks; near the breachway to the Sound, quahoggers in waders pulled clam rakes on tidal flats. On a day as tranquil as this, I found it difficult to conjure up a massive clubhouse as described by Flanaghan or pavilion on the barrier beach, never mind a tidal wave. Flanaghan shook his head and said, "Haversham Golf Club is the third attempt to have a golf course on this land. Hard to believe."

I didn't say what I thought. First, the Masons, then Windmere Country Club, and now Haversham Golf Club? Was there a jinx on the land? Maybe because it once belonged to the Quonnies...?

CHAPTER TWELVE

"Ollie Randall never had a chance…," I said.

"Well, he set it off, didn't he," Charlie replied.

We were well into a lunch of ham rollup sandwiches and fruit salad in a spacious country kitchen at the rear of the house. Charlie had asked for wine but like us settled for iced tea.

Flanaghan wondered, "How …, why …, would you set a fire in a building full of fireworks and stay inside? Was he a smoker? Drops a butt and…?"

"Had to be drunk," Charlie said without pity. "Randalls are all drunks. You should see how they lived. Falling down house, lean-tos, chicken coops, rusted out truck bodies, all jumbled together. Lay abouts and drunks!"

Flanaghan's usual friendly demeanor dissolved at Charlie's comments and I had no idea what kind of signals I was giving off, but it was enough for Dani to leave the table and return with a plate of warm chocolate chip cookies. Then, without my asking, Charlie seemed compelled to give us his recollection of the night of the fire.

He had been home, alone, he said, watching a DVD. Dani had taken their two daughters to check out a summer camp on Martha's Vineyard where they would be counselors. Dani nodded firmly in agreement. The night was clear, with a full moon and a blustery wind off the Sound, the kind that would 'blow off Grandma's bloomers,' he said oddly. About ten, he heard the first siren and then several more. Curious, he got into his car, reached Route 1 as a Dunn's Corner ladder truck roared by and he followed it to the clubhouse. "By then, flames were shooting out of the windows on the second floor, the roof was on fire, with the wind blowing debris everywhere in showers of sparks. I mean *showers*! It took *forever* for fire trucks to hook up to the hydrants and start hosing it. Then, there's a *tremendous* explosion. Positively shook the ground! Blew the roof of the maintenance building right off. Right about then, the new manager shows up and admits there were fireworks stored overnight. The chief pulled his crew away because there's explosions every few seconds, the whole sky lit up with rockets screaming overhead." He stood and his palms went upward. "End of the clubhouse!" And without a change in tone, "Algy, how about a quick game of pool…?"

That was enough for Flanaghan. He left the table, went upstairs and returned with a briefcase and a typed list of questions for me to consider. "The softballs," he muttered.

Reluctantly, I agreed to Charlie's request for a 'quick game.' How typical of Charlie to postpone something unpleasant. We left the kitchen for a spacious family room on the other side of the house, complete with a customized home theater and a new eight foot Brunswick table with heavy legs and maroon cloth. A rack was set and eight ball was the game. Charlie gave me a cue stick and asked me to break, which I did, sending balls to all sides of the table and pocketing two solid colors. I pocketed another ball and then obliged my host by missing an easy shot.

As I suspected he would, Charlie began to make his plaintive case. "Algy, *you* can see how absurd all of this is." His tone intimated that *I*, of all people, should understand that he was getting the shaft. As he spoke, he set up for a cross table shot.

I had to ask, "When you granted the option for your land, you didn't have *any* idea it was to go to Calibrese?"

His wobbly shot got a striped ball in a side pocket and with a grin of satisfaction, he stood to face me. "None! No idea at all!

This … Silverman said his principal wanted the land because he was going to develop a very exclusive subdivision, only eight houses, on part of Randall's property which he had under agreement. Maybe I should have pressed him but right then, after the Newport … problem …, before I really got established here, the option money came in handy."

Charlie, although obviously a careless player, pocketed two more balls and smiled. One of the great things about pool is that anyone who doesn't rip up the felt experiences a rush after pocketing a few balls. He missed the next shot with an expletive and shortly, four of my solid balls disappeared off the table. I could have run out the string but didn't, leaving the eight ball in play.

"I found out about Calibrese the same time as everyone else," he continued. "The whole town was in a panic. Everyone thought Calibrese was going to stick a casino right in my backyard, and then along came the Watch Hill folks and I thought of Calibrese's land and matched them up. Algy, I saved Westerly from a casino! Back then, people would stop me in the street and thank me!"

There was no pretense in his voice; he believed that he had been a hero.

He resumed play while he described meetings of the Building Committee. Every major decision or purchase had a name attached to it: Fred Giles, the vice chair of the Board, insisted on the lap pools; Josh Crotty was addicted to mahogany; Howard Kittery insisted the Club use the fellow who built his wine cellar in Palm Beach; James Slocum had a thing for the 'right' look in the Players Grille; Missy Wheatcroft was an expert on window decor. The Committee meetings revolved around what members saw at other clubs, or read in golf magazines, or had whispered in their ears by spouses or architects or designers, meeting after meeting, with checks flowing under Charlie's signature as Club Secretary.

Charlie won and insisted that he would give me a chance to 'get even.' I agreed because he was into the Club's leadership and membership. One thing I discerned during Charlie's ramblings was that while the founders of the Club, the Board, and the members of the Building Committee were mostly Watch Hill 'old money' as Charlie described them, the bulk of the membership was 'new money,' Goldman-Sachs bankers, hedge fund geniuses, venture capitalists, the Wall Street gurus who were buying up Watch Hill and Weekapaug 'gray ladies' and remodeling them beyond recognition or tearing them down to the foundation and beginning again. These groups seemed to have reached an accommodation such that the 'old money' would be the face of Haversham Golf Club, while the 'new money' would supply the bulk of the membership and provide the cash. That arrangement seemed to be an acknowledgement by newcomers that a huge second home, beach club privileges, or a forty foot boat didn't equal acceptance in a tight-knit summer colony. I suspected that the 'old money,' as it always had, would allow 'new money' to supply the necessary cash, and would play its role of heritage, prestige and authenticity, unless and until the game became too costly, or worse, embarrassing. Then, watch out!

Eventually, we went up to Charlie's office. Flanaghan's twenty-odd 'softballs' were short and so were the answers. 'Who approved purchases? The Committee approved every one.' *Nota bene*, I scribbled; Charlie, if necessary, should name Committee members so the blame gets spread around. 'Can the purchases be traced? We are confident that we can, despite the loss of records. The architects and interior designers approved the purchases too? Yes, every one. The hiring of the manager? Not our committee.' And they continued. Charlie was clearly weakest on insurance issues and the insurance claim process. I suggested that he leave these issues to others and, generally, tried to tamp down his optimism about how he would perform by pleading with him to practice his responses. As for the rumor, Flanaghan had written out his defense—it boiled down to 'no way'—and I insisted he respond according to the script. After ninety minutes of coaching, I left, assuring an uncertain Dani that Charlie would do 'just fine,' wondering if he would.

∘ ○ ∘

"Developments," Flanaghan said importantly.

I was in the loft, dressing in formal wear for tonight's premier Commencement Week event, the Honoree Dinner when he called.

"Tom Junior came up with a pretty good lead on the source of the rumors about Charlie. I had him checking land records on all of the purchases by Calibrese and the Club, to get it in chronological order, and see if Charlie's option fit in, like he told us. There are transfer tax stamps that represent a percentage of the sales price on each of the deeds so a little math and we can figure out selling prices. Charlie's 'little finger of land' went for six hundred grand! Seems like a lot of money for a landlocked six acres."

"That's public information, right. That's how it would have been reported in the newspaper?"

"The price for the property when it was sold would be in the newspaper but not the purchase price under the option. For an option, all that's recorded is a memorandum that says the land is subject to option and for how long, without tax stamps or a recital of a sale price. In other words, nobody but Calibrese and Charlie would know what price the option agreement actually stipulated."

Meaning, I thought, the option price could have been a dollar or six hundred thousand or anything in between! And with Charlie's known predilection for misleading even friends…? "We need to see Charlie's copy of the option agreement."

"I did. He gave it to me. Says six hundred thousand. He didn't get a penny more, at least from the closing."

"So …?"

"Westerly's Registry of Deeds is next to the Clerk's Office in Town Hall. Seems Calibrese's local lawyer, Dino Sinese, a good guy but a talker, has been spending a lot of time there the past few weeks doing abstracts of all of the property owned by the Randalls, Calibrese's remaining acres, the Club properties, and surrounding parcels. And property up near the Indian Swamp. Tom is bumping into him everyday and finally sees what he's up to. I mean, he's not just going back in the records sixty years, he's going back forever and taking his time about it, having coffee with clerks, making remarks about how Charlie's option memorandum didn't state the sales price, how much Charlie's land went for, 'seems like a lot of money for six landlocked acres, ….' Drop a few nuggets like that, a few shrugs, and the next day, it's gossip at the coffee shops in town, eventually reaching the ears of those concerned."

"Why?"

"Not sure. But it's Calibrese, alright. How did Charlie do with you?"

I replied that while Charlie promised to get the answers down pat, I gave it a fifty-fifty chance he'd pull it off.

"And here's another thing that makes the gossip sound plausible. Before the closing of the golf course land, Charlie didn't seem to have a pot to piss in, had mortgaged the family's house up to the hilt, and in Westerly, if you're a Fessenden, that's news. The six acre sale paid off a lot of debt, plus some. And the sale to the Club made real estate prices in that area jump! Just in time for Charlie to become a big time realtor with an inside track to the Club membership. Poor bastard had it made and he could thank Calibrese for that. Now, he can blame Calibrese for whatever happens. The old bastard giveth and he taketh away!"

CHAPTER THIRTEEN

The Honoree Dinner is the best ticket during Commencement Week.

At the black tie affair in Grafton Hall, a three story, Romanesque building set back from The Green, guests are escorted up a grand staircase to an oblong, oak paneled dining room that could have been in Windsor Castle. At each of the ten tables with ten seats, there would be an honorary degree recipient or one of the eclectic Commencement speakers chosen by the graduating class and the graduate schools, along with Trustees, donors, politicians, senior staff, and faculty. This year's honorees were the Secretary General of the United Nations who would have his say about world poverty and the wealth of nations tomorrow on The Green, a Nobel Prize winner in physics, a Supreme Court justice of a decidedly liberal bent, an alumnus who ran the world's third largest bank from the U.K., a former president of Mexico, and a Pulitzer prize winning historian. The Commencement speakers, a little more colorful, were the president of Doctors Without Borders, a best-selling graphic novelist, an environmental architectural activist—famous for the grass on the roof of his headquarters and building designs that reminded me of crumpled paper balls—and the founder of Phoenix House, a drug rehab program. I noted that in addition to being prestigious, the group was ethnically diverse and included three women.

At seven o'clock, in black tie, having braved a crowd of media, clusters of video cameras, the just curious, chanting Students for a Democratic Society, the Young Socialist League, Young

Republicans, Greenpeace, and others born for placard waving, as well as a phalanx of security guards checking I.D.'s, I entered a room resplendent with gleaming china, sparkling crystal ware, silver candelabras, and glorious long-stemmed flowers in elegant vases that permitted guests at the round tables to see one another. Each place setting had been prepared with infinite precision; delicately shaped napkins imitating Japanese origami faced one of the University's collection of priceless, Georgian period Seddon chairs. Elegantly garbed guests were being served champagne flutes from silver trays by a waitstaff in formal dress.

The invitation and seating were matters of campus and corporate politics since they were in the discretion of the President and the Provost. I was anxious to see if my seating request—at the same table as a movie mogul alumnus who was a *huge* giver and rumored to be famously witty and profane—had been honored. I was in transit around the tables when the Provost beckoned to me.

"Your truce has been fractured," he muttered darkly. "The manager of the Faculty Club just called me. Somebody from there printed out Sonny's bills and sent it anonymously to the *Journal*. With all the late notices and the dunning letters! Sonny will be ballistic."

"Ugh!" Sonny Russo's membership in the Faculty Club was a source of frequent concern to College Hall. At any one time, he would be overdue more than any other member, using his membership to impress his gang of limo-riding sycophants as he put our face in the *merde* during boozy parties in the Club's private rooms. Over time, gracious reminders from the Club's management had gotten progressively tougher and, eventually, I drafted one or two zingers that were more demanding. Ironically, Sonny was a member only because the Club's bylaws stipulated that whomever occupied the office of mayor of the City of Providence was an *ex officio* member of the Club, which meant any occupant of that office, at any time. Unfortunately, the bylaws didn't cover the issue of what to do with a mayor who didn't pay his bills. If it had been up to me, the Club would have kicked him out early on and risked the publicity but the Club's board demurred, fearful of reprisals like increased real estate taxes or limits on the full liquor license the Club enjoyed.

"He'll assume we did it to embarrass him," the Provost continued.

"He should be embarrassed."

"That's not the point!" His steely eyes met mine, giving me the message, 'Move on this. Two more days of Commencement Week.'

"What can I do?"

"The reporter wants a statement from us. I told the Media Office 'no.' I want this left at the Club level. The manager told the reporter that membership charges are private. The reporter responded 'stonewall' and 'what's the University got to hide?' 'Stonewall…!' "

"It is." My evident disagreement wasn't appreciated by the Provost, even as he had to acknowledge and warmly smile at one of the guests. "Should we call Sonny?" I asked.

"Yes." There was a momentary silence.

"Me?"

"Yes."

"When?"

"Now."

∘ ○ ∘

I left Grafton Hall to make the call since I was not carrying my BlackBerry. I barely noticed the security people, the remaining media and hangers-on, and sign holders as I crossed The Green to College Hall. Maybe, I thought, if I can get through to Puppy

Dog, explain the facts, make such amends as possible, I could make it back in time for dinner. If I had gotten a glass of vintage champagne before the Provost caught me, this would be going down easier.

Puppy Dog answered on the third ring. The background was loud conversations and music, no surprise because Sonny and his cronies traveled in a pack. He recognized my voice, asked me to speak louder, and I practically shouted what I had to tell him.

"What-t-t-t!" Then, a noisy exhalation. "Sonny's here. I had better tell him now. Where are you?"

"My office."

"I'll call you right back."

Five minutes went by during which I managed to get hold of an apologetic Faculty Club manager, sure that the culprit was a female student graduating on Saturday who lived at the Arts Quad and helped with billing. He said the reporter had Sonny's charges going back at least four years, with all the polite and then insistent letters to the Mayor for payment. Sonny had an 'over-ninety' balance of over six thousand and change as of the end of April, including a bill for a Christmas party for Russo loyalists and another for a sumptuous dinner for political intimates in March. Nobody else in the entire club membership came close.

I finished my conversation with the manager as my office phone indicated an incoming call from Puppy Dog's cell phone. Only it wasn't him.

"You know who this is?" The voice was barely under control.

I knew.

"What are ya trying to prove?"

What kind of question is that? "Apparently, a student working at the Club printed out your file. Everything. Including the letters. The University had nothing to do with that...."

"I'll look like a *cavone*. Do you know what a *cavone* is?"

I did.

"You make me puke! You're breakin' my balls! I do something nice for you and gotta spit in my face."

It didn't take much imagination to see his face twisted in anger, reddened by the brandy he favored, his rotund body shaking in anger.

"I...."

"Let me tell you somethin'. I'm not going to forgot this. Tell Danby that. I don't care about your fuckin' commencement. I don't need your fuckin' buildings...."

"We told the *Journal* this was a private matter. We're not putting out a statement."

"Oh-h, that fixes it right? The Mayor's a fuckin' jerk and you ought to be thanked for not puttin' out a press release?"

"What else can we do?"

"Fuckin' apologize!" he shouted. "Fuckin' apologize would be a good start. After that, kiss my ass. Then, I'll think about it."

This is what Providence has for a mayor.

Puppy Dog's shout pierced a burst of profanity, then the clatter of the phone hitting something hard. After a few seconds of raised voices, Puppy Dog got back on the line.

"The Mayor is upset."

"Where are you?"

"Napolitano's." Sonny's hang out on Federal Hill.

"Could you explain that we're not 'breakin' his balls....' "

"Lot of good that will do."

"The President's upset about this, too."

"Let him show it."

I didn't want to go there.

"I'll brief him. Whoever did this will be found out. I don't know if any law has been broken...."

"Great. What we need is to have the *Journal* think they have a whistle blower who gets fired because of the story. We want a one day story and that's it. But believe me, you got trouble!"

He hung up.

"Shit!"

CHAPTER FOURTEEN

It was now eight-ten. The delicious soup and stylized salads would have been cleared and the main course was likely being served by white gloved staff. The glassware would have been filled and drained and refilled with superb American wines. Intelligent, lively conversation sparked by our guests of honor would brighten every table where all would be basking in enhanced self images. Over baked Alaska, coffee, ports, and dessert wines, a short welcome from President Danby would charm all, and everyone would be out by nine-thirty. A time-honored schedule. How rank would it be to interrupt my table with excuses, even if I managed a happy face.

• ○ •

I gave a security guard a handwritten note describing the blasts from Sonny for the Provost, left The Green for my Mini Cooper parked in the driveway of Temple House, and was soon in the traffic of Fox Point. The area's rapid gentrification was on display during this hour after sunset as coffee shop and bar patrons spilled onto sidewalks, galleries and antique shops remained open for tonight's Gallery Night trolley tour, and new restaurants, for some reason mostly Indian and Japanese, and pizzerias seemed busy. Jimmy's, housed in a pre-nineteen hundred clapboard building, was virtually the last remnant of the Portuguese-Azorean neighborhood of my youth.

I left my tuxedo jacket in the car and with my black tie loosened,

ened, I probably looked like an off-duty sideman as I entered the aroma infused restaurant and took a stool at the counter facing the open hearth kitchen. Young Jimmy's wife, Maria Catarina, née Sousa, whose grandparents landed at the India Point docks—not two blocks away—on the sailing vessel *Esmerelda* before World War One, handed me a menu. She said, "Nadie give you the boot? You look terrible. Manuel says try the *amejoes na cataplana*." I said, "Fine," thinking if the forthright Maria Catarina said I looked terrible, I did. "I'll get you a glass of Bucelas."

With my head braced by the palms of my hands, I played out possibilities of the Faculty Club debacle. Would Sonny's minions make the next two days miserable? The *Journal* wouldn't likely hit until Sunday because any story big and political would be saved until then. So, maybe Sonny would wait. But maybe not.

"Something interesting upstairs," Young Jimmy said as he slid on to the stool next to me. "A couple of pretty good players are in town. Emilio Salazar and Cong Choi. Know them?" I vaguely recalled the names but if Young Jimmy said they were 'pretty good,' they were. Young Jimmy had rising pool stars in for exhibition matches before they played at Foxwoods or Mohegan or the Greenwick Downs ESPN tournament show. They also got a dinner, and some 'extras,' along with the status that came from being good enough to be invited to play by Young Jimmy, a legendary player from the meager purse days before television decided pool had an audience and Las Vegas and Atlantic City held big money nine ball tournaments. Young Jimmy learned his craft, as he often said, from people who took your money, never smiled, and didn't care if the door hit you in the butt on the way out.

"Nine-thirty, they play," he said and left me as Maria Catarina arrived with my wine.

Across the counter, I watched Maria Catarina's cousin Manuel brandish a *cataplana* for one. "For you," he smiled, and I remembered that Maria Catarina once explained that Sousa family chefs use measurements of 'a little,' 'some,' 'enough,' 'plenty,' and 'a lot,' in their zesty cooking. One of their implements is the *cataplana*, basically two skillets hinged together that when shut, fit together like clasped hands. In went chopped tomatoes, onions, sautéed linguica, green peppers, garlic, and 'a lot' of herbs and spices, heavy on the cumin, together with a splash of white wine—all of this was for the sauce known locally as 'gravy.' Then, freshly opened littlenecks in their shells, a cup of what I guessed was fish broth, a few minutes of sizzle within the *cataplana* turned several times over the flames, and the dish arrives in a soup bowl, with the cooked littlenecks bubbling in 'gravy.' Wonderful!

Manuel brought the steamy bowl to the counter in gnarled hands that ignored heat. I ate hungrily, with compliments to the chef, my napkin tucked in my open shirt collar. When I left the restaurant at nine, I felt more like myself. In fact, as I climbed the back stairs and entered numbers in the key pad by the door, I was looking forward to seeing these 'pretty good players.'

A good crowd, maybe forty members, was in attendance, some at the bar, some in upholstered observation chairs as tall as barstools with a crossbar to fit feet, others in deep conversation near the tables where the pros were warming up.

I walked behind the bar and got a Bass Ale from the refrigerator, popped off its cap, and walked through the lounge toward the tables. The Club is distinguished from the local pool pits by what it is not: it is not public, the walls are unadorned by beer signs, there are no fake Tiffany lamps over tables, and none of the nine foot tables sported Red Sox or Patriots logos. Most Club members are forty to fifityish males, with employment ranging from university deanships to plumbing, with a sprinkling of young professionals. We pay our dues to play in pleasant surroundings on well-maintained tables, without interruption, with a minimum of small talk and noise from adjoining tables, or for the challenges of the house league and annual championships, or membership in a very good travel team that plays in tournaments throughout New England and New York. Being Providence, there are also sporting members who rarely are seen with cue sticks in hand and frequent the Club only if 'something interesting' like tonight's match was scheduled. These are, no surprise, gentlemen who wager.

I watched them in discussions near the pros, wondering who they were favoring tonight. I would not inquire because I never bet on pool. Never. Not because of scruples but because betting on pool is a fool's game unless the players are kept honest by the amount of prize money or a guaranteed stake. They tell me the matches sponsored by Young Jimmy are on the up and up, and Jimmy's is not a smoke filled betting dive like those so vividly portrayed in *The Hustler* and *The Color of Money*. But who knows?

Alec Ferguson was watching the diminutive Choi loosen up at a table, taking what appeared to be random shots concentrated on his form. Ferguson is my age, angular, taller than me at six-four or so with an odd face that reminded me of pitcher Randy Johnson's, triangular with little chin. A heart specialist at City Hospital, he plugs in the stents and does the angioplasties and bypasses that make him the heart surgeon Rhode Islanders seek out, one of the few members allowed to take or make a call in the Billiard Club. I like him immensely, especially his analogy between pool and surgery: both, he says, give immediate satisfaction when you fix a problem and win, both take practice and patience, and as he says, if you are good, it's 'cool.' I didn't think Alec knew I was standing beside him until his head moved a notch toward me. "Smooth delivery. Watch his elbow. Perfect arc."

I did. Choi was a lesson.

"Want a game? Eight ball?" Why did I ask that? Was I still antsy?

"Sure," he replied.

We chose a table away from the action. A touch of a wall switch adjusted the cone of lights over the table, we choose cue sticks from the visitor's rack, and I asked Alec to break the rack which he did smoothly, sinking a solid ball, and then ran off three solid shots before a miss on a long carom shot. Remember that, I thought, long shots. I chalked up my cue stick tip, suddenly feeling too loose for someone who fancies himself a finesse player who feels the geometry of the table but struggles with the physical act of striking the cue ball exactly where planned. My first shot wasn't crisp, even though the nine ball slid into a side pocket. Three more shots and we were even when I missed a cross table shot and left the cue ball in a spot for an easy shot for Alec to put away, which he did quickly. He missed another long table shot which gave me an opening, and with aplomb, I finished off the table. Alec acknowledged my win and began racking for another game when Young Jimmy approached us. He cautioned, "You don't want to take away from our guests, do you?"

Alec put his stick back in the visitors' rack, as did I.

"Before their match, they'll play with members." That was an invitation.

Alec said, "Sure" and I said, "No."

"Come on," Alec said. "If I can get creamed, so can you."

A bad idea but what the hell! Beating Alec was an ego charge. Alec took his own cue stick from the members rack, walked over to Choi, and was introduced to the pro. I took my tournament Viking from the same rack and followed Alec, wondering what had happened to Salazar. Choi and Alec agreed to a best of three games, nine ball followed by straight pool, ending with eight ball with house rules. A voice next to me grunted, "We do the same." Its owner moved to a Brunswick table closer to the bar.

Hello. Nice to meet you. Thanks a lot.

Most of the onlookers retreated to the observation chairs near the Ferguson-Choi table; I noted that the sporting members didn't seem much interested in my match, no whispered wagers were evident, which was fine by me. Young Jimmy followed us and racked the balls while I appraised my opponent. He was one of the new pros who mistook image for personality. His shaved head came with wrap-around shades that covered some of his indoor complexion and yesterday's beard. He stripped off a black leather jacket to a high neck, black tee shirt exhibiting a body builder's chest and arms; his black slacks were held by a black belt. His cue stick was a black Schoen with an ivory colored inlay. Seeing his costume, I remembered he had been written up in *Billiards* or maybe *Inside Pool* as a comer, but was not up there, yet, in rankings. From … New Haven? His nickname, a necessity in today's world of professional pool, was 'Zorro'.

Salazar removed his sunglasses and let me break the nine ball set up, and I embarrassed myself by not getting a darn thing in. It took Salazar all of three minutes to finish the game. I never got another shot! One down!

He broke for straight pool. Since it was to be a quick match, we played for twenty-one. He took eleven balls before my fingers rested on the cloth. The few members who had drifted over to watch us, probably to get a line on Salazar's shooting, decided that Choi and Ferguson were more of a match. Young Jimmy observed the massacre and failed to offer me any sign of encouragement. When I missed pocketing the six ball on my third shot, Salazar took over, right through the next rack. A hosing! Young Jimmy scowled as though he should have asked someone else to engage the pro.

Two down. We should have stopped but since Ferguson and Choi were in a real match in their second game and Salazar obviously enjoying whipping me, he racked for our third game. I was embarrassed but figured the slaughter would be over quickly.

Eight ball isn't popular with the pros; it's too common, has too many house rules, and it is too easy to get beaten by a few lucky shots. The savvy tournament guys all want nine ball. But to show his confidence, Salazar let me break and I pocketed two solid balls, with a third ball gone moments later. A fourth shot was an easy pocket, followed by a decent carom shot for the fifth ball. I was playing rapidly and smoothly, barely taking time to chalk up between shots, into my finesse game; a glance showed an opponent who didn't look very happy. A long table shot dispatched the sixth ball which happened to be the six, and the seventh shot was a given. All I had was to pocket the eight ball in a side pocket, a difficult but not impossible cross table shot, and be redeemed by a shut out. As I draped over the table, I could see a striped ball was a bit of trouble in my line but I could still smack the eight ball home. That's when Salazar walked past me with a whispered sneer. "A hundred says you miss it."

Only Young Jimmy could have heard. I didn't answer. Nor did I hesitate in setting up my shot. In pool halls, silence to a challenge, a bet, means assent. I aimed. I *felt* the shot, the precise angle of the cue ball and the eight ball. The side pocket looked as wide as the Grand Canyon. Only, I missed.

Salazar finished off his balls in rapid succession, with nary a chalking between shots. He came to his eight ball shot. A double bank, difficult shot, but not impossible, to get the eight ball into his designated pocket. He passed by me to take up his position. I muttered, "Five hundred says you don't drop it."

His head jerked back at me, his eyes narrowed, and a curl edged up his thin lips. He approached the shot, drew a bead on the cue ball, struck it forcefully, and I watched the eight ball crash into the far rail, rebound to hit the closer rail, and drop neatly in his pocket. The eight ball could have been on strings.

I had been suckered. Oldest trick there was. Get the mark exercised, make the bet, execute the shot. But it was bad form for one of Jimmy's guests to scam a 'Friend of Young Jimmy.'

Young Jimmy had caught the action and was dismayed at Salazar's gambit as he mentally added the one hundred and the five hundred to Salazar's exhibition money. That's the way it's done; Young Jimmy adds wagered money to the exhibition pot for his pros, you pay Young Jimmy later on. Young Jimmy whispered to me, "How could you be such a mark. You know this game…!" and left me at the table.

Salazar stared at me from across the table, his face in an oily, stick-it-to-you, leer.

CHAPTER FIFTEEN

A call from Fausto Tramonti early in the morning is rarely good news for the recipient.

I was at my desk in College Hall at seven-thirty with the *Journal*, a cup of acidic coffee from the machine in the canteen, and a Seven Stars Bakery chocolate crueler brought from home, spread on my desk. Upon arrival, I had e-mailed the Provost a blow by blow description of my conversations with Puppy Dog and Sonny Russo and received his reply to 'stay the course' and let Sonny make the next move. No surprise there. Also, I had reached Tuttle to advise him that because of the Faculty Club imbroglio, Sonny had an excuse to change his mind about cooperating; Tuttle's reaction, in contrast to the Provost, was sulphurous, but I urged him to follow our script of cooperation unless it failed. As I hung up with Tuttle, Fausto called me on my BlackBerry from his office. His voice bellowed over the speakerphone he always used.

"Councilman Ferrucci," he began, "was with Sonny last night when he called you. Sonny was bouncing off the walls." Fausto, I thought, should have been thrilled by Sonny's embarrassment but his tone was measured.

"Sonny was extremely … unpleasant, let me put it that way." I sat back ready to get into more detail when he said, "Oh, more than that! He is *pissed*, at you! You personally."

I gave him the background but Fausto seemed both well informed and somewhat indifferent. I asked him if Sonny might screw up Commencement. Smart, shrewd and the real politician of the family, Fausto understands these things.

"You and Tony sometimes forget he didn't get to be mayor by being stupid. Corrupt, yeah, but not stupid. You'll get your payback. But not right now. He won't want his retribution and his bill paying to be connected. Next week, the week after, it starts."

He paused, maybe to sip his usually available espresso. "Anyway, I called about Charlie. Benno found out that the State Police want to talk to Charlie because Charlie had to call in the Westerly cops when … the burned guy ... threatened Charlie when he got fired. Charlie said some choice things in return, according to Benno. And the burned guy …."

"His name is Randall."

"… had a run in with Dani that morning and Charlie was furious. She said she told you…."

With that admission, I might have expected something like an apology about what had been withheld from me, but Fausto doesn't hear what he doesn't want to hear, and never apologizes, at least to me. Actually, there has always been a sense of his tolerance of me in our relationship, and it had been there since Tony brought me home as a new friend. Fausto, then a LaSalle Academy senior, wasn't sure he liked his brother's East Side buddy. Once, I put that down to jealousy, and later to his suspicious, ornery nature, and now, I thought it was all of the above.

"Once Charlie gets going, you don't know what he might blurt out. Somebody could twist this, make it seem like he had a motive to…." Fausto's voice trailed off in distain; he admires brains, toughness, and loyalty and Charlie was deficient in all three. "I gotta get him a criminal defense lawyer."

"What about Flanaghan?"

"He's already got his hands full."

"Who?"

"I was thinking of a guy in Jerry Franks' office."

That was the reason for the early call. Jerry Franks. The brothers knew about my run-in with Jerry Franks, Rhode Island's star defender of the Mafia, drug lords, and indicted politicians, a mean, ugly fight with, literally, a mean, ugly lawyer.

"Not Jerry himself!" Fausto protested. "Too close to Sonny. He's got a guy in his office, a wanna-be almost as good. Joe Laretta."

"You get him somebody like Franks and the Club's members will suspect Charlie's in real trouble. You're escalating this…."

His response betrayed annoyance. "Not the people we care about."

I didn't have to ask 'who.' Culturally anchored in his community, the 'people' were from Providence neighborhoods, graduates of parochial schools, LaSalle Academy, Providence College, now the political lawyers, councilmen, and judges who frequented the Aurora Club, summered at Bonnet Shores and the Pier, and enjoyed the steakhouse atmosphere of The Capital Grille. They were not members of Agawam Hunt Club, or the Hope Club, and certainly not Haversham Golf Club.

"According to Benno, the Staties think the burned guy …."

"Randall," I said impatiently.

"Yeah, yeah, … set the fire. His threats are enough for motive, it's his cracked skull that's the problem. So, it could be that somebody clocked him and then set off the fireworks, maybe thinking nobody could tell that he got a fractured skull. Problem is that Charlie was alone at the time. No alibi." He took a deep breath for emphasis. "Laretta's good, Algy. I've been sending him criminal defense work the past couple of years. Got a lot to lose if he screws up. So, trust me."

I would defer. Hiring Laretta was a family decision, had been discussed with, and agreed to, by his brother. This call was to let me know—I was that close to Tony—that it had to happen, whether or not hiring Franks' protégé was offensive to me.

The office phone rang and I asked Fausto to hold. It was the Provost from Grafton Hall at the last meeting of the Board of Trustees for this academic year. Since today's meeting was planned to be serene, self-congratulatory, and kept to a tight schedule by the President so that the Trustees could get on with this morning's Honorary Degree ceremony, the call meant something within my bailiwick had been unexpectedly raised by a Trustee. In the background, someone was speaking as the Provost whispered, "We got a question on the Arts Quad." He mentioned one of the Trustees, a California Court of Appeals justice. "She's urging the Trustees to create a special committee to deal with the 'incursion,' as she calls it. I don't see any momentum for it, but I don't want the Board jumping into this if I can avoid it."

I thought, 'Mind crossing your fingers?' "Do you want me over there?"

"No, it would give her honor the opportunity to ask more questions. I want to be able to say that you and the Mayor's office are dealing with this, that you have a promise to revisit the Protocol over the summer, and we expect that should give clarity to both sides. Nobody has said anything different, right?"

I agreed—technically that was true—and he hung up.

I got back to Fausto, who was talking to someone in his office. "Sorry about that," I said. "Duty calls."

"No problem. I'm going to call Charlie...."

"Some advice. Wait until after the Sunday meeting with the members. Don't add anything to his angst. Nothing is going to happen until next week anyway."

Fausto considered the point. At the membership meeting, the audience was my turf. "Okay. Makes sense. I'll wait. Suppose you call Laretta? Bring him up to speed...."

"Fausto!"

"I know, but we gotta do what we gotta do. Don't be pissy

about this. All the pols know about Charlie, that we've bailed him out before. They expect us to take care of our own, but nobody wants to be embarrassed by their friends. We're at a critical time trying to get support from these guys and Sonny's kicking the crap out of us…."

"Franks hates me, I have no use for him, so why should I call his associate."

Fausto practically growled, "This isn't Franks! I'll let Laretta know you're going to call. He'll understand." Then, "You know, we need you to do this. It's important."

There was an exhalation of uncertainty before I agreed and hung up. Damn! I'm closer to Tony than my own brother. But this was turning blood into—what was the *Times* puzzle word I discovered on Sunday meaning a smelly, viscose liquid—ah, grume!

Both fists hit the desk, throwing anything loose into the air, sending a shock of pain through my hands. I needed that. I was overreacting to Fausto's pushy personality. 'Laretta.' The name was familiar and suddenly I had it. Giacomo Laretta is the political don of Providence's Eighth Ward, a boss sometimes in opposition to Sonny for arcane reasons only a Providence politician could understand. Runs a popular family-style restaurant down the hill from St. Bart's Church. In its back room, Fausto said, political careers had been made and lost. Joe Laretta must be a son or nephew!

∘ ○ ∘

The Provost called minutes later indicating that the Board of Trustees' meeting had adjourned with no action on the Arts Quad, despite her honor's admonitions not to let the police 'trample' on University and student rights. Thanks! Everybody is an expert when it comes to telling the cops to bug off from two thousand miles away.

With the Honorary Degree ceremony beginning to ramp-up outside on The Green as two thousand folding chairs were being opened and aligned, I was now off duty and I examined my options. I could hang around for lunch and then attend my class 'meet and greet' function at Bancroft Hall, to be followed by a forum on health care issues moderated by two classmates, one a member of the House of Representatives, the other from some think tank from Berkeley. That would be the 'Carter' thing to do. Or, I could get ahead of my weekend chores because Saturday would be taken up by Commencement, and Sunday was the membership meeting in Westerly.

"Ugh!"

I had to admit, I *was* in a put-upon mood, angry at myself for my greenhorn play last night at Jimmy's, how I let Fausto cajole me into briefing a Jerry Franks' associate, none to happy about my upcoming role as a shill on Sunday. And, I wasn't particularly keen for my class function where forty or so academics, lawyers, stock-brokers, and class officer types, were likely to be full of themselves. Although, honestly, that wasn't the complete rationale. I dislike reunions. I am sympathetic to the views expressed last year in a letter to the *Alumni Record* that reunions are depressing, making many of us feel downright inadequate compared to the speakers or seminar leaders or award recipients. After ten or twenty or more years from graduation, we haven't advanced the cure for cancer, made a scientific breakthrough, written a Broadway play, or been elected to national public office. We live lives and careers out of the limelight and rarely make the *Notes* section of the alumni magazine until we marry, send kids to Carter, retire, or die. So, why spend even an hour ill at ease, with others in the same predicament?

I walked home, selected the Mini Cooper, and drove to the WholeFoods Market at University Heights, then Wayland Square with my laundry, and finally, up to Federal Hill. At Tony's Colonial Market, I bought links of sweet sausages for Sunday dinner, a wedge of sweet gorgonzola, and some cured capicola for panini, and walked the block to the former tenement that housed Gasbarro's World of Wine.

"Hey, wrong day!" Marco called out from behind the counter. He wore his trademark white shirt with sleeves rolled up to the elbows.

"Yeah, I know. Commencement is tomorrow."

"Right."

Marco was a year or two ahead of me at Carter but already focused on wine and his family's business. "I want you to try a brunello. Just came in. I tasted it last year when Carla and I were in Montalcino. It took me all this time to get it. I opened a bottle for friends. Come on back."

I followed his slight figure the length of the store into a windowless office with fake knotty pine walls lined with ancient metal file cabinets, family photographs, wine posters and memorabilia, books on wine and food, and a large, poorly executed Tuscan vineyard scene. Two security television screens faced his cluttered desk from over the doorway. I sat in front of him, not revealing I knew this invitation was for more than a taste.

"Hey," he said, leaning over his desk, "I hear Tony's gotta problem in the family." His eyes left mine to squint at the monitor to above my left shoulder.

I shrugged. "Sonny's always got something to piss him off. Tell me about the wine."

"Sure, sure," he said, and opened a cabinet behind him, withdrew a loosely corked bottle, and selected balloon shaped glasses from a shelf. "1995. A good year everywhere in Italy, and it's got another five to ten years before it blooms, but taste this!"

He rattled on about the Podere Salicutti vineyard, the owner's family, how he had lunch under an arbor by their vineyard, how the antipasto was prepared, how he had regaled the *padrone* with stories about some nasty, avaricious wine distributors in the States, how lucky Gasbarro's was to have the only hundred cases in New England. Meanwhile, he had filled my glass and I began the ritual, holding the glass to the light, swirling the black cherry colored wine, inhaling the rich 'nose,' and finally tasting. He was right, it was delicious, tannin in balance with an unidentifiable fruit. He joined me with a taste. "Powerful, serious wine," he said. "Can't serve anything with it but beef or a good, thick veal chop."

I savored the wine's subtle aftertaste and thought, Nadie shares a bottle of this with me, and she surrenders.

"I'll put a case away for you, right?"

"Sure." I looked and sounded offended.

"I gotta ration these," he said defensively, and probably meant it.

Holding my glass to the light, the 'legs' on its bowl evidencing the wine's richness, and knowing an expensive case of wine was worth a trove of information, I said, "Marco, a lawyer by the name of Laretta?"

A black eyebrow was raised in question. "Jerry Franks' guy?" He shrugged. "Good on his feet, tougher than nails, already has got a reputation. Father is Giacomo. You've heard of Giacomo?"

"Thanks," I said as he offered another taste. Marco looked up to the screen to my right, and blinked twice. "And, hey, you're not going to believe it, he's in the store! He's there." He pointed to the screen which showed the back of a man at the wine bins with a salesman, Cousin Frank. Marco pushed back from his desk, "I'll get him for you?"

Decision time. I tell him 'no,' and he wonders why, or I tell him 'yes' and I get the promised phone call over with. I finished the wine. "Why don't you introduce me."

We left the office, Marco secure in the thought that he had sold a case of choice brunello at a nice price, with the bonus that something interesting must be going on. In front of bins of Ovietos and Pinot Grigios, a tall, darkly handsome man about forty in a light gray, well-cut Italian suit, wavy black hair, straight nose with flaring nostrils, was listening to Cousin Frank describe the lineage of the bottle of Gavi in his hand. Marco interrupted, "Joe, I want you to meet a good friend of mine, Algy Temple."

Laretta's eyes flickered before he put out his hand.

"Nice to meet you," he said smoothly. "Let me take care of this. Then, maybe we could meet for a minute?" Marco's eyes widened; there was clearly more to learn as Laretta took the bottle of Gavi that Cousin Frank was holding. "A half case, Frank, with the others. I'll be back."

I followed Laretta out to the parking lot and a new black Mercedes 500C. "Let's get outta the sun," he said as the door locks popped. The car had that brand new, musky leather smell that is an aphrodisiac to me. The engine was turned on, no louder than a hum, as the air conditioning flowed. "Fausto said you would call, could give me an insight into the … situation."

In the next few minutes, I told him what I knew about the 'situation' including what Dani told me about her incident with Ollie Randall, Charlie's jealous temper, and the circumstances under which she told me. I tried not to editorialize about his client and that was hard. I said Charlie didn't have an alibi, as far as I knew, for the time of the fire or just before. As I gave him details of Charlie's description of the fire, I got the impression the lawyer was sizing me up.

"I saw you once in federal court, when you were defending Textron in a class action. Marty Berlin was on the other side...."

That pleased me. I had been lead counsel in a multi-million

dollar case over allegedly defective brake parts. I won.

"… and in our office. Jerry was defending that black kid who got popped in New York. I can't remember his name…."

"Lavelle Williams."

"Yeah, that was it. Jerry ended up having a thing for you. However, that doesn't affect me. I haven't met Fessenden so I have to wait until I see and hear him. Fausto has Benno Bacigalupi looking into this because Charlie doesn't have an alibi."

Oh, how dumb was I! That's why Benno was on the case! Not for the insurance claim or the rumors but to bolster the case that the 'burned guy' remains the Staties' choice for perpetrator. So much for saving Charlie's reputation, or even Dani's embarrassment!

"I suppose the club members will be all over him. You're helping out? When's that?"

"Sunday. A membership meeting."

"What are you supposed to do?"

"Be there. Ask some questions he can answer, if need be."

Laretta's face broke out into a smile. "Hey, what are friends for?"

My head went back in agreement, finding I liked Laretta. He had the rough charm of the Hill, with the unusual quality of directness, and radiated confidence without Franks' deviousness. Fausto—and I should have realized this—had made a good choice for Charlie.

"You used to be with Champlin & Burrill?"

"Eighteen years. Before that, two years with Manhattan District Attorney. Found out that being a prosecutor wasn't going to be my career."

He nodded. "I was with the Attorney General for five. Had enough and I had a family. I applied to Champlin & Burrill but didn't rate an interview. Got back a form letter that my law experience didn't meet their 'needs.' Now, they got a full blown white-collar criminal law guy in Jimmy Bryan. Former assistant AG. The best." He laughed, or at least snickered. "The practice changes, doesn't it. Here we are in my Mercedes up on the Hill, and I'm talking to Alger Temple and I've got a client by the name of Charlie Fessenden."

A man who gets it, I thought.

CHAPTER SIXTEEN

I went home and put away my purchases and laundry, went downstairs, and practiced pool, mindful of my foolish play last night and the challenge for me in this year's Club tournament only weeks away: don't get eliminated in the first round! My name was etched on the senior's plaque next to the bar at Jimmy's only because the perennial favorite, Alec Ferguson, was out in the second round on some fluky play by a banger who ended up being my opponent in the championship match. Alec, I thought, would deservedly regain his senior flight championship this year.

Close to four, I went up to the loft, discovered a *Law and Order* marathon on A&E, and during a commercial punched in Bill Tuttle's cell phone number. He was at the Smithson Sports Complex which would soon be rocking with the music and gyrations of the annual College Dance. The Honorary Degree ceremony had gone off without a hitch, he said, and his sources had heard nothing to indicate a squeeze play by Sonny. "Whatever you did, worked," he said appreciatively. I didn't feel obliged to respond.

Then, Nadie called. She would be back later than expected tomorrow; her mother needed an 'excursion' and Nadie, being the dutiful daughter, would take her to a Radio City Music Hall matinee. I told her about the Faculty Club debacle and she responded smugly by asking how the University could tolerate Sonny Russo ignoring his bills! My explanation didn't lessen her suspicion of duplicity in College Hall. "The Mayor and his goombahs eat and drink their fill and then stick it to you by not paying the bill. You cut him slack that nobody else gets. At the same time, he sends in his thugs to make a show at the Arts Quad. And nothing is done about it! What hypocrisy! The faculty won't buy it! I bet the *Journal* already has a dozen quotes. The administration will appear as conniving, enabling, and … pusillanimous."

Okay, she was right. Enjoying the convergence of targets, but right. Quickly, I asked after her mother and Nadie was immediately on to her quarrelsome Aunt Ida who seemed to dominate Nadie's mother. I also told Nadie about my genealogy search. Almost with empathy, she said, "Maybe now you'll be a little less dismissive of their cause."

She might have meant federal recognition? But I asked, "Casinos?"

"Whatever."

Ah-h-h, 'whatever.' That wonderful word that blends implication and indifference. Don't go there, I told myself. And I didn't. I promised I'd pick her up at the Amtrak Station and she said she'd call before the train left Penn Station to verify her time of arrival. I told her I missed her, which I did, and she responded with an "I love you."

That is usually enough to pick up my day.

Usually.

∘ ○ ∘

Being a bachelor as well as a son living in the same city as a surviving parent means an open invitation for dinner if the request comes early enough. As Nadie had reminded me. Tonight, I was welcome at six sharp, the dinner hour of the elderly.

Because of my presence, we would use the intimate family dining room off the kitchen. As I came in through the pantry door, I heard the whine of the stairway lift from the central hall which meant my mother was on her way down. When she arrived, cane in hand, she was wearing one of her many cardigans, this one a hand knit light blue that matched her eyes. I kissed her properly, left cheek, right cheek, left cheek a second time and helped her into her chair at the table. Sylvia, who stands no taller than five-three and whose girth is her own business, rolled in a roast and side dishes on a cart and joined us. I filled wine glasses from a bottle of Red Truck—my mother has her thrifty side—and was permitted to carve.

Not surprisingly, my mother was full of animated conversation as to her trip to Beaufort, her childhood home, visits to a favorite cousin's home on the Broad River, how the town was now a favorite moviemaking location, 'like Providence,' she said, and the status of the restoration of her family's in-town house to be occupied by Beauford County's historical society to which she was a major and anonymous donor. Eventually, she asked me about Commencement Week activities and I gave her a rundown on this year's celebrities and events; she seemed taken aback by my casual, even diffident, attitude, and said so. Point taken.

The conversation went on like that, back and forth, with Sylvia joining in with nostalgic vignettes from when Temple House and Commencement Week were joined at the hip. After nearly fifty years of residence with us, Sylvia is 'family' but her biological family, the Odums, are descended from slaves freed by Providence abolitionists during the Revolutionary War when slave holding was legal and prevalent and Bristol and Newport were major slave trading ports. The Odums are also part of the history of Carter University, proudly supplying its first African-American graduates and first tenured black faculty member.

As we finished dinner, I told them about my research on Nathaniel and Issac Temple, the gruesome death of King Philip, Nadie's thinking on the Quonnies of today, the proposed casino, and why I had consulted my grandfather's family history. My mother's eyes blazed with interest since she shares many of the same sympathies as her good friend Nadie.

"Sounds as though both sides were brutal to each other," she said of the war, "a clash of cultures and *no-body*, individually I mean, was to blame. You cannot help who you are. History let's us pause over every *ter—rible* event and too often without context. We can't forget *that*. Look at us. We had slave holders, and worse, slave traders, in both of our families. Can't imagine anything more *ap-palling* … but that's what it was. That's the way they lived, and it was *legal*, God forgive us. Of course, other Temples were abolitionists, from before the signing of the Constitution. The Quakers held meetings against ratifying the Constitution in this house because it didn't abolish slavery! John Quincy Adams and Frederick Douglas stayed here. By then, the Temples were on the side of right, even as my kin were getting ready for Fort Sumter."

Sylvia poured herself the last of the Red Truck and my mother, obviously enjoying our conversation, suggested I open another bottle, which I did in the kitchen as I heard Sylvia begin to hold forth in her soft, level voice. As I returned with the wine, Sylvia was saying, "… with all the bad times in history, you can't live there! You got to deal with today, how people are, and not with the past." Her glass was lifted, I poured, and she took a generous drink. "If you thought about injustice all the time, like some want to, you'd always be a victim or acting guilty or totally oblivious to wrongs. Can't really do that. You have to get on with it."

My mother, her face slightly roseate from the lively discussion as well as the wine, added, "I can tell you, down in the Carolinas, they pushed back the native people *hard*. When I think about the Gullahs on the islands 'round Hilton Head! Lots more back in the mountains past Greensboro. Strange though, as I think of it, we never learned much about them in school. Like they were never there. Nobody seems to pay much attention to these folks until they decide they have some rights."

Sylvia, getting a bit lively, made a remark about the 'get-rich-quick casino' schemes of promoters in league with Native Americans. My mother demurred and addressed us with the aplomb and confidence of a sophisticated, Southern lady of a certain age. "While I can't *think* what was in Congress' mind to let any tribe have a casino any place they'd like to. I imagine a lot of them are in places where you might not want to spend an *aw-ful* lot of time. But here, I suppose they do real well. I suppose they're using their riches to benefit the poor among them ....?"

Sylvia, showing her Baptist heritage, wouldn't give an inch. "Maybe they do but casinos are taking money from poor people. We have folks from the church down at that place in Greenwick all the time! Others go on to Connecticut. I don't care about high rollers who can afford it, it's the people spending their Social Security checks and their welfare money and their kids' school tuitions on a fool's game...."

Sensing it might be time to change the conversation, I picked up on what my mother said about local history and the original inhabitants of Rhode Island. "It's strange isn't it, you can live your whole life in a place like Providence and never learn about the people who lived here before Roger Williams or the battles that were fought right here, hundreds of people killed and wounded, how Providence was mostly burned to the ground during King Philip's War. It's almost as though the only thing you learn about Rhode Island in school is that it's about the size of an iceberg off Greenland or a forest fire in California, or a Texas ranch."

The spark that ignited in her eyes indicated I had struck a chord with my mother. She asked me if I thought that a school program about the native people would make a difference in terms of social interaction of Rhode Islanders and an appreciation for all the succeeding waves of immigrants. I replied it would have to be more than bare bones history because each immigrant group would harp on its own disadvantages. "It could be 'victim of the month.' "

"You can be so cynical, Algy! I think Nadie's right some times. Your father wouldn't…."

Sylvia touched my mother's hand. "Ginger, you're too hard on the boy. He's still learning while we're happy to be still living!" She raised her glass and laughed loudly, her ample bosom shaking, ending the maternal lecture.

∘ ○ ∘

When Sylvia went into the kitchen to prepare an ice cream dessert, my mother put her hand lightly over mine. "I think Nadie's going through some difficult times. She's unhappy. Am I right?"

The two were great friends. Before Nadie, when I'd be in desolate affairs and uninterested in a permanent relationship, my mother kept to a reserved politeness. But with Nadie, my mother made it clear that my continued bachelorhood is an unfortunate state in a generational family. After all, my brother had 'produced,' what about me?

Before answering, I tried to recast in my mind Nadie's jumpiness, momentary irritability, sometimes inflexibility, in the context of the Byzantine politics of a Carter academic department.. "Not unhappy, just frustrated."

"More than that," she countered knowingly. "She's not at ease with herself. Have you been listening to her? Demanding?"

Me? Demanding? Be more empathetic, more supportive of her causes? My lover is a hairshirt when it comes to victims and fails to distinguish between victims and underdogs.

"Talk to her," was my mother's final admonition. "She'll tell you in time."

○ ◯ ○

After a slice of homemade pound cake with vanilla ice cream and a dram of Calvados—the family's liquor of choice as an all-purpose cold cure and toddy for a night cap—and some assistance with the dishes, pots, and pans in the kitchen, I left Temple House around nine-thirty and walked home. Street lights were glowing and the curbs of Benefit and Prospect Streets were lined with cars. The night was full of stars without wind and the muffled sounds of music from the College Dance carried over the rooftops of the East Side. By now, complaints would be registering on the University's 'hot line,' with local councilmen, and the precinct cops at the Brook Street sub-station. 'It's once a year' was our standard excuse; not much of a response to those with cranky, wide-awake children. At Congdon Street, I entered the kitchen and checked telephone messages. Only one, from Tom Flanaghan, leaving his home telephone number.

"I think we're gonna have a busy day tomorrow," he said. "Ugo Calibrese called me."

"What?"

"Heard that we were poking around. Said if I had any beef with him, about how his land was put together, he was going to be in Watch Hill this weekend and I could ask him face to face. Said to bring you along."

"Me?"

"He dropped it so-o-o casually. Which means he's interested big time. To me, he wants to show off, put me off the scent. You…?"

"I don't get it…." How did he know of my interest? Was this the Sonny Russo connection? A little embarrassment for me? But why bother? "We're going. Unless you advise otherwise."

"Not me. This could be a good show, you two together. A clash of cultures…."

"Thanks."

"Sorry. Figure on one o'clock at my office. My guess is you'll be out of the membership meeting no later than twelve. By then, they'll need their Bloody Marys."

CHAPTER SEVENTEEN

It never rains on Commencement Day at Carter University. Never.

Except this year.

A deluge.

I awoke to the sound of rain on the roof, with the *pat, pat* of drops from a clogged gutter. When I pressed the gizmo on my bed stand that opens the window blinds, it was drizzly; by the time I was dressed in academic garb and on my way to The Green, it was a downpour, my umbrella giving scant protection from wind-driven, pelting, sheets of water that whipped the East Side. Despite the maelstrom, the police had been busy. The cross streets to Angell Street were closed by rows of police sawhorses, 'Do Not Park' notices were stapled on curbside trees and poles, orange cones diverted traffic, and cops by the dozen in yellow rain gear were evident. The graduation 'special detail' meant coveted double overtime; maybe, when it came right down to it, Sonny, despite his loathing for us, wouldn't mess with their checks.

At The Green, two thousand Carter University graduation participants with raincoats, slickers, ponchos, and umbrellas, braved torrents of rain while being organized into groups by volunteer marshals for the celebratory march down the Hill to First Congregational Church. At nine o'clock sharp, a shrill whistle sounded and the honorary Grand Marshal, his top hat and cloak covered by glistening plastic, grasped the dripping University mace and stepped off, accompanied by the Sheriff of Providence County in a protected topper and brilliant green sash over his raincoat. Directly behind them, under streaming umbrellas, were the poobahs of the University led by the Chancellor and the President in floppy red hats right out of *Richard III*, followed by the Provost with the Trustees, and then senior staff including me, faculty members who cared enough to brave the rain, alumni with Carter Cats baseball caps grouped by class, and finally, the happy, noisy, hung-over, whooping and hollering graduation class, with their droopy bouquets, rain-blurred placards, and banners ranging from the overtly political to 'thank you, Mom and Dad.' As we stepped off to the cadence of the booms of bass drums echoing against The Green's brick and stone facades, the graduates, in unison, discarded whatever rain protection they wore over their flowing black gowns and put on their mortar boards, leaving piles of clothing and cover-ups to the vagaries of the weather and our maintenance crew. You gotta love 'em!

Our ranks squeezed through College Arch on to Angell Street where camera flashing and video taking well-wishers were standing four deep. Some within my group, as our shoes sloshed through puddles, grumbled 'why do we do this' and 'instead of catching pneumonia, we could be inside the Sports Complex' and 'what's the big deal of a march down The Hill?' I let the complainers pass me by so I could join the ranks of the graduates. They are the answer. Forget the rain! Experience the cheers in many languages, kids leaving the march to embrace family members and pose for photographs and videos, waving at everybody and anybody, singing, music of all kinds. Even the most everyday grungy, sappy, MP-3 fixated, over-indulged, and barely tolerant of parents kids were into it. In their excitement and delight in being graduates, only a Scrooge would not be caught up in the joyous, liberating moment.

And then, just as the graduates crossed Benefit Street, the rain stopped as though it had been turned off at a faucet. By the time the marchers were funneled into the church or rows of folding chairs on its wet, slippery lawn, a sharp sunlight flooded the scene along with a sense of beneficence.

Oh, ye of little faith.

∘ ○ ∘

A noted Holocaust survivor delivered the baccalaureate address, managing to evoke pangs of great sorrow along with the herald of expectation as only one who has suffered mightily could do. He was followed by President Danby's gracious, humorous, and mercifully short address of encouragement to graduates. At eleven-thirty, we trudged back up the Hill in a brilliant sunshine that caused steamy black graduation regalia to be carried rather than worn. At The Green, graduate school deans led their charges to various campus locations for luncheons, speeches, and diploma distributions, while the rest of us found places in rows of chairs, wiped dry I might add. Before things got too raucous with champagne showers, an African-American graduate brought the crowd to its feet in her valedictory address that reminded classmates of words from a popular professor at their freshman convocation, an early, eloquent plea not to dismiss any knowledge as irrelevant because of possible career choices. Then, diplomas were distributed, we heard brief good wishes eloquently spoken by President Danby and at the stroke of one, it was over: four years, if not more, at Carter University, a quarter of a million dollars of tuition, board, fees, grants, loans, and expenses later. Slowly, reluctantly, already nostalgic graduates, with frequent embraces and hugs, accompanied by their guests, filed through The Green's many portals to dining halls or to lunches downtown or on Thayer Street or back to the Quads or apartments to finish packing, leaving the Carter cocoon.

I exhaled deeply. Commencement Week was over! Sonny Russo had not ruined it. You did alright, Alger Temple. Doesn't make any difference if anyone appreciated it or not. Good on you!

I lingered for a few minutes for conversation with colleagues, and then threaded my way through the rapidly thinning crowd toward College Hall where I was approached by two smiling young women, former interns in my office who also volunteered in a legal aid group I mentored. One was going to attend Yale Law and the other Virginia Law. I congratulated them and spoke of my pride in their accomplishments; early on, they had picked up on Danby's passion for civic commitment and I knew they appreciated the privileges and responsibilities accorded to a Carter education. Their beaming optimism pumped me up even more; I was proud that I had helped make a success of their four years at Carter, capped by a successful Commencement Week.

In my office, I took off my gown and finally paid attention to the vibrations of the past hour emanating from my BlackBerry. Its screen told me my repeated caller was Puppy Dog. Well, Commencement Week was over, Puppy Dog, over! Just a little too late!

° ○ °

Five minutes later, I walked down Bowen Street, avoiding the puddled sidewalks where plane trees and maples continued to drop rainwater, in tune with a half-remembered 'summertime dreaming' Beach Boys song that popped into my head. The air had been washed, retaining its after-rain smell, my spirits were high. That lasted until I spotted the police cruiser in front of my house.

I rapped on the cruiser's passenger side window. It slid down with creaks, as though grit was in the rails. "Officer, can I help you?" I said into the darkness of the car's interior. Only a blue short sleeve shirt was visible.

A large head with a dark brush cut and black eyes craned out of the shadows to see me. "Are you Alger Temple?" The voice had spent years in growls.

"That's me. What's the problem, officer?"

"No problem. I'm supposed to let Goldbloom know if you arrive." He reached to a handset on the dashboard. It crackled and he said, "Seventy-two. Tell Goldbloom that Temple's home."

Static, unintelligible voice, and more static.

"Just tell him, okay?" he responded impatiently.

More noise and words that made little sense to me but to the cop something that needed a response. "Look, give him the message! I'm goin' back to patrol." He slammed the handset into its dash holder. The window went up an inch and stopped. His head was again visible. "The Commissioner's friend, right? The guy from the University …?"

I acknowledged that I was.

"Let me tell ya somethin'. I'm on the force … twenty years. Never had a commish that wasn't just a stooge set up by a mayor to do the awards and stuff. Tramonti …, he's trying to do something. Got a set a balls. You should hear the crap Sonny and McCarthy put out about him. Probably shouldn't say this, but …."

I shoved my hand into the car. "I appreciate it."

"Vinnie Greco." He took my hand and leaned forward to display a wide face with substantial nose, square chin, and a wide grin. "Do me a favor. Don't pass it on."

"I understand."

"Puppy Dog must need to see ya. I've been sittin' here for an hour. Whatta waste of time for me to be sittin' here for that asshole. That's what's wrong. Ya know what I'm tellin' ya?"

I agreed, said goodbye, and entered my house. Mrs. Pina was in the living room and looked up from her vacuum cleaner to cluck at the wet I had brought to the hall. "E-e-e!," her hands went to her pile of thick gray hair. I said, "Sorry," complained about the rain of the morning, told her the place looked spick-and-span, and escaped further admonishment by asking after her grandson who is our district councilman and her pride and joy. I changed clothes quickly and went into the kitchen to make a sandwich. When the front door chimes rang a few minutes later, I figured it was Puppy Dog and barely beat Mrs. Pina to the door.

Puppy Dog, in his other suit but same straw fedora, breezed by us into the central hall. "I called four freakin' times …!" he complained and then he saw Mrs. Pina. She appraised him in a single glance, looked at me quizzically, and with her nose pointing at the ceiling, went back into the living room. I love her!

I led him into the kitchen where he stood at the center counter, his hands stuffed into his trouser pockets. There were transparent pimples of sweat on his oily, carrot-shaped nose. "You avoiding me? You gotta get on the *Journal*!"

He followed me into the den. I said over my shoulder, "Look, we're not putting out a statement. That's it."

"That's not good enough."

"What could we say anyway? Sonny doesn't pay his bills on time?" I sat on the divan and he didn't. He went to the windows, took a deep breath, and addressed me in the reflection of the glass.

"Better get off that," he snarled. "You just got away with your Commencement. Now, you owe!"

I almost went for his bait by firing back in anger. Usually, my best tactic in dealing with Puppy Dog is to let him ramble while I remain silent. It irritates him enough to fill the void. But not today. He was on my turf, had chased me down, not the other way around. That realization helped my voice remain calm, almost pleasant. "Leon, do yourself a favor. Leave it…."

"Put the word out that the billings get screwed up sometimes, especially when there's a big party. You sent the bill to City Hall, not his address for political things. Anything, something...."

"How about the truth...."

"Bullshit! The truth is the Mayor's got a problem so you got a problem."

"What's that supposed to mean?"

"Simple. Sonny takes the hit for a day. Okay? But then he turns it around on the University, and you and Tramonti get accused of a conspiracy against him. The Mayor's protecting taxpayers so you try to embarrass him because you're Tramonti's buddy. It's all a political set up by you. Sonny's gonna get through it. He pays the bill ... clerical problem, whatever, ... somebody takes a fall in the organization. But, you, you're goin' to take a hit. Only chance for you is that Danby starts thinking about how the Mayor gets paid back for not making you—and I mean *you*—the issue. These goddamn buildings for instance. What's the fuckin' delay? And it's time to take care of a coupla other ...."

"I can't believe what you're...."

"Hey, tough fuckin' titty! I'm just the messenger. Grow up. This is politics."

By now, I was pacing the den behind Puppy Dog who remained facing the windows. My stomach was so tight with anger, I could hardly talk. Providence politics is a blood sport and Puppy Dog and I had been in a lot of battles, but this time his threat was personal. I couldn't remember if he had ever used a vulgarity addressed to me. Something is up. What? Why? It made me emboldened.

"Okay, you tell Sonny this. Maybe you should use very simple words so he'll understand. First, no apology. We're not putting out a statement. That's it. Tell him this *is* 'politics.' The Faculty Club is separate and apart from the University. Other than an annual subsidy, it runs itself. If Sonny wants to take advantage of its hospitality as an *ex officio* member, he can. That's in its charter. But if he runs up a bill again, he gets tossed, with lot's of publicity about what a welsher he is, and that's a hell of a lot better than a story about how Sonny got to be a member in the first place."

"What…?"

"Oh, please! Any *Journal* reporter willing to dig would find it, how the Club was denied a full liquor license for years and, bingo, Sonny puts in the fix and the License Board says 'yes.' "

Abruptly, Puppy Dog turned to me, his face in a disparaging sneer. "You don't have the balls to go there."

"After years of applying and no license, Sonny's guys on the Board get the Mayor's nod and they vote for the special club full license, but only after the club's charter got changed making the mayor of Providence an *ex officio* member. Who's idea was it for the *quid pro quo*? I don't know and don't care. It happened long before me and it's history as far as I'm concerned. But to a *Journal* reporter…? Tell Sonny if he tries to do anything to me, one thing out of line that he can't prove, there'll be lawsuits and subpoenas and depositions and everything he doesn't need. Especially on those jerks at the License Board. He's got more to lose than I do if that story comes out."

Puppy Dog turned and snarled, "You wouldn't dare push a load of crap like that. You know you can't prove anything…."

"Right." I moved closer to him, my lips zippered, my eyes showing the matter was closed. I knew Puppy Dog—and Sonny—wouldn't risk the *Journal* delving too deeply into the machinations of his flunkies on the License Board.

He flinched! A gulp bounced his Adams apple two inches. "So, you're threatening the Mayor…."

"I never threaten. You want the buildings, they're yours. All clean and nice and Italian. But if Sonny gets nasty, *presto*, they disappear! If he's got a cover story for the Faculty Club exposé, use it. We won't deny it."

His mouth opened and he showered me with a mist of spit. "That's a threat! It is! That's what I'm telling him. Nobody threatens Sonny Russo."

Puppy Dog marched out of the den, tripping on the last stair to the kitchen in his haste, slamming doors on his way out. I remained in the den, still feeling feisty. I had been so ballsy! The rumor about the License Bureau, all secondhand to me and old news for some, but a great twist on the expenditure story that Sonny wouldn't like. Who asked who and for what? When did it happen? Sonny's first term, six, seven years ago? Would anybody care? And the buildings. He *needs* the buildings!

CHAPTER EIGHTEEN

Having learned the hard way that the better lawyer is the prepared lawyer, I wanted to brush up on insurance law before tomorrow's Haversham Golf Club's membership meeting in case I got involved in a colloquy with a knowledgeable member.

After a lunch of thinly sliced capicola on a hard roll from Mrs. Pina's cousin's bakery and a hard boiled egg washed down with a Bass Ale, I went upstairs to the loft and logged into our office's online library to an insurance treatise, *Kaplan on Insurance*. 'Important Points' was the heading on my yellow legal pad as I made notes from relevant chapters:

'(1) Policy Construction—in favor of the insured. If there is doubt as to whether coverage exists, such doubts should be resolved in favor of coverage. Good!

(2) Policy Binders—not as good as a complete policy but if the parties agreed as to what the policy was going to provide, a binder would be 'binding' on the insurance company. See World Trade Tower cases. But, the intended insurance had to be proven by a preponderance of evidence. Could the Club do so?

(3) Type of Policy—a commercial business policy should cover liability to third parties, fire damage and other casualties to buildings and contents, and have appropriate endorsements for 'business interruption' due to any calamity that shut down revenue. Any exclusion from coverage should be strictly construed against the insurer. Good!

(4) Breadth of Coverage—the building would be insured to replacement value up to a 'cap.' If the 'cap' was less than 80% of

the loss, that would trigger a 'co-insurance' clause which requires the insured to pay a portion of the loss. Awful result but unlikely here.

(5) Building Contents—had to prove what the insured owned and that it was destroyed in the casualty. Up to Charlie and the accountants.

(6) Arson—doesn't affect the collectability of insurance unless the fire was set by someone with an interest in the proceeds. Assuming it was Ollie Randall, no issue.

(7) Business Interruption Coverage. What did it include for a private golf club? Protection from revenue loss from the Club facilities? From members paying dues and guest play? From the pro shop sales? Delays in payments of dues? What about continuing costs for salaries during shutdown and repairs? Any separate cap on damages? Watch this one!

(8) Subrogation. If a third party was negligent and caused the loss, the insurance company would have all the rights of the Club to sue to get back any money paid out. Maybe the fireworks company, or Ollie Randall's estate—if there was one?

It all came down to this: the binder would refer to standard coverages and amounts of coverage and maybe a general description of the types of insurance. The adjusters, the lawyers, and the insurance company would have to agree as to what coverage was applicable under standard policies, conditions of the underwriting, and the quote, and any special endorsements standard for a ritzy golf club. That was the legal side. The practical side was what could be proven.

∘ ○ ∘

I showered, as much to get the legal clutter out of my head as anything else, and then watched the five o'clock news on Channel 11 whose video-cam truck followed today's graduation events. After thirty seconds of celebrating graduates and close-ups of President Danby and guests, Chief Daniel Patrick McCarthy, looking official in a white shirt with brass collar emblems, shoulder boards, shiny badge, and black tie, smiled into the camera. He answered a reporter's unheard questions by saying his 'men' were happy to see the end of this class, a bunch of 'smart alecks' and 'troublemakers' who had no respect for 'law and order,' who sneered at the citizens of our fair city!

Goddamn it! How had the 'buffoon of the year' gotten air time to besmirch our graduates? My guess was that Channel 11 had this interview in the can when they showed up at graduation. A Puppy Dog shot across the bow, whether we had a truce or not.

I gave the Chief his due by clicking off, although that didn't quench my frustration. To whom could I vent? It was three hours before I picked up Nadie. Not even a Gordon's gin martini and crackers with *dolce* gorgonzola helped as I scanned the *Journal's* 'Lifebeat' section for some early evening diversion. As the last of the setting sun flooded downtown with golden light, tonight's WaterFire would begin with eclectic music while flaming braziers transformed the Providence River into a glowing path for party boats, gondolas, and thousands of Riverwalk strollers. Not quite up for that. What else? The Pawtucket Red Sox at home against the Ottawa Lynx at McCoy Stadium? I would have to leave in the seventh inning. Stay at home with the package of Netflix DVD's unopened on the hall table?

I opted for dinner at Jimmy's.

∘ ○ ∘

At the Billiard Club, the pool tables were dark and only a table of card players and a few members watching a golf tournament on the plasma screen occupied the lounge. I went behind the bar for a Bass Ale and took the bottle to a table at the far side of the room, snapped on the cones of table lights, and set a rack of balls. I barely noticed the woman who entered the Club and busied herself behind the bar until she walked over to my table, Heineken bottle in hand. She was tall, a redhead with curly hair, thirtyish, looking attractive in a white blouse and dark trousers, one of the few female members I didn't know by sight or name. She said, "Hello." Her voice was a touch breathy. "Bethany Reins," and she put out a slender hand. The name was vaguely familiar.

"Hi. Alger Temple."

"I'm in the women's flight for the tournament. Thought I'd get in some practice." Her voice was a flat Midwestern.

"Had the same idea."

She took a step into the table lights. "Want a game? Nine ball?"

It was so natural and innocent. If she had been a guy, I wouldn't have hesitated to say 'yes,' so I wouldn't for a woman? Some female company wasn't going to compromise me.

We played two games of nine ball. She was pretty good and I played better than I might have. Go figure. There wasn't a lot of conversation, just banter as to good and bad shots, the upcoming tournament, and that many women were disinclined to play the game seriously because unlike golf, it was widely viewed as either too macho or seedy. She seemed sincere and pleasant; during the second game, she mentioned she began playing pool with her dad and brother in the family's basement rec room in Akron, Ohio. I said I had been a player since I was a teenager, told her how I was introduced to the game by Young Jimmy and his friend, now Police Commissioner Tramonti, describing Jimmy's Billiard Club when it was a neighborhood Irish bookie joint owned by the infamous politician and tavern owner James Aloysius Hannigan. Before I knew it, I'd asked her to join me for dinner.

We went downstairs and the restaurant's hostess, Maria

Catarina's niece, placed us at a red clothed table in the center of the busy dining room, a little conspicuous, but what the hell. We ordered calamari and the pizza special of the day, *molto* tomatoes with chopped green onions, paper thin chouricco, and mushrooms and decided to split a calamari appetizer. I ordered wine and our waitress was soon pouring glasses of Quinto da Aveledo. She was talkative, about her family and growing up in Ohio, and as she went on, I appraised her. Close up, she wasn't especially pretty, a touch overweight for her height but with a warm smile showing white even teeth, a nice complexion, hair that was more amber than red in the subdued restaurant lighting, with striking blue eyes. A plate of golden calamari with chopped hot banana peppers and red sauce arrived and I was going to ask her about her job when I remembered who she was! An investigative reporter for the Journal.

"Hey," I interrupted her abruptly. "Is this really a coincidence?"

"What do you mean," she said, her eyes widening.

"Are you on the Faculty Club story?"

"That's me," she said without reticence or abashment. "And I don't stalk people."

I betrayed disbelief as I made a show of pushing away my plate.

"Sorry, that's hard to believe."

"I wouldn't abuse Jimmy's like that."

"So, can we have dinner and not mention the Mayor or the University?"

"If you want."

I pulled back my plate, but couldn't let the awkwardness dissipate. "I imagine the Mayor's not too happy."

"Actually," she said with eyes that didn't meet mine, "he's been cooperative. I didn't expect that. Claims it's a matter of administrative miscue. He knew we were on a story about how he spends his political action committee money, the dinners, the 'meets.' As for the Faculty Club, it's no secret the University is his pet peeve, so why does he spend any time and money up there? Can't be just the food...."

She was eliciting a response. I stabbed a calamari.

"Oh, come on," she continued, smiling now. "It has to be because he enjoys making everyone there uneasy. By the way, I'm a Carter graduate, ten years out now. The University has been and will always be his target. It's a wedge thing for him."

"An undeserving one," I responded.

"He'd debate that one," she said. "After all, he does have a point about real estate taxes. The University owns some of the best real estate in town and doesn't pay any taxes...."

I couldn't let that go by. She is, after all, a reporter with the newspaper of record in Rhode Island. If Sonny's canards and aspersions had burrowed into her craw, then we were in trouble. So, I responded with a defense of the University's property tax exemption, how the University supports the community in a hundred ways, and that the University has never discounted the idea of good faith negotiations to deal with payment for civic services, but was not going to negotiate under Sonny's blustering threats. As I went on, a professional hardness developed in her eyes and I realized I had taken the bait.

"Hey, what I'm saying is off the record, right?"

"Not to worry."

"When is the Faculty Club story likely to be published?"

"Never know...." She looked up as someone approached from behind me.

"Hey, this is a surprise," Tony Tramonti said too heartedly. "Mary and I are having dinner in the other room. How ya doin', Bethany."

She smiled and I saw familiarity. She said to him, "You've been friends for a long time."

Tramonti's face radiated a politician's goodwill. He put his hand on my shoulder. "From what, eighth grade ….?"

I nodded agreement, feeling a little put upon as he added more flesh to my story of Young Jimmy's father's pool room, how we learned to play the local variations of pool games with Young Jimmy, when allowed to by the off-duty cops, the politicians, and the lunchbucket guys who barely tolerated our presence in their smoke saturated sanctuary.

She said to me, "And now you're supporting your friend's bid for mayor?"

"Hey," Tramonti smiled with a knowing, insider wink, "that's premature."

"C'mon, everybody knows you're going to run against Sonny."

"Right now, I have a full-time job with the Department and …"

"But that's a prelude. You're gonna run against Sonny …."

"Well, some might say," he said, his smile fixed, making me further unsettled. "Good to see you, Bethany. Algy, we'll talk. Gotta get back to Mary."

Ms. Reins didn't let go. I half expected a tape recorder to pop out of her handbag. "… with Alger Temple one of your biggest financial supporters?" That sally must have come from Sonny Russo and betrayed her story angle. "You know how things are in Providence," she continued, "everybody knows everybody or is related to somebody. Here's Alger Temple, University Counsel at Carter University. The University has a Faculty Club. It's nominally independent of the University but gets subsidized one way or the other. Any mayor of the city is a member because it's in the by-laws of the Club. When this mayor doesn't pay his bills, who composes the dunning letters? Alger Temple, who happens to be best friends with the Mayor's political rival, the Police Commissioner. We get an anonymous tip from someone at the Club for a story that could put Sonny in a bad light because he doesn't pay his bills on time. Or maybe at all. Could that have been a set up? Come on, guys, don't you owe me something more than 'it's been nice talking to you, Ms. Reins.' "

"It's been nice to talking to you, Ms. Reins," I managed to mutter as the pizzas arrived. Tramonti laughed, slapped my shoulder, shook his head in innocent wonderment at the two degrees of separation that is Providence, and walked away.

We ate in silence. I finished most of the wine and I didn't say another word until I was on my last slice. "You know, that was kinda crappy."

She said, "I realize that. Just happened. Nothing personal."

"No, but is my involvement with Tony part of your story?"

"Sure. Of course. You did write the dunning letters, didn't you."

"I edited a couple so that they were appropriate in addressing the Mayor."

"But you did do it?"

"Yes."

"Sonny especially didn't like that."

"Can't help that. Part of my job." I signaled for the check. "Well, it's been … interesting," and asked the waitress to split the bill which seemed appropriate. After we paid, I offered my hand which she shook weakly and I left her at the table. I went upstairs and had my best practice in a month!

○ ◯ ○

The night was warm and in the distance, music from WaterFire wafted toward me. I put the top down on the Mini Cooper and took Benefit Street to avoid the crowd thronging the streets at WaterFire. I crossed Angell Street, took a left at the Old State Capitol to the bridge over the canal to the Capitol Center side—the asphalt challenged side—of the Amtrak station. Nadie was waiting outside the spare domed building. She waved and smiled when she saw me and I felt better.

We went back to Congdon Street and it didn't take long for us to shower and head for bed. There wasn't a lot of conversation before or during. It was happy, pleasurable lovemaking, intense and then quiet. We shared a large pillow as her girlish body coiled into me, with her hand on my stomach and her right leg barely on mine. Her eyes closed and her breathing became almost inaudible wisps of air. Then, a car door slammed, a reveler laughed, and she murmured, "What was that?"

"Nothing," I said. "A car."

She uncurled and left the bed for the bathroom and came back, turning off the reading light and scooting up next to me. I stroked her hair.

"What's happening in South County?"

"Nothing happens in South County. It's all farms and beaches and land trusts and ..."

"You know what I mean."

"Go to sleep. You don't care and there's not much anyway. Seems like the Tramontis are going to stay embarrassed." I pressed closer to her warm body and inhaled the perfume she wore.

"How about your truce?" She had become chatty.

"Held," and she took my nuzzling face in her hands.

I moved up her body and kissed inside her ear but she shook me off. She wanted to talk, and she did, a lot, about sexist colleagues and departmental policies. Realizing this was the end of snugginess, I moved to turn on my reading light, half listening to her defense of positive psychology in case there was a test. To tell the truth, I'm not much into any kind of psychology, a thought I had never expressed to her. I did however once say something of the kind to a friend, an Italian Dominican friar on the faculty at Providence College. He responded that philosophy, not psychology, was the key to the human condition if you believe that striving for 'good'—whatever that is—was man's ultimate desire. Psychology was a tool to that end but could become a distraction, even a dead end and not an avenue, toward 'good.' Was Nadie's positive psychology any different?

Sensing my distraction, she elbowed me. "Are you listening?"

"Is that all that's been bothering you?"

She sat up with an expression more quizzical than miffed. "I guess it shows," she sighed. "Damn!" I thought she might continue, putting my mind to rest, but all she said was, "We have Italy in one more week. It will be wonderful to get away."

• ○ •

Later that night, I awoke and found her facing me, her pale face placid in sleep, all animation calmed, her breaths soft. We had been content for too long, foolishly postponing a needed discussion as to our future. Now, while she experienced a serious professional issue at her department, something unspoken and almost invisible, was forming like a fog. Would it harden into something impenetrable? Did I have a choice but to press for an outcome? Would Italy be another postponement of the inevitable discussion?

I need more. I could gladly accept a rollercoaster of a life with Nadie; it would be better than the mannered ambiguity I saw in some couples, or reverting to the category of 'single man usually available,' and casual relationships. Once having tasted the real thing, anything else would be insipid.

At the right moment that Italy must provide, I would press for an answer.

CHAPTER NINETEEN

Despite Ms. Reins' prediction, I was up early to retrieve the *Sunday Journal*, expecting a headline like 'Russo Stiffs University' or 'Carter Gives Russo Special Deal,' with a side bar 'University Counsel Is Tramonti Supporter.' But it wasn't there. Instead, a banner headline shouted 'Verona, Our Sister City Comes for Festa,' the first of a four part series on Verona's history, culture, architectural heritage, food, and wine, replete with color photographs of its Roman amphitheater, the Castelvecchio, and Piazzo Erbe.

Sonny must be in hog heaven! The *Journal*, usually his nemesis, was supporting his *Festa Verona*!

In anticipation of the attire of the male members of Haversham Golf Club, I was dressed in a white open collar shirt and tan slacks. I put a light green blazer over the back of a counter stool, made a breakfast of diet-busting eggs benedict and espresso, and kept my interview with Ms. Reins to myself. Why ask for trouble? Nadie, with a bowl of yogurt mixed with granola, announced a day of computer research and dinner with some sympathetic female colleagues, and a night at her apartment. Her prickliness had returned and when I said I was waiting for the Faculty Club story, she said in a voice that combined amusement, irony, and derision, "So am I. Can't wait to see how College Hall's high and mighty handle this one."

I kept my nose in the newspaper as a 'high and mighty' should when faced with a wellspring of informed opinion.

◦ ○ ◦

It was ironic, Charlie said when I picked him up at his home in my dark green Range Rover, that the membership meeting would take place at the Wynomet Golf Club, a venerable nine hole golf course which for years served the summer colony's golfing needs but was now outshown by the grander, eighteen hole Haversham Golf Club. Charlie was pale but firm jawed, bright-eyed, and loquacious and I wondered if he had prepared himself with a couple of well-disguised drinks.

Within a few minutes, we were in a parking lot full of luxury sedans and SUV's. We entered a low slung clubhouse clad with weathered brown shingles and a lounge area that led to a larger room where rows of metal chairs faced a cloth-draped table topped by a small podium, a pitcher of ice water, and glasses. Charlie, dapper in a light cream linen jacket, pink knit shirt, brown slacks, and penny loafers, walked briskly through the lounge, getting a noticeably tepid response to his greetings, and I realized that his clothes didn't reflect the somber subject of the meeting nor the sobriety of a man responsible for other people's money. Ugh! Flanaghan and I blew that.

I lingered in the lounge where coffee and tea urns were doing a brisk business beneath prints of Scottish golfing scenes and mounted antique golf clubs. I tried to capture the mood of the members and wasn't surprised that those few whom I recognized and gave my story about being Nick's proxy were not belligerent, despite being frustrated by their Club's predicament. It was also evident that those members present would not be mistaken as diverse. The younger men were dressed in Brooks Brothers Country Club, with 'moss' or 'taupe' or 'heather' knit shirts, and chinos tied by colorful striped belts; the older gents wore blue or green blazers, light colored slacks, with open collared, button down, white or light blue shirts. The women—blond or streaked blond through age fifty, short-clipped, gray hair thereafter—appeared to have shopped en masse at a Lily Pulitzer trunk show for their pastel clothes and accessories like canvas tote bags.

Near to eleven, I went into the meeting area to sit in the empty second row, ready to lob my softballs if necessary; the members filled in toward the rear as if in church. Charlie had removed clipped sets of documents from his briefcase, with the cheat sheets we had prepared on each topic on top, and placed them neatly in front of him. He had that too eager salesman grin as he found a spot on the ceiling that caught his attention. How would he do? Would he remember or read our scripted responses like '... still working diligently on the insurance issues,' '... confident as to results despite adversity,' '... dedicated to opening the course for play,' '... enough money for operations,' '... the bank seems to be cooperating,' etc., etc., etc.

At eleven on the dot, five middle-aged men, obviously the Board of Governors, attired in blue blazers with a pocket crest that was likely Haversham Golf Club's logo, entered from an adjoining room, followed by Gordon Ackley, their lawyer, the only one with a briefcase. The group arrival signaled a pre-meeting without Charlie, which was not a good sign. They took their seats at the table with cursory acknowledgements of Charlie's presence.

The microphone at the podium squealed a few times as a spare, balding man with wispy eyebrows, narrow but prominent chin, unsmiling lips, and a ruddy complexion called the meeting to order with the demeanor of someone used to handling a gavel. Taking half lens glasses from his blazer pocket, he placed them at the crown of his broad forehead while the others at the table turned over cardboard name plates bearing their last names—Soames, Spencer, Giles, Shattuck, and Towner. Neither Charlie nor Ackley apparently rated name plates. The speaker introduced himself portentously as 'your chairman, Archie Soames,' named the others at the table who waved or nodded perfunctorily, and made the point that this was an 'informational' meeting with no business to be decided.

What followed was a brief, matter-of-fact update. With his glasses now placed in position, he read from notes. Since most everyone in the room had been at the site, he said, there really wasn't much to say about the calamity. The fire had probably been set by a former employee lately identified as the fire's victim. The negligence of the newly hired club manager in permitting temporary storage of paper goods under the porch and fireworks stored overnight in the maintenance building was inexcusable and had caused the Board to terminate him, for cause. "I'm advised by counsel not to get into these issues today, for obvious reasons."

Someone behind me said in a stage whisper, "What 'obvious reasons?' " but that didn't intimidate the chairman. With spirit in his voice, he reported that the carts and larger course equipment had not been damaged, the golf course was in great shape, and, "Within two weeks, we'll be open for play!"

His announcement engendered a smattering of applause that broke the tension that had fixated the room. For their hundred and fifty grand initiation fees and fifteen thousand in dues, at least they could play!

"Importantly, as I'm sure you'll remember, in addition to the opportunity to play a golf course which is one the finest in New England, we will be protecting your investments in the Club and our lease of the adjacent lands when we commence golf play before the fourth anniversary of our closing on the purchase of the land. Otherwise, the Club would have to decide whether to buy the leased land or pay a substantial increase in rent for not doing so, or relinquish it to the owner. Your Board believes none of these alternatives are desirable and by opening the course before July third, none, I repeat none, are required."

That Hobson's choice evoked a few 'I didn't hear that befores' which Soames ignored. I wondered how many members had any clue about 'Charlie's deal' when they sent in their applications. "Your Board," Soames continued, "has put in countless hours since the day of the fire to ascertain both our financial position and our ability to realize on your investment this summer." The other Board members nodded in agreement. "And I'm pleased to announce that our hosts here at Wynomet will again lend their clubhouse to us for some social events."

Half-hearted applause followed.

"Lastly, we will collect our insurance and rebuild our clubhouse! And he paused dramatically to build expectation, "we will do it without an assessment!"

"Now, we're talking," someone said loudly and at that, the room erupted with acclaim. Members stood, clapping, slapping each other on the shoulders, and generally expressing relief. Waspy bonhomie had replaced the dour atmosphere.

"We'll be having our annual meeting in our new clubhouse next summer!" More applause. Archie Soames was on a roll. He smacked his palms together loudly, then dramatically ripped off his glasses and raised them above his head. "It's going to be the best golf club in New England!" The applause was deafening.

As enthusiasm died down, Soames collected his notes, cleared his throat, and said too evenly for my comfort, "Now, we'll hear from our Club Secretary, Charlie Fessenden, followed by our Treasurer, Clyde Tower."

Soames took the microphone from its stand and it was passed on by two Board members to Charlie on the far right of the table. From where I sat, Charlie's forehead looked damp and his face was slightly flushed but he started off fairly well. "I have been working on this project for over four years," he said in a tight, controlled voice, "waiting for our plans for the club to be realized. I walked the land many times when it was still a designer's dream, suffered through the delays caused by the regulators, seen our clubhouse take shape, and was filled with expectation for our opening. Like you, I feel the pride of our accomplishments and the deep distress caused by the fire."

So far, so good.

"Despite all of our financial records and computers destroyed in the fire, I'm pleased to report to you today that our backup documentation and the hard work of all concerned will let us reconstruct our financial status as of the night of the fire. It has been a Herculean task involving the Board, myself, accountants, Mr. Ackley, ... but we are almost there."

Murmurs of approval.

"The Club took over the insurance responsibility for the clubhouse from the building contractor just days before the fire. We obtained an insurance binder on the clubhouse and maintenance building from our broker. For purposes of the limits on the casualty, ... er ..., fire insurance, the Building Committee used its best estimate of final construction costs as well as its estimate with respect to the cost of all purchased items of furniture, fixtures, and equipment, what they call 'f f & e' in the insurance business. All of that information was being inputted into our computer system when the fire—."

"You mean, you're not sure of what we bought? What's goin' on?" The stage whisper had become a resonant voice from behind me. I turned around and identified the speaker two rows back, sitting by himself. He was about forty, balding, swarthy, with a long narrow nose in a face that was squeezed together like a prune; his leather jacket over a striped shirt with an open collar was strikingly out of place.

"No, I ..., I ..., didn't say that," Charlie stuttered and I heard the first crack in his resolve. "We will soon have final numbers. Of course, as soon as you buy something, it depreciates …."

The voice rang out again. "You mean you can't tell us if we have enough insurance to pay off the bank and rebuild the clubhouse with all of the 'f f & e?' Is that what you're saying? Are you goin' to build it and furnish it out of insurance proceeds, or not?"

C'mon, Charlie, time to turn it over to the lawyer! His mouth opened, but he didn't utter a sound. Finally, he coughed out, "We know, for sure, that the insurance covers our debt to the bank and what we spent for improvements and furniture and equipment. The questions that remain open relate to …."

Gordon Ackley relieved the floundering Charlie. "Let me take the question. It's mostly legal." Charlie gladly passed the microphone down to Ackley. "There are always several issues in collecting insurance," Ackley said with the assurance of an accomplished lawyer. "Because the fire was arson and there's an ongoing investigation, there'll be a delay in settlement, no matter what. Then, as in the case of any casualty policy, we have to identify what is to be replaced with respect to the building and its contents, and we have to show what we paid for things …."

The loud mouth behind me interrupted. "In other words, we don't know, right now, as we sit here, how much we're gonna get and if there's enough…."

Before Ackley began his answer, Charlie shrilly addressed his heckler. "I didn't say that! Nobody said that! You heard the Chairman! We have sufficient insurance to protect the Club's interests! We have bound coverage for every cent of our losses!" If only he had stopped then. "We also have business interruption protection. We may have an issue on what that might include since the binder …."

Hands went up all over the place. Soames stood up and took over. "Let's take these one at a time," he said, and he and Ackley did, and fortunately, the questions were obliquely asked and in some instances idiosyncratic like 'will we still have mahogany in the Grille Room' diffusing the effect of those of real concern which were deftly handled. I got to ask Charlie two softballs which were answered as though he had forgotten all our careful preparation but for the most part, Soames controlled the microphone, occasionally handing it off to the lawyer, and they ignored Charlie's attempts to interrupt. The members, except the persistent loud mouth, seemed reluctant to take them on directly, and there was not a single reference to 'Charlie's deal' or the alleged kickback.

Just before noon, after assurances from the Club Treasurer that the Club had liquidity and that a lower dues schedule, reflecting the loss of the use of a clubhouse, was under consideration by the Board, Soames finished up with an upbeat prediction that the course was in 'great shape' for play, an announcement that the bar was open, and a motion to adjourn. As the Board members stepped forward, each seemed to pick up three or four questioners as they moved slowly toward the lounge. Charlie remained at the head table sorting out his papers, trying to appear busy. Nobody approached him.

Feeling empathy toward him, I went up to Charlie. "Who's the guy who interrupted?" I asked.

Charlie didn't answer my question. His face had lost the darkness of anger and now reflected dejection. "It's all of these rumors, that's what's doing it. They don't trust me, don't want to hear from me. Some think I'm dishonest and others think I'm somehow responsible for the fire." His eyes pleaded for understanding. "Algy, what the hell am I going to do?"

I couldn't answer and repeated my question as to the identity of the loudmouth sitting behind me. "That," he said with disgust, "is Lawrence Silverman. Calibrese's front man. The guy who got the option from me. He uses the membership that Calibrese got as part of the closing on the land."

Charlie filled his valise and we went into the crowded lounge where voices were demanding Bloody Marys and Chardonnay from beleaguered bartenders. Archie Soames, his face in a glower, beckoned to Charlie who deflected the chairman's evident ire with my introduction. Instantly, Soames turned on an appreciative smile as he recalled working with my brother when he—Soames—was in investment banking at J. P. Morgan. Then, he asked if he could speak to Charlie alone and feeling the need, I headed for the men's room.

The conversation at the urinals and sinks was more pointed than at the meeting. 'Sounds like we got screwed on this lease deal, if you ask me,' 'I'm gonna talk to my own lawyer,' 'I heard the lease was Fessenden's idea so the deal would close and he'd get his land sold,' and 'What the hell were they thinking?' and so on and so forth. As I rinsed my hands, Gordon Ackley approached me. "Didn't expect you to be here," he said almost in a whisper. In the mirror above the sink, superiority was playing on his lips. He began to slick back his longish gray hair as I explained my role as proxy.

"Oh," he said suspiciously.

I asked him if the clubhouse fire affected the deadline of July third.

"The trigger in the lease has nothing to do with the clubhouse. Just the course being constructed, all the DEM permits in place, playable, and they actually play by July third. It's not quite that simple but …."

I pushed the button of the hand drier and wrung my fingers in its hot air. "If the leased land isn't of much use, why do they care."

Ackley's brow wrinkled as though my questions indicated more than a casual interest. "Truth is, back then, it wasn't, although some on the Board wanted enough land to put in another nine holes someday. That was one of the arguments that Charlie used to persuade the Board to go forward. Later, during the permitting process, out of left field, and you have to wonder about that, DEM required the Club to control all of the leased land or no permits because they are in a single aquifer, with the water running north up to the Indian Swamp in Greenwick. In essence, DEM said, if you fool with one, you damage the other and if the Club didn't control that leased land, no permits. So 'Charlie's deal' actually made the Club possible because it meant the Club had control of the land through the lease and didn't have to got back to renegotiate with Calibrese. Just unbelievable luck if you ask me."

I hadn't.

"July third? Getting a little close, isn't it?"

He seemed to take my comment as an accusation. "We're on it. Despite DEM, I might add. Sent down its people the day after the fire. That pond over by the first tee? DEM said it caught debris and ash from the explosions and fire. Suspended the permits until they tested. They didn't find anything, of course. And it seems that someone—no names necessary—dropped the proverbial dime."

He didn't have to say who. This is Rhode Island!

CHAPTER TWENTY

Tom Flanaghan was waiting for me in his parking lot. He wore an open collar white shirt so I felt appropriately dressed for our interview with the mysterious Mr. Calibrese.

After a recap of Charlie's disappointing performance at the membership meeting, I followed Flanaghan's black Cadillac past the Three Fish Fountain, and then along the Pawcatuck River to Beach Street and winding Watch Hill Road. The traffic was light, and the sun sent heat waves off the exteriors of vehicles heading toward the shoreline. The river, sparkling and wind-rippled, widened as we drove south; swans dotted the water beyond young marsh grasses, cat o'nine tails, and clumps of beach roses along the road. At Westerly Yacht Club in Avondale, power boats on trailers were poised at ramps on what was likely a perfect launch day. The drive was so scenic that I lost my concentration until a rusted out Jeep Cherokee with a cluster of saltwater rods on its roof barely missed my right fender as it roared out of a public boat landing. My annoyed horn blast immediately engendered a middle fingered salute; what could I expect from someone whose bumper stickers proclaimed 'I'm a local, don't hassle me!' and 'The new white meat-Piping Plover.'

Watch Hill needs no municipal signage at its entrance; suddenly, protective hedges are thicker and tightly clipped, flag poles stretch taller, and elegant cottages sit on knolls behind stone walls and elaborate *Architectural Digest* landscape designs. The village reeks of laid-back ambience, privacy, tradition, and class, and is your mind's eye version of the generational homes of the discretely rich. So unlike Gilded Age Newport, according to friends and relatives who summer in the village: Newport is all about what you own and how big it is; Watch Hill is about how long you own it.

A sweeping, descending curve led to Bay Street, the village's commercial center at the water's edge, where restaurants, cafes, and boutiquey stores still draped with bunting from Memorial Day weekend were doing a brisk pre-season business. Day-tripping families, holding ice cream cones, shopping bags, and toddlers, crowded the narrow sidewalks and promenade facing Watch Hill Cove. A sharp left took us by the Flying Horses Carousel, past the granite lighthouse facing Fisher's Island Sound and Napatree Point, to the crest that gave the village its name. Two driveways later, almost across from the Watch Hill Chapel, Flanaghan's Cadillac entered the gravel driveway of a brown shingled house with a white trimmed porch and sharply slanted cedar roof, a building conspicuously missing the dormers, balconies, cupolas, and towers that denotes Watch Hill 'style.' A green Jaguar Vanden Plasse sedan with Rhode Island license plate 'UG-1' and a Hummer 3 were in the driveway. We left our cars and approached the house, with Flanaghan remarking, "The views of the Sound and Block Island from up here on the bluff are spectacular!"

The front door was opened by a middle-aged Latino woman and Flanaghan identified us. She barely nodded as she ushered us into a central hall. Two narrow, wall length windows without curtains gave minimal light at either side of a fifteen foot wide staircase. The maid asked us to wait and padded away; I used the moment to check out the 'spectacular' view, which Flanaghan, if anything, had understated. Over a low brick wall that gave a modicum of protection from a cliff of rugged ledge, a strand of golden beach was speckled with colorful blankets and beach umbrellas. Offshore, a score of white hulled boats, many with blue canopies, rolled in the chop; further out, a three masted schooner was under full sail toward the pork chop shape of Block Island. Flanaghan came behind me and used both arms to express the breadth of the panorama. "What did I tell you!"

The maid returned and led us briskly through an overfurnished room, the kind with two ormolu clocks not keeping time, large gilded mirrors, smelling of polish and wax, and with the feel of being unlived in or a project taken on but long ago abandoned. Our steps made no noise on its thick brownish carpet as we followed her to a sliding glass door and outside into dazzling sunshine.

What I saw, I didn't expect in Watch Hill, a *terrazza* from Southern Italy. An aquamarine swimming pool was at our left, the breeze breaking its surface. The paving stones surrounding it were pink and blue, inset with tiles of red sea horses and green fish; its pool house was a pale yellow and roofed in orange tiles. Above us, over the house's windows, were pinkish awnings with green stripes. To our right, a fountain splashed with water from spouting dolphins, next to a faded green umbrella advertising 'Martini e Rossi' shading a chaise and side table. A gruff, unwelcoming voice called from its shadows, "Gentlemen, join me."

Our host did not rise to greet his guests: "Please, sit," he said and Flanaghan and I took seats in cushioned wicker chairs with the sun in our faces. We refused an offer of cold drinks and the maid picked up a plastic cup from the table that may have held yogurt, and left. As a *Wall Street Journal* weekend edition slid to the tiles, Ugo Calibrese pushed himself straight against the back of the chaise. While his facial features remained indistinct, I made out a large, oval head topped by a prominent pompadour, a loose floral shirt that didn't disguise layers of belly fat, faded green shorts above legs that were thin, pale, and hairy, and white feet stuffed into black loafers. As Flanaghan introduced me and engaged in pleasantries, I put on my RayBans. With my eyes adjusted, I discerned sunken, pockmarked cheeks below the egg shaped lenses of his sunglasses, and a nose—a guess said it was once fleshy—that was snubby. A ruined face. Cancer surgery, leaving him a frog …, no, a toad …, dressed for vacation?

"Tom, we've had no business for years." Ugo Calibrese's voice was even and his lips barely moved. "Now your making inquiries about me. And you, Mista Temple. I'm surprised that you're involved in Westerly stuff." His nasal accent was too determined, of a variety only a Rhode Island talk radio host would appreciate, with an 'in your face' tone dismissive of status.

My response was that I knew Charlie, and my brother was a Club member. There followed a grunt as a hand blotched with liver spots reached for a glass of water garnished with a lemon slice. Like Puppy Dog's, I thought.

"How long have you been in Watch Hill, Ugo?" asked Flanaghan, ever the ice breaker, maybe knowing the answer would flatter.

Calibrese finished a long drink and held the glass in his lap. "Eighty-two. So what's that, … goin' on twenty-five years? Nobody wanted these barns then, with the village fallin' to pieces, but for a guy from the North End, havin' it was sayin' somethin', ya know what I mean, Tom? My wife, may she rest in peace, wanted the place, so I fixed it up for her, made it a real show place, put in the pool …. I knew we didn't fit in with the summer people. We were just 'locals,' Tom, right?" Then, a flash of remembrance trembled his voice. "After she died in ninety-two, I only kept it because of her." He took another sip and put the glass on the table. Recovering, he said, "Hey, did you tell him about that Windmere Country Club….?"

"I did," he said.

"Third time a charm, right?" he responded with a laugh that turned into a hacking cough that brought him forward in the chaise. He used a handkerchief and removed his sunglasses; I saw toughness etched in the lines that sagged from his eyes before he put them back on. "Whadyaknow about Westerly, Mista Temple?" His voice was an accusation. "Not just Watch Hill. The town! What it was like growin' up here? Tell 'im, Tom, how the ownas of the quarries treated the dagoes they imported to slave in the quarries while they made millions. How the Irish didn't let their daughters date any eye-talians. And the old yankees? How they hated all of us?"

How to answer? And Flanaghan didn't.

"So, anyway, let's get to the point," Calibrese said, suddenly business-like. "You know I gotta lotta property in Providence. But nothing in my home town. My business associate, Larry Silverman, had an idea. He's upstairs in the office but he'll be down in a few minutes. A lotta money was beginnin' to move in from New York, ... here, Weekapaug, Shelter Harbor. He figured on some upscale subdivisions if we could get access to a pond and beach. Took years of lookin' around but we finally got Admiral Duffie's property. Larry kept me out of it 'cause some people in Westerly can't get over *anybody* from here leavin' and makin' a few bucks!" There spoke a man with a grievance. "Then we got some other small parcels, but nothin' that got us on a pond until old man Randall died. Larry had tried to buy his land for years but the old bastard was havin' none. His two daughters were his co-executors and they sold the land, provided their brother could stay in that crappy house and trailer until the land was developed. All told, I bought almost six hundred acres," he said proudly, and then his voice lowered, "but I needed a piece of Fessenden's land to make it easier to link up the two largest properties." His voice lowered another notch and he directed it to me. "Didya know the Fessendens used to run this town? Owned a piece of everything, a couple mills, the bank and the largest quarry...."

He coughed again. For a moment, I thought he might spit into his glass, either from phlegm in his throat or spite, but he recovered and said, "Tom, I know you. If bullshit was money, you'd be a millionaire. You think that I'm behind these … rumors … about Fessenden making a few extra bucks when I closed the deal. C'mon, why would *I* do that?" he asked with a falsetto of innocence. "Pay him more…? I already agreed to pay the pompous prick …," he put up a hand toward me, "… oh, excuse me, he's your friend …, more than the land was worth, and that was before my neighbors decided that they wanted a golf course. So I says to myself, I gotta talk to Tom and get him off my ass?"

Flanaghan asked, "You took the option on Charlie's land despite the Quonnies claim…."

"Listen, I've been dealin' with Quonnies for years. Even since I took over the track. I got a lot workin' for me. When they got the idea to have the feds recognize them as a tribe, they needed cash to hire consultants, lawyers, and lobbyists. I thought about it. Foxwoods started with a single family; the Mohegans had only a coupla people, so why not the Quonnies? A long shot, a bet. But …" and now there was a trace of a grin in his tone, "that's what I do." Another sip of water. "Geez, why am I tellin' you this? Who cares, right? Anyhow, Oaky Gardiner says if I backed 'em and if they're successful, the tribal council would do a deal for a casino at my track 'cause Quonnie land is shit, all swamp, bugs, deer ticks, and not much else. Then, when they file their application, they included Fessenden's land! Didn't tell me! And I needed that property." His eyes strayed impatiently toward the house. "Where the hell is Larry?" he said loud enough to carry to any open windows. "It all kinda came together. Hadda stop the nonsense, especially when my neighbors decided they needed a golf course. So, I got the tribe to drop the claim, I sold some land to the Club, and I leased some more. That's it."

Flanaghan, clearly sensing an opportunity to further flatter Calibrese's deal making, asked, "Why the lease?"

Calibrese hunched forward, and for the first time, his face was completely out of the shade. It had the pallor of someone ill. "Yeah," he said, clearly recollecting a triumph. "So why did I make that deal? 'Cause I had to make sure they were goin' to finish the golf course, giving the rest of my land better value and I didn't have to sit on it, costing me more money. I give 'em four years from the date of the agreement. Four fuckin' years! Tell me that's not fair! July third. I always remember the date 'cause it's my weddin' anniversary. My wife and I use to come here for the day. Their lawyers in New York had to send down all the papers here for me to sign, which seemed to drive'em nuts." His face screwed up into a smile. "So, this summer, they either get the place up and runnin' or they pay me a lotta money or I get it back. Or, maybe we negotiate somethin'." He shrugged. "Who knows?"

That last comment left a sense of a good deal made and his relishing of another deal that might cost his 'neighbors' something more valuable than a few bucks. Since he would have neither their friendship or respect, he would have their acknowledgement of his power over their Club's future.

The glass door slid open. "Here's Larry. You ask him."

The loudmouth from the membership meeting came outside, taller than I would have thought, thick through the middle where khaki trousers were held up by brown suspenders. His sharp edged face showed no emotion; his dark eyes were razor slits in the sunlight. As though to protect his employer, he stood silently facing us as he was introduced, affecting a look of distance and disinterest. "Larry," Calibrese said in a question that sounded rehearsed, "what did you give Charlie Fessenden extra when we closed on the option?"

"Nothing."

"Did you pay Fessenden a penny more than what he was supposed to get under the option deal?"

"No."

Flanaghan said, "Seems like a lot of money for only six acres...."

"You know, 'location, location.' It helped pull all of Ugo's land together. We could have built without it but...."

I said, "No promises, nothing...?"

Calibrese's sunglasses came off quickly and I saw black eyes that glistened with intelligence and purpose as Silverman became swarmy. "Ugo's got land adjoining the golf course and some across Route 1, and the rest of the Randall property. Very developable. Water views from some, views of the golf course from others, some with access to Wynomet Pond and the barrier beach. He's got plans for upscale subdivisions in there. Nothin' like it in Westerly. Gotta figure we'll need a lot of help to get a subdivision through the town because there's always opposition to anything near the water. Charlie wanted an exclusive brokerage to help us out. If Charlie can be helpful, why not?"

"So why start rumors that...?"

Calibrese interrupted loudly. "Hey, I didn't say I did! I can't help it if Fessenden's got a perception problem 'cause he had a piece of the deal when it all closed. Look at me! The town's got a perception problem with me 'cause I am one of their own and I got out of here and made a few bucks. Freakin' jealous!"

Silverman started to say something as if to caution but Calibrese waved him off and shuffled his legs off the chaise. "Too bad, it's all perception, ain't it," he said cuttingly and I didn't need anything else to convince me he was behind the rumors. Charlie, the ass, had given Calibrese the opportunity to set him up, and he used it. What was his motive? That was for us to figure out.

The interview appeared to be over as Silverman excused himself and went back inside. Calibrese said, "Tom, you're a Westerly guy. You're not satisfied, right? You wanna know how it all came together, right? Why the Quonnies gave in? See, I got nothin' to hide. Oaky Gardiner's expectin' you, right after here. Ask him about how it happened. In fact," he said and turned elaborately to me, "he wants to meet you, too. Somebody from the University said you're interested in the Quonnies."

My mouth opened more than the second needed to give Calibrese the lift he sought from my reaction.

We stood to leave. Calibrese didn't give up the chaise. To me, he said, "I know Young Jimmy Hannigan. From before. When he was a player. Probably no pool hall north of Philly didn't know him."

One up again. "Great player," I replied. "We've been friends for over thirty years." Was I one-upping him?

"We have pool tournaments up at my track. ESPN shows 'em on cable. I sponsor young players on tour, too. Ever hear of Emilio Salazar?"

"Yeah," I acknowledged. Word gets around fast in Rhode Island. Ugo Calibrese liked having information, to gaff someone, or rub salt in a wound.

"Hey, he's a pro. He's supposed to win, right?" he said with false humor.

● ○ ●

We found our way through the house to the front door and outside. Flanaghan got in his car, turned on the engine, and his window slid down quietly. "Ugo's positively shrunken. Must be he's got something wrong."

I was upset enough to hope he was right.

"Do you want to tackle Oaky?" Flanaghan asked, in a tone that suggested it would be a waste of time. "It's a little after one-thirty.

Take us thirty minutes to get to his place. Don't know what it gets us. Ugo's clearly behind the rumors. You heard him. He denies it to tell us that he is but we can't prove it. Oaky's been prepped to tell us Ugo backed the Quonnies and got them to release their claim for the clubhouse land. All up and up."

Not going was not an option to me, not after Derek Kirk had whetted my interest in the Quonnies and my latent suspicion about Ollie Randall's motives in setting the fire. And what had Kirk told Oaky Gardiner about me? "Maybe we'll get a history lesson," I responded. "Or something about Ollie Randall that might help Charlie?"

"No way. Quonnies stand together. Never snitch on another."

One thing I learned as a trial attorney was that you never know unless you ask.

CHAPTER TWENTY-ONE

Flanaghan asked me if I was hungry, and I was, and suggested we stop at The Cooked Goose, a deli he enjoyed in Avondale. We were shown to a patio table and put our jackets over the backs of the ice cream parlor chairs. We ordered herb-infused chicken salads and iced teas and Flanaghan, ever the storyteller, said, "Ugo's got a 'chip.' "

" 'Chip?' "

"On his shoulder. Both shoulders! Guys like Ugo grew up during the Depression and the war in one of the mill or quarry villages. Westerly had a few back then. Those places were self-sufficient, insular, whole families, aunts, uncles, grandparents from the old country, all living within a block or two. You played, went to school and church with cousins you saw everyday, your mother shopped in the village store that carried about everything, you were expected to work in whatever mills or quarries supported the village, marry someone from there." He stopped for a moment when the iced tea arrived and he doused his with three packets of Equal. "Grow up that way, poor, ill-educated, and you live suspicious, ready for any snub or remark. It's like an acid that eats at you. Families like Calibrese's never forgot a hurt; animosities and dark memories never get erased, could go on for generations." He took a long drink. "You can hear it in his voice. Forget what he said about his wife; he bought into Watch Hill as a sharp stick in Westerly's eye!"

∘ ◯ ∘

Once again, I followed Flanaghan through the center of Westerly, then on Route 3 in Hopkinton to Route 95, and north to the first exit on to a hill and gulley country road marked Route 33. Modest houses set back from the road were widely spaced among rock strewn pastures and fields; fieldstone boundary walls blotched with lichens, stretches of pines, and ponds with stumps rudely protruding from their waters, made the occasional subdivision raw in contrast. At a fork in the road, the highway continued to the left past a sign pointing to 'Greenwick Village-Settled in 1648' below a flashing video billboard touting slots, bingo and dog racing at Greenwick Downs and golf at Greenwick Greens; to the right, the road narrowed to a single lane past a rusted metal signs for 'Indian Swamp Road' and 'Low Town.' We took the right and immediately the land sloped off and after a half mile of potholes and frost heaves, we crossed back under Route 95. Abruptly, at the bottom of a hill, Flanaghan slowed and turned on to a dirt trail where, hammered to a tree, a roughly lettered sign with crossed arrows and a deer in silhouette demanded: "Stop. You are entering the lands of the Quonochontaug Tribe. Admittance past this point is governed by the regulations of the Quonochontaug Tribe. For information, Quonochontaug Tribal Headquarters, 500 feet."

The trail wound around moss covered boulders, stands of saplings competing for growing space, patches of briars and vines, and over culverts between swamps. A line of utility poles with sagging wires accompanied the trail. The Cadillac's taillights brightened every few seconds as Flanaghan slowed at every puddle and mucky rut; the Range Rover automatically shifted to four-wheel drive and maneuvered as though born to the terrain. After a minute or two, the trail ended at a gravel parking area in front of two ramshackle buildings. Flanaghan drove toward a shabby

South County farm house with a pitched metal roof, paint curled clapboards, and a porch three stairs off the ground. Above the front door, a slice of log with block letters read: 'Quonochontaug Tribal Headquarters.'

Flanaghan parked and I pulled in next to him in the space between the house and a one-story building clad with dingy, gray aluminum siding, with a Budweiser sign over its stoop proclaiming 'Oaky's Tavern.' A half dozen neon beer logos glowed in blackened windows; on its roof, satellite dishes were grouped like toadstools. Six or seven non-descript cars and pickups, alike in their muddy fenders and grimy windshields, were nosed in at its front, along with two shiny motorcycles that must have been wiped down since arrival. A spotless black Chevrolet Avalanche was parked conspicuously by itself opposite the tavern; its sparkling chrome wheels, sun roof, and running boards meant it was 'loaded' as a car salesman might say, 'pimped up' as our kids would say.

A lanky man, maybe sixty, with a long face, sloped forehead, and leathery skin, his steel gray hair tied into a ponytail, opened a screen door in the house, watched us approach, and sat in an overstuffed, badly stained parlor chair on the porch. He wore a white short sleeve shirt and non-descript baggy trousers; a bandana at his scrawny neck was held by a turquoise, silver, and bone choker. Flanaghan addressed him from in front of the steps. "It's been a while, Oaky."

"Yes, my friend. How ya' been?" His voice was not unfriendly but reserved. Intelligent, dark eyes nestled under thick white eyebrows.

"This is Algy Temple. Algy, Oaky Gardiner."

"Sit down, if you will," he responded, motioning to a rocking chair and a canvas camp chair. We climbed the pine board steps to the porch; I shook his outstretched hand and sat in the camp chair as Flanaghan lowered his bulk into the rocker. "Something cold?"

We declined.

There was a moment of silence while he sized me up. This was a man whose face gave away nothing. "You want to know about *Mouwneit*? Means 'assembly place.'"

"That's it," I replied, realizing I wouldn't dare mispronounce the word.

Oaky's eyes swept to a muffler-deficient Dodge Ram 1500 '4x4' sitting high off the ground on the raised axles and oversized forty inch tires of an off-road vehicle, its fog lights on a bar over the cab, pulling to a stop in front of the tavern. It was only a year or two old but had already collected a fair number of scrapes and dents. A mud-caked dirt bike was chained to a frame attached to a roll bar. Oaky's hand went to a cell phone at his belt; he punched in a number, checked the screen, and replaced it in its holster as the driver swung out of the cab and struck a cowboy pose, his thumbs hooking into pockets of washed out jeans. He was short, stocky, and broad chested, his tobacco brown, round face shadowed by a black Western style hat with a white tipped feather in its band. Two dark braids fell over the shoulders of a denim shirt and leather vest; the sunlight caught something that flashed in his ear lobes. I waited for him to call to Oaky; instead, he turned and entered the tavern.

Oaky ignored what had to be an insult. "Our people always claimed *Mouwneit* as Quonnie land. A long time ago, we had a camp there, a smoke lodge, and every year, corn and hunt ceremonies. The old ones told us they went in wagons with their families. Every year June and October." He leaned forward, smacking one hand in his other, for emphasis. "Let me repeat. Every year! The one thing that all real Quonnies have in common. Except for poverty. Ask your professor friend."

I ignored the reference to Derek Kirk and said that the tribe's withdrawal of its claim made Haversham Golf Club a practical possibility.

"It's no secret why we released the claim. Had to." Pause. "Sure you don't want somethin'?"

We declined again and he stretched his arms out toward clumps of scrub oak and cat o'nine tails visible across the parking lot. "All of this land out here, a couple thousand acres, was our ancestors, people forced into the swamp by the whites, before anybody cared about 'record' title. Nobody wanted it and we took it. Three hundred years of scratching out a livin'. Even today, most of our people are poor, under-educated, victimized because of color and racism." He put one lanky leg over the knee of the other and his voice smoothed. "Ugo's our biggest employer, our biggest backer too. I hated to give up *Mouwneit* but Ugo said all it did was to stir up another town with some powerful political support and money to fight us. Ugo convinced the council. Didn't know then that Ugo was buying land around there." His face gave up a grimace. "Shoulda guessed."

Flanaghan interjected, "Ugo told us he gave the tribe financial backing in return for a casino deal at his track."

"Shi-i-t-t!" He wiped a thin hand across his face and addressed Flanaghan directly. "Ugo said that? *Gave...!* He *lent* us the money! Every penny is a loan! Ugo gave us nothin'! He said we had to give up *Mouwneit* or he'd back out, so we did. I figured there was a few jobs on the line, too. A lot of our people didn't like it." His gaze shifted to the tavern. "That one that just went in? Freddie Jones. Calls himself 'Magua' Jones. He and his family led the opposition when we gave up the claim...."

"Was Ollie Randall against giving up the claim?"

Oaky jerked his head around to look at me, his stare betraying a half second of surprise. Oaky's eyes were black—and maybe it was reflected sun—with sparks. "Ollie Randall was with Jones 'cause *Mouwneit* was Randall land until they lost it in a foreclosure to the Fessendens. Ollie was the last with the Randall name but he and his father, Darius, were always fightin' and when the old man died, his sisters inherited the land and sold it to Ugo. Ollie got a few bucks which he blew in no time, bought that Dodge swamp buggy Jones is driving, and got the right to live on the family property, in that beat up trailer...."

"That's Ollie's pick up?" Flanaghan asked.

Oaky's face squinted back at him, maybe hesitant to answer a question about a Quonnie. "Yeah," he said slowly, "Freddie must think it's his now 'cause he always drove it after Ollie lost his license sometime back. With those tires, and that frame, could go most anywhere out in the swamp. I guess it must be part of Ollie's estate, ... might be all of Ollie's estate." He leaned forward toward me and I couldn't help but return this serious man's stare. "The Jones's are among the last Quonnies living close by here. A few in Low Town, a couple further out. But his parents live close to town, a mile up on 33, good people, but couldn't handle Freddie. Nobody could. He left home at fifteen and lived down by the Wood River in a shack when he dropped outta school. I think that's when he got crazy, living out there, all alone, with the *wallahs*. But nobody, I mean *nobody*, knows the swamp better than Freddie, every creek, marsh, back trail, ..."

Flanaghan had reacted to '*wallahs*' and now asked, "*Wallahs?*"

"Spirits of those who died out there...."

Oaky's cell phone buzzed. He picked it out of the holster, listened, and stood up with an agility of a man half his age. "You wanna see what I'm up against? Why we don't have respect?"

We followed Oaky's long, purposeful strides the length of the porch, down some stairs, across a few feet of gravel to the side door of the tavern, and into an airless, dark room filled with cardboard cartons, beer signs, boxes, and folding chairs. A metal beer keg with an open top held three or four baseball bats on end; Oaky grabbed one and opened the door to the tavern.

It was smoky, dank, and ill lit, had walls of pine board, a floor of cracked linoleum, and the acrid odors of sweat and joints smoked not long ago. Country and western music competed loudly with the blare of a television over the bar but the noise didn't muffle the curses and angry shouts coming from a pool table close to the front door. Freddie Jones had both hands on a cue stick across his chest; five or six unshaven beer belly look-a-likes in boots, jeans, fake combat fatigues, tees, key chains, and bandanas, were mouthing off across adjoining tables. Between them, a muscular, maybe six-four and pushing two-fifty, body, with no neck, in a black tee shirt emblazoned 'Quonnie Security' was smacking a blackjack into his left palm. Each repetition was a soft explosion and I remembered a cop once telling me, where there's a sap, watch out for brass knuckles. I guessed this angry walking refrigerator was Peter Gardiner, Oaky's son. I could see that you do not fool with Peter!

Oaky bellowed, "Freddie!" from halfway across the tavern.

All of them turned to us, open mouthed, except Freddie Jones who responded in a voice dripping with contempt, "Hey. Stop everything! The *Great Sachem* has arrived!" The cue stick dropped to the table and his arms flew back into the chests of two allies in mock dismay. "Careful, boys," he sniggered, "you don't want to offend *him*!" His hair was loose over his shoulders and his expression was beyond mean. He saw Flanaghan and me behind Oaky, "Who these suckers?"

"None of your goddamn business."

"Look like a couple of white suckers to me." His buddies laughed nervously.

Oaky moved a step closer to the pool table that separated him from Jones, his hands firmly gripping the barrel of the bat, his head lowered so as to be seen by Jones beneath a metal fluorescent light fixture hanging from thin wires above the table. "If you got a problem, you deal with it at the Council. Not here."

"Hey," Jones addressed Flanaghan and me, "you tourists. You down here to see the natives?" A smirk grew, showing a mouthful of bad teeth. "Welcome to the reservation," and he bowed dramatically. "You wanna play some pool? 'Indian' pool? C'mon over here. C'mon, I'll tell you what's goin' on. Petey," he said dismissively to the mound of rippling muscles still flipping the sap, "get the tourists some beer." Peter glowered and the sap hit his palm harder but everyone else's eyes, even Oaky's, were on Flanaghan and me. Nobody had expected the challenge. Flanaghan grabbed my elbow but I shook him off.

You never know when ego will take over. Look what happened at Jimmy's only two nights ago! It lurks there and when you feel put on, it wants you to do something about it. A cue stick lay on the table next to Oaky. I picked it up, looked down its less than perfect shaft, and the group around the table parted to let me through.

"Hey, o-kay! C'mon, sucker, I'm gonna give you a lesson." He stumbled toward me drunk, or close to. As I chalked my cue stick, his face came within six inches from mine; his breath was a sewer.

The table was beat up, the cloth worn and ash stained, and had picked up the tavern's humidity; the cushions looked hard, cigarettes had burned into the wood rails. At one time, it had been coin operated but now the pockets held plastic cups to catch the balls. The light fixture over the table had one fluorescent tube providing a bluish light. The balls were racked for nine ball and Jones decided he had the right to break. As he drew back his stick, he eyed me. "Do you know who I am?"

"Freddie Jones."

He jerked up, his face contorted by rage. "Don't call me that! That's a slave name. Call me Magua!"

"Okay…, Magua."

He broke the rack and had the luck of two balls being pocketed, which produced a wider smirk, his favorite, maybe only, expression. His stance, arm arc, and follow through showed fundamental weaknesses and I knew I would beat him. He wobbled in an easy shot on the six ball but left the cue ball in an awkward position for his next shot which he missed. "Shit," he complained and whacked the table with his cue stick. "Ever hear of Magua?" he snorted as I checked my shot.

"Yes." I straightened and faced him.

"What?"

"Magua fought off a bunch of drunks aiming to burn out the Quonnies. A … warrior," I said, trying to pick the right word for a rogue and a robber and a brave man.

Jones' face scrunched up to let me know I was stupid. "More than that! He was a rebel! Protected his people, could have taken all of this land back …."

I didn't reply and quickly took out four balls and realized my next shot was a double bank and with these bounceless cushions, difficult. I had been working quickly and precisely, beginning to get the feel of the table and there was even some drawn-in breaths from those watching when the balls dropped. But my audience, I knew, were almost caricatures of themselves, alcoholic, petulant, waiting for the next act, whatever it was. I bent over for my shot and when he moved closer to me, I smelled a body that hadn't been recently touched by soap. "Magua took what he wanted. Didn't care nothin' about nobody. Angry, very angry. Like me," he said and straightened up. "I got his blood. I hear him in me. I feel it." His face raised to the plank ceiling, his whole body shuddered, and he screamed what had to be his version of a chant. His two buddies started banging their hands in a rhythm on the other table.

Nobody, not me, nor the Gardiners nor Flanaghan, nor any of

the others moved. I said to myself, 'Watch out, white man!' and used the moment to purposefully miss my shot.

Jones' writhing stopped. Suddenly, he became calm and managed to get in two balls before he awkwardly flubbed his next shot. I purposefully missed a long table shot and the game went back to him. Somebody gave Jones a bottle of Bud but neglected me.

"You know Calibrese?"

I said, "Met him once. Today...."

"Oaky's buddy, ya know," he said pointing the cue stick at Oaky, causing Peter Gardiner to glower. "Yeah, we had a good thing goin' until we were sold out. We give up *Mouwneit*. To fuckin' Ugo! We give up our rights! We give up our ...."

Behind me, I could hear the righteous slap of the blackjack begin. Peter Gardiner growled, "Finish the fuckin' game!"

Jones, his face full of loathing, muscles in his neck and shoulders tensing, his eyes going hard, clutched the butt of the cue stick and held it upright. "Petey," he shouted, "the old man buy you that Avalanche outta what he got from Ugo ...?"

Peter Gardiner knocked me into the table in his scramble to get at Jones and I barely missed the arc of the sharp-edged light fixture which Jones swung into Peter Gardiner's face. The blackjack fell to the floor as Peter Gardiner grabbed his nose and mouth, blood gushed on his hands. Enraged, he yelled, pushed me out of the way and rushed at Jones who brandished his cue stick like a staff, slashed the air, and caught Peter Gardiner on the side of the head. He went down. Two of Peter Gardiner's pals lunged over the table at Jones who deftly flipped one on the floor like a stunt man in a Rambo movie and the other got a knee caught in his groin. Again, the cue stick flashed as Peter Gardiner, blood dripping from his chin, struggling to his feet, deflected the blow to the knuckles of my right hand. I turned away in pain, when its butt smashed into my upper back with a *thwack* that went right down into my rib cage, knocking my glasses to the floor. My last look at Jones was him brandishing a knife with a six inch blade as Flanaghan grabbed me around the waist, pulling toward the door and....

Whoom-sh!

The discharge of a sawed-off shotgun at close range is a combination of earsplitting bang and swoosh. Oaky Gardiner, planted in the open doorway, had fired off one barrel outside, and now pointed a gun with a shortened, tape-covered stock at the combatants caught in slow motion as they disentangled themselves. Peter Gardiner, despite his injury, had the head of one of Jones' allies in his armpit; he gave his captive a full fist in the face, and dropped him. Three others disentangled from a pileup on the table with one grasping half of a broken cue stick.

With Flanaghan at my elbow, I wobbled toward the door, my right hand numb, my back ringing with the pain from what could be a bruised rib. But Oaky waved us away with the shotgun which he leveled at Jones.

Jones stared for a long moment and then lowered the knife, probably back into his boot which was blocked from our view by the pool table. But he wasn't a cowed by the shotgun. His chin went out in defiance. "How much Oaky? Are you ever goin' to tell the Council? How much did Calibrese pay you? For our...."

Oaky took a step forward, the door slammed shut, and he pointed the shotgun at Jones, who laughed manically as he slowly came around the table, hands at his side, to within a few feet of Oaky.

"You gonna off me in front of them?" He shrugged toward Flanaghan and me. "C'mon, you must be gettin' old." Then, he lurched forward to press his chest into the shotgun's barrels. "Go ahead, old man. I fuckin' dare ya!"

I froze. There was a moment when, with the smell of gun powder, the anger in Oaky Gardiner's face, and Peter Gardiner's shouts, I was afraid Jones might have challenged the wrong man. Instead, Peter Gardiner, his lips bloody and puffing up, got behind Jones, put him in an arm lock and propelled him forward. Oaky hit the push bar of the door and Peter Gardiner wrestled Jones into the parking lot. I found my glasses, followed Flanaghan outside to the stoop as a thrashing Jones was thrown inside the cab of his pickup. Two other brawlers, one whose nose had swollen and was bleeding from a cut above the eye, and the other holding his stomach, mounted motorcycles under Oaky's watchful eyes; seconds later, their engines caught in a roar, tires screeched, and in a spray of dirt, they headed out of the parking lot. Flanaghan and I turned to go back inside, when the solid crunch of metal into metal stopped us. Peter Gardiner swore and ran toward the Avalanche as Jones' high-wheeled pickup came off its rear deck and smashed into the trunk of Flanaghan's Cadillac before it careened out of the lot. Peter Gardiner ran back to the stoop and grabbed for the shotgun but his father held him off. Flanaghan ran to his car, swearing, his fists clenched and shaking at the disappearing pickup. I was lucky that Jones didn't have time for the Range Rover.

Despite everything, Oaky was a reservoir of calm. He said to me, "Jones is crazy. Drunk, he's worse. You better go. And be careful. He's got everything all twisted. Thinks he's a born again Magua…! And a long time ago, the real Magua took out some white boys on the very same trail."

"I heard the story."

"Believe it," he said and took me by the elbow to where Flanaghan was inspecting the Cadillac's damaged trunk, his face sweaty and furious. "It's hit and run and I'll get the bastard on that. Where does he live nowadays?"

Oaky paused. "Don't know."

Flanaghan glared at Oaky, realizing that Oaky, despite everything, would protect a Quonnie. I heard Oaky Gardiner hiss, "I gotta get'em under control."

CHAPTER TWENTY-TWO

The sawed-off shotgun jolted me awake. Oaky Gardiner had it aimed at me and some fine sense of nerve, some faculty of perception, warned me to awake.

"Oh-h-h!" A turn to my left side produced a stab of pain where the cue stick had connected with my ribs; the fingers of my right hand stung as if caught in the closing of a door. I needed Nadie next to me, sympathetic, loving. But could I tell her what happened without taking heat for being in a bar fight?

Then, I remembered that last night, while prone on the sofa and stuffed with Advil, I had given myself today off. Not just because of my aches and bruises, but because after a Commencement Week that included Puppy Dog and the Arts Quad, Sonny Russo and the Faculty Club, hapless Charlie Fessenden and the membership meeting, *Mistah* Toad of Watch Hill and a brawl at Oaky's Tavern, I deserved a day of blessed idleness. Who would care if the University Counsel played hooky?

I hunched up on a pillow and saw sunlight invading the spaces between the window shades and frames, creating slivers of vertical brightness across the loft to the shelves of mysteries and thrillers that lined the wall from the entertainment center to the bed. Slowly, still fuddled by painkillers, I levered off the bed, slipped on a cotton robe, and my hand went to a line of Lauren Estelman's shoot 'em up, Detroit crime novels. What about *Down River*, a breezy Amos Walker yarn with a couple of slick murders, imaginable bad guys, assorted sleazes, and women out of a bad dream. As my hand went to the book, my eyes went to the shelf above and a two-volume anthology of Sherlock Holmes adventures. I pulled out Volume II and opened to *Hound of the Baskervilles*. I read:

> *'October 16th. A dull and foggy day with a drizzle of rain. The house is banked in with rolling clouds, which rise now and then to show the dreary curves of the moor, with thin, silver veins upon the sides of the hills, and the distant boulders gleaming where the light strikes upon their wet faces. It is melancholy outside and in. The baronet is in a black reaction after the excitements of the night. I am conscious myself of a weight at my heart and a feeling of impending danger—ever present danger, which is the more terrible because I am unable to define it.'*

Ah, perfect! A Victorian classic thriller with well-placed clues, the bone chilling atmosphere of the Dorset moors, and a direct and understandable mystery along with mayhem and murder. After two more Advil, I took the book to the recliner, snapped on the reading light, managed to find a comfortable position, and began that more famous than read story. Time went by quickly and I should have ignored the insistent buzz from my BlackBerry that began during Chapter Four. By the time I found the device in trousers that didn't make it into the laundry chute last night, the caller had gotten my recorded message. The call back phone number wasn't familiar to me but a three-two-two was a South County call and therefore likely to be either Flanaghan or Fessenden. It was neither; my caller was Chief Richard Grace of the Greenwick Police Department.

"I got a complaint here. Tom Flanaghan says you're a witness to a hit and run by Freddie Jones. Said that you were at Oaky's Tavern in Low Town and a fight broke out. Freddie deliberately crashed into Flanaghan's car and took off. That right?"

"Yes."

"What the hell were you guys doing at Oaky's?"

After a second of hesitation, thinking the Chief already had

Flanaghan's statement, I said, truthfully, "Research on the Quonochontaugs." No response. I continued, "One minute everything's fine and the next thing I know, we're in the middle of a bar fight and …."

"Everybody walks away? Then, Jones takes it out on Flanaghan's car?"

"Something like that."

Silence followed until he said, "Not a place to spend a Sunday afternoon. Especially with a guy like Freddie Jones. Delusional, know what I mean, should've been locked up a long time ago. A beer short of a six pack. The hair, the outfit, …. Crazy!"

A police radio interrupted and he responded before getting back to me. "Freddie's been out of the Army for maybe … two years. Since then, I've had him in here a half dozen times for fighting, drunk and disorderly. Oaky, as tribal leader, always bails him out, even though Jones gives Oaky and his son Peter a lotta noise. Just as well 'cause Freddie's not somebody for a twelve by nine cell. Ripped out the cot once, another time the sink. Have to listen to how I got 'no jurisdiction,' he's a 'free' man, mouthing off about some Quonnie hero named Magua. Sometimes, he thinks he is Magua. And these cockamamie war chants…? He knows that I'm going to get him for the fires up there in the swamp. Ever since he came back, anything vacant in or around the swamp has been popping off, unless it belongs to a Quonnie."

A coin dropped.

"Well, Mr. Temple, here is my advice. Stay away from Oaky's. In fact, stay out of Indian Swamp. You never know when Freddie or one of his gang will decide your invading Indian country. Remember that."

I would. "Yes, sir," I said and added "and thank you."

I put away my BlackBerry. My adrenaline was pumping, my mind racing. Holmes and Watson and murder on the Dorset moors; Freddy 'Magua' Jones and fires in Indian Swamp, a delusional psychopath and a hero-in-his-own-mind Quonnie, an Emperor Jones consumed with destruction of enemies. Crazy enough to burn down the clubhouse on the 'signal hill' occupied by a despised enemy?

The grandfather clock in the hall downstairs began its clangs to eight o'clock. Marcie, an early arrival at College Hall, would be at her desk. I used my BlackBerry to tell her that I wasn't coming in, to give me a call if anything important occurred, otherwise I'd see her in the morning; if the office got too quiet, she should put a suitable message on the answering machine and close the office after lunch. Then, I called Flanaghan.

"I filed a complaint last night," he said, "and this morning Dick Grace called. Told me the same story about Jones. I checked with Benno. Says he's looked at State Police and Fire Marshal records as well as police reports in Westerly, Charlestown, Richmond, and Greenwick. Over the past eighteen months, there's been a slew of fires in and around Indian Swamp. Cops think that anything worth saving was taken before the places were torched. Here's the angle. About a month ago, a fire was reported near the Charlestown-Greenwick line, with cops from both towns converging on the site. The Charlestown cops stopped Randall's pickup on a back road not two miles from the fire. The driver was our friend Mr. Jones. Had Ollie Randall with him who was shit-faced. In a field sobriety test, Jones seemed to be okay. According to the report, the pickup had a dirt bike in the back, registered to Jones, and a gas can, which in a swamp buggy in the boonies, is no surprise. Both claimed they had been at Oaky's; the cop checked it out later and was told they had been there drinking, causing a ruckus, until a few minutes before they got stopped by the cops." He paused. "No surprise there. Not sure what it all means but Benno's still digging."

∘ ○ ∘

Why was I compelled, despite aches and pains, to visit the ruins at Haversham Golf Club? Was it that Sherlock Holmesian thing about the 'scene of the crime'? What did Rumpole of the Bailey say about the necessity of defense attorneys visiting the *locus in quo* to get the staging and the scent?

Ninety minutes later, I was in my gleaming black Charger heading into Westerly on Route 1. The spring morning, infused with the shiny green vibrancy that suddenly pervades South County in June, raised my spirits, just as ibuprofen, Ben Gay, frequent changes in position, and flexes of my right hand—now a pretty purple just above the knuckles—mitigated the effects of yesterday's pummeling. I took the winding private drive past the parking lot and bag drop to where, only days ago, white pillars marked the clubhouse entrance. And found them gone, replaced by a yellow, truck-mounted crane hoisting blackened girders into waiting dump trucks. I left my car not far from a front-end loader shoveling what appeared to be the last of the debris from within the foundation, and walked toward the first tee. Since my previous visit, rolls of turf had been laid on what had been the burnt-out embankment, and impatiens, looking incongruous in their pinks and whites, were in beds smelling of compost; flowering rhododendrons, lilacs, and forsythias shielded double rows of hay bales that ringed the knoll. On the tee, yardage markers and benches had been installed; from a nearby green, mowers made sounds like swarms of angry wasps, and fairways stretching to the north were bathed in a light from the noon sun that eliminated shadows and turned the ponds into glass.

Okay, what had I come to see? Would I recognize it?

The cart path to the remains of the maintenance building was now free of police tape and I followed it down the slope past trees that had been pruned since my visit. The crane and loader hadn't gotten here as yet and the remaining masonry walls showed spaces where the garage entrance and a single window had once been. As I had before, I tried to figure out how Randall got inside. Window? Could he get in a window with a back brace? Were the garage doors open like the pump house? Unlikely, too close to the Clubhouse and would have been picked up by a security patrol. Was the security system already burnt out? Did he set a separate fire inside with gas, or with a fuse from some fireworks, and then couldn't get out? Wouldn't he have arranged his exit from inside before setting the fire? Or was it unintended, from a cigarette butt as Flanaghan suggested, or because he had been so drunk as Charlie wanted to believe? Or, was that when Jones came in?

My ruminations were interrupted by a bark from Shadrach, this time on a long retractable leash. At the other end of the leash was Charlie Fessenden.

"Algy, what are you doing here?" He approached rapidly, dressed in a maroon pullover sweater, jeans, and a cap with the Club's emblem. Despite his hearty greeting, his face was set in the same grimness as when I left him yesterday.

"How about yourself?" I said and remembered that, on purpose, I had not told him that I would visit Ugo Calibrese yesterday.

"Taking Shadrach for a walk. Dani's not riding today … feeling a little punky … so I said I'd take him 'walkies' and come up here to see how things are progressing. Fausto called me yesterday afternoon. I have to go to Providence tomorrow to meet another lawyer." He shook his head. "Can't believe Fausto's so insistent that I have a Providence lawyer with me just to answer a few questions from the State Police." He said that with the petulance of a teenager complaining about a visit to a frosty spinster aunt.

"It's a good idea."

"Sure, sure," he said dismissively.

"Tell Laretta everything, about you and Ollie Randall and …."

His eyes left me to turn to the vista of fairways at my left. Sheepishly, he said, "Dani told me she called you about the scare Ollie put into her. That bastard! Goddamn it, Algy, that was the last straw, and then he shows up drunk…."

I could have pursued that point—was being drunk the reason he was fired? Instead, I asked, "How do you get up here?"

"Past the corral, through a strip of Randall's …, Calibrese's …, land, up the back road past the pump house, then through the woods along the eighteenth fairway. It's about a fifteen minutes walk." He took off his cap to wipe his forehead with his sweater sleeve and I saw his hair, usually not a strand out of place, was greasy and unkempt. "Archie Soames doesn't want me up here…." His voice caught. "Asked me to resign as Club Secretary which I have done. I ….," and he turned back to me. Tears were welling up in his eyes as his hand reached for my forearm. "Algy, you've been such a good friend. I can't tell you how I appreciate it. I know you are doing it for Tony, but …!"

"Not just for Tony."

"Well, for Dani then. I know that's the reason."

I hesitated before I said, "It seems to me you're getting a raw deal and, well, I don't like it."

I expected a show of appreciation for my support but he wasn't listening from inside his well of self pity. "Sometimes, I don't know what to do. I don't have anybody I can talk to. The Tramontis think I'm a failure, someone that they have to bail out, like I can't do anything myself. I only stand for it because of Dani. Dani's wonderful but she's not practical. And relies too much on her brothers." He took a long, dispirited breath. "I had something good going here. Really good. I was a success! Now, it's all over…."

"It's not over yet," I lied because *if* it was known that Charlie asked for an 'extra' to get 'Charlie's deal' closed, it would be, and changed the subject. I gestured toward the fairways and made a comment as to the course's elaborate irrigation scheme.

"Engineering marvel," Charlie said quickly, momentarily perking up and selling the Club as he had done with prospective members. "Ingenious system. Depends upon the pumps for sucking out the water from wells and ponds and sending it back into the creeks and swamps. If the pumps fail, the irrigation system stops, the waters aren't charged, the recycling ponds don't fill…."

"I had no idea." I feigned interest since I was trying to keep him from slipping back into his self-centered doldrums.

"Come on," he said, "if the pump house is open, I'll give you the tour. Leave your car here. Have lunch with Dani and me and I'll drive you back."

I didn't resist his invitation; after all, why the hell *was* I here?

● ○ ●

We followed a well-behaved Shadrach past throbbing diesel dump trucks to a wide asphalt trail that probably accommodated maintenance trucks and tractors. It wound around the height of a modest ridge that sloped east to west, a natural point for the gravity flow that must help with the irrigation. Through groves of pines pungent with resin and with last year's needles making a brown carpet, past cairns of boulders and broken ledge likely grubbed out during the construction of the fairways, Charlie mounted his hobbyhorse about the obstacles the Club overcame to obtain environmental permits. The original course design, he explained, contemplated that the swamps and ponds were to be used as water hazards or were to be redirected to line fairways, with wells tapping into abundant ground water providing irrigation. Seemed elegantly simple to all concerned until the world famous course designer and his engineering team met reality at the Department of Environmental Management.

The answer from DEM, after months of prodding during an ominous silence, was 'no.' The ponds, creeks and swamps, it pointed out, eventually became the southern end of the Indian Swamp, an 'ecologically sensitive' area. Any change in the volume of water from the golf course property would disrupt the swamp forever. If there was going to be a golf course, there would be no change in ground water levels, meaning the Club would need a closed or 'looped' irrigation system. That brought howls from the Board and the course designer, but eventually they threw up their hands and the course was reengineered with elaborate use of dikes, culverts, aerators, and tunnels that controlled the flows of surface and ground water, with the pumps the key to its functionality.

"The engineering cost was a quarter million alone," he blustered, "but it didn't pass muster. The DEM now objected that fertilizer and herbicides would affect the ecosystem of the swamp no matter what happened in the 'loop,' and that errant golf balls would attract golfers into the marshy 'fly-overs' from some tees to fairways, making 'habitat management' unmanageable. Bad enough, but then the Rare Species Society found a fern that was indigenous only to the Indian Swamp and someone from URI discovered a rare salamander that *had* to be protected."

Although they eventually got through the fern issue with a designated 'forever wild' patch of land and the salamander crisis with culverts to its breeding areas, the Board decided to go the political route to speed things up. "That's what everyone thinks you do in Rhode Island, and this one time, they were flat out wrong. The staff at DEM was fighting with the Governor about something else so when his office intervened on our permits, we got into deeper shit ..., pardon the expression."

We had been walking for almost five minutes. Where was this pump house?

Finally, the Board got smart and hired a local engineer with environmental credentials and political clout and a deal was reached. The Club would have a closed, pressurized system which would irrigate from designated ponds and wells, aeration would be provided to the ponds, a continuous filtration system would be installed, and a state of the art monitoring system would check on the pumps and fertilizers, solvents, or any other gunk that might get into the eco-system. "Cost a ton! And DEM still has it in for us. The relationship is poisonous. Their multiple permits require activation of the system at all times between March and November. If not, the permits are yanked, golf is suspended or terminated." And then, he pointed to our left. "There it is."

Through a line of cedars, I saw a building designed like a country barn painted red with white trim. A radio antenna or maybe a lightning rod, exhaust pipes, and air conditioning units dotted its roof. Our trail led up to its garage doors and then down a steep incline into trees. A section of metal tank was visible on one side of the building. As we got closer, I heard the rhythmic hum of large machinery. Charlie pulled on Shadrach and stooped to release him from the leash.

"It's that important! That's why I came up here the night of the fire. Just to check ...."

"What...?"

CHAPTER TWENTY-THREE

I wrenched Charlie to his feet. His face was inches from mine, his eyes amazingly wide.

"You told us you were home all night! Then, you heard the sirens…."

Charlie shook off my grasp. Limply, he said, "That wasn't completely true."

"Don't tell me!" I marched toward the pump house, furious at another deception, barely able to keep my temper in control. He caught up to me and it came spilling out.

"I … left out some details. Nothing important." He touched my arm but I didn't break stride. I couldn't bear to look into those lying eyes. "Dani and the girls were away. I'd gone to a cocktail party earlier, went home about nine and watched a movie, had a couple of drinks. Dani telephoned me and I must have slurred a word or two. She asked me if I had been drinking and I said 'no' and that started an argument because she had been all over me about the booze. After I hung up, Shadrach had to go outside. I put him on a lead and went up by the corral. That's where I thought I saw a flicker of light, a flashlight maybe, maybe a tail light, up by the pump house. With the leaves not all out yet, you could see right up there on the ridge. Nobody should have been up there. And, I knew the security patrol didn't extend that far. All I could think of was that son of a bitch Randall doing something up there…."

"Why didn't you call somebody?"

"I … didn't have my cell phone with me and …."

What? It was always attached to his belt. "You could have gone back to the house and called."

"I know," he said with his head down, "I wasn't thinking clearly. Must have been the booze. Anyway, I took the trail, just like this morning. Before I got here, I thought I heard voices, then a door slam. As I got closer, I realized that Shadrach might start barking and …, so I decided to go back to the corral, tie him, and come back."

We had reached the front of the pump house. Machine noises from inside were loud, intense, and regular, reminding me of the engine rooms of ships I experienced during my stint in the Marine Corps. Two concrete steps led to the only door; 'no admittance' was painted on an upper panel. When the knob didn't give in to his hand, Charlie said "I didn't think anybody would be here because there'd be a maintenance cart or a truck out front. Come over here so you can see the pumps," he said and peered into the only window in the building's front.

Despite a reluctance to follow a direction from him, I joined him at a triple glazed window with a manufacturer's label on one corner pane; my fingers found gouges on its frame that had been painted over. A dim light inside illuminated three huge, parallel machines painted a pea green, maybe twenty feet long and six or seven feet high, set within concrete piers, each with rows of pipes, valves and cylinders. Digital lights showed on a control board and computer system near the door.

I muttered, "Impressive," because it was.

"All automatic and controlled from here. Those pumps are hybrids. Use diesel during the day and electric when full power isn't needed, like at night. Or, you can change it around if it's cheaper. Program and check the pumps once in a while. They keep the pressure in the lines all over the course and power aerators in the ponds for the wells without drawing too much water.

Almost completely self-contained, except for an agreed amount of filtered water that you could probably drink that flows through a drainage tunnel into Indian Swamp."

I backed away from the window and faced him. Might as well hear it all. "So, when you came back …."

His chin went down to his chest like a little boy expecting a spanking, and croaked out his story. "I left Shadrach and started back up here. It was quiet, no noise at all, no lights except for that one over the door"—he pointed to a spotlight fixture—"that's on a timer. As I approached, I saw the door was open a crack. Shouldn't have been." He gulped and hesitated long enough for me to wonder if he had recollected something he wasn't going to tell me. "I was about to go inside when I heard the sirens coming from Dunn's Corner and thought of the clubhouse immediately. I ran up the trail, think I even forgot to close the door."

"What about an alarm?"

He walked away from me, maybe to avoid my question. "I thought of that, too. Maybe nobody heard it and it went off after a time. Or somebody forgot to turn it on. I knew the Club was having problems with that system, in fact all the security systems for the outlying buildings. Come over here," and disappeared around the corner of the building.

This forced disengagement was getting old but I followed. The ground behind the building fell away quickly to a pond that was connected to the pump house by large steel pipes two feet or so in diameter, each held by a metal frame set close to the ground; two led toward the pond and two out toward the course. Behind the pipes were three huge steel tanks, with yellow 'hazard' signs. Charlie put his hand on the nearest tank marked 'Mega Green Only.' "Fertilizer. It's liquid catfish gurry from Mississippi. Nothing, absolutely nothing, chemical, one hundred percent natural! Unbelievable stuff. We're not allowed to use anything else!"

He shrugged and pointed at the larger pipes. "High-pressure aeration and recirculation. That smaller one contains the power cables. Those two boxes contain the back-up generators in case the electricity goes off." Two immense orange boxes stenciled 'Kumasu' were behind a chain-link fence and a tank marked 'Diesel'; each generator box had an exhaust pipe that extended upward over ten feet. "We've got our own electric substation up by Route One, that's how much juice it takes to run the system, with underground cables up to here. The pumps got to be on twenty-four seven."

Interesting but a typical Charlie diversion. I didn't give up. "So…?"

"Didn't even get to the knoll when I saw the flames," he responded. "Turned right around for home!"

"Why?"

He took a step toward me, his face reflecting shame. "Because I was in a goddamn panic! That's what you wanted to hear, right?"

"I don't get that."

"Algy, everything I had built up here rested on the success of the club. My future was literally going up in smoke. I didn't want to be the first on the scene. I couldn't take the … responsibility." He was holding back tears unsuccessfully. "I went back, got Shadrach into the house, and had some … coffee. Then, because I knew people would expect it, I drove over like everyone else."

"Didn't you tell anyone about the lights, the voices, the door left open?"

"In the excitement that night, it didn't seem like a big deal." He hesitated. "I could have been wrong about the lights or the voices, I mean. Maybe the light was from over the door. Maybe the voices were my imagination. Sound carries out here in ways you wouldn't expect and the wind was really blowing. And, goddamn it, Algy, I had been drinking! How could I be sure?" He shook his head plaintively. "A day or so later, though, I mentioned the door to Joe Pontarelli, a groundskeeper, the guy who takes care of the pump system. He kind of dismissed it. He said maybe one of his people could have left it open by mistake and came back later to close it because nobody reported it. Or, I was wrong." Charlie's voice was whiney. "And maybe I was."

"You didn't tell anyone else?"

His eyes flashed back. "Who? Who wants to talk to me besides the accountants? And, I didn't press it with Pontarelli. He's a tough wop, sarcastic, disrespectful, always seemed to have a comment on everything, the kind who mutters to himself. I guess he must be good at what he does if he got hired. All he seemed to care about was the course and the pumps. Didn't want anyone near his precious pump house."

I followed Charlie back to the front of the building, trying to stay on message, remembering I got into this mess to protect Dani. "Make sure you tell the whole story to Laretta. Everything, including the noise, the lights, the voices, the unlocked door...."

He stopped me short. Fear surrounded him like a fog. "I ... I have to tell him I ... panicked?"

"For crying out loud," I answered sternly, "give him the goddamn facts! You went back to investigate and by that time, there were sirens everywhere, flames leaping out of the clubhouse. I think that's what really happened, right?"

"Yes," he said with uncertainty. "I'd like to think that."

Shadrach had returned to his master and Charlie led the way down the ridge line. Near Charlie's boundary line, the asphalt path ended in a dirt track that seemed rarely used by anything with four wheels. Despite my disgust, I needed one more answer, if for no one else, me. "Calibrese says you asked to be the exclusive broker on some of his properties near the golf course if the Club deal went through."

He jerked his head toward me. "No, that's not what happened! Silverman suggested it to me. Sounded great!"

"Just before you closed the deal?"

"Well, around then."

"Did you see a possible conflict?"

"What conflict?"

I gave up.

◦ ○ ◦

It was two-thirty by the time Haversham Golf Club was disappearing in my side mirrors. Lunch had been made bearable by Dani's presence. Charlie sat morosely at the table, eventually complaining of a headache and leaving Dani to drive me back to my car.

It clouded up during my drive home and by Schartner's Farm near Route 4, the windshield wipers were in a steady rhythm. In a few minutes, I was on Route 95 weaving impatiently among the trucks thundering north through a drizzle. I should have retanked on Advil but I forgot to ask for the muscle relaxer before I left Fessenden's and that didn't help my disposition nor thought process. Do I tell Fausto the latest? Could I rely on Charlie telling Laretta? The pump house event, or non-event, didn't seem very relevant to anything we were interested in except Charlie now had another deception on his record. But maybe, the pump house was a stop on Randall's way to the clubhouse? Why? At least now I understood the reason for Charlie's lies. Charlie knew that *if* he had called security—I didn't believe he didn't have his cell phone with him—perhaps, the fire might have been prevented or at least contained by a 911 call. Why hadn't he made that call? Because he was drunk or close to, or too scared? No matter, but if the Board found out about his inaction, he was toast!

I also realized that I wanted a satisfactory resolution to what happened that night, how Randall killed himself. Something Charlie said was waiting in a part of my brain to catch up with a conclusion. I touched the visor button for the door opener of my garage, put the Charger away, walked up East Street around the corner to my house, and felt my BlackBerry vibrate. I checked the number and it was Fausto Tramonti.

I answered by saying, "Hold on" and went to the second floor bathroom for two little red pills. It was a full four minutes before I was back on the phone and this time, I was aggressive. The whole situation was giving me the proverbial headache. I opened the conversation with, "Not even a call to ask if your brother-in-law survived the membership meeting?"

"You shoulda called *us*…!"

'Shoulda called *us*? That response was classic Fausto. Always on the offensive. I could picture him at his desk, his face in a frown, his hands fluttering in the air over the speakerphone. "What's going on?" I continued heatedly. "You didn't tell me that Randall scared the bejeezus out of Dani right before Charlie got him fired. You didn't tell me about the Calibrese connection. Or, since Charlie hasn't an alibi until he arrives at the fire, that's why you hired Benno and Laretta!"

Fausto's silence meant he was surprised by what I knew and was thinking about how to handle the inconvenience of truth. "You weren't supposed to get that far into it," was his muted response. "The idea was for you to help get Charlie through the membership meeting. No further involvement. That was it."

"So you and your brother decided how much I was supposed to know?"

"Cheap shot, Algy."

Ugh. "You better hope Laretta's as good as you think."

"Why? There's something you're not telling me …?"

It gave me pleasure to relate how Flanaghan and I met with

Calibrese and learned about Charlie's 'arrangement' with Calibrese for future real estate commissions. Fausto's response was a curt, "Who knows besides you?"

"On our side, Flanaghan and me. Now you."

"Shit." Then, "Why did you meet with Calibrese? Why didn't Flanaghan ask me?" He was about to shoot the messenger. "Chrissakes, Algy, what are you doing? Nobody's asked you! Stay out of it!"

That jab riled me. I planned to also tell him of our misadventures at Oaky's Tavern but decided not to since he was so patronizing and dismissive.

"Damn," he said, "you can be a stubborn bastard!"

Being a stubborn bastard, and now an angry, stubborn bastard, I hung up. Maybe that should have made me feel better, but it didn't. I felt stupid.

∘ ○ ∘

Nadie arrived around five with a bundle of groceries and an overnight bag. After some discussion about dinner, we decided on tuna steak which I would prepare on the CharBroil grill on the patio, together with a salsa, and a tomato and parmesan salad. I mixed a Ward Eight cocktail for her and a Negroni for me. As I grilled and sipped my aperitif, she sat at the breakfast bar and I told her about my run to Westerly, that I had decided, which was true, that Charlie Fessenden's problems were no longer any of my business. Her eyebrows arched in a question and then she seemed satisfied that I was becoming 'unglued'—her term—from the troubles of Mr. Fessenden. With a bottle of cool Santa Dama Chianti, we shared our *rapido e simplici* meal, with Nadie full of new thoughts from her guide book and the internet for our itinerary in Italy. I guess I was getting goofy because I responded to everything she said in my limp Italian, which loosened her too serious, tour director demeanor. Maybe, in my foolish repartee, I was also covering up for my bruised hand, the latter having been explained as the hood of the Charger falling as I checked the oil.

After we cleared the dishes and glasses, she went upstairs while I scrubbed the grill. I followed some time later with two espressos. A black and white Turner Movie Classic was on the Sony as I put the espressos on the table in front of her. Katherine Hepburn's elegant face was profile to profile with a 'what's his name' leading man from the early forties. Maybe John Lund? The film was of a *Philadelphia Story* genre; she wore an evening gown, he had a three-piece tuxedo, and ballroom dancers flashed by in the background.

I slumped into the sofa and saw that Nadie was engrossed in the film. No surprise considering her notions about America's upper class, especially its women, and what better screen representation of the type than Ms. Hepburn with her good cheekbones, hair artfully exposing a delicate brow, her clipped speech, graceful use of words, and wispy mannerisms. With her tennis racket, or golf club, or martini, or in a 'first woman in the job' role, she epitomizes an aristocracy of tone, money, and culture that captivates Americans, whether in a Wasp or in a Kennedy. And that phenomenon troubles Nadie, a child of Brooklyn, with social activism in her DNA and anti-elitist to the bone. Time and again, she is drawn to a sociological examination of the 'why' of American class. Hadn't she read de Tocqueville at Radcliffe? During our early days together, I sometimes wondered if, deep down, the 'why' was the reason she hooked up with me in the first place.

Nadie interrupted my musing. The movie was over and Ms. Hepburn was being interviewed years later. "Isn't she lovely?"

"Yes…?"

"That voice …," Nadie said. Ms. Hepburn must have been eighty at the time of the interview, still clear eyed and beautiful, reminding me of my mother, as the actress reflected on her later movies with Spencer Tracey and John Wayne. "You know," Nadie whispered as though the actress was sitting across the room, "she was Tracey's mistress for almost two decades."

I said I knew that. Should I add Howard Hughes too? "But were they happy?"

Nadie turned to me, surprised. "I don't know," she said thoughtfully.

"It could have been two decades of frustration, sneaking around, excuses, hideaways…."

"Yes, it could have been," she said, with a gentleness that was unexpected.

The interview ended. Nadie started to surf channels. "Why do you suppose he married Dani Tramonti?"

"Huh?"

"Charlie."

"How about love."

"I mean in addition to love."

"I don't get it."

"He's a dummy but not all dummies are dumb when it comes to their own inadequacies. He must have seen Dani as someone beautiful, probably an ardent lover, and with all the money and power that her family brought to the marriage."

"Well, that's rather cool," I replied.

"Think about it," she said. "I bet he could have married any number of girls from his social set. But he didn't. He married into a traditional Italian family. Albeit, a wealthy Italian family. There had to be another reason."

"And you call me a cynic!" I complained. "A rich guy marries a beautiful girl from money and somehow it isn't romance. Dani loved him. He couldn't love her? Nadie, it makes the world go 'round. People fall in love and they get married. They really do!"

Nadie used the remote and clicked off the television. She stared at the screen, then let her hands comb through her hair. Seconds went by in silence before she said softly, "You know I love you. But, it's a different time. Someone like me has a separate life and a career from yours. I can't be …, enveloped …, subsumed in you …, like it is for Dani. Sooner or later, that's what you would expect…."

"Not so!" I exclaimed. "We could do it."

She exhaled deeply, leaned over, and took my hand, held it for a moment as though unsure of a response. The next thing I knew she clicked the remote and we were watching a rerun of *Seinfeld*.

The moment was gone.

CHAPTER TWENTY-FOUR

Behind the *Journal's* 'Lifebeat' section, Nadie's towel turban was barely visible across the breakfast bar. "Listen to this! That new cable show, *The Hill*, starts tonight. 'Violence, treachery, politics, infidelity, bribery, backstabbing, set right here in Providence!'" Pause. "Seems like they've got that right."

No response required. Nadie's cynicism toward my fair city was ironic since she enjoys living and working here, its great restaurants and cultural attractions, with Boston only an hour away. I sipped my espresso. Out through the den, I saw the new apartment and condo towers in WaterPlace in the heart of the bustling self-proclaimed Renaissance City. Why hadn't HBO, and Showtime, and Hollywood bought in? Because, Nadie the Psychologist once said, Providence is schizoid, having both an exciting, vibrant, stimulating personality and a corrupt, self-absorbed, *noir* personality living together, a condition unrecognized by natives and long-term residents, evident to newcomers. I'm paraphrasing, of course, but you get the idea. The 'good' Providence is what I hope for, but 'where the old world shadows hang heavy in the air,' is more titillating.

I heard a few more quotes about *The Hill* – I assumed from her evident interest that we would catch a few episodes—as I breezed through Part Two of the *Journal's* Verona series focused on its superb restaurants and local cuisine. Someplace along the way, I wondered aloud when the Faculty Club article would break, which brought Nadie's retort that maybe the story had been killed by some 'friend of the University,' reflecting her suspicion of the *Journal's* publisher, part of Providence's elite, don't you know.

I dodged that bullet and closed the newspaper with the clever remark that it was a day closer to our departure for Milan. Nadie responded by bestowing a radiant smile because *I* was the one who brought up Italy.

● ○ ●

Maria Lopes knocked and came in to my office with a handful of photographs of her nephew's graduation, including one of him in the uniform of an Army second lieutenant standing next to his proud auntie. I had been frequently reminded by Maria that the nephew was off to Boston University Law School before his active duty service and that she hoped for my assistance when he applied to Providence law firms for summer employment. Once again, I acknowledged that I would do so if his grades were up to snuff. She sniffed and said, "Not to worry!"

The rest of the morning was routine through to a noon conference call with lawyers in the counsel's office at Dartmouth and Princeton on the timely subject of overlapping municipal police and campus police jurisdictions. It was soon apparent that the issues faced in Princeton, New Jersey and Hanover, New Hampshire had little relation to the way we do business in Providence, Rhode Island. When the call wrapped up with promises of more information sharing, I told Maria that I would be back after two and walked to Thayer Street for a late lunch at Geoff's Deli. The day's special was a 'Judge Fortunato,' heated Italian cold cuts, pickles, hot peppers and mozzarella on Italian roll. A stool at a window was my vantage point to watch the sparse sidewalk traffic with a *Providence Monthly* and an Orangina. As I finished, I found myself thinking of the delights of Bellagio, Lake Garda, Verona, Trieste, the Maserati I had rented for the trip, and then, more somberly, of last night and Nadie's indecision. That thought would not go away, even in expectation of Italy's many splendors.

○ ◯ ○

When I returned to College Hall, the light was on in the President's first floor office.

Charles Danby looked tired. Commencement Week is a rough stretch for everybody in College Hall but toughest on the President. Being the gracious host for the luminaries, alumni, and Trustees, giving a last 'all' for the graduates, being 'there' all the time and 'on' all the time, is wearying even for a vigorous man like Charles Danby. As I knocked, he took off his glasses, pushed aside a document he was reading, and thanked me for a difficult week dealing with Sonny, Puppy Dog and the Faculty Club story. I related my ambush by Ms. Reins. "Enterprising," he laughed, not at all alarmed. "Sounds like a graduate we can be proud of." Then, "I'm sorry if it gets personal for you."

I nodded wanly. I admire Charles Danby, not only for his singular achievements during his brief tenure, but because he is a good man. He then said he was about to leave with his daughter, a graduating senior, on a 'road trip' from Providence to Florida, with no itinerary, reservations, or plans, stopping when and where they felt like it. "Can you imagine not being scheduled for two weeks?"

The pleasure of the thought was written largely in his happy expression. Martina Danby, a remarkable young woman, bright and very loyal to her father, had been his unofficial President's House hostess since the death of his wife shortly before he took office. "You know, she's signed with the Peace Corps. Thinks it's going to be Tanzania for the first year, training volunteers in the second. Then graduate school."

"You must be very proud of her."

He pushed his chair away from the desk and turned away to face a window and the towering trees of The Green. "I'll miss her terribly. She was my link to her mother in so many ways. I don't know if I could have gotten through the first year without her. She was my extra set of eyes and ears on the campus. I'll never have that again."

His secretary knocked on the doorframe, announcing a phone call. "By the way, Sonny sent me this," he said and handed me a contract for the city's use of the South Water Street buildings for the 'Sister City' events. The formal letter that went with it noted a need for repairs and clean-up and the City's willingness to move expeditiously on permits. I wondered why it went to the President and not to me.

"Pressure's on Sonny to produce something positive," I said.

"Maybe the 'truce' can continue?"

"I doubt it. There's neither goodwill or veracity in anything related to Sonny." I said I'd review the contract before I left for Italy with Nadie. At her name, he smiled. "I heard she's shaking the tree at Psychology. Good for her." Then, he rose, came around the desk, and took my hand in both of his. "Algy, you're part of what makes this campus work. We've got something good here. You and Artemus, the rest of our senior staff. I'm gratified."

I think I blushed.

◦ ○ ◦

A few minutes later, I felt like Nostradamus. Maria and Marcie, on summer hours, had already left the office. Stuck to my computer monitor was a message on a yellow Post-it in Maria's careful penmanship: "Call Mr. Tuttle!"

"Your truce is about to end." The 'I told you so' bite to Tuttle's voice wasn't hidden. "I called the Traffic Division this afternoon for a status report for the movie people. Guess what? We're not getting any support. We get *nada*. Those huge vans and trailers they got, all the trucks with the special lighting? Vince Nardello, the traffic guy I deal with, said if they're gonna park, it won't be on the city streets. And that schedule of street closings we gave them, with the 'no parking' schedule, forget it!"

Why would Sonny mess up Providence movie-making? Screw up Leonardo DiCaprio and Alec Baldwin and Toni Gillette coming to town? Sonny *loved* hobnobbing with movie makers, posing with film stars, dining with directors on Federal Hill, showing up at sets with a cashmere overcoat around his shoulders like an impresario. Had the Faculty Club issue, or my threat to expose his pay-to-play politics at the License Bureau, overcome his urge to be in the lights?

"Maybe somebody didn't get the word?"

"There is no 'word'! I've known Nardello for years. He's got his orders directly from McCarthy!"

"How much time do we have?"

"I've got to talk to the production people tomorrow morning if there's going to be a problem."

"Let me try Puppy Dog," I said. "Don't call them until I've gotten back to you."

Paula Ciccone's familiar recorded message greeted me: 'Mr. Goldbloom is either on another call or is outta the office. Please leave your name and number.' Note that it didn't add '... and he'll return the call.' Who else? I couldn't call Chief McCarthy for obvious reasons. That left Tony Tramonti.

"No, I haven't been 'ducking' you," he answered breezily. "You've been terrific. I owe you, the family owes you."

"Here's your chance to repay," I replied. "The Traffic Division is under orders not to cooperate while the DiCaprio movie is filmed on campus. The production people arrive next week, ..."

"What do you need?"

"Their vans and trailers got to be on Mary Street, Angell, Waterman, probably Brook and Hope, and side streets while they film. Parking bans and the side streets blocked off when they need it. It's all in the fact sheet and schedule we gave the Traffic Division weeks ago. Which they approved! Those trucks and trailers have got to get in and out and be on the streets. Cops directing traffic...."

"And Nardello blew off Tuttle?"

"Right."

A long, breathy pause. "Okay. What I want you to do is leave a message for Puppy Dog that you called me. If you don't get cooperation by tomorrow, it's *force majeure*, you'll cancel the movie's use of the campus...."

"I can't do that!"

"Listen, tell him that! He doesn't know what you can or can't do. The movies use union guys. Lots of 'em. The Teamsters drive the trucks, the IBEW has the lights, the Carpenters Union is all over that place, the Laborers are the service people, carting, loading and unloading, everything. Plus, the police and fire details. Nobody will like it if they don't get hired, with all that overtime and star power, not to mention the free food. Say that since he's not around, you had to call the Commissioner. Meanwhile, Fausto will get some calls made to appropriate guys in the unions."

I didn't respond immediately. There was enough of a silence for him to say, "Algy, it's simple. If Sonny screws you, it's no problem for anyone but the University. If he screws the unions, and the cops and fire lose their overtime details, it's his problem. They have to know what Sonny's threatening to do, that his vendetta against the University will cost them jobs and money."

Ah, Providence politics at its best.

He hung up.

I left the required message for Puppy Dog and called Tuttle to tell him about Tramonti's move. "The Commissioner's got street smarts," he said appreciatively. "He's gonna be a great mayor!"

His comment was meant as a tip of the hat to me, that my relationship with Tramonti would eventually bear fruit for the University. So, why did it leave me cold?

I went home.

◦ ○ ◦

The bricks seemed to radiate heat as I took a glass of chilled Pinot Grigio and the latest Sue Grafton 'Alphabet Murder' mystery with me to the patio. I raised an umbrella against the brilliant four o'clock sun; the cooling breeze that had been coming off the Bay most of the day had died, and there was no masking of the murmur of traffic, even when I played a CD of *Madame Butterfly*. In the distance, the granite facades on two new condo buildings in Capital Center had reached their sixth or seventh floors in their race to penthouses.

In the shade of the umbrella, the cushions of the chaise were soft, the wine was dry and cool, and finding my place in the book, I got comfortable. Nadie complains I'm shamefully envious of the thrills and spills of my fictional heroes and heroines and it is true I tend toward mysteries in a series, where over time the character of the detective becomes more robust, discernable, and human. A series makes me feel like an insider as my favorite detectives learn their craft, find their slants on the state of the human condition, develop personal traits helpful and hurtful, and confront their inner devils. Except for Parker, they even age.

I guess I dozed off after a few pages because I awoke with a start as two squirrels fought a territorial war in the patio's dogwoods. I roused myself and went into the kitchen and found that before leaving for the campus, Nadie had posted an underlined *Journal* obituary to the door to the hall:

> *Angelo Columbino, 64, of Napoli Drive, Johnson, a retired tavern owner and a former mob enforcer, died Saturday at St. Joseph's*

Hospital after a short illness.

Born in Providence, a son of Domenic ("the Dom") and Maria (Fiori) Columbino both of Cranston, he had lived in Johnston for fifty years.

Mr. Columbino owned Pace's Tavern, Providence, until recently.

He served a five year federal prison term for extortion after he and Felix ("Happy") DelFusco were convicted of shaking down Providence bookies in the early 1980s.

Mr. Columbino was an associate of the Marfeo crime family.

The funeral will be held Wednesday at 9 a.m. from Parkside Funeral Home, 1010 Park Ave., Cranston, with a Mass of Christian Burial at 10 in St. Maria's Church, Birch Street, Johnston. Burial will be in Peace of God Cemetery, East Providence.

Nadie's postscript? "Only in Providence!"

∘ ○ ∘

I was in the den when I heard the front door open, the kitchen door's swing, and the click of heels across the kitchen's tile floor followed by the plop of a bulging leather shoulder bag landing on the divan. Followed by herself. I asked if she wanted some wine.

"No."

"Some chips and salsa?"

"No."

"A fat lip?"

"No!"

I almost repeated Danby's remarks about her 'shaking the tree' in her department but stopped in time. She might take that as a prelude to interference. Independent Nadie works alone! I asked about dinner and maybe watching the debut of *The Hill* and got a pouty 'I don't care' response.

Giving up on commiseration and empathy, I told her about

the problems with the movie production and my calls for help to Tony Tramonti, which elicited a hand slap on the divan. "Providence!" she declared. "Nothing is ever on the up and up. You can't get anything done without some politician putting his thumb in it." Oh, she was on a toot! "And how does the University Counsel deal with it? You do it by politics!"

Hm-m-m. Perhaps I should read up on positive psychology!

She got up from the divan and took the three stairs up to the kitchen. "Don't you ever get sick of it?" she said over her shoulder.

"Look, there are certain realities in my job."

She changed her mind about the wine; I heard its gurgle as she poured. "So, you play into *their* politics," she said. "You think you can beat them because they're so awful and Tony is your friend. But if Tony is elected, is it going to be any better? Aren't you going to call him for favors? If an ordinary person has an issue, will he or she still have to know a someone to get it resolved? Is that going to change?"

"Somehow, incrementally, for the better. I thought the idea was to do the best you can…."

The phone rang, breaking into her retort. Nadie answered it quickly and reacted with a covered receiver and a mouthed, "Charlie Fessenden."

Ugh. What timing!

I went up to the kitchen and took the phone. After a 'hello,' I barely got another word out.

"I went to Laretta's office. Right out of *Goodfellas*! Characters all over the place. This receptionist, a blonde bombshell—you should see her—takes me in and I wait for him in a conference room with terrible artwork. I mean God awful! Laretta like he could be … well, you know," his voice lowered, "a *consigliere* to the Godfather!"

"He's a very competent lawyer and deserves your respect and absolute candor."

"But, you can understand why I wasn't comfortable …."

Ugh!

"Anyway, things are looking up," he said brightly. "Ackley reported to the Board that negotiations with the insurance company are going well. The Governor tees off on Saturday, *two weeks* before the July third deadline. Everyone will feel much better…."

I agreed. What else was there to say.

"Algy, Dani and I appreciate your efforts. You and I are cut from the same post." I cringed. Nadie could not be told. "We'd like to invite you and Nadie down here tomorrow for dinner. I know its last minute, but the kids are in Narragansett with their grandparents for a few days. I've already invited Tom Flanaghan and his wife and they're coming. It'll be a good party. Let us say 'thank you' properly."

I should have immediately excused us on 'short notice' but instead I asked Nadie what she thought and was surprised by her nonchalant, "Sure, why not." It was too immediate and direct. Was she spoiling for a fight with Charlie? I responded to Charlie and we agreed on six-thirty at Charlie's home. I hung up and turned to tell Nadie about the arrangements but she was in the den retrieving her shoulder bag. "I'm going home. I'm terrible company tonight. I'll get some Chinese on Thayer Street."

"Are you sure?" I asked and then, "Why did you agree to dinner?"

"Because, we are leaving for Italy in two days and I want to hear from Charlie and Dani that your services are no longer required. I'll be ready by five-thirty. That should be plenty of time, right?"

I said it would be. She came forward, gave me a quick kiss on the cheek, and left.

CHAPTER TWENTY-FIVE

Shortly after Nadie left last evening, just before *The Hill* began with two 'fellas' gunned down on Acorn Street, Fausto Tramonti telephoned, informing me of a meeting with Joe Laretta and Benno Bacigalupi at Fausto's law office in the morning at eight-thirty. He didn't mention my hang-up of his last call; in fact, he was off the call with a 'gotta go' before any further explanation.

Which was why I was in barely moving traffic in a sodden downtown where a morning rain grayed the city. Drivers seemed even more impatient and ruthless than usual, pedestrians scurried to avoid the splash of cars, and buses blocked streets, doubling the time from College Hill of Providence's East Side to Broadway on Federal Hill on the other side. I stop-started, seeing the frustration build in the faces of other drivers as we advanced a few feet and fell back, waiting for someone to lose 'it' in the lines of cars stalled between Francis Street and the bridge over Route 95. Rhode Islanders honk at any car that doesn't move a nano-second after a light change or at any pedestrian dashing between cars clogged in traffic so there was a chorus of angry horn blasts from near and far over the sounds of rain spatting the Mini Cooper, the wipers, the defrost, and NPR news on the radio. To make things worse for me, my back started to ache. Not a good beginning for a session with Fausto.

A hundred and fifty years ago, Broadway was planned as a tree-lined thoroughfare linking downtown to the sprawling West Side.

By the eighteen nineties, it was Providence's widest avenue and the prestigious address of mill owners, lawyers and physicians, downtown merchants, and bankers. Broadway never quite recovered from Depression-era dislocations, and after World War Two, the neighborhood's mansions were chopped up into apartments, the stately oaks and elms became diseased and dust laden, and a place of middle class pride deteriorated into a shambles. But through benign neglect, which came easy in Providence, Broadway escaped urban renewal plans and was reclaimed during the real estate boom in the eighties and thereafter. Now, its trees are cared for, the sidewalks maintained, professional offices like those of Fausto A. Tramonti, Esq., and elegant condominiums have replaced tawdry apartments, and you couldn't touch one of the mansions for under seven figures!

The striped parking lot behind Fausto's Victorian was stained with the rainbows of oil when I pulled in fifteen minutes late. I parked between Benno Bacigalupi's car and Fausto's white Maserati Quattroporte sporting a single digit license plate that signified Rhode Island clout, and dashed through the wet to rear stairs. I had been here many times, usually in a conference room where he held regular lunches with 'Tramonti people.' These worthies included ambitious young politicians like 'Junior' Lucca, the smart-alecky councilman from Federal Hill and son of former Senator Lucca; a disaffected union leader; a wealthy Tramonti cousin who manufactures costume jewelry; a Latino councilman with a laundry list of grudges against Sonny; and 'old timers' Frank Rotundo, a state senator who works for Tramonti Corporation in 'public affairs'; and Charles 'Knocko' O'Reilly, vice chairman of the state party. In such a seasoned group of Providence pols, you can imagine how much weight is given to my East Side political insights. How many times did I hear, 'Ya don't get it, Algy, ya just don't get it!'

Fausto's secretary, Eva, was coming out of his office with a tray holding an espresso pot; she held the door open with one foot and I entered what was once a mill owner's living room, lavishly furnished, with a crystal chandelier and marble fireplace. Benno, in a dark suit and sitting rigidly in a leather chair in front of Fausto's mahogany desk, acknowledged me with a flick of an eyelash as I took off my Burberry and put it on a sofa. Fausto stood by the desk, his squat wrestler's body, curly black hair, and wolfish demeanor bespeaking his roots; he wore an immaculate starched white shirt with gold cuff links and a Pucci tie, and his trousers were likely part of a Canali suit. He held a tiny white cup. "Joe Laretta is on the line," he said pointing to a speakerphone.

Laretta said, "Like I said, Charlie authorized me to speak to you. I told him he did well…." From the background noise coming through the speakerphone, Laretta was in his car.

"Mistake," Fausto muttered gruffly into the speakerphone, and sat behind his desk. "He'll believe you."

Laretta ignored the comment. "I had him prepped, dressed right, so all he had to do was tell a straight story with no edits, no sidebars. He called Randall a 'villain.' 'Villain?' The smirks on their faces at that? Anyway, he went through how Randall got fired for showing up drunk. They had statements from witnesses who saw the ruckus and the Westerly cops who took Randall off the property, including his threats against the Club and Charlie. They knew Randall's history, that he was a drunk with a couple of DUI's, suspected of selling stolen goods…."

Fausto interjected, "And everything backed up Charlie, right?"

"All the Staties were interested in was tying Randall to the fire. They're pretty much convinced he set it and didn't get out in time because he was drunk." He paused. "Don't ask me how you test for alcohol level when he had to be mostly charred bones. Charlie said that Randall could have known about the temporary storage under the porch, even though that was a last minute thing, if he was snooping around. And, he could get through to the clubhouse on the back trails from his trailer easy enough. Not so sure if he knew about the fireworks because that was a last minute deal. One Statie asks why Charlie got Randall hired if he was a troublemaker. Charlie answered it was because Randall lived nearby, knew the land like the back of his hand, and was mean enough to frighten trespassers. In other words, to neutralize him. But the Statie asked if he was a troublemaker, why take the chance?"

Good question. One we hadn't asked.

"Charlie hems and haws and there is a long pause, like maybe something might be coming out. Because, he says, it might keep Randall from getting the other Quonnies riled up while the clubhouse was being built on their 'signal hill.' So that brings out a slew of questions about the 'signal hill' and the Quonnies. They hadn't focused on that angle. Bingo! Not only did they have a dead, drunk suspect who was fired by the Club and hated the Fessendens, but now they had an added revenge motive."

I hesitated to ask a follow-up but I couldn't leave it alone. "Did they ask Charlie about the night of the fire?"

"Yeah, but just as a prelim. He said he joined everybody else when he heard the sirens. Which is true. Didn't ask about where he was before. And he didn't volunteer anything."

I almost continued with something like 'Charlie should have told them about the pump house' but didn't; he was Laretta's client, not mine. My question, however, prompted Fausto's frown and a question directed to me. "Why are you asking?"

I ignored him. Despite the veneer of modernity of his automobile, his spacious office, and fine Italian suits, Fausto carries suspicion like a sledge, which often annoys me.

"And," Laretta continued, "it was over, one guy yawning and

the other guy tapping his coffee cup impatiently, and I'm putting my pad away when Charlie volunteers that he couldn't think of anyone who gained from the fire. Not even Ugo Calibrese!"

Fausto lurched forward in his chair, spilling his coffee.

"They asked him what he meant and he went into Calibrese's leased land deal. But since Ugo only benefits if there is no golf play on the course, and that starts in a couple of days, it's not an issue. Charlie was trying to stir up trouble for Calibrese, a pay back, he told me later. I never saw it coming. Jerry Franks has represented Calibrese. That could have put me in a compromising position."

Fausto swore in Italian and hunched over the speakerphone. "So, bottom line …?"

"I think they'll file it away as a fire set by a vengeful drunk. They've got Randall with motive and opportunity. Probably will stay that way unless they want to look for an accomplice, which according to Benno could be that buddy of his, the crazy one."

Fausto looked up at Benno with a 'what's going on' glare as a car horn sounded and a muffled vulgarity came over the speakerphone. Laretta said, "Traffic's terrible. I'll be late for court. It's over, I think," and he left the call.

Fausto punched a button on the speakerphone console. He used a paper napkin to delicately blot the drops of coffee on his trousers. I looked out a window to the sputtering traffic on Broadway, not wanting to watch Fausto's face as his mind worked through an evaluation of where he was, and what to do. Benno, of course, remained inscrutable. Finally, Fausto, his voice evidencing decision and pride in his selection of Laretta, said to Benno, "Looks like that's it. Laretta's good, huh?" When Benno didn't reply, Fausto, annoyed at the lack of expected concurrence from the detective, switched his attention to a topic that concerned me. "By the way, don't worry about your movie. People from Local 252 and a couple of councilmen had a meeting with Sonny, the Chief, and Puppy Dog last night. Sonny said it was all a scare, just to let you know what he could do, if he wanted to. Put you on the hot seat for a day or so. According to my source, he was showing off."

Fausto scowled; I had been the occasion of another insider's victory for Sonny.

"Thanks," I said warily, now with the impression that Fausto was thinking the University, and me in particular, were rapidly becoming political liabilities, or, at the very least, nuisances.

"I wanted you to know," he said firmly and stood in our dismissal. Clearly, releasing Benno and me from our assigned tasks had become his next order of business.

I started to rise from my chair but Benno tilted his head to me and spoke in his modulated voice. "Ain't that simple. You should know what happened that night in case they decide to go further when they know what we know. Because I think they will. Suppose they ask Charlie if he had a personal run-in with Randall, like a few hours before he got fired? Because maybe Randall told somebody else?"

Fausto interrupted gruffly. "Benno, I only got a few minutes before I got a client coming in. Where's this going?"

Benno slowly raised his eyes to Fausto. "You're paying me a lot of money. You ought to listen."

I don't think I've ever heard anyone address Fausto Tramonti like that. But, to my surprise, Fausto, despite his glare, sat and folded his fingers over his stomach.

"I told you some of this before," Benno began. "Over the past eighteen months, there's been fourteen known fires set in or near the swamp. But here's the thing. Not one at a property owned by a Quonnie. According to the local cops, a Quonnie buddy of Randall, Freddie Jones, is responsible, with Randall helping out. Jones is a certifiable nut case. He was released from the Army's stockade about when the fires began, in there for biting off somebody's ear after some unflattering remarks about Indians. He also poured lighter fluid all over the guy's bunk and set the barracks on fire. The Chief in Greenwick figures Jones and Randall would torch a place after they boosted anything of value, copper flashing, metal pipes, bicycles, small refrigerators, beat-up air conditioners, all kinds of crap. They sold the stuff to junk yards or off the back of Randall's truck in the boonies, like a traveling Salvation Army store...."

"Yeah, yeah," Fausto said with exasperation.

"Every Friday night, Jones and Randall are at Oaky Gardiner's tavern, usually with some other troublemakers, mostly relatives of Jones. On the night of the clubhouse fire, a Friday, Randall and Jones don't show up. But the night before, they do, all the time giving each other high fives, until they got shut off and tossed. When the Staties were asking questions about Randall's whereabouts on the night of the fire, they didn't ask Gardiner or anybody else about the night *before* the fire, according to Gardiner. Just the night of. You gotta ask the right questions to Quonnies because they don't volunteer."

Fausto's face flushed with impatience. "C'mon, c'mon, who cares?"

"You do," Benno replied calmly. "Oaky Gardiner, the tribal leader, had always protected Jones, bailed him out a few times, because his family's a solid minority on their tribal council. But right now, Gardiner's not happy with Jones or his relatives." Benno glanced at me and maybe his lips had a trace of a knowing smile. "So, he tells me something interesting. Said it was tribal history but I got his meaning. The Quonnies set ceremonial bonfires on Fessenden's land, the 'signal hill' that Fessenden referred to, where the clubhouse got built. Guess who ignited those fires every year? Seems like this is a privilege that belongs to the Jones family because they trace their lineage to a hero named Magua. They'd collect all kinds of combustibles, take it through Randall's property, haul it up to the top of the knoll, get all dressed up, do a lot of whooping and hollering, and then a Jones would set it off!"

Benno's eyes were now half closed. He had it all worked out in his mind. Fausto's big leather chair creaked as it came forward. "Benno, you're probably right. For all I know, you're absolutely right. So what? I don't give a shit! Unless getting Jones picked up helps us to direct attention away from Charlie." He paused to consider that. "Nah! Just going to prolong it."

I asked, "You said they would steal things before...."

Benno continued to stare down Fausto but addressed me. "No one knows if anything is missing at the Club, right? I've been thinking the fire had to be a two man job. Too much for a little guy like Randall." His head slightly tilted toward me. "I think Jones and Randall decided on a boost at both buildings and a helluva bonfire. Could have used a pickup through the back trails from Randall's trailer. Figured they could smash and rob, set the fire, stash whatever in the swamp or at Randall's place. Look, I've been out there. You could hide half of Providence in there. So, that means they're together. Get it? Charlie doesn't have an alibi but he doesn't need one if Randall was with Jones!"

Fausto's fingers drummed the table. "Look, can you guys get this! The Staties aren't gonna pursue it! We don't care why he did it or who if he had help! All we gotta know is that they don't come after Charlie! I know what I gotta do...."

I agreed with Benno. "What if Calibrese found out that Charlie had a run-in with Randall...? The rumors on the land deal would be small potatoes...."

"Fahgettaboutit." Fausto responded. He might as well have said, 'Stay away from Calibrese,' and then, realizing he had come at us too shrilly, he became as silky smooth as his suit. "It's over,

Benno," and he extended his hand over the desk. "You did a great job! The burned guy did it. We don't need to know why. Or with who. Let's drop it, okay!"

Benno stood, bringing Fausto to push away from the desk and come around to us, his presence and personality filling the room. "Send me your bill. Charlie's okay, the Indians got trouble, life will go on."

Benno left Fausto's office without a response. Fausto smiled and shook his head as though I would understand his reaction. "See? That's his problem. Goes off on stuff we don't care about. Can't let things go." I stood and he raised his arm to my shoulder and said I was a 'true' friend. "We've done what we can do."

Why did his slap on the back as I left his office give me a chill? Why did I remember a line from a Mafia movie, a don saying 'screw your friend, marry your enemy.'

∘ ○ ∘

I approached Benno in the parking lot as he was opening his car door. The rain was now a mist. I asked him for a moment of time and got in the passenger seat. The car smelled of the Pine Tree deodorizer hanging from the rear view mirror. His face was stony, his lips in a straight line. "Something stinks," he said. "Don't know from under what rock. Why shut down on Calibrese? It's killing Fessenden."

I wondered about that as well. Maybe Fausto agreed with my assumption that Calibrese—even for Sonny—wouldn't push Charlie's conflict to a complaint at the Real Estate Commission because he would be involved. Or, maybe Fausto figured Charlie's reputation was a lost cause and it was time to move on. In any event, my interest in what happened the night of the fire remained unabated. So, I told Benno that Charlie had lied as to his activities the night of the fire, that there were noises, lights, and maybe voices up at the pump house, that the pump house door had been open, and that Charlie later mentioned the security lapse to a greenskeeper who brushed him off.

Benno rubbed his eyes with his thumbs in consideration of new information. "The out buildings like the pump house were tied in by a wi-fi system to the central station in the clubhouse that wasn't operable as yet. Shoulda had audible alarms. I didn't check with the alarm company if they had a record of anything going off out there." Then, he added, "So, you're saying the fire gets set and nobody would notice if the pumps weren't on, not for hours. The pumps are off and DEM pulls the permits. Ugo wins big time." His voice trailed off. "What's the name of the greenskeeper?"

"Pontarelli." I noticed the slightest reaction to the name.

He reached into the back seat and withdrew a battered brief-case, opened it, and found a set of papers clipped together and headed 'Personnel.' He flipped pages until he found 'Joseph V. Pontarelli—Assistant grounds keeper.' "Before he got the job, he worked at Calibrese's course up in Greenwick. I was surprised coming from a public course he could get a job at a first class place like Haversham. Goddamn, I'm slipping. Should have looked further!"

Benno's eyes dulled in his evaluation, then abruptly, he shook his head and shuffled the papers back in the briefcase. "No. It doesn't work. Calibrese is too smart to get involved in something dangerous like setting a fire as a blind for shutting down the pumps. Not for short money. It's too obvious. If the pumps are shut down or vandalized, just before the trigger date on the lease, somebody's gonna point a finger at him. And, someone—a Randall for instance—could rat him out. Nah, he'd never put himself in that position, always plays his cards close to the vest...."

Benno's reluctance to connect the dots made me impatient. I knew that squint-eyed, revengeful toad *was* involved! "But," I argued, "Pontarelli must be his guy on the scene while the Club gets built. Suppose…," Benno was already shaking his head 'no,' "… Pontarelli riles up Randall after he gets fired. Pontarelli must know about the temporary storage, the fireworks, …."

"A clubhouse fire doesn't revoke the DEM permits," he replied rigidly. I told him that the DEM had tested the pond after the fire after a false report had been received, but he dismissed the thought as a tick on an elephant. "Calibrese's not going to risk an arson charge to shut down the pumps!" He was dogmatic.

"Benno, I want you to be working for me. Not Fausto. Is that a problem?"

"I just got fired," he answered, slowly, his eyebrows arched in question.

I explained what information I wanted, some that was directed toward the fire, some more as to the nature of political intelligence. "I gotta lot on Calibrese already," he said, his eyes sparking with renewed interest. "All his connections, going back years. Whatever you need to know. But not about his Westerly background or his dealings with the Quonnies or Pontarelli. It'll take a few days."

"I'm leaving for Italy day after tomorrow for two weeks. I need whatever you have when I return."

"Okay."

We talked about his fees, hourly and daily, and I accepted. I left his car, saying I wasn't sure why I wanted the information.

"I never know what's useful until it kicks me in the ass," he replied and put his brief case on the vacant passenger seat. "You gotta have imagination. Get as many facts as you can about the people involved. Something might work." What I might have expected from a gimlet-eyed, hardball detective right out of Hammett, Block, and MacDonald. "Nobody appreciates that anymore. Investigations aren't just logic. It's goddamn shoe leather!"

CHAPTER TWENTY-SIX

I collected Nadie in the Range Rover at her apartment. She was smartly dressed in a colorful short sleeve Bolivian knit sweater over black shirt, and dark green pants. Pearls decorated her kissable ears, under tied back, glistening hair; a pink and green Vera Bradley bag hung over her shoulder. She was happy, almost loquacious; an *Eyewitness Guide Book To Northern Italy* was withdrawn from her bag and as we drove south in heavy traffic streaming from Providence on Route 95, she clicked off a number of 'must sees' at Lake Como, Verona, and Padua; I made agreeable sounds. The way she rambled convinced me our excursion in *bella Italia* would soothe the 'whatever' that was bothering her.

Thunderheads darkened the horizon and gusts of a cooling wind came off the Sound as we arrived at Pond House. Dani, at the front door to greet us, embraced me and then, more guardedly, offered her hand to Nadie who was polite. Good! I was surprised when Nadie hung on my arm when we followed Dani into a living room with comfortable looking seating; a shell motif was evident in the bases of hurricane lamps, decorative glass jars, along ceiling borders, and in dark blue drapes complimenting pale blue walls. The Flanaghans were standing by a granite slab fireplace under a large, well-executed pastel of a rugged shoreline, beach roses, and tall grasses. Our hostess introduced Nadie to the Flanaghans; Charlie was at a drinks table, loudly announcing that he was mixing 'adult beverages.' I noticed Jean Flanaghan's kind, intelligent eyes in her round freckled face and that her comfortable clothes signaled that she didn't care if she was as stout as her husband.

Nadie requested a Cosmopolitan and I settled for a beer. I didn't realize that Charlie was one or two drinks ahead of us until he joined us with our drinks and loudly declared—out of context and over our small talk—that he was 'confident' that the insurance company was about to 'capitulate' on an appropriate settlement to fund the clubhouse's restoration, that he always knew it would 'come out alright.' Flanaghan and I shared a silent acknowledgement that his pronouncement did not have to be affirmed by us. Dani steered the conversation away from the Club with weather talk as she passed hors d'oeuvres; I probably stuck my foot in it when I asked Flanaghan to tell Nadie about the Windmere Country Club. Flanaghan did so, patiently ignoring Charlie's frequent and boorish interruptions. When Flanaghan got to the manslaughter trial of the club's manager, Charlie stood abruptly and with a splash from his cocktail wetting his cuff, declared righteously, "He deserved it!" and walked to the drinks table to replenish his glass for the second time since our arrival.

Jean Flanaghan had listened patiently. As her husband finished, she said quietly, "Tom didn't tell you that my Uncle Joe was the busboy at the clubhouse." That brought forth 'oh's' and a silence; Charlie was open-mouthed. "He would have been twelve or thirteen. My grandfather never got over it, blamed himself, because ordinarily he would have been at the Club as its bartender but he had been loaned to an event in Watch Hill. The manager got through by clinging to a part of the collapsed clubhouse and riding the flood across the Pond into Randall's fields. They found him the next morning, clothes mostly ripped from his body, and drunk on a bottle of something that followed him ashore. That, of course, didn't help him locally. People wondered."

Nadie asked, "I don't understand why they didn't leave before it was too late...."

"The Depression, Nadie, the Depression!" Charlie interrupted.

"They were afraid to lose their jobs! He kept them there!"

Jean Flanaghan's voice gave away the discomfort of a guest disputing a host. "Looking back, a lot of mistakes were made that day, decisions that cost lives. Should he have been imprisoned, lose everything, because of his ignorance of a horrific, once in a hundred years, storm?"

∘ ○ ∘

Through a dinner of mesclun salad, grilled swordfish steak, early peas, Yukon Gold mashed potatoes, and ample pours of wines from Sakonnet Vineyards, Jean Flanaghan, gently encouraged by her husband, matched his storytelling skills with a repertoire of tales of huddled families miraculously saved from the ravages of the hurricane, ordinary people turning into heroic rescuers, the spiritual revivals of those who survived ordeals, and nature's eventual healing of the storm-ravaged coastline. It didn't take Nadie long to give away her profession by asking why her stories had happy endings, to which Jean responded there were too many tragedies like her Uncle Joe's for a dinner table, leaving Nadie momentarily abashed.

As dessert plates were being cleared, Westerly was invaded by lightning and marching booms of thunder as rain swept in from the Sound. Jean Flanaghan indicated her desire to leave but Charlie insisted that we accompany him to the 'observatory' and 'observe' the 'lightning show' over the Sound. The women declined and Dani ushered them into the living room for coffee; Charlie led a curious Flanaghan and me to the second floor gallery and up a circular metal staircase.

The 'observatory' was sparsely furnished, seemingly designed for the sole purpose of three hundred sixty degree views through wide casement windows. A ceiling fan went on with the overhead light which revealed a brass telescope on an eye-level stand aimed toward Block Island. Charlie explained his grandfather's fascination with the shipping on the Sound and its frequent storms, calling the octagon-shaped room a 'whimsy,' as jagged slashes of lightning streaked the sky and reflected in the white capped surface of the pond. Wind and rain, maybe hail, lashed the windows and pummeled the roof, thunder cracked every few seconds, creating a sense of danger you could see, feel, and hear. A lightning bolt lit up the sky to the north toward Route 1; Flanaghan said 'a thousand one' when the room trembled in the following thunder.

One of the women called from the base of the stairwell, demanding our return. I was ready to go downstairs and said so, when Charlie spotted the blaze. "Look over there!" he shouted, pointing north toward Route 1. "There's been a strike!" A faint, yellow glow appeared above the tree line. "Could be …," his voice lowered suddenly "… Randall's."

In his reflection in the window, his mouth was agape. I took his elbow but he resisted. "I'm fine, … fine," he stammered, his face strained and damp, and shook off my hand. "I better call Dunn's Corner," he said and followed Flanaghan down the stairs.

The blackness and sheets of rain were seared every few seconds by lightning followed by cracks of thunder. I wrongly assumed that the torrents of rain would quickly quench the fire; instead, flames licked upwards, dancing in the turbulent winds. Then, the lights went off, eliciting a collective gasp from the second floor, followed almost immediately by a buzz of relief as they flickered on. I heard Dani's thin, not very reassuring, voice say that generators had kicked on, that electricity loss happens once a summer, and we were not to be concerned. I went down the staircase where Charlie was on the telephone, giving directions to what I assumed was the Dunn's Corner Fire Department. He said 'yes' several times, then hung up, shaking his head excitedly. "They'll never get a pumper into Randall's from Route 1. The road over the wetlands collapsed since they sold the place. But will they listen to me? I told them the alternative is to come through here and up the back trail…."

Dani interrupted. "If it is Randall's house, at least nobody lives there … with Ollie gone. I can show them the trail if the truck comes in through here." Then, "But the gate, if it's locked…." She stared at Charlie.

"I still have a key," Charlie said, hesitantly, reluctantly, "unless they changed the lock." His face was pale, sweaty, uncertain. "I … should check."

The thought of Charlie out there alone was none too comforting. Flanaghan immediately volunteered to go with him. I joined in, thinking Charlie's in a daze and Flanaghan's out of shape. Charlie said, "There's storm gear in the boathouse. I'll get it," and he left us.

"Don't be a hero," Nadie said to me earnestly, taking hold of my arm.

Me?

◦ ○ ◦

In yellow slickers, with rain hats tied under our chins like three old salts, we left the house clutching large flashlights. My eyeglasses were useless in the rain and I slipped them into the slicker's jacket pocket. Our beams bobbed in the pelting rain ahead of our heavy-footed strides. Charlie led us past the barn and corral on the trail which had dissolved into a river of mud. Lightning seemed to be marching to the east as we wound around windswept brush and trees groaning in the gusts, our slickers squeaking as our arms and legs pumped forward, our shoes filling with water in the muddy ruts. At the golf course boundary, we took a sharp right and in a few strides faced closed wooden gates in a high picket fence. Charlie used a key to open a large Yale lock and left it hanging on its hasp. Flanaghan and I swung the creaking gates open and latched them by hooks to two sturdy wooden posts.

Without hesitation, I continued on and slogged up a treacherous, slimy incline toward the glow above the trees, thinking no fire apparatus is ever going to get up here, what was Charlie thinking? A lonely siren pierced the noises of swirling rain and wind, then a distant horn bleated rhythmically every few seconds, calling in volunteer firemen. Charlie followed me, demanding loudly that we return to the house; Flanaghan, not in any kind of shape for this kind of effort, was far behind, calling my name. At the cusp of the ridge, I stopped to regroup. Flames rose from behind a line of trees on the other side of the ridge and despite the rain, the wind blew sputters of burning wood and acrid smoke at us. Charlie had a few more steps to reach me, cupped his hands to his mouth, and yelled, "It's gone. We can't do anything. Let's go back!"

Cra-a-a-ck! Dazzling light. Molded together in one nuclear second! My head spun, my ears deafened, I was conscious of the air smelling of ozone and that I had been thrown into bushes. Slowly, I gained purchase, staggered upright, unseeing, and my mind grappling with the thought that lightning had struck over the crest of the ridge. My fingers went to my eyes and I realized they were open but all I saw was black, except for sparks that flew around in circles like a pinwheel. I blinked, blinked again, rubbed my eyes, and was slowly regaining my night vision, when a dot of light became Charlie's flashlight. Another stab of lightning, this one further away toward the north, brought a shattering crash, and Charlie was next to me, his arms over his head. "My God, my God," he was screaming.

Flanaghan caught up to us, his slicker cap off and his hair sopping wet and falling into his face. "Too goddamn close!" His eyes took in mine as Charlie fumbled at the clasp on his slicker jacket and he croaked out something nonsensical about '911' as his cell phone appeared in his shaking hand. He had to be in shock and I began shaking his shoulders when, from somewhere near the fire, a truck engine cranked, cranked again, and caught in a roar.

We left Charlie fumbling at his cell phone and struggled a few feet over the ridge to a bend where brush grew like hedges and a row of boulders narrowed the trail. Only a hundred feet away, a building was engulfed in flames, the swirling wind flinging golden scraps of fire from its burning roof on to a trailer brightly illuminated by the flames. Silhouetted against the blaze, a truck, with headlights off, leaped on to the trail. Mud, ruts, and fallen branches didn't slow its charge toward us. I took a step forward, waving my flashlight frantically, expecting the driver to see the beam, my yellow slicker, and brake. No such luck! Fishtailing in the mud as it gained momentum, it came right at me, its engine roaring, its huge off-road tires spinning and slipping in the mud, its transmission grinding. Flanaghan, yards behind me, screamed, "Holy shit" and must have gotten off the trail. I hesitated, still waving an arm while getting a beam of flashlight into the cab, convinced it would now slow. Fog lights over its cab flashed but instead of slowing, it lurched forward as I caught a glimpse of a white mask with red and black slashes at the mouth and eyes.

I was trapped! Boulders on one side, thick brush and vines like a wall on the other, the truck filling the width of the trail, already scraping rock and brush. I was conscious of my body wanting to turn although retreat was impossible; my feet stuck in the wrong direction. Again, I waved my arms madly, and with the truck close enough for me to see the ram emblem on its massive metal grill, I dropped to my knees and dove forward on to the grassy hump between tire tracks. My eyes closed as my chest hit the ground, my nostrils and mouth open to the wet grass, my arms stretched straight ahead, one hand grasping tufts of weeds, the other the flashlight. My body flattened as the engine's roar overcame any other sound. Please, God, nothing loose in the undercarriage. Please, God, don't let it slide.

The engine's roar deafened me, then came the raspy grind of the transmission, the creaks of its struts, a flush of warm air on my neck, the fumes of exhaust. And it was gone. I turned to my left side in time to see reflectors brighten in the light of the fire and disappear over the rise. I struggled up, lost my balance, and went down, my shoulder grazing something hard. Flanaghan, swearing and shouting my name, staggered toward me, and yelled, "Gesus…!" He grabbed my arm as I scraped mud off my face and spat out dirt.

"Freddy Jones," I managed to say as he helped me to my feet.

"Who?" Charlie approached, his arms flailing like a punch drunk fighter, clutching his cell phone with one hand, his flashlight in the other, but seemingly unscathed and unaware of my near death experience. "Did you see that? Goddamn fool almost hit me!"

There was no time to explain. Jones was escaping, I was sure, not as a fire victim but as a fugitive. I shook Charlie by his shoulders. "The truck is either going up to the path to the Club or into your property. Call Dani, tell her to lock the doors, get everyone upstairs, and don't let anybody in. Then call 911. Tell them a truck is leaving the scene of the fire at Randall's, nearly ran us over, is going toward your house or up to the Club. Tell them it's Freddie Jones. Important. Freddie Jones. Then, get up to the pump house in case the truck is there. If it is, call us, don't go in, and get back to the house."

In the glare of the flashlights, rain dripping from his yellow slicker hat mixing with sweat, his tiny pupils and sagging mouth made him seem incapable of comprehending my directions. "God, you're a mess," he complained to me loudly.

"Do it!" I screamed.

Charlie's eyes widened and his voice became robot-like. "I'll call Dani. I'll call 911. I'll check out the pump house." He seemed none too steady but since he wasn't a hero, I figured he wouldn't get too close to a problem, if there was one.

We left Charlie and fought our way up the ridge in a night filled with sirens and fire engine horns as the storm rumbled away and the rain began to abate. We hadn't gone fifty feet when we heard the smash of metal meeting something hard. I picked up my pace, leaving a panting Flanaghan slipping in the mud. After a turn of the trail, my beam shown on the reflectors of the truck, its right fender and rear wheel off the trail and smack up against a slab of ledge, the door on the driver's side open. The only sound was the ticking of the engine cooling. I approached cautiously, looked in, saw the windshield was a swirl of cracks; a black hat, with a feather sticking out of its band, was on the seat. Flanaghan, painfully out of breath, his chest pumping his slicker jacket up and down, reached me. I told him to follow me back to the house when he could. He acknowledged by weakly raising his flashlight.

With the meager light of a single beam, the trail was treacherous. More than once I tumbled into deep, rain filled ruts before I reached harder surfaces by the corral. Had Charlie ..., Dani ..., called the police? Would they be on their way? Where was Jones? What was he doing all painted up? Acting out Magua?

That thought gave me the second wind to sprint past the barn, around the driveway, into the front yard of the house. I banged on the door. "Dani, it's me, Algy. Let me in!" I yelled as a clatter erupted from within the boathouse across the lawn!

An obviously frightened Dani unlocked and opened the door, with Nadie and Jean behind her. "Go back inside," I said intently, pushing them back into the front hall with my hoarse whisper.

Dani's hands went to her mouth as she saw my mud streaked face. Jean Flanaghan touched her arm "Where's Tom?"

"Coming. Don't worry. Charlie went up to the pump house, checking it out."

Nadie said intently, "Charlie called us. He didn't make much sense. And we called the police, too."

Another crash came from the boathouse, maybe something being thrown in frustration, that the women didn't hear. "Lock the door and get up to the observatory," I ordered. "Now!"

Nadie grabbed my arm. She realized I was going back outside. "Don't go, Algy. Wait for the police," she pleaded but I had a head of steam and left them, waiting at the closed door until I heard the click of a lock. Next to the door was a set of light switches. I snapped them all up and the front yard, walkways, driveway, and boathouse were bathed in floodlights that reflected off a mist creeping up from the pond.

What the hell *was* I going to do! With the boat tied up at the dock, Jones must be searching for an ignition key or something to wire it. I didn't have a weapon and was matched against a walking mountain of grievances, an arsonist escaping a fire, wearing war paint. With half an idea, I ran to the Range Rover, fumbled for my keys in my trousers pocket, started up the engine, put it in gear, peeled across the lawn, and rammed its steel framed brush grill against the boathouse door, effectively barricading any exit. The modest shed shook visibly on its foundation causing whatever was loose inside to crash to the floor, producing an unintelligible shout.

Only then did I realize that I hadn't a clue as to whether the door to the boathouse opened out or in! In, and it was over; hammering blows to the door told me; thank God, it must open out!

I remained behind the wheel, not sure of my next move, as the bangs and thumps and screams of anger continued from inside. The boathouse glowed in the floodlights except where the Range Rover threw its shadow. Siren wails seemed closer and I thought

'Please be the cops!' when with a smash of glass and splitting wood from within the shadow, the shutters in the lone window of the boathouse flew open.

Bam! The right headlight exploded. I ducked down across the passenger seat.

Another *bam*, and a thud of pierced metal.

Bam, and *dnang* as a third shot ricocheted in a whine off the hood and the windshield above me splintered into frost around a hole the size of a dime.

A moment later, I heard more glass being pulverized and realized there must be another window facing the dock!

I hunched up to reach the door handle and it didn't budge; somehow I had triggered the all-door lock mechanism, great for safaris, not so great for instant evacuation. I fumbled at controls above the armrest, heard the snap of the door locks, and had my feet on the ground when *wham*, the windshield showered me with diamonds of safety glass. A horrendous, twisted face appeared in its jagged hole, jerked away with a scream, and *wham*, what was left of the windshield disintegrated.

To get to me, Jones would have to go around the rear of the SUV, giving me precious seconds of margin, and I began a sprint which lasted two strides; my right foot jammed into something hard and I fell forward; my arms stretched to break the sprawl as I hit the wet grass. I rolled over and braced myself with one hurting hand to get to my knees, looking up into floodlights that were suddenly blocked out. Jones was standing over me, the floodlights a penumbra on his bare shoulders, his hands grasping something raised high above his head….

Bam!

I waited for the pain of the bullet.

"Put it down!" Flanaghan roared. "Freddie, put it down!" Jones turned his face into the light, red and black stripes arching over his bulging eyes, white mouth drawn back in anger and surprise, and I knew he was deciding whether to swing downward or challenge the voice with the gun. My arms went up to protect my head as my body curled away in the longest seconds of my life. From five feet away, I staggered up, holding my gut, and saw Jones, in all his painted ugliness, a boat oar poised high above his head.

I stumbled to Flanaghan's side. "Freddie," he shouted past me, "put the fuckin' oar down!"

Jones complied, slowly, lowering it until the paddle end touched the grass.

"Drop it."

As he did, his eyes widened in recognition. "The fuckin' pool player!" he screamed.

CHAPTER TWENTY-SEVEN

Not two minutes later, a pair of Westerly patrol cruisers, spouting the amplified angry, raucous shrieks that get attention, careened into the yard, throwing up driveway stones and grass as they converged on the boathouse, their red, white and blue lights transforming us into Cirque du Soleil players, their headlights blinding us. From behind open doors, garbled commands were shouted to "Freeze" and "Drop your weapon." Flanaghan let his gun slip to the grass and was hustled away toward the cruisers as a uniformed cop took over Flanaghan's bead on Jones whose arms were folded tightly over his glistening, hairless chest. Some rough handling by two cops ignited a screaming chant as Jones was searched, forced into handcuffs, and pushed into the rear seat of a cruiser. Seemingly ignored, I picked up the oar only to have an aggressive voice from behind the light yell, "Drop it." As a hand holding a shiny blue steel gun appeared, I obeyed.

The Range Rover remained in the floodlights, a film of wet on its exterior. The driver's door was open and the interior light showed its bashed-in windshield. Closer inspection revealed a bullet hole in the hood and I didn't have the heart to inspect the damage underneath.

While we had been playing heroes, the three women had wisely remained inside the house. They now rushed to our rescue, their excited voices explaining the circumstances over the sounds of crackling hand sets. Confusion reigned until a sergeant arrived and told us all to shut up because he wanted to hear from Flanaghan who made our story sensible—the fire in the woods, our rush to the blaze, Jones escaping the scene, the crashed truck, my half-ass attempt to keep Jones trapped inside the boathouse, and Jones' attack. As I listened, the reality of what happened got through to me. Did I do that? My stomach, still hurting from whatever I landed on—it turned out to be one of several pieces of jutting ledge in the lawn—made my breath shallow as the bludgeoning-with-oar scene in *The Talented Mr. Ripley* came to mind. A cop interrupted Flanaghan to report that Jones had a handgun stuck in his belt, empty of cartridges but with three spent shells in its chambers, and a six inch blade in a boot. The sergeant snapped an order for Jones' arrest and two cops piled into the cruiser that held him and drove away as another cruiser noisily arrived.

Flanaghan stayed with the sergeant who released us to the house. The mist had now gathered in droplets of drizzle as we went inside. The thought that if Jones had another bullet, I might be lying out there in the car or on the wet grass was clearly getting through to me. A hall mirror reflected my mud-crusted face flecked with bloodied scratches, and Nadie handed me a damp hand towel from a lavette; I wiped away grime and felt the stings of cuts and bruises. She began to berate me for my foolish bravado, but her words belayed her evident concern. I dropped my slicker on the lavette's tile floor and removed my soggy shoes. I offered no defense, in fact I would have agreed if asked, when Charlie, drying his hair with a towel, appeared from the kitchen. I had completely forgotten about him! Dani embraced him; her breathless update on our fracas with Jones seemed to perplex him.

"Well, good. Good," he said, patronizing our experiences. "My 911 calls got action. And, by the way, someone *was* at the pump house. That's what took me so long. Guess who?" Pause. "Joe Pontarelli!"

"What?" I managed to cough out as Charlie headed into the living room and the drinks table. We followed him.

"I can't tell you how relieved I was because it could have been another crazy Quonnie." He filled a tumbler with Dewars. "He was at the generators, in the headlights of a maintenance cart. Had the casing off one but they seemed to be working fine and I could hear the pumps. When I shouted to him, I thought he was going to soil his drawers! When he recovered, he said after the electricity went off, he drove to the pump house because they've been having problems with the generators not switching on automatically." He took a large snort of his drink and wiped his face with his towel. "I told him about the fire at Randall's and that goddamn Quonnie in the truck, and that seemed to shake him up even more. Then, get this, he screamed at me that I shouldn't be up there! To get the hell out! Swearing, and shouting at me, he put the cover back on the generator case, got in the cart, and took off! Didn't even offer me a ride home. I had to trek back through all that mud!"

Indignation reddened Charlie's face as Flanaghan, shaking off water like a sheep dog, burst into the living room, complaining that the 'new' cops hadn't a clue and fortunately, his old friend Sergeant McNulty had arrived. The police, he said, were setting up security near the boathouse. Charlie, gawking at him, made the mistake of extending his Scotch which was taken from Charlie's hands and emptied in a swallow. "McNulty says the pumpers did get through from Route 1, despite a couple of shaky culverts. The house is gone, the barn mostly, and the trailer is scorched. And I'll tell you what I think, if we hadn't been up in the observatory, the whole shebang would have been ashes before anybody reported it."

I was barely listening to Flanaghan, so focused was I on Joe Pontarelli's presence at the pump house. Nadie grasped my arm, saying to all that we were leaving, and pulled me toward the hall. "What possessed you to go out there?" she whispered. "He had a gun! Algy, a gun! You could have been killed!"

I excused myself for the lavette when Dani gave me a pair of dry socks. I heard Jean Flanaghan, whom I would have thought never raised her voice, doing so at her husband, both for his heroics and for owning a handgun she knew nothing about. Meekly, Flanaghan confessed he had it in the glove compartment of his car because of Jones' behavior at the 'incident' at Oaky's Tavern. What 'incident'? And it turned out that Flanaghan, like me, hadn't been very candid about our adventure last Sunday. Flanaghan, fortunately, gave a sketchy description, emphasizing the damage to his car and what he said was Jones' crazy behavior, as I joined them with my face washed, hair wiped, and shoes cleaned and back on.

"You were there, too," Nadie said, quite likely thinking of my bruised hand and sore back of the past few days. "Can we go now? Unless you have to go down to the police station."

I looked at Flanaghan for an answer. His brows arched and his eyes seemed to brighten. "Nah, nice thing about practicing law in the same town all your life, you get to know what the cops want. I'll file the complaint against Jones. Charlie'll come down with me." Flanaghan got up and withdrew a set of keys from a trousers pocket. "Here, take my car. We'll get AAA here in the morning, get yours towed to your dealer. I'll get somebody to go up to Providence and pick up mine. We'll drop Jean off at home, and go on to the station...."

"Yes," Charlie added, assuming an air of responsibility. "Of course, we'll take care of it." He put out his hand to me. "I owe you again, Algy. If he had gotten the boat ..., it was gassed up ..., can you imagine? He would have raced down the Pond to some inlet or landing, maybe smashing it up on the rocks, or getting out through the breachway into the Sound. I could have ended up with no boat!"

Thanks, Charlie, for thinking about me.

∘ ○ ∘

On the way home in the big black sedan with the smashed rear deck, exhausted and yet adrenaline-wired, I explained what I knew about Freddie 'Magua' Jones and my suspicion that he might be an accomplice of Ollie Randall in the clubhouse fire. Nadie listened in a grumpy silence. She remained angry that I had not been candid about my first encounter with Jones. Later, as we neared Providence, she said off handedly, "The sachem, what's his name, he'll be happy. With Jones in jail, that will be one less tribal council vote against his casino."

I agreed. "Oaky Gardiner may be the only winner tonight."

∘ ○ ∘

Oakland 'Oaky' Gardiner was not a winner. His son Peter Gardiner was dead, discovered in Ollie Randall's trailer by Westerly firefighters. Flanaghan telephoned us with the news from the Westerly Police Station within five minutes of my turning the key in the front door lock. "It's Peter all right. All the cops know Peter. Won't tell me how he died but there was gun play. Jones hasn't been charged yet but...." His pause was full of meaning.

"After we left Oaky's on Sunday, Peter followed me out of the swamp and stopped me. Steaming mad! The fight embarrassed him. He wanted to make sure I was pressing charges. He told me Freddie was holed up in the swamp, that sooner or later, Jones would come for whatever he and Randall had boosted from out of Randall's, and ..., are you ready for this..., he was going to 'fix' Freddie good."

Nadie, listening by my side, picked up most of his conversation. "I thought Westerly was a nice, peaceful town. Now Providence, I understand. Drive-by murders among gangs, a Mafia on-purpose, or an abusing husband, that's par for the course...."

She stopped. "Sorry. No pun intended."

I ignored her.

○ ◯ ○

The next morning, I learned that Tom Flanaghan was born with blarney and guile. On its web site, the Westerly *Star* reported that through Charlie Fessenden's efforts, the Westerly police had captured Freddie "Magua" Jones fleeing from the scene of suspected arson and homicide. Charlie led 'friends' on a trek through a fierce thunder storm to assist firefighters gain entry to Randall's burning house and trailer, only to face Jones escaping Randall's trailer. The police captured Jones at the boathouse because of Charlie's timely 911 calls—and there was nothing about my 'daring do' or Flanaghan's timely arrival or gun shots. I realized Flanaghan had laid it on with a putty knife. If the Tramontis were paying him to save some scrap of Charlie's reputation in Westerly, Tom Flanaghan deserved a bonus on his retainer.

Nadie, of course, wasn't satisfied with my candor and slowly dragged the truth out of me as to the incident at the tavern and our trek to Randall's trailer. Despite her upbraiding over our espressos, I detected pride in her voice, mixed with a concern that was heartfelt, reminding me of when she, and I, had subdued the 'Carter Stalker' only a year earlier, when we felt like John Steed and Emma Peel of *The Avengers* for a few days, even though she fit the part more than me.

She left Congdon Street after breakfast to finish packing. I exercised, got cleaned up and walked to the office. I marked up the proffered contract with the City for the buildings on South Water Street and asked Marcie to clean it up and send it to Puppy Dog just before I returned to the office. She knew whom to call during the next two weeks and that the international cell phone I planned to pack would be for emergencies only. Before I left

College Hall to begin my own packing, a Westerly *Star* reporter contacted me on Jones' capture. I followed Flanaghan's lead, giving Charlie accolades for his steady nerves, concern for those in harm's way because of the fire, and the capture of the fleeing Jones. I was barely a witness to it all. That almost made me swallow my tongue but I got through it.

∘ ○ ∘

Nadie and I left Providence at four, baggage stacked into a Lincoln Continental limo, on our way to the seven-forty, nonstop Delta flight from Logan Airport to Milan. While Nadie fussed about passports, and a forgotten book, whether and when she should take one or two Ambien sleeping tablets for the flight, and then became engrossed in her guidebook, I got to the sports section of the *Journal*. 'Play,' according to the golf writer, would be initiated tomorrow at the 'snake-bitten but exclusive new Haversham Golf Club,' with the Governor taking the inaugural tee shot. I folded the newspaper and leaned back in the comfortable leather seat, watching the traffic into Boston slide by. I hoped it would be a cloudless, South County beautiful, day when the members played their new course. Maybe, some of the good feeling would slop over on to the 'brave,' 'concerned,' and 'unselfish' Charlie Fessenden, alleviating some of the obliquity of 'Charle's deal' and other failings in remission.

Unless Ugo Calibrese had other ideas.

CHAPTER TWENTY-EIGHT

As you climb out of the sun-drenched Lombardy plain toward Lake Como, the heat dissipates with every meter in gained altitude. To the north, golden lights play off snow-tipped mountains, and you smell—you think—the camellias, azaleas, and verbena that rush by as you use the silky six speed gearshift of the Maserati Granturismo more frequently.

The lake sits like an upside down wishbone in the foothills of the Alpi Orolie, a water filled gorge created by an ancient glacier. At the cusp of the lake's two arms, elegant Bellagio, the summer retreat of Italian nobility since the sixteenth century, faces the northern stretch of the lake. There, the water becomes turbulent as it decides whether to flow southwest to Como or southeast through the narrows to Lecco.

While the scenery was guidebook beautiful, I was engrossed in driving. The V-8 Ferrari engine purred in muscular echoes and the refined suspension and superior braking flattened the curves of the S-231. No GPS system or electronic foolishness on the dashboard of this piece of metal sculpture from Pininfarina. Even Nadie, usually oblivious to automobile artistry, raved about the car's sinuous lines, its luscious leather seating, the rosewood panels on the dashboard and doors, the Bose sound system, and the unexpected massaging seats. During the next ten days, I would drive this gorgeous car, experience its power and learn its secrets, a perfect holiday extra for an automobile buff.

Close to three in the afternoon, I pointed the car into the sweeping curves of the palm lined boulevard from Piazza Mazzini into the stone courtyard below the warm yellow facade of the Hotel Florence. Two uniformed staff quickly took our luggage as hand in hand, we climbed the marble stairs of the eighteenth century palazzo of the Borremeo family. The reception requirements were little more than signatures and a flick of passports and we were whisked to the top floor in the filigreed cage of a silent elevator.

Our suite was baroque opulence. Nadie opened double glass doors that faced the shimmering lake; curtains billowed in a breeze that was clean and sweet and smelled of water. The canopy bed, frescoed ceilings, and antique furniture, the marble bath with all of the amenities, the vista of the sky-tinted lake and snow-capped mountains from the balcony, and the prospect of passionate lovemaking, were transforming. Nadie's radiant smile was full of expectation.

∘ ○ ∘

It was our third day in Bellagio, a day off from touring the lake's many attractions and exploring Bellagio's graceful arcades for *caffe latte* and *connetti con marmellata* breakfasts and long lunches. We lay on cushioned lounge chairs on the hotel's stone terrace, dressed in shorts, with me in a polo shirt and Nadie in a light sweater. The temperature was cool for eleven o'clock late in June, the sky milky, and the morning mist hadn't cleared the lake's surface, giving it a mysterious quality, especially as ferries suddenly appeared and disappeared. The hotel's courteous staff had been by several times, seemingly fixated on whether or not to open the sun umbrellas, inquiring 'was the *senora* comfortable,' and 'would the *senor* like to reserve for luncheon or dine *al fresco*?' I was in my reader comfort zone with the latest Janet Evanovich in my lap, a pot of espresso and a plate of almond cookies on the table beside me. Nadie was reading a fearsomely thick tome. I was considering ordering lunch delivered to the terrace—an antipasto, vegetable *ravoli al dente* and perhaps peach melba—when I heard a deep exhalation. Nadie's book closed, her sunglasses went to her lap, and she said, "The night of the fire, when you and Tom and Charlie went off to war, Jean Flanaghan told us something that just popped into my mind."

These out-of-no-where, change-the-mood events, are a Nadie 'thing.' I bent a page corner and closed the book. On the flight to Milan, we mutually promised there wouldn't be any talk about her new course or Charlie Fessenden or the Quonnies. "*Mia cara*, do I want to know?" I was in my Italian lover mode.

"Yes, I think you do," she replied. "The people who died when the tidal wave hit the clubhouse? In the hurricane? Jean's uncle, remember?"

"Sure," I grumbled, feeling the mood dissipate.

"When people realized that two waitresses and the boy, all local people, had been killed, and the manager, who kept them there, was still alive, it didn't take long for the Washington County prosecutor to get calls. The victims' families couldn't sue the promoter or the club because of the bankruptcy and they only got a few dollars out of their workers' compensation checks. Jean's grandfather and grandmother got nothing because her uncle was a minor. And of course, they were devastated by the loss of a son...."

She stopped for a moment to see if I was paying attention. By now, I was.

"The manslaughter charge against the manager was that he put their lives in mortal danger by maintaining 'unsafe premises.' The cook who survived was the only witness against him. Said she tried to convince the manager to close before the tidal wave hit but he was insistent they stay."

The lawyer in me reacted. "Seems a stretch. Like Charlie said, unless he was Simon Legree snapping the whip, and they were in fear of their lives if they disobeyed, I don't know that was enough to try him for manslaughter...."

"Well, they did. Jean said it was the only hurricane related criminal case brought in all of Rhode Island! And he was convicted. And here's the point. Charlie Fessenden's grandfather was the foreman of the jury! And, two years later, he bought the golf course land, including where Charlie's house is located, at foreclosure. Charlie Fessenden's grandfather!"

I hoisted myself up in the lounge chair as Nadie continued. "It was obvious that Dani didn't know. When Jean realized that, she was apologetic about bringing it up."

Wheels within Rhode Island wheels. "What was the manager's name?"

Nadie paused. "I think it was Higgins ... or maybe Huggins. I'm not sure."

"Still," I said, "the conviction of Higgins, or Huggins, and the purchase of the real estate had to be...."

"You're going to say coincidental, right?"

"Yes."

"And that's not all of it. Dani went out of the room for the coffee and Jean said the grandfather was one of the town's big shots, whom Jean said her family called a 'swell.' When was the last time you heard that word? Big car, servants, a mansion overlooking the river, owned a lot of real estate, and the last operating quarry in Westerly. A year or two before the hurricane, middle of the Depression, he closed it. Without any notice. Shut down, throwing fifty people out of work without any kind of severance. The workers' rioted when they couldn't get their tools or their back wages, and he had them blacklisted from any employment in Westerly. But the 'swell' was still doing fine, driving a big Packard, trips to Florida...."

"Nadie, callous, yes, …."

"Just think of it. This … 'swell' … closes down the town's last quarry, a lot of people lose their livelihoods, then he puts the manager away, and buys the club's land at a knockdown price so he can build his house where three people died in his front yard!"

Class was rearing its ugly, complicated head! "I don't know and I don't care."

"Higgins or Huggins … whatever his name was … was a victim of prejudice and Fessenden's cupidity…."

"Ugh!" Taking up the cause of the manager, an outsider, an underdog, put upon by a 'swell' taking advantage of status and money and ignoring a tragedy, was essential Nadie.

"Jean said Westerly talked about it for years. People wondered if the manager got a fair trial. The Fessendens were disliked by ordinary people because they were snobs, for the way they closed down the quarry, treated their employees. Was the grandfather trying to make himself popular by putting the manager away?"

Better stop it now. "Look, you didn't hear the witnesses, you weren't in the jury room, you don't know anything about it. And we're on vacation and it isn't Charlie's fault—or my fault—if his grandfather was a rapacious, insensitive jerk!"

"Do these people have blood in their veins? Put somebody away for years! Build your house where three people needlessly died? Take land from people … the Randalls … that owned it for hundreds of years because they're down on their luck? People like Charlie, they go through life never having to pay for how they got there, their history…."

"That's just it, Nadie, it's all history. You're making Charlie out to be one of your 'types.' "

O-o-h, I shouldn't have said that but it sailed right by. She put her sunglasses on with a snap that signaled irritation. "You're ready to excuse perfectly outrageous behavior because either it was too typical of the time or it touches too close to home."

"That wasn't very nice." Why was she pushing this?

There was a long silence and then she said, "It's just … oh, I don't know. It's just there." She picked up her book and muttered, "I'm sorry. Forget it."

I went back to Janet Evanovich and her beat-up city, lowlife bail bondsman, crazy relatives, and spirited heroine, but Nadie had struck a chord. Despite sharing my mother's and Sylvia's take on 'getting on with it,' maybe I did excuse too easily. After all, Charlie is a dunderhead beside being a liar, and likely as avaricious and insensitive as his grandfather. But would the grandfather, the 'swell,' have manipulated the system by playing to local prejudice in the jury room? Did that explain why Westerly would easily believe rumors about a Fessenden?

And, what happened to Higgins-Huggins? I'm not sure why but after lunch I called Benno.

∘ ○ ∘

A few days later, I made my self-imposed single call to the office. After routine questions, Marcie said that the lead story in the *Sunday Journal* was Ms. Reins' report on Sonny Russo's extraordinary expenditures for food, drink, and travel. Every one of Providence's great restaurants made the list, from Al Forno to Z Bar, along with some of Boston's finest eateries—we're not talking just North End eateries but Lockovers, No. 9 Park, Capital Grille and L'Espalier for example—with limo rides back and forth. Sonny even took some of his cronies and contributors to Las Vegas for a convention or two. Of course, the well-publicized trip to Verona was there, with Providence real estate entrepreneurs Ugo Calibrese, Vincent 'Vinny' Malofante, and Salvatore 'Sally' Veramma; 'governmental representatives' Senator Silvano 'Silk' Zenga, Representative Tommy Regan, and Councilman

Christopher Ferrucci; and the *capo regimes* of Sonny's organization, notably Nick 'the Angel' Buonnatti, all paid for by 'Friends of Russo.' But nothing on the Faculty Club!

That came on Monday, a factual listing of the bills, the amounts overdue, the policy of the Faculty Club when member payments were not current, and a litany of the many fights between the University and Sonny. A sidebar referred to me and my role in the dunning letters, which were printed in full, with a paragraph about my friendship with the Mayor's political rival, Police Commissioner Anthony Tramonti.

As Nadie predicted, Tuesday's paper brought the faculty's reaction. Ms. Reins had scrounged up representative comments on what was referred to as 'Sonny's special dispensation,' all scathingly critical of the Faculty Club, College Hall, and the Mayor. An investigation by an independent forensic accountant was the demand of Professors Ambrose Kyle and Merten Aggassey, two pain-in-the-ass fussbudgets, 'sparrow farts,' Derek Kirk calls them. The Mayor's response was that it was all a mix-up by his campaign staff and since the account was now current—it was paid the Monday after Commencement—so what's the big deal? Was this a University plot to embarrass him while he fought for tax fairness and upheld drug laws?

Marcie said the Provost's reaction was that it wasn't 'too bad,' which I took means no heads were rolling at the Faculty Club and my association with Tramonti, well-known in College Hall, wasn't deemed poisonous. But what was troubling was a press release from the Mayor's office in the middle of the flap that the University would be donating the use of the three riverfront buildings for the 'Sister City Festival' as Verona's visit was now billed. Since nothing had been signed with Sonny, the press release 'one-upped' the University: if we denied the press release, it would look petty; if we accepted it, we were giving into Sonny's pressure. The

Provost decided the University would put out a statement of support for the event, including the use of the buildings, without mentioning the Mayor.

Nobody asked me but I knew we had lost leverage. My Protocol revision was history. Carter University would supply the buildings, was publicly supporting the Mayor's project, and gotten little in return.

Puppy Dog's grin must be from ear to ear!

○ ◯ ○

Days went by as it only can when every day is exhilarating. The weather remained superb, Nadie was relaxed and loving. The ambiance of Bellagio was followed by a long, snaky, drive through Lecco and Bergamo to our next hotel, the Locanda San Vigilio on the beach at Lake Garda. For the next few days, we took day trips, the first being across four miles of water by hydro boat to the walled town of Asolo for lunch at the sixteenth century Villa Cipriani, followed by an afternoon piano concert on the lawn of the historic Villa Barbero designed by Palladio. The following days, the Maserati smoothly got us to the increasingly dramatic north where rocky cliffs and pine-filled slopes hugged the shoreline. We enjoyed wine lubricated lunches in Bardolino, explored castles, took the cable car to the summit of Monte Baldo for its views of the Austrian Alps at sunset. Then, after a day of spa treatments and a late dinner prepared over an open fire at the rustic Antica Locanda Mincio, we left in a morning mist and drove through ghostly shrouds into the Veneto plain, to Verona.

Providence's sister city!

Our hotel, the imposing Baglione, was on a quiet street behind the fourth century Arena. We registered and went out to the Piazza Erbe where stalls, shaded by colorful umbrellas and canvas awnings, sold everything from suckling pig in bread rolls to fresh picked fruit. We took our luncheon purchases to a wine shop, bought a bottle of chilled prosecco, and picnicked near a charming fountain in the middle of the Piazza as Nadie outlined our walking tour. With a breeze shaking the dust of the old city, we braved the heat through colonnaded streets to the Adige River by the Porte Scaligero, the gardens of the Castelvecchio, then to the Piazza Brà and its enormous Arena where banners for a performance of *Aida* flapped in the wind. After a stop for gelato, I stood beneath the balcony of the Casa di Giulietta, where Nadie waved from the simple, marble fronted balcony and like thousands of swains, I heard 'Romeo, Romeo. Where for art thou?'

Nadie had one more stop, the immense, thousand year old Romanesque church of San Zeno Maggiore. I remained in a rear pew as she joined a tour of the church. I was perplexed. How was Providence going to compare with this sophisticated city of classical images and architectural splendor, where culture exudes from every arcade and square, with delicious surprises around every corner like a box of chocolates. I love my hometown and there is plenty to see and appreciate but it would take more than a few cleaned up buildings, a WaterFire, and our wonderful restaurants to compete. Verona is a city of evident pride.

And that's when I got the idea!

For our second day, we had planned a side trip to Padua. I claimed fatigue over breakfast in our room and even a raspy throat, and encouraged Nadie not to miss Padua's many attractions. After some complaining, she changed to button cuff gray capris and a white shell shirt, borrowed a couple of hundred euros for treats and the lunch and rendezvous, she said, she planned with her Italian lover, and caught a tour bus from the hotel, leaving me while I attended to business. She was back at five, enraptured by the stunning cathedral, Giotto's frescoes, and the pleasures of the Antico Brolo where she lunched on its signature ravioli stuffed with zucchini flowers. I disclosed my digestion was fully repaired and we dined at the justly famed Il Desco, a sixteenth century palazzo, where the menu varies from smoked oysters and game to its wonderfully flavored Amarone wine risotto.

The next morning we took the A-4 *autostrata* from Verona around Vincenza, Padua, and Venice, experiencing the pastel colors of the flat Veneto plain against the dramatic, distinctive limestone peaks of the Dolomites. With my RayBans on, wearing Nadie's present of a cashmere sweater, and sitting beside a beautiful woman in one of the world's most handsome cars, I felt like Marcello Mastroianni in *La Dolce Vita*. More than once, as we drove north on secondary roads, Nadie expressed frustration with Italian road maps whenever I asked for directions or a location, and then complained of my macho tendencies when I pulled over to read it myself. Immediately, we were joined by uniformed and very formal *carabinieri* in a black Lancia who seemed more interested in the car, and then the *bella senora*, than in any infraction of Italy's traffic laws. Eventually, we were waved away with a warning for something, and after more miles of hardwood trees and two lanes barely wide enough for truck traffic, we reached Udine, all pink limestone, fountains, and dramatic wooded hills.

We spent a pleasantly cool evening there and traveled on to the hill town of Cividale del Friuli where our hotel looked down into a dramatic ravine crossed by the Ponte del Diablo, the Devil's Bridge. There, after a dinner of capron soup, local turkey stuffed with chestnuts and carrots for me, and a fresh lake fish for Nadie, the following morning, we met our guide, arranged for by Nadie, who led us on a day long walking trip toward Gorizia through foothills, vineyards, and limestone plateaus to a grove of pines where his beautiful associate had laid out a picnic lunch of *prosecco di valdobbiadene*, cold pasta, and luscious peaches. We ate and napped and I expected to be driven back to Cividale del Friuli by our guide, only to be delighted by Nadie's surprise of a night at a country inn!

She said she knew she would be surfeited by hotel and restaurant food by then and had been tipped off by a colleague as to La Casa Pescheria. At a bench table in the atmosphere of a workingman's tavina, our meal consisted of small sardines with glistening oil and vinegar, hard crusted bread with a white local wine, *spaghetti alli vongole* with a mound of tiny clams, oil and garlic, and then a *coda di rispo*, baked in white wine, zucchini and rosemary. It was memorable; any Italian cook would bless such food by the knuckle of the first finger of the right hand pressed into a cheek, a quick turn of the hand, and a smacking of lips.

Trieste was our last stop, with a suite at a five-star hotel, a former Jesuit retreat house, with splendid rooms and sweeping views of the Bay of Trieste. We tramped around the city and the Venetian castles that dotted hillsides and villages nestled into the coastline as far as the Croatian border. We read, we slept, we were tourists, we enjoyed each other's company, we loved. Nadie was relaxed, with the renewed spontaneity of someone ready to move on.

It was time for my question.

One night after dinner on a terrace at the hotel, high above the moon-drenched sea, as romantic a scene as I could conjure, we shared Negronis, the perfect drink for a star kissed night, then dined by candlelight. *La luna, mi amore.* Her eyes were wide and moist, and seemingly, only for me. We were in a lover's harmony. I ran my fingers lightly over hers and she said 'I love you' with her eyes. "*Carissimo.* I love you madly," I said softly. "Let's just do it."

Nadie laughed that I hadn't formally proposed in over a year, which was formalistically true. Still, her voice was breathy; I thought her breasts rose under her blouse ..., my imagination? She repeated that she loved me, but wondered ... again ... if marriage was a practical necessity anymore for people like us. Why can't we just go on as we have, enjoying one another when together, missing one another when apart?

My response was that you either want to marry, to pledge lifelong love, affection, care and support, or you don't. This isn't about logic, it's about commitment. And, I knew we had to commit, or terrible as it might be, one day we would move on.

She leaned over and kissed me on the cheek. I made up my mind that was not enough.

CHAPTER TWENTY-NINE

After the glories of sun-drenched Italy, a drizzly midnight arrival in Providence caused by a three hour delay at the Venice airport wasn't particularly welcoming. While Nadie dumped laundry into the up and down washer-dryer next to the bathroom on the second floor, I deleted a cascade of e-mails and mowed through telephone messages for mortgage refinancing, telephone services, cable offerings, and a myriad of charitable opportunities, down to a call from Tom Flanaghan from only two days before. Then, I logged on to *Projo.com* and found Ms. Reins' articles, including two columns of Sonny Russo's expenditures at various restaurants for his 'political' meetings. While the Faculty Club made the list, he obviously favored Federal Hill, including familiar names like Napolitano's, Aromas, Fiori's, Mezza Luna, Frankie's, and Nana's. Asked why he went to the Faculty Club, Sonny said he liked the 'atmosphere' and while the food was 'okay,' he wanted the University to know he was 'watching.' Incredible!

Nadie wasn't much interested in the stories and we went to bed by one-thirty. She was grumpy and not looking forward to a long promised Fourth of July family weekend on Fisher's Island. In the morning, I got in some pool drills while Nadie went off to the gym and then to her apartment to check mail and messages and restock clothes. At two forty-five, I picked her up for the drive to the ferry in New London. As the *Sound Queen's* horn blasted the harbor and the squat vessel left the dock with a shudder, Nadie stood at the ferry's prow, determined to enjoy fifteen minutes of sparkling, green-blue water, her sleep-reddened eyes protected by large, dark glasses purchased at the Armani shop in Bellagio. I left topside for the coffee bar below deck, and privacy. Flanaghan was at his home when I called.

"Been a lot of interest in the Quonnies and Jones since you left. A reporter from the *Star* had a feature story in the can on their 'signal hill' and federal recognition and that ran the Sunday after the Gardiner murder. Got picked up on the wire services which led to a story in *USA Today*, and we got a history of the Quonnies including an ambush led by a Magua in the *Journal*, and the division in the tribe between the swamp Quonnies as the 'true' Quonnies and Gardiners' group in for the casino money. Haversham Golf Club took some hits for where it built the clubhouse but no mention of Charlie as yet." He took a breath and exhaled slowly. "But get this, Jones wants to talk to you."

I was incredulous.

"He specifically asked to talk to you." Flanaghan's voice crackled with suspicion. "Had the public defender call me."

"Why me?"

"Haven't a clue. Besides the murder charges, Jones also has the assaults on Charlie and me from the night of the storm. Multiples on that. I kept you out of it as best I could. All told, including the assaults, gun charges, resisting arrest, my car, …, you know, he managed to club a cop in the station, too …, he's got …," he apparently looked at something, "… sixteen charges, fourteen of which are felonies. By the way, the autopsy shows Gardiner wasn't killed by the gun shot, just wounded, not even life-threatening, and he had lacerations and bruises, an eye swollen shut, but cause of death is smoke asphyxiation. The bullet which went through his thigh was found in the trailer. From Gardiner's own gun. The one Jones used at the boathouse."

"Where is Jones?"

"ACI. And get this! Calibrese hasn't gone away. He's filed a declaratory judgment suit yesterday in Washington County Superior Court against the Club for possession of the leased land. Says the Club is in default under the lease because it only got 'temporary' permits, not 'permanent' permits, by July third. They pay him increased rent or he throws them off. Gordon Ackley must be pissing down his leg because he assured the Board that the threat was over when they started playing golf in June."

"Has Calibrese got a case?"

"Don't know. Nobody's saying much. I read the complaint which contains the wording in the lease. After mandating actual 'golf play,' it says 'available for golf play on a permanent basis ....' If the permits are temporary, is it 'available' on a permanent basis? Anyway, the suit will jerk them around for awhile. Wouldn't be surprised if that's why Ugo's doing it. Then, look for an arrangement. Press hasn't got it yet but the *Star* will sooner or later. When the Club members hear about it, Katie bar the door!"

∘ ○ ∘

At ten on the following Tuesday, after a three day weekend of bike rides, board games with my brother's children on the floor of the billiard room, family meals and cookouts, and the Fisher's Island Golf Club's annual 'Begin The Summer' fireworks display over Long Island Sound, I drove into the parking lot of the Adult Correctional Institution, the ACI, located off Pontiac Avenue in Cranston. The seven acre compound contains four penal facilities reflecting varying levels of supervision and crime, ringed by a sixteen foot fence topped with coiled razor wire. Those awaiting trial, if not charged with a major felony, would be housed in the unadorned, dormitory-like, Intake Center and, if they didn't make bail, in Minimum Security, an antiquated building of brick and barred windows, with its own fencing. Jones, charged with murder, didn't get bail and was held in Maximum Security—'Super Max'—a granite faced fortress in the center of the complex, looking like a bad dream out of *The Shawshank Redemption*, reeking of meanness, violence, and cupidity.

As a court-appointed defense lawyer during my early years of practice, the ACI was, and is, a doleful place, populated by psychotics, druggies, and chronic offenders, maybe half of whom—those with some mental capacity—claimed innocence, or that they had been pushed into pleading to lesser charges by incompetent counsel, or were victims of one sort or the other. My clients liked having a former Manhattan D.A. as their defense attorney and I did what I could for them, even as I grew to hate the assignments. Were any innocent? Probably none that I represented, and if there were one or two, they were likely guilty of something equally as heinous.

Visitors to the ACI enter the Intake Center where they are identified, searched for contraband, and their names are run through the Bureau of Criminal Investigation. After that, they are funneled into a waiting area reminding me of a shabby bus station in its rows of stained wooden benches, grimy walls, and meager lighting. Some artsy soul long ago hung now faded inspirational posters shouting 'Courage,' 'Duty,' 'Pride,' and 'Love,' below idyllic photographs of beach and mountain scenes. This morning, probably on most mornings, poorly dressed, gloomy looking women of various ages crowded the benches while toddlers clung to them or played on the scuffed tile floor with toys and dolls. I stood out like a sore thumb in my suit and tie and should have known that I would.

I used the time to call Derek Kirk. "Aye, yew've been away, laddie. As have I. The internet is crackling about Freddie Jones, a/k/a Magua. Peter Gardiner has become a renegade deserving of elimination, complicent in schemes of his father with the white man, while Jones has morphed into a revolutionary."

"A what?"

"I'm an anthropologist. I study man in varied situations. But I could study some swamp Quonnies forever and might not understand them. For hundreds of years, the whites, when not trying to kill 'em or take their land, have been trying to get them to look and talk and act and think and pray like whites. For the swamp Quonnies, the Jones family in particular, it ne'er took. Here's a chance to tell their story and there's a resonance among some radical eastern Indians, especially the young who feel the power to say 'no,' to take back what was taken. And with the internet and blogs ..., yew should read the 'Magua' blog...!"

"But he's a criminal...."

"Yew haven't been listenin', Sonny Jim. Jones may be an accused murderer and arsonist but some see him as a warrior! Over the top, maybe, but a victim of white man's avarice. Yew know about victim identity, do yew not?"

Ugh. How could I not! In all of its many colors, it is part of campus life, the privilege of dressing down a former oppressor.

"They say Jones struck back at his tribe's enemies with fire, their tribal weapon against oppressors, and that includes the golf club that built a clubhouse on sacred ground. On a level for some with their heroes taking over Alcatraz Island or the riders of the Sioux in the Dakotas. A war that is ne'er over."

He told me more about the internet chatter and then we ended the conversation. Derek's seeming acceptance of Jones' emergence as a hero irked me; I was suspicious there was a scholarly piece of research being formulated.

Another fifteen minutes passed, with a failed attempt to read a month old *Time* with its cover missing, and the attention of a gap-toothed, pretty Latino girl about four who decided I needed company. When 'Olga Temple' was announced over the staticy public address system, I approached a glass window in the far wall of the waiting area. A disinterested, uniformed female guard cheerlessly checked my driver's license and directed me to a metal door which opened electronically and admitted me into another waiting area where I was frisked by a jelly-belly guard sporting a Fu Manchu mustache. There were two exit doors, one marked 'Maximum-Medium' the other 'Minimum-Intake.' The guard finished with me and grunted through clogged nasal passages, "You's not an attorney?"

How to answer "Yes, I'm not an attorney" or "No." I said, "No."

"Didn't think so. Never saw ya before. But you dress that way." He opened the metal door to 'Maximum-Medium' and led me down a corridor to another metal door, this one with a wire enforced window at eye level, and unlocked it. I followed him into a dingy, low ceiling room with bare cinderblock walls, divided lengthwise by a plexiglass panel with cubicles every few feet on either side; a metal counter ran below the divider and held microphones. Overhead, fluorescent tubes buzzed in a reluctant effort to emit a harsh light; the air was close and stale with a trace of disinfectant. Most of the metal chairs in the cubicles were occupied by participants on either side of the panel wearing earphones; 'Magua' Jones, as I now thought of him, was in the middle cubicle staring straight ahead. Guards, two men and a woman, were on station behind the prisoners; one, particulary burly and angry looking, was closer and directly behind Jones.

Jones didn't bother to drop his eyes from the stained, dimpled ceiling tiles above me as I pulled out a chair. Like the other prisoners, his uniform was orange overalls over a denim shirt; unlike others, his hands were manacled. His huge head had been shaved so when he finally lowered his head to mine, and opened his mouth to a wide, superior smile, I thought of a jack-o'-lantern.

"I did not think you'd come." He spoke so slowly that I was

taken aback. Through my earphones, his voice could have been generated in Bangladesh.

"Well, I did."

Silence. "Surprised?"

"Yes," I responded.

"Did ya hear the people are rallyin' around me? Four hundred fuckin' years of being screwed. They are waking up! Because of me! They didn't know about Magua but now they do." He jerked his head toward the guard. "They don't know what to do with me, shit or go blind. 'Cause they can't touch me." He tapped his forehead. "I'm in here."

Those onyx eyes apprised me carefully. His smile drained and his large features squeezed together in consideration. "I think you wanna know what happened the night of the clubhouse fire."

"Are you going to tell me?"

"Maybe. Those assault charges...."

"Why me?"

" 'Cause the more ya know, the more ya gonna wanna know."

I didn't expect this. Maybe some horse-cockie bravado, maybe something about the fire at Randall's trailer, or an apology for trying to kill me?

His head went back so that he was looking down his wide flat nose at me. "Those assault charges. Fessenden and that fat lawyer. I need'em dropped."

I was intentionally careful. "If you tell me anything at all about that night, I'm not your lawyer. I can go right to the A.G. on this."

He didn't hesitate at that.

"Let's see what you do, man. How's your buddy Fessenden? The 'hero.' "

For the record, I didn't agree to anything, didn't get the chance to even consider doing so or respond, before he began.

"Ollie was going to get even. Finally!" Jones' manacled fists hit the counter in front of him. "Fessendens took his land, our land, too, then Calibrese got what was left when Oaky Gardiner sold us out. Fessenden gives Ollie a nothin' job to keep him quiet. Ollie took their money so as to laugh at 'em. Do nothin' and get paid? Why not? But, he couldn't be bought off! He wasn't a scumbag like Oaky."

Jones' loud voice provoked the guard behind him to touch his shoulder with a baton. "Fuck off," Jones muttered and with a second of hesitation, the guard retreated. Jones threw his head back, his eyelids dropped, and his pupils moved up under them, leaving a sliver of white.

"Clear night but windy as hell. Must have been blowing thirty at least. Full moon. I showed up at Ollie's trailer, already he's drunk, messed up on his pain pills. He was laughin', so far gone he could hardly stand up. I couldn't make out everything he was yellin' but he says we're taking the bike, not the truck."

At that, Jones inched closer to the glass.

"The moon was so huge, it was daylight. Ollie's holding on tight but was so goddamn out of it, he almost fell off at every turn. We come up to a barn and he yells to stop. He gets off the bike, takes a screwdriver out of his jacket, uses it like a pry bar to dig up the sill, and smashes in the window. But the door is unlocked and Ollie walks in! No alarm! Goes over to the window, smashes some more glass, and opens it. What's goin' on, I ask him, but he's so shit-faced, he laughs, says he'll tell me later. Inside, there's these big machines, making a clackety-clack racket, down in this pit. He goes down the stairs into the pit and grabs a bunch of levers and yanks them down."

"He what?"

"Yah, he shut the machines down. Laughin' and swearin', and drunk as shit. 'What the fuck is this,' I ask him, 'what are we gonna do' and he says 'we done it.' He starts up the stairs from where the machines are set in, and he trips, his head slams against a concrete stair, and shit, he's out cold! And …."

He stopped, his eyes becoming focused on my face.

"The pump house is four …, five hundred yards away from where his body was found…!"

His voice rose sharply. "I'm telling ya, that's the last time I saw him!"

"You left him and …?"

He answered carefully, "I never saw him again!" Disbelief strained to get out of my face as his black eyes fixed on mine, and continued, "He couldn't have gotten up the ridge and into that building by himself. Through a window? With that brace? No fuckin' way!" Sanity momentarily filtered through his wild expression. "So, how does he end up killed in the fire?"

"Are you saying somebody got him up there? And left him to…."

"Yeah, some … body," he smirked. "Somebody who didn't like Ollie."

"Why are you telling me this?"

"I think you gotta reason to find out how Ollie got up there. And I don't want anybody to think I killed a brother. When you do, I bet you wanna make a deal so I don't happen to drop a name. No assault charges means no name." A maniacal grin replaced the sullenness.

The guard came over and ran the baton across the back of Jones' chair. Visiting time was up. Jones' face had developed an oily sweat. He whispered into the microphone, an ugly leer in his voice, "You think on this. I'll be waitin'!"

∘ ○ ∘

I left the prison and sat in my car. It was eleven-fifteen. Why would Magua Jones claim that Ollie Randall wasn't with him at the clubhouse fire? No, that's not quite right. He said he left Randall unconscious in the pump house. Did Charlie tell me he went inside? No. Did Charlie say that the pumps were off? Goddamn it! He did say it was 'quiet,' but it's never quiet if the pumps are churning away!

CHAPTER THIRTY

Charlie Fessenden was in his real estate office. I telephoned that I would meet him there but not why, and forty minutes later, I pulled into a strip shopping center near Dunn's Corner across Route 1 from a credit union, a Benny's, and a WalMart. Sandwiches and sodas were being delivered from a Subway in the shopping center to an office under a sign of a stylized wave and buoy for 'Sound Real Estate, C. E. Fessenden, Realtor.' A large window facing the parking lot was covered from the inside by photographs and descriptions of expensive South County properties.

As Charlie paid the delivery kid, I entered a sparsely furnished reception area with several desks and chairs, none of which appeared to have been recently occupied, plastic ficus trees, and posters of South County beaches on the walls. Charlie, laden with a bag of food and cans of soda, led me into an inner office with Haversham Golf Club renderings on its walls. A 'for sale' sign associating 'Sound Real Estate' with a New York auction house lay against a closet door. Charlie's salesman grin was back.

"Let me tell you, it's been a very interesting few weeks," he began, rubbing his hands together, reminding me so much of the scheming car dealer played by William H. Macy in *Fargo*. "Most of the insurance issues are tied up and we're on our way to reconstruction! Of course, I'm not directly involved any more, it's all architects and engineers and auditors and insurance people, et cetera. and the new club manager, and ," he added, "that's okay by me." Charlie's evident relief continued as he began work on a tuna melt wrap and a Sierra Mist. "Things have been so different since we captured Jones!"

"We…?"

"The members, the Board, I can't tell you how much they appreciate it. No telling what that crazy could have done. Suppose he got into the pump house…?"

"We?" I repeated and was ignored.

"Only cloud in the sky is this surprise lawsuit Calibrese filed on the lease. Ackley's told the Board it's a holdup, but I heard he didn't tell them, absolutely, one hundred percent, slam dunk judgment for the Club. The Board didn't like that but for now, it's all 'Calibrese's an extortionist' and 'stiff upper lip.' "

Impatiently, I interrupted. "Charlie, the night of the fire. You went up to the pump house, right."

He stopped in mid bite.

"And you went inside the pump house, right?" He hadn't exactly said that to me, only that the door was open.

"That's true. I did go inside." His voice had become less assured.

"The pumps were off…."

Silence.

"Ollie Randall was there."

◦ ○ ◦

Mechanically, he put down the sandwich, pushed away from the desk, got up, walked to the office door which he closed for no apparent reason, came back, and sat bolt upright in the other chair on my side of the desk. His hands were trembling violently, but his grin remained, as though he couldn't get rid of it. "How do you know?"

"Jones told me this morning." My voice remained calm, despite my anger at his lies, his disloyalties, for being Charlie. "Said he had been there that night with Randall, that Randall stopped the pumps, was so drunk that he fell and hit his head, knocking himself out. Jones said that he left Randall there." I could have added, 'tell me he's lying,' but I didn't. Why bother?

He worked himself up to clear his throat and, avoiding my eyes, stared across the desk. "I went inside the pump house, to investigate, like I told you."

He hadn't.

"The pumps were off! Off! Critical that they be on all the time. Six hours off, unscheduled, and the permits are yanked. They got electronic printouts that the DEM checks. Each pump has a cut off switch and they were all on 'off.' I flipped them back and the pumps went on, and there's Randall, in the pump well, staggering to get up, bleeding at the scalp, his face contorted with anger. He started screaming, he was going to 'get me,' and I …." His voice trailed off.

"And…."

"I was next to a tool bench when he came at me. I grabbed a monkey wrench to frighten him, only he lunged at me and I swung it and hit him. On the head."

"You what!"

"Self-defense, Algy, self-defense! What was I supposed to do? He fell, made this terrible groan! I thought maybe I killed him but he had a pulse and was breathing. I got his blood on my hands. I started to get sick. All I could think was to get out of there. I started to and then I knew I couldn't leave him. Suppose he came to and stopped the pumps again. There was a maintenance cart inside, its key in the ignition. I dragged him over and dumped him in its bed, drove up the path along the ridge, the same one we walked. I thought if I got him up to the clubhouse, I'd get to security people and I could explain what happened and …." His eyes teared. "Algy, I was going to be a hero! I was going to deliver him, that's why I didn't use the cell phone. The guy who stopped the crazy Quonnie from shutting off the pumps!"

"Why didn't you tell us?"

His eyes widened, a plea for understanding formed in his voice. "Algy, listen to me!" he shouted, grabbing my hands. "I pulled into the maintenance building. All the key rings to the carts have a door opener, and I drove inside. I left him in the cart, and started up the knoll to the clubhouse to get security…."

I tried to advance the story. "You left the garage door open?"

"I guess so. I didn't see the fire until I got beyond the trees that screened the maintenance building from the clubhouse and by then, flames were shooting out of the windows, the porch was on fire, there was burning stuff flying all around in the wind. I've never seen anything like it! I knew it was too late, Algy! I knew right then it was all going…."

His voice quivered in remembrance.

"I got as far as the first tee and saw somebody jumping around, dancing, waving a torch or something on fire, screaming over the noise of the fire and the wind. I yelled, at least I think I did, and whomever it was turned but I don't think he could see me or maybe in the noise of the fire and wind didn't hear my voice. By then, I was in a complete panic, Algy, it was an inferno, and sirens were wailing, then, fire truck horns. Close by. The maniac …, it had to be Jones, I know now …, disappeared into the blackness, toward the maintenance building. I couldn't go back there so I ran back to the pump house, went inside, found the wrench, cleaned up the place up, and went home. Believe me, I was so scared, I never thought about Randall until I was back at the pump house! I said to myself Randall would wake up in the maintenance building and sneak off. I didn't know about the fireworks, believe me. I thought Randall might come after me or I'd get charged with assault, so I threw the wrench into the woods. I got back home, washed up, and like everyone else drove over to the fire. I planned to tell what happened, that Randall had turned off the pumps, tried to kill me, and get him arrested. But before I could find anyone to talk to, the fireworks blew up the maintenance building. What if Randall was still in there? I couldn't very well say I brought him there." His voice pleaded for a touch of understanding. "Could I?"

After all his lies, I found it difficult to appreciate what might well be, finally, the truth.

"If you went into the maintenance building in the cart, why didn't you trip an alarm system?"

His eyes opened.

"I didn't think about that. That system was controlled from the clubhouse. The fire must have knocked it out. I never thought about that until now."

"At the pump house, did you notice a window had been smashed? Or anything else which indicated a break-in?"

"What...?"

"Something jimmied, broken...."

"I didn't notice." He began to collapse before my eyes. "The door was open...." He grabbed my hands. "Algy, what should I do? How can I explain my silence!"

"Tell Laretta. Immediately. Tell him everything and instruct him not to tell Fausto. Listen to him! And don't tell Dani."

His eyes pleaded with me for more but I had no more to give.

∘ ○ ∘

I was tired, deeply tired, and troubled as I drove back to Providence. The sun had disappeared behind puffy carpets of gray with pinkish edges. I fought my fatigue with an attempt to fit it all together. Jones and Randall had planned to do damage at the clubhouse, maybe boost what they could before setting a fire, but Randall, at the last minute is thinking pump house for some reason. Randall knocks himself out inside the pump house, Jones leaves Randall in a rush to set the fire, maybe with the thought to pick up Randall on his way back. Charlie Fessenden comes upon Randall in the pump house, he's attacked, clunks Randall on the head, puts him in a cart, and drives him up to the maintenance building. He panics when he witnesses the fire roaring out of control and Jones dancing around the flames. Jones sees somebody, later figures it might be Charlie, which is why he gets to me. Jones either doesn't know that Randall is in the maintenance building when he, Jones, sets off the fireworks or more likely, some debris off the clubhouse gets into the maintenance building through the open garage door, and ignites the fireworks with Randall inside. Charlie, having gone from a hero in his own mind by returning power to the pumps to an enabling, although unwitting, factor in Randall's death, is too ashamed to admit his involvement.

What's unexplained? Why is Randall suddenly focused on the pumps when Jones believes the clubhouse is their target? Charlie tells Joe Pontarelli about the unlocked door at the pump house and is shrugged off. The window is repaired, the sill repainted. Why was the door unlocked? Why the fake break-in? Because, if the pump house was Randall's target, and it would be difficult for a brace wearer like Randall to get through the window, the door had to be unlocked and the break-in fabricated!

Trying to piece it together was like when you are a kid and you have those cute little Scotty dog magnets and you try to force them together at similar poles. No matter what you do, they jerk, turn, and continually fuss their way out of alignment.

I was getting a headache.

○ ◯ ○

"Higgins—Huggins?" I called Benno as soon as I returned home.

"Higgins. Spent three years in the can, let out to join the Army in forty-three. Wife divorced him while he was in jail and moved up to Providence with their daughter. Lived for years in a trailer park in Richmond, got by as a carpenter, then as a janitor in the school department. Wife died and daughter got married. After the daughter's husband got his in Vietnam, Higgins moved in with the daughter and her son in a tenement in Mount Pleasant near Triggs Golf Course. Took care of the kid while she worked in jewelry plants around the city. Apparently, the kid and the grandfather were close. Married name….?"

"Yah?

"I don't know how you do this. She married a Vito Pontarelli."

He let that sink in.

"Are you thinking what I'm thinking?"

"I don't believe in coincidence," he replied sharply.

"And Calibrese?"

"You have good instincts. His old man worked at Charlie Fessenden's grandfather's quarry, along with three uncles and a parcel of cousins when it got closed down. The Westerly *Star* did a story on the lockout, people showing up for work, the gates closed, security guards and cops with dogs. One of Calibrese's uncles and a security guard got into a fight because the uncle wanted his tools out of the quarry house. Started a melee involving the whole family and a bunch got arrested for assault and trespass. Fessenden prosecuted the uncle, his father, and some relatives but eventually the charges got dropped. But the Calibrese family got a bad reputation because of the fight and had trouble getting jobs until the aftermath of the hurricane when everyone got clean-up work. That's something a Calibrese's not likely to forget. Understand me?"

I did. Long before the clubhouse fire, fate allowed Ugo Calibrese to work out a scheme that would wound an avaricious, not very bright, Fessenden. Simple, elegant, and rewarding revenge for the way his family was treated decades earlier, the snobbery, as he saw it, of his Watch Hill 'neighbors.'

"Is this a waste of time?" I said.

"Probably," said Benno. "Let me tell you why. At the time of the fire, Pontarelli is in a gay bar in New London. Plenty of witnesses."

"That takes care of one possibility. But only one."

"Why are you doing this?"

"I don't know." Pause "You know that."

"Yah, I guess I do."

I was going to leave it at that when he said, "I don't know if you can use this but there's some other things you oughta know. About Calibrese," and I listened to the ex-State Police detective go through years of speculation, rumor, and underworld talk, on Ugo Calibrese. When he was through, all I said 'thank you' and 'can you put this in an e-mail to me.' His every surmise was a nugget for me, every set of facts a string of pearls.

How could I exploit this?

I went into the kitchen and took a bunch of green grapes from a bowl in the refrigerator, a welcome home present from Mrs. Pina, and went out to the den. I wanted to talk it through with Nadie but that wasn't going to be possible. She'd say 'call the police,' and if I didn't, I'd be protecting Charlie, and therefore Dani, or would it be for Tramonti or maybe a whole 'class' of people. I had come so far alone. I had to work it out by myself.

◦ ○ ◦

After an early dinner, Nadie had nodded off twice watching television on the sofa and by ten, she was asleep in our bed. When I slipped in an hour later, her breath was shallow like the sounds of waves in a conch shell. On the table next to me was a Ross MacDonald thriller from the early seventies, *The Goodbye Look*, taken from the shelves of the game room at Fisher's Island over the weekend.

For a few moments, I stared at the cover of the tattered paperback with its psalms of praise for the author … 'better than Hammett and Chandler at their best,' 'best living writer of the mystery thriller' and similar blurbs from reviewers. I've read every Lew Archer novel at least twice. Why? Because Archer burns himself out trying to discover the truth about what happened at a precise moment in time and place even though he knows the real world defies absolutism, that a lot of details never get filled in or don't make sense, that no reconstruction ever gets it quite right. The novels move forward, scene by scene like in real life, messy guessing games about motive and opportunity. Archer sorts it out by asking questions, uncovering lies, getting his hands dirty, maybe losing a scruple here and there. Usually, he thinks he has it all figured out, and then it unravels; he follows another line of inquiry but remembers he created the line in the first place. He doesn't try to cram all the facts into logic and miss a better idea. Real life.

And, there is the part of his investigation that is personal and has little to do with the client or size of retainer; he satisfies a sense of justice and tries not to do harm.

Plus, he played snooker!

I went downstairs, poured a drink of Macallan, and spent the next few hours trying to apply Lew Archer's approach to link the death of Ollie Randall, the cowardice of Charlie Fessenden, the crimes of Magua Jones, and the cunning of Ugo Calibrese. Justice for whom? Who would be harmed? I was soon fighting myself. When an opportunity comes to cut corners, my conscience mans the barricades.

The next morning, I read Benno's e-mail report at the office and I knew what I would do. Even if Lew Archer would do it cleaner, and better.

CHAPTER THIRTY-ONE

Ugo Calibrese took my call and seemed almost indifferent to my request to meet. He said eleven o'clock at Greenwick Downs and was off the phone. That made my neck prickle with apprehension. Here's a guy who's out to ruin Charlie Fessenden, who resents people like me, and he says, "C'mon over."

○ ◯ ○

A gigantic video billboard on a stanchion hawked jackpots and daily drawings as greyhounds danced, horses pranced, slot machine cherries lined up, and dollar signs paraded. Like 'South of the Border' signs along Route 95 in Virginia and North Carolina, a series of message boards followed with flashing arrows pointing to 'Parking Lot C, Free Parking,' and 'Lot B, VIP Valet Service, Dog Track.' Over the crest of a hill, completely out of context in its bucolic setting, an enormous, stucco box painted a bilious yellow, with a forest of satellite dishes on its flat roof, rudely pushed out of a modest hill. 'Lot A' was along its nearest side where Greyhound, Peter Pan, Pawtuxet Valley, and Conway buses lined up against the building like little piggies at the sow.

A discrete sign directed vendors to a parking lot at the far side of the building so I continued up the highway and saw it was actually two lots, one marked 'Executive' and the other 'Others.' A bulging arm with a faint bluish tattoo protruded from a security booth. At my approach to the barrier, the arm extended up to a brown short sleeve shirt. "This here's private," said a voice from the shadows.

"I've got an appointment with Ugo Calibrese."

A shaven head, square, with no neck and the potato nose of someone who had taken a few punches, leaned out of the booth. An unlit cigar was jammed into a corner of a mouth rimmed by meaty lips.

"Nobody toll me," he said importantly.

"Why don't you check it out?" I offered.

"They're supposed ta tell me!" A cell phone went to an ear that might have been half again the size of my own. "Shir-lee, there's a guy here ta see Ugo." Long pause. "Yah suppostah tell me!" and the cell phone clattered against something hard as the barrier swung up. He leaned out of the booth far enough for me to see 'Guido' stitched on his shirt over a logo of three cherries against a blue seven in a white oval. "Yah see a black Jag down there? Park there," he said. I did as I was instructed, parking next to Calibrese's car, locked the Charger, and walked back to where Guido, now wearing sunglasses, was amply filling a folding chair next to the booth. He didn't bother to look up from the *Daily Racing Form*. "They shoulda told me," he mumbled.

From under an old fashioned marquee, the kind with bulbs that turn on in sequence, with neon dollar signs and slot machine cherries, a faux marble foyer led to a desk where a greeter, an aging plump blond in a tight fitting Greenwick Downs polo shirt, hailed me with "Hi, how ya doin'?" I continued into a cavernous, over air-conditioned slots palace where rows of hundreds of video slots converged on an ersatz volcano spouting colored steam into the rafters. Strings of spotlights made looking up painful. Metallic, whirring, and ding-dong sounds mixed with the ca-chings of jackpots that seemed augmented by an audio system also pumping out Dean Martin ballads. There were, I noticed, no clocks and no windows.

A quick survey of the slot players revealed that the vast majority of patrons were over-weight, sixty-plus women squatting on seats attached to the machines, grimly hard at work as though at stamping machines in a piecework factory, with fingers wearily at 'bet' buttons or grasping one-armed bandit cranks. The honk of a Clarabelle horn behind me and the brush-by of an obese woman in an electric wheelchair ended my inspection. Not quite a geriatric ward, I thought, but at least senior day care.

Ubiquitous signs directed patrons to 'Smoke Free Slots,' 'Bingo,' 'Dog Track,' 'Horse Pari-mutuel,' 'Restaurant Row' and 'Pool Stadium.' A large security person—they all were large, and I thought of Peter Gardiner—with a radio at his hip and a ring of keys on a black belt looked me over as he sauntered by. I asked for Calibrese's office. "Second floor," he said with a shrug toward the rear of the slots floor. He accompanied me to an elevator where he punched numbers on a keypad and pressed the number two on the elevator's control panel.

Apparently, nobody was welcome there; even the elevator doors opened with reluctance. In the tiny reception area, a curly haired man about forty, with muscles born to heft under the now familiar polo shirt, was on a cell phone. He was, according to his shirt I.D., 'Carmine.' He closed the phone when I asked for Calibrese. "Shirlee's on her lunch break," he sniffed and like ace parking lot attendant Guido, Carmine, thinking this 'suit' was an unwanted salesman or pain in the butt government official, eyed me suspiciously as he made a brief and inaudible call on his cell phone. Then, he escorted me down a corridor with stagnant air and floors that squeaked noisily, likely plywood under industrial carpeting. One wall of smoked glass overlooked the gaming room below. I peered down at the sea of winking lights and asked Carmine if this was a typical midday, midweek crowd. "Actually," he replied like a person who rationed goodwill, "not as many as usual. Probably runnin' some promotion at Foxwoods or Mohegan."

At the end of the corridor, Carmine pushed through swinging doors into a suite of two offices; its reception desk held two empty Dunkin' Donuts coffee cups that could have been there for days. At a half-opened door, Carmine knocked, and left me.

The shades in the office were drawn, nothing adorned the walls, and the furniture looked dusty and cheap. A double bulb ceiling fixture gave scant illumination. Music from the slots hall was audible from a speaker on a shelf behind Ugo Calibrese who sat at a desk devoid of paraphernalia except for a blotter, a telephone console, and a black and white photograph of a woman with a pleasant face and too many ropes of pearls. He wore an unbecoming brownish, long sleeve shirt that couldn't disguise his bulging breasts and made him look even more the toad. Or was it Jabba the Hutt.

"Have a seat," he said sourly. I nodded, noticing that his black pompadour was an unconvincing hair piece, and took a chair set back a few feet from the desk. From a score of Mafia movies, I knew the first thing you do when you meet an adversary on his own turf is let him know that you honor his hospitality. I also knew that any shallow banter would be a poor attempt to hide weakness in my position. "Thank you for seeing me," I said to no response. Then, "I have to tell you that I'm impressed."

"By what?" he said evenly.

"I always thought it was a dog track, with some bingo and slots attached. Now I find out it's a casino with a dog track attached."

He grunted and waved his hands dismissively. "Casino? No fuckin' way. The players, they go out to Foxwoods or Mohegan. Poker, blackjack, craps, high stakes games which I don't have. I'm penny ante. Lotta nickel and quarter slots. Everything is video, no table games. I gotta get the day people, the bus operations, the seniors, the meat and potatoes guys on a lunch break, with cheap buffets and lots of door prizes. Otherwise, I die. Half of Rhode Island goes to Foxwoods and Mohegan and spends the real dough. We get the scraps."

Okay, what next. "As I said on the phone, I'm not here on behalf of anybody. Just myself."

"Yeah-h-h."

"I mean that. Nobody knows I'm here."

"Sure, sure," he responded. "What do ya have to say?"

It crossed my mind that he might think I was there as a behind the scene representative of Haversham Golf Club. That could complicate things.

"Your lawsuit against the Haversham Golf Club? I want you to drop it."

He noisily inhaled and laughed like an old car cranking up until he coughed. "Sure, sure," he said wiping his hand across his mouth. "Okay. Is that all? Don't ya want I should do somethin' else for ya? C'mon, I'm in a generous mood."

My play. "The Commissioner doesn't appreciate the rumors you started on his brother-in-law. You don't need the next mayor on your case."

"*You* say I did?" The words were uttered with heavy, well-spaced emphasis. "*You* and Flanaghan? Why would I? What do I care about a pompous ass like Fessenden?" His face screwed into a self-satisfied, almost smile. "Hear he got canned. Nothin' to do with me. That was from his own kind. And ...," he leaned forward slightly, his finger raised in emphasis, "I got no beef with the Tramontis. I have no problem with the police. Everything I do is clean. And, my money says Sonny gets reelected."

"Fausto Tramonti's ...."

His right hand smacked the desk. "I don't give a fuck about Fausto Tramonti!" He was too dismissive. "Ya got somethin' else?" His mouth had twisted, his eyes were barely open, his head pushed forward toward me.

Well, that took care of bluster and bluff. Was my growing pessimism leaking into my chest showing up in my face?

I moved my chair closer to his desk. From my jacket pocket, I pulled out the list of restaurants, bars and clubs from the *Journal* article on Sonny's expenses, with notes and materials from Benno's research. "Seems like you are in the recycling business."

"Huh? What recycling business?"

"You lease Café Oltranto on Atwells to Vincent Villucci and Paulie Vallone is your tenant for Croziano's. Both big contributors to Sonny. You own, among others, Napolitano's and Aroma's. I could go on. Your restaurants, clubs, bars, your friends' places, are where Sonny holds his big fundraising 'times.' All these places take in a lot of cash at the Mayor's parties because of huge markups on drinks, food, etc., all of which Friends of Russo gladly pays. But that's no problem because a lot of money is coming in. It's like Sonny is your salesman, a silent partner, getting a piece of the action with the contributions you raise from all your tenants, your buddies, their buddies, all bundled up in big paydays for Sonny, that goes through Friends of Russo and on to your places and those of your friends. It's clear how the money gets recycled. A complaint to the Ethics Commission...."

If it hadn't been his own office, he'd be walking out. His hands were flat on his desk, like he was going to spring. "What is this shit, some kind of fuckin' half-ass blackmail? If it is, you're a fuckin' amateur! I say show me and ya show me nothin'..." His eyes narrowed. "This is all fuckin' Bacigalupi! He's been on my case for years. I heard you guys had him on the payroll. Well, fuck him. You tell that skinny-assed dick to take his 'recyclin'' and stuff it up his ass!"

Okay, we go on. Obviously, I wasn't going to get anywhere with a Bertie Woosterish 'I regard your answer as unconvincing and inadequate' or 'we'll pass on that.' I had to show my hole card. I said as casually as I could manage, "Joe Pontarelli."

"Huh...?" His face was a squint of surprise.

"P—o—n—t...."

"Whaddabout him—" and was interrupted by a public address announcement that Mrs. Tilly Campignato of Cranston was the winner of the one hundred dollar 'Greenwick Greenback' hourly drawing. Calibrese turned off the speaker on a shelf behind his desk. "What's Pontarelli got to do with anything?" he responded with some real curiosity.

"He works for you for almost ten years, then moves over to Haversham Golf Club as a groundskeeper. He's your eyes and ears on the grounds. That's a smart move, like getting Silverman as a member to keep tabs on the Club. He's got to know that if the pumps that run the irrigation system are damaged or shut off, DEM comes down like a ton of bricks on the Club and they close the course. If that happened before July third, it triggers your lease deal."

Hot button! Calibrese's breath was taken in slowly, his face scrunched up into a scowl. He barely sputtered, "Listen to me ...."

"The night of the clubhouse fire, Ollie Randall, the guy who got cremated, walks into the pump house. The door isn't locked. For some reason, the security system isn't on or is disengaged, still he made it look like someone got in by jimmying a window. After the fire, Pontarelli, when told the door to the pump house was unlocked that night, doesn't investigate, doesn't seem to have mentioned it to anybody—and whatever damage Randall did, got repaired by Pontarelli, all on the q.t.—"

"And...?"

"And weeks later, a night when the electricity is knocked out during a thunderstorm, there's Pontarelli at the pump house, this time fooling around with the generators. They're both on, as they have to be to keep the pumps running if the electricity is off. So, why does he have the protective cover pulled off one…."

"Where's this goin'?" he hissed.

"It gets better." I think my voice remained modulated, maybe I forced myself to grin, but I had the ice of anxiety in my gut. "Everybody in Westerly knows all about the Windmere Country Club and the '38 Hurricane. The manager, Higgins, took a manslaughter rap for the deaths of three people, including a kid, who didn't get out of the clubhouse before it was struck by the tidal wave. While in prison, his wife divorced him, took away his daughter. After he got out, he never had a decent job again."

Calibrese's fists pounded the desktop. He practically shouted, "What's that got to do with Pontarelli?"

"Higgins' daughter married a Pontarelli from Providence and moved up there. When her husband was killed in Vietnam, Higgins moved in to take care of his grandson Joe. Higgins must have told his grandson his very sad story, that because he was an 'outsider' in Westerly, he was the only one jailed in all of South County…."

The mind of the toad was working, even as he threatened, "Make some fuckin' sense or get the fuck out of here!"

"Sure, sure, here's the payoff. The foreman of the jury that put Higgins away for years, cost him his livelihood, his reputation, his family, was Charlie Fessenden's grandfather."

Calibrese retreated in his chair. His eyes narrowed as his intelligence overcame his spite. But he couldn't help muttering, "A high-hat fuckin' asshole…."

"Who ill-used your family when he closed his quarry in Westerly, had your father and uncle arrested…."

From the slits of a second ago, his eyes opened wider than I thought possible. "Keep my family outta this! What would *you* know…?"

My voice was as calm as a psychologist on Prozac. "Think about it. Pontarelli, in your employ for ten years, gets a job at Haversham Golf Club. He knows if the pumps shut down, DEM pulls the permits, they can't play golf, and you get the cash or increased rental or the property. You win big! Charlie Fessenden's 'deal' kicks in. The members—including your Watch Hill 'neighbors'—are forced to pay you more or lose their investment. So, whom do the members blame while they pay you? Charlie Fessenden. He's ruined. You get a windfall and Charlie Fessenden takes a fall."

"What is this shit about pumps? I don't know fuck about pumps." The way he said it, his palms up at me like fans, made me wonder if, indeed, he did!

"It's about perceptions, Ugo. Like you told me. The perception is going to be that Pontarelli's your guy and he was trying to corrupt the pump system for your benefit before July third. Somehow the fire is part of this, maybe as a feint or cover, but shutting down the pump system is what this is all about."

He gestured at me in dismissal but I kept marching forward. This was the moment when my face, voice, gesture and clarity of point—the summation—had to be told as a story; if anything struck Ugo Calibrese as 'off,' it was over.

"But, there's another scenario. Maybe Pontarelli, solely out of personal revenge because of what happened to his grandfather, stokes Randall with the idea of shutting down the pumps, closing the golf course, so that 'Charlie's deal' ends up in Fessenden's ruin. Probably never wanted the risk of arson on such magnitude as a diversion or suspected Randall would have arson in mind. But, the clubhouse *is* torched, Randall's body is discovered, and the pump system remains on. What's going on, Pontarelli asks himself. He checks out the pump house and sees that Randall did fake a break-in but something prevented him from shutting off the pumps. Pontarelli's reaction is to immediately repair the damage because nobody's the wiser, until Charlie Fessenden, the object of his revenge, tells him the door to the pump house was open the night of the fire. But Charlie is too naïve, too immersed in his own problems, to make anything out of it. Pontarelli thinks he's clear."

Calibrese's mouth opened, spit escaped from the corners of his lips, but he didn't interrupt.

"Now, the next part could go either way. After the fire, somebody anonymously becomes a 'whistle blower,' a good citizen who complains to the always watchful DEM that debris from the fire and runoff from the ruins seeped into the wetlands and ponds. Maybe the fire would accomplish what Randall hadn't achieved, the suspension or termination of the DEM permits."

Calibrese's hands moved to the center of the blotter, squeezing together as though he clenched a rubber ball, or maybe my neck. Could it have been Ugo Calibrese, or someone working for him, not Pontarelli, who had been the 'good citizen'?

"But DEM tests and the Board has a lawyer on top of it, so it relents. It could have ended there. Two strikes and no contact with the ball. But it doesn't. Two weeks later, the night of the fire at Randall's trailer, lightning knocks out the electricity to the Club, and Pontarelli senses another opportunity. There's still a few days to go before the critical anniversary date. If the backup generators don't operate and the pumps stop, nobody is likely to know for hours because the central security system for the pump system was located in the clubhouse … and that's gone! He scurries up there in the middle of the storm, he gets the housing off one of the generators to muck it up and shut down the pumps, when up pops Charlie Fessenden! He can't believe it! Charlie thinks Pontarelli's doing his job, and Pontarelli has enough sense to alibi his way out. Again, he breathes easily."

With that, I got up from my chair and stood behind it to look down at Calibrese. His hands had receded to his girth.

"All in all, I say it was Pontarelli, acting on his own, figuring if there's any blame or surprise, it falls on you. Especially with Randall now dust in a jar someplace. But that's my take. The Club's Board will take a different tact. Because of your lawsuit, they'd be willing to pursue any angle that would damage you, call into question your motives. When they know about the link between Pontarelli and you, the fake vandalism at the pump house, his sudden appearance there during the storm…?"

Long seconds ticked by as we stared at one another. I had nothing in reserve. He could crush me with a dismissive wave or a call to Carmine to escort me out. But he didn't. His hands went to the arms of his chair. He was icy calm; his voice low. "You're tellin' me this crap so I give up the lawsuit?"

"And the rumors stop. Charlie Fessenden's done nothing wrong, no 'opportunities' are disclosed." I spread my arms wide. "Look, I see you as a businessman. In business, you take losses. You try to turn them into opportunities. Make a business decision. Walk away from the lawsuit, from the rumors. There's less of a chance of Club opposition when you go forward with your subdivision plans. Build up a little goodwill. And it was Charlie Fessenden who convinces you …."

At Fessenden's name, Calibrese's face registered an anger that was visceral. He seemed to be barely breathing, so full of hate that the very name brought out his deepest bile. A whitish tongue wet his lips and I figured I had been evaluated and found wanting. And then, there was a 'tell' in poker jargon, a fidget, a tic. "What kind of guarantee can ya deliver?" he muttered.

"Only this, Benno Bacigalupi will be all over Pontarelli like a cheap suit."

Calibrese stood, ponderously, with the aid of the chair's arms. A knee bone clicked as he straightened to no more than five-four, his belly hanging on the edge of his desk. From somewhere in that bloated body, a sound that was supposed to be a laugh managed to erupt with a spray of spit. "Tough guy, huh," he grunted in derision. "A fuckin' East Side tough guy." A kiss-off was coming.

"Benno will talk to Pontarelli," I replied smoothly. "Given the alternatives, he'll quit his job at Haversham, and move away. What I know, stays here. No guarantee, of course, on Pontarelli. But Benno would be persuasive. No doubt, he'd remind Pontarelli how upset you would be if you learned you had been set up to take the hit as he satisfies his personal revenge...."

Calibrese's fingers crawled over his pompadour and it slipped; his brows furrowed, his jowls tightened like they were muscles he could flex. In that moment, the kid from the mill village in Westerly revealed himself, born with nerve and little else other than a heritage of family pain and discrimination, clawing his way out of a society run by Fessendens and their ilk who despised his kind. "Got it all figured out, eh? I get rooked because Joe Pontarelli's old man got a raw deal. Because *you* say I got a lot to explain because Pontarelli once worked for me?" He shifted his stare away from me. "I'm not shittin' in my pants because *you* come up here to save your phony friend. He makes me puke! When my ass was sticking out of my pants, Fessenden was eatin' off golden plates! What do ya know about quarry work? Fuckin' dirty, back-breakin' work, where you got fingers, arms, legs crushed, got killed. And *you* come in here to push *me* around?"

He sat down heavily, his eyes drilling into me, measuring me, and considering facts that only he knew. During his rebuke, I hadn't moved. My bet was that Calibrese wanted, needed, power more than anything, more than money or respect, had always risked everything to get it, and now he needed to keep it. It was all business now.

Slowly, his face broke into a surly smile. "How's it feel to have your hands dirty, Mista Temple, trying to shake me down, to make a deal to save the reputation of your shithead friend? That's what *you* think I'd do to you, right?" At that, he cackled. "Geez, I'm *really* surprised! *You* want to play at being *me*." He looked at the ceiling. "Wait outside. Five minutes, and you'll get an answer." I thought that there was a serious, pinched, shadow on his face.

Dismissed, I left his office for the corridor window over the slots room, looking down through a haze of smoke at the rows of blinking machines. Pretty easy business in Rhode Island: you install slot machines that the state owns and leases to the operator, the marks play, and you take a cut. A sure thing once they get off the bus. Carmine rushed by me into Calibrese's office and in less than five minutes, he returned; if he was muscle, he didn't seem to be looking to bash my face in.

"Ugo says go back in," and left me.

Calibrese was at his desk, his chair facing toward a filing cabinet to his left. He was rolling a black cigar between his fingers, a lot calmer, a look of resolution on his face. Maybe even the ghost of a smile.

"You're a stand up guy, right? You want me to trust you and your kind because I should," he said mockingly, addressing the file cabinet. "So, I'll tell ya what. I'll make *you* a proposition. A game of pool. If you win, I drop the lawsuit. And if you lose, life goes on but you keep your stories to yourself." He turned to me and pointed the cigar at my face. "If you don't, I'll make life fuckin' miserable for Fessenden. Either way, Pontarelli's out of here and I never hear his name again. You take care of that."

I asked against who?

The cigar was dropped on the desk. "Emilio Salazar's downstairs practicing for tonight's ESPN match. He'll play ya. Now." He turned to me, his face in a sneer. "Wanna play or are the stakes too high?"

CHAPTER THIRTY-TWO

The pool 'stadium' was a brightly lit television studio with a two row 'gallery' on three sides of a nine foot Brunswick Gold Crown table. One large lens camera rested on guides above the table within a panel of dazzling lights; five or six mini-cams were fixed at various heights and angles to cover shot and ball movements, players, and spectators. An unshaven Emilio Salazar was leaning against the table, in his 'Zorro' mode of black leather jacket over a black polo shirt above black trousers. He rolled his ebony cue stick between his palms. "I don't get this, Ugo. Why am I playin' him?"

"I said so," he replied curtly. "Play him and beat him."

A plain-Jane maple cue stick with a leather butt wrap that looked suitable for my stroke was in a revolving stand off the set. After rolling it on the table to test its trueness, I held it like a rifle and sighted down it while slowly rotating it. This was all for show because the match was absurd; Salazar had taken me to the woodshed not four weeks earlier and I hadn't played a game in weeks! If I lost, Calibrese would be sticking pins into me, now and forever. And, if by some miracle I won, would Calibrese keep the bet? I never bet on pool, right!

I took a few shots to get the feel of the table which, no surprise, was of tournament quality with new cloth that would slow the roll of balls. I asked for a shaper to round off the cue tip, another delay which seemed to irk Salazar.

"Stop foolin' around. What are we playin'?" Salazar said.

I replied, "Straight pool."

Salazar, expecting nine ball, was caught off guard, but recovered and snorted, "Old man's game. For an old man. Makes no difference. Your ass is grass."

◦ ○ ◦

Straight pool is basic pool, elegant, uncomplicated, and requiring control of the cue ball since most of the shots are short. You use each of the fifteen numbered balls, you shoot at any ball you want to, and every ball counts as one point no matter its number, so it makes for a fast game. Before a match, players agree as to the number of 'points,' whether it be twenty-five or one hundred twenty-five. Whoever sinks the designated number of balls first is the winner. Importantly, every shot is a 'called' shot which means that the shooter calls out the pocket and you continue to shoot until you miss, at which time your opponent takes over. When only one object ball—the 'lone' ball—is left on the table, there is a pause; the fourteen balls that have already been pocketed are reracked with the front position, on the foot spot, left vacant. The shooter continues to play and usually tries to pocket the 'lone' ball with a shot that also has the cue ball streaking across the table to break up the reassembled rack, allowing the shooter to have a variety of shots for the next shot. Sounds easy? It is not!

So why did I choose straight pool? Straight pool plays to my strength since I grew up on straight pool at Young Jimmy's father's pool room where it had the inelegant name of 'numbers.' And because it is a game of finesse. That's all I had going for me.

◦ ○ ◦

"Everybody out of here," Calibrese yelled to those working cameras, booms, and other television paraphernalia who had stopped work to sidle toward the table. With audible resentment, they left as Salazar collected balls into a rack as Calibrese flipped down a seat in the front row of the gallery. Maybe Salazar wanted an audience to show off to because he took off his jacket and slammed it on a seat next to Calibrese. Delaying the inevitable, I slowly followed his lead, took off my jacket and tie, loosened my shirt collar and folded my jacket carefully over Salazar's. I made the point to smile at Calibrese who didn't respond, then took up more time to shake talcum powder on my hands. I could sense Salazar's impatience grow, could I hope for a slight advantage from that? I muttered it was bright enough at the table for sunglasses, conditions familiar to Salazar but not to me, and asked Calibrese if the lights could be dimmed. "No" was his answer.

"Water?"

"Over there," he said, pointing to a Poland Spring dispenser.

Salazar, who had been in the shadows, impatiently stamped the butt of his cue stick on the floor. "Lag or flip for it?"

That was a reference to the opening break. Either we could do a 'lag' which means we each shot a ball against the far rail and the ball closest to the shooter's rail got to call who was to break, or we could flip a coin. Pros usually 'lag.' Okay, I can be difficult and I needed a fifty percent chance. I reached into my pocket for a quarter and said, "Call it."

The quarter left my thumb and in mid air, he called out 'heads.' I caught it, slapped it back on my right wrist. Damn, it was heads!

"Number," he said. The first to pocket the 'number' of balls wins.

I answered without thinking, "Thirty-eight."

"Thirty-eight? Wha-a-at?"

I retorted, "Shoot pool." Right out of *The Hustler*.

Oh, he didn't like that! His mouth puckered and his face dissolved into a supercilious sneer. "Did ya hear that, Ugo? Thirty-eight! You didn't pack your lunch, did ya? This isn't gonna take any time at all."

He chalked his stick, put the cue ball in position behind the lead spot, and sighted down his stick, ready to break, when I called out, "I want to check the rack." A *tight* rack is a grouping of balls touching all their neighbors in a proper alignment on the table. A *loose* rack not only absorbs the power of the cue ball but gives a shooter the opportunity for spins that might get into a pocket. Your opponent usually racks for you and vice versa; I had let him rack without checking it, not too smart when you are playing with a pro. I took the plastic triangle from the hook at the bottom of the table and hovered over the rack. The two ball on the foot spot seemed a millimeter off. "Well, looky here," I said aloud as though dramatically surprised, "not as tight as it could be." I put the triangle around the balls as Salazar came over, his face holding rage.

"Are you calling me ...?"

"No," I replied icily. "How would you know who was going to shoot first?"

From the shadows, Calibrese said impatiently, "He's right. He should check the rack. Shut up and play."

Salazar stiffened and turned to stare into the darkness. Neither of us could see Calibrese's face, just his plump body and egg shaped head in the shadows. Salazar swallowed the insult and resumed his shooting position.

Anyone who watches pool regularly, especially nine ball tournaments on television, expects a rack to be broken with balls spreading out in all directions, usually one or two being pocketed at a minimum. Not the way of straight pool. Straight pool often begins with what is called a *safety* shot. The cue ball hits a corner ball which, in a perfect world, bounces off a rail and ends up behind the balls in the rack, while the cue ball returns to the front of the rack, creating an almost impossible shot at the freed ball that can lead other players into a mistake or a foul. Salazar shot and nicked the far left corner ball, the nine, and watched it spin against the rail, and angle off behind the rack. Meanwhile, the cue ball bounced off the side rail and returned halfway down the table. It was a wonderful safety shot. I couldn't call the nine—the ball behind the triangle of remaining balls—because I'd never get it in. If I simply smacked the cue ball into the rack, I couldn't call a shot which would be a foul. Two fouls and the game is over. My shot had to hit an object ball that touched a rail cushion, otherwise, it also would be a foul. No wonder a lot of straight pool players say that if you win the toss or the 'lag,' let your opponent have the opening shot.

I thought of mimicking Salazar with a safety shot of my own, when a close examination of the rack showed the two ball, still at the point of the rack's triangle closest to me, to be slightly out of position. If I read the alignment correctly, it might send the one ball at the right corner of the triangle into the corner pocket. I called the shot and heard Salazar smother an arrogant chuckle. I set, aimed and hit the two ball squarely, sending the one ball to speed toward my called pocket but with more of an opposite English than I intended. It struck the cushion at the angled opening to the pocket, and smartly went back into the rack where a trio broke from the set.

So, I had begun the match with an amateurish misplay!

Salazar wasted no time. In seconds, those three balls, followed by six more disappeared. Finally, he had a shot that wasn't going to be simple. The cue ball was behind a cluster of four balls. Six balls were left on the table, five to get in, one to be the 'lone' ball. He called the eight ball in the side pocket, and made it but again left the cue ball at a tough angle for a next shot and I recognized a flaw in his play. He was striking balls too hard, slamming them instead of finessing them, because he wanted to humiliate me, vindicate his skill with Calibrese, and get the game over. He called the three ball in a corner pocket, a double carom. He chalked, aimed and struck the cue ball. The first carom worked, the second didn't, and, finally it was my turn. At ten-zip.

My first three balls were easily pocketed. The fourth shot was a long table shot on the seven ball near the far rail, barely missing the cue ball on its return, and falling in a corner pocket. A good shot, not spectacular, but good at ten-four. That left me six balls behind Salazar and the lone ball on the table. Time to rerack.

Calibrese appeared with the triangle in his hand, picked balls out of the pockets, and pressed the balls toward the base of the triangle, leaving the front spot open. Salazar muttered to me, "Gonna check 'em?" Calibrese snorted before he returned to his seat.

I took care of the 'lone' ball, but left the cue ball five or six inches in front of the rack, without spacing balls in the rack for any kind of next shot. Not a good place to be. As a practical matter, only from either ends of the base of the triangle can you expect a ball to catch a corner pocket, and I had already missed that shot. I realized I was going to have to commit a foul, which would cost me a point. I aimed carefully and tucked the cue ball into the vacant front spot.

"Cute," Salazar cracked as he walked by me, "but watch this." Could he get the cue stick down on the cue ball with enough force and spin to smack a ball into a pocket? I gave it one in ten and watched him arch over the cue ball, drive it into the rack, and the nine ball rifle into a corner pocket. A marvelous shot, almost a trick shot, the cue stick striking the top of the cue ball, spinning it into the balls forming one side of the triangle, pocketing the ball as called.

In two minutes, he pocketed every ball except the 'lone'—making it thirteen in a row—taking little time between shots before burning them in. It was twenty-three to four! I felt perspiration running down my back, my hands needed more talcum. While Calibrese, who squeezed a smile into his toad-like face, racked the balls, I took a cup of water from the dispenser, took a long swig and put the paper cup in the drink holder in the arm of the seat next to Calibrese. When Calibrese was finished, he loudly announced the score, adding that if Salazar pocketed the next fifteen balls, it was over.

Salazar was beaming confidence and promptly made an ego mistake. He took down the 'lone' ball but his carom shot, in breaking the rack, left the cue ball within a clutch of three others. A difficult over-the-hand shot was his only possible shot and he missed. Twenty-four to four and my turn.

Blessed by what is known as a 'sweet' table, I took as much time or as little as needed in moving around the table, putting in one after another, feeling my confidence grow with each pocketed shot. Salazar retreated into the shadows and it was as though he wasn't there. When I had it down to the 'lone' ball, this time, *I* called out the score, "Twenty-four to seventeen." I heard Calibrese swear as he racked the balls.

That moment of confidence dissipated with the first shot in game four: I missed pocketing the 'lone' ball. Worse, the cue ball smacked the side rail, ricocheted into the rack with enough momentum to spread most of the balls.

Salazar came back into the light with determination. When he saw the spread of balls, he grinned but that dissolved when he realized the cue ball was again nestled within a cluster of three balls. He took his time examining his options and executed the shot brilliantly, pocketing the 'lone' ball, spreading the rack out further. The five ball was quickly gone, the eleven on a long table shot, then the thirteen at the side pocket where I stood. He had reached twenty-eight; there were ten balls left, plus what would be the lone ball, on the table. He was now in reach of victory.

Salazar passed by me to sight the remaining balls loosely grouped in the center of the table. I smelled both his cologne and sweat. Maybe the only satisfaction I was to get was that this game against the 'mark' wasn't as easy as anticipated. All I could hope for, however, was another mistake.

It turned out it wasn't a mistake; it was simply a difficult shot. The one ball banged off the side rail at an inlaid mother of pearl diamond spot and barely missed the corner pocket. Salazar swore in disgust; that was followed by a 'hrrumph' from Calibrese loud enough for Salazar to angrily stare into the shadows.

I blocked Calibrese's view when I went for my water cup and analyzed ball position. My host's impatience was audible. As I circled the table, I knew to stay alive, to be within striking range, I had to rattle off a skein.

The first four balls fell easily, then, on the fifth shot, I called the corner pocket and the four ball went in; unfortunately, the cue ball banged off a rail, hit the thirteen ball and I scratched! The scratch cost a point and the four ball was spotted. Twenty-eight to twenty. There was a chortle from beyond the lights.

Salazar was quick to take up a position. A ball quickly disappeared, leaving six on the table. Another ball dropped. Salazar is *cruising* at thirty to twenty. Then, a tiny mistake.

Chalk is used to help create English on the cue ball; chalk up the tip of the cue stick and you've got a better chance to have the surface of the cue ball spin the way you want. Every good player knows that; every good player knows when not to do it. I noticed that Salazar had been chalking after every shot. That meant that his cue stick tip gets a tiny bit caked and chalk marks appear on the cue ball, which I spotted. I wondered when it would make a difference and this time it did. He used English on the next shot, the cue ball kissed exactly where it was supposed to, but as the six ball went in to the corner pocket, the cue ball slowly rolled across the table to a side pocket where it was the classic 'hanger.' I inhaled and saw it fall in. He had scratched! Lost a point! Twenty-nine to twenty.

Calibrese's palm slammed a seat as he said something inaudible to Salazar, set the rack, and went back to the shadows.

I took care of business and pocketed four balls, and more importantly, and luckily, left myself with the 'lone' ball in perfect position when we started the next game at twenty-nine to twenty-four.

I surveyed the table, taking my time. Salazar said something to Calibrese that caused another 'hrrumph.' The 'lone' ball was ten or twelve inches below the rack on the right hand side of the table. If I hit it as hard as I could, slamming it into the side pocket, and at the same time sent the cue ball to break up and spread the balls in the rack, I would have a chance to run out the table.

I backed away from the table for another gulp of water and felt perspiration running down my back. Was it showing? Calibrese was at my side. I expected a goad or a con, but his voice betrayed a grudging respect. "I gotta tell ya, I haven't seen a straight pool match in years. That's all we played at the Italo Club in Westerly when I was a kid." He glared at Salazar. "Not like these guys. Everything is nine ball because it's quick and … there's so much money." That last bit was for Salazar who was at the other side of the table, his left hand at his hip, his right hand clutching his cue stick with its butt between his legs. His eyes blazed at the rebuke, and I suspected Calibrese's backhanded compliment was a 'double con.'

I wiped my hands on my trousers. I took deep breaths, set up slowly, sent the 'lone' ball into the side pocket as the cue ball hit the side rail, then the far rail, and slammed into the rear of the rack for a break as wide as I could have wanted. Twenty-nine to twenty-five, and the cue ball nestled in a loose triangle of three balls!

Was it over?

Picture this. Salazar had made a similar shot earlier. I stood behind the shot for longer than I should have, using the chalk, blowing away the excess, trying to think about whether an opposite spin might put a ball into a pocket. Calibrese left his seat to stand close to the table; Salazar held his cue stick rigidly across the table. Expectation was rising; they saw I had one, very difficult, if not impossible, shot. Which I called.

I heard Calibrese's wheezy breaths as I bent forward. This could be it. I struck down on the cue ball, spun it to the right to hit the three ball off the side rail, and slowly, more slowly than I can even imagine, it rolled toward the corner pocket, the white circle in the red ball appearing in each revolution as momentum dissipated, before it struck the angled edge of the pocket, and fell in! So focused was I on the three ball that I didn't pay attention to the cue ball which slid across the table and fell into a side pocket. A goddamn scratch! I lost a point and turned play over to Salazar. Twenty-nine to twenty-four. Nine more balls pocketed by Salazar and it was all over!

Is there a patron saint of pool players? Couldn't remember any. There should be because I needed help. I had to do something to break his momentum.

"Ugo," I said nonchalantly after another swig of water, "I can't imagine having so much fun on a weekday."

Salazar's face crackled with anger. I was a wise ass! He was gonna whack me. Just what I wanted him to do, get really pissed at me. With the balls tightly grouped, he realistically had a choice of two shots, both difficult but not impossible for a professional. He lined up behind the shot that I thought was the easier of the two, then he positioned himself for the other. But he looked at both again, and again took position for the more difficult shot, the nine ball off the side rail, across the table, and back into a corner pocket, a shot that required finesse, concentration, and a little back English. Anger and pride were leading to indecision. Salazar bent over, aimed, shot, and … missed.

A 'fuck' came from the shadows. If I made every shot and the next 'lone' ball, fourteen straight points, …

I'd like to say that I then played my best pool, called my shots coolly, with nonchalance, a steady hand, and a noble heart. But that wouldn't be true. For the first three shots, comparatively easy shots, my shirt stuck to my back, my face felt wet with perspiration, my hands were wiped countless times on my trousers. My glasses fogged up and I walked away from the table, took them off, and used a handkerchief on its lenses. I knew I needed to catch some calm.

Calibrese knew it too. "Fer Chrissakes…!"

And suddenly, as I set up my shot, I was on 'dead stroke,' the most dangerous moment for a finesse player like me whose play is all in the geometry of the balls on the table. I didn't fight it off. Two more balls were pocketed; nine to go. The ten, two and six balls slid across the table into pockets, each time leaving the cue ball in alignment for another shot. All easy. I was cruising, I was *there*! Five more, including the lone ball. I could do it! I was fluid and crisp and had finesse. The eight ball disappeared and the eleven ball was an arrow in the center of a side pocket. The nine ball was a carom shot that I almost misjudged but rattled in; the two and thirteen were easy pockets. I shouted out the score thirty-seven to twenty-nine, something very boorish, and sat next to Calibrese and gulped down the rest of the water. Calibrese got up, slowly, muttering to himself, to rack the balls for the last time. If I got the 'lone' ball in, the rack would not be broken.

The final shot. Another wipe of my glasses and I was back at the table when I realized I had left the 'lone' ball, the seven, an inch or less from a rail at mid-table, with the cue ball no more than twelve inches away but at almost a ninety degree angle. Thirty-eight, I repeated to myself. I can do it. Thirty-eight. The cue ball couldn't touch the rail, it had to kiss the seven ball so that it would roll parallel to the rail down the length of the table, hit the angled cushion at its outer edge, and fall into the corner pocket.

And then, as I plotted the shot, I sensed my 'dead stroke' leak away. Oh, God, why now? When I was cruising! Thirty-eight. C'mon Algy! I checked the tip of my cue stick, chalked it, wiped the excess away, took a deep breath, set up, aimed, and shot.

It was all slow motion. The cue ball touches the seven ball and the seven ball begins its roll toward the corner pocket. I saw the slightest deviation from the parallel in the first rotation. A fault in the cloth? I stroked it too hard? With English? Calibrese came to the table. Salazar stood behind me. There wasn't a breath among the three of us as the ball brushes the pocket's angled cushion.

It dropped in.

Could I have avoided my exultant 'Yes!' Did I emulate Tiger Woods on the first hole of a sudden death playoff? I plead guilty. It was not the way to behave, even here. I placed the cue stick on the table and saw my opponent staring at Calibrese's purplish face. "What the fuck! You can't beat this amateur?" Calibrese shouted.

"Shit lucky! Whoever heard of playing to thirty-eight?" he responded, more plaintively than I would have expected.

"Thirty-eight or thirty-eight fuckin' million, ya should've crushed him."

I put out my hand to Salazar. I lied, "Honored to have played you again."

Salazar's mouth opened and I expected a nasty response but he walked away. Calibrese leaned into me, looking up at me with icy eyes, holding the frustration of a sure thing becoming a bad bet. "Ya expect me to welsh…?" His square chin went forward, his eyes burning in his stare.

"I hadn't thought about it."

"… expect me to take a dive because that's the kind of person ya think I am?"

I didn't reply.

"I'll tell ya, I didn't get where I am without being stand up. Ya know what I'm sayin'? What I say, I do. Remember that. Whatever else ya heard about me," he said, "you remember that. And the people I make a deal with, they better be stand up, too. Always." He waddled from the room.

I picked up my jacket and tie and made it to the door when Salazar touched my arm. His face had eased. "Thirty-eight. Why did you pick thirty-eight?"

"I don't know." I touched my forehead. "It was rattling around in there."

CHAPTER THIRTY-THREE

Archie Soames retorted 'when pigs fly' when told by Charlie that Ugo Calibrese would drop his lawsuit, and swallowed hard two days later when the lawsuit was dismissed, with prejudice. Which meant that Ugo Calibrese was a 'stand up guy' in a way I probably would never understand.

The Board responded with an e-mail to all members—forwarded to me by both my brother and Charlie—that gave Charlie Fessenden 'full marks' for 'his cooperation, his guidance, and determination' in resolving the litigation 'at no cost to the Club'! And the chatter among the members? According to Charlie, nothing but back slaps at the Club.

It was time to swallow the Kool-Aid.

○ ◯ ○

Benno called me at the office.

"Pontarelli's gone. I checked his apartment this morning, like everyday since I talked to him on Friday. Checked with his landlady, and the post office. No forwarding address. My hunch is that he figured Calibrese ... or somebody else might be calling. No surprise there. I'm not lookin', am I?"

"No."

"There's something else you oughta know. Fausto's made an accommodation with Calibrese. He's supporting council members that Fausto thinks eventually might swing to his brother, the ones on the fence over stayin' with Sonny, so he can't be accused by Sonny of welshing him out. We're talking serious dollars. Tony Gugliami in Ward Four, Rhoda Sanchez in Ward Seven, Antonia Luso in Ward Eleven. And Joe Laretta's father? There's been talks."

P-s-s-h went the last gasp of air from my good government balloon. That reliable nudgy feeling after Ugo Calibrese's name surfaced weeks ago had been justified. Fausto Tramonti played hardball, I knew that, would do anything to get his brother elected mayor. Would the 'accommodation' mean a post-election collaboration with Calibrese and company? Was Nadie closer to the truth than I?

I thanked Benno, told him to send me his bill and reminded him of confidentiality. That comment was received as offensive and I apologized quickly.

I pushed back in my desk chair. I felt a pang of conscience. Conscience is like a horsefly at the beach, a barking dog at dawn, a yellow jacket at a picnic—not to be ignored but dealt with. I was reminded of a Rhode Island aphorism: In Rhode Island, you can be guilty, not guilty, or guilty with an explanation.

° ○ °

A reluctant Tom Flanaghan informed the Attorney General's office that he would 'prefer' to drop the assault complaints against Jones. The Attorney General was none too happy but Flanaghan is an important party cog in South County so a deal was worked out under which only a single assault charge would be held pending the result of the murder trial. If I owed Jones anything, I felt he had been paid back. He was on his own.

Charlie and Laretta then went to the Attorney General where another deal was struck. Despite prosecutorial ire about withholding material evidence, Laretta played his cards neatly, pointing out that Charlie had not lied to the State Police, was not an accessory to any crime, and had done the 'right thing' by capturing Jones and cooperating in the prosecution in the Gardiner case. Charlie's silence had 'pained' him but he lived in fear of Jones and it was a 'courageous' act to come forward, even belatedly. The handshake deal worked out was if Jones was convicted of Peter Gardiner's murder, there was no need to get into the clubhouse fire, especially with the prime suspect dead. If Jones got off on the murder charge, Jones could be charged as an accessory for the fire, with Charlie as the prime witness, along with the remaining assault charge.

As for the continuing saga of 'Magua' Jones, the 'victim-hero' refused to enter a plea at his arraignment and disrupted the court with war chants that infuriated the judge, brought in the sheriffs, and ignited a melee with Jones' family members and supporters. With the media now fully engaged, Jones placed a curse on Haversham Golf Club by telephone at an event staged by relatives in the Indian Swamp, complete with a fire ritual. That was followed by the ACLU representing Jones in lawsuits for religious sessions for Native Americans at the ACI and changes in hair length regulations. He also acquired a flamboyant defense attorney, a Rosebud Sioux who affected a ten gallon hat with feathers, and more beads than Gerry Spence, who filed multiple motions—all denied—to throw out the case on jurisdictional grounds because his client was an 'unassimilated native,' not subject to state or federal laws but only the jurisdiction of his band. Meanwhile, picketing by rights activists at the ACI and the courthouse, Jones' delusional claims to be the reincarnated Magua, and his backers' accusations of guard brutality, brought out nutters of every kind and stripe whose rants filled talk radio airwaves with evil bilge. Tensions rose. This, in a population that until a few months ago had never heard of the Quonnies!

At trial, covered by *CourtTV* whose last appearance in Rhode

Island was Claus von Bulow's murder trial, the circumstantial case against Jones was soon punctured with doubt; when it came right down to it, the prosecution's case consisted of evidence of bruises on Peter Gardiner's body, Jones' escape as related by Flanaghan, Jones' possession of Gardiner's gun, and motives of hate and revenge against the Gardiners. The defense countered that there were no witnesses to the actual shooting or alleged struggle, the fire was the likely result of a lightning strike at the old homestead, and Peter, not fatally wounded, died from asphyxiation in a trailer that, according to a Quonnie friend of Randall's, had a warped door frame so that the door often stuck, something Peter might not know, possibly couldn't overcome. How Jones got Peter's gun was somehow lost in the evidence shuffle and courtroom antics of defense counsel. Jones never said a word in his own defense and I wondered if the jury was going to get past his scowling demeanor, beads and feathers, his unshorn hair, or the nightly television scenes of demonstrators, including Carter University kids, denouncing the 'show trial' of a Native American.

The jury hung. Rather than immediately retrying the case, the Attorney General decided on the accessory prosecution for the clubhouse fire and the single assault charge, looking for a plea bargain on all charges of twenty years with a minimum to serve of twelve and mandatory psychological treatment. While generous considering the evidence, Jones refused the deal, savoring another opportunity to play victim. By then, word had leaked about Charlie's proposed testimony but in Westerly, any taint of Charlie Fessenden's weakness had been washed by the detergent of Charlie's efforts in the capture of Jones, the Club being opened for golf play, and Charlie being instrumental in the dismissal of the Calibrese lawsuit. Charlie, now thoroughly believing and often embellishing his role, was happily selling real estate to new and prospective Haversham Golf Club members.

Joe Laretta was engaged to ensure his client had a short, straight, believable, and well-rehearsed story of the night of the fire. But what saved Charlie was that the reincarnated Magua didn't survive to his arraignment. Within two months of the murder trial, he was found hanging from a noose of bed sheets in the lavatory of the prison laundry. Laretta later told me that Jones' enemies inside, both inmates and guards, were legion, and that hatreds multiplied as he became a self-proclaimed 'white hater' who angered a group of white supremacists inside, and disparaged black and Latino inmates as 'slaves.' Which group did the deed remains unknown.

Some people are better off dead, I thought, when I heard the news. The world is a better place without him.

Then, I heard Nadie's voice, 'Who are you to judge?'

● ○ ●

Ironically, Magua Jones, even in death, was not through with Haversham Golf Club; maybe his curse laid on the Club might not prove effective but was prophetic. Within a month of the opening the new clubhouse, the Ninth Circuit Court of Appeals determined that the Religious Freedom Restoration Act, or RFRA, which Congress passed in 1993, meant the federal government was required to demonstrate a 'compelling interest' in any action or permit that would 'substantially' burden a religious practice of Native Americans. The case caught the attention of Jones' activist counsel who filed a suit in United States District Court claiming that the presence of the clubhouse on *Mouwneit* would effectively terminate a significant cultural event for the Quonnies, i.e., their ritual fires, and that the federal government hadn't considered RFRA during the permitting process. Even Plastic Man would have trouble stretching facts that far since the Quonnies were not federally recognized, no permitting authorities were aware of any Quonnies claim, the Quonnies had long ago released their claim to the land to Ugo Calibrese, and the only federal permit involved was one related to water discharge under the federal Clean Water Act because the Indian Swamp eventually flowed into the Pawcatuck, a boundary between two states. Nonetheless, knowing how things can go, the Club couldn't ignore the suit, confirming to Gordon Ackley that he had a client that was an 'evergreen,' a source of much joy at Brinkley & Alley, especially after the Jones family began to agitate to put *Mouwneit* back into the band's petition for federal recognition.

Of course, these events were in the future when on a humid day in late July, with bus fumes coloring Kennedy Plaza's air a yellowish brown, I was summoned to City Hall by a telephone message from Ms. Ciccone. Puppy Dog sat at a corner of his desk so he could look down at me.

"How did you do it?" he asked, his eyes burning with indignation.

"How did I do what?"

"Sonny has a lot riding on this festival. This is a big deal! It's got to be a huge success!"

"Well, I hope it is. I brought my draft of a revised Protocol...."

"Some ..."—he was so mad he couldn't get it out coherently—"... flunky from the Italian Consulate in Boston called Sonny yesterday. The Italians gonna cancel! Said they're not coming unless the University is a 'co-sponsor' and certifies everything is ready...!"

"Really," I said archly.

"You did something, goddamnit! You were there!"

One afternoon in Bellagio, I had called my brother. As an international investment banker, he always knows somebody—or somebody who knows somebody—of local importance. Within an hour, he was back to me with an appointment with an Italian automotive magnate whose family's name even I had heard of, an important star in the Italian political firmament, who, luck would have it, was at his villa north of Verona. Yes, I would miss the attractions of Padua with Nadie.

I arrived at the entrance of Villa Santori near eleven, pushed the button in the gates' security console, stared into a blinking camera, and stated my name. The gates electronically opened to a gravel lane shaded by umbrella pines leading to an immense, post card beautiful villa surrounded by gnarled oaks and groves of walnut trees. I was greeted by a middle-aged man in a white, loosely flowing shirt and black trousers, a solid figure with carefully coiffured black hair and a square, slightly Germanic face. In charmingly accented English, he invited me to tour his vineyard, pleased that I knew something of the wines of the Veneto and Friuli. He explained that he grew mostly Pinot Grigio, Chardonnay, and Pinot Noir grapes for his private use, particularly for a blended *rosato* prosecco of which he was particularly proud. Under a *loggia* by a swimming pool, we enjoyed his wine in stemmed glasses with fluted rims; it was a splendid *frizzanta*, salmon pink, dry, with an almond finish. That led to a delightful lunch of soup, antipasto, eggplant stuffed tomatoes, slices of cold roast with caper sauce and figs, served with vintage Valpolicella and Amarone while I explained my 'problem.' He responded with a shrug here, a nod there. He asked me where Sonny's family came from in Italy and I told him I thought it was Apulia. He sniffed, and again, a shrug.

It was obvious my host possessed *sprezzatura*, the Italian art of effortless mastery of a subject, a situation. With his napkin waving in the air, Verona, he said, is a city of history and of character, urbane with multi-talented citizens, including world renowned artists and designers, and a cuisine prepared in a Northern Italian style that was the 'envy of Italy.' An official exhibition in Providence—'where is that by the way'—would have to be done with 'respect.' He was sure his old friend, Mayor Pontaloni, would agree. Persons in the government could be prevailed upon. It was a matter of honor that if Verona were to become *familia* with a city 'in the States,' it must be appreciated that Verona's culture can be exhibited only in the most appropriate of locations and with venerable and honorable associations. Otherwise, how could there be 'respect.'

Our luncheon ended with *millefoglie*, a pastry baked with strawberries and whipped cream, a large espresso, and a sweet wine for the digestion. "Don't concern yourself," he said before we finished. "It will be as you desire."

"You're blackmailing!" Puppy Dog spit out.

I didn't respond. Where had I heard that before? Was I getting good at it? I wouldn't deny that I was experiencing *schadenfreude*, the unholy joy of an enemy's hurt. But few things in life are as enjoyable as a hypocrite's discomfort.

"Sonny almost told him to go to hell, you know that? After all this work…!"

I grimaced.

"Sonny … hates you! He's gonna stomp on your ass one day. He had Ugo Calibrese in his office when the son of a bitch from the consulate calls. He told Sonny to lay off you. Why was that?"

A surprise!

"That was nice."

"You are really pushing it."

"The revised Protocol," I said as I handed it to him. "I need the

Chief's signature. Then, you get a festa." I looked up at his gargoyle face, knowing I had both a revised Protocol and a 'truce' through the last day of the festa. But after that...!

∘ ○ ∘

I left Puppy Dog's office, giving Paula Ciccone an unexpected high five. City Hall didn't feel so tawdry because I, for once, left as a winner.

I stopped for a doppio espresso at the Starbucks in the old Hospital Trust building and took the hot, acrid brew across the College Street Bridge to a bench on the cobblestone walk in the park facing the Providence River. The corridor from Route 195 was busy with traffic; without a breeze, a haze would soon be hovering over the downtown. Under the shade of maples, with the ebbing tide sending ripples to the granite abutments, I reflected on a month of deals, strokes and counter-strokes, 'stick it in your eye' politics, and compromises. I sipped the espresso slowly and realized that this narrow section of the river is where the Bay was once choked into what was the Great Salt Pond of the Narragansetts. What had Derek Kirk said about the leaders of the local tribes and bands—all deal makers—until King Philip? Maybe if *he* had made a deal…?

∘ ○ ∘

That evening, in the semi's of the Billiard Club's tournament, I lost my match to Alec Ferguson. I managed to win one game in the best-of-five which gave me at least the patina of being able to keep up. After I lost, Young Jimmy joined me at the bar. I soon had a Heineken in front of me; Young Jimmy was drinking San Pellegrino. He said, "A couple of weeks ago, a guy from back when called me. Ugo Calibrese. He wanted to know if you were a stand up guy."

I hardly batted an eye.

"And...?"

"I said I've known you for a long time. Longer than I've known him. You don't always go with the flow but you keep your word."

"Ah, shucks!"

"I told him the truth," Young Jimmy said with a conviction that made me feel honored.

I replied, "If he ever calls you again, tell him I know what that means."

Young Jimmy raised his eyebrows.

∘ ○ ∘

I got home about ten. Nadie was upstairs on the sofa watching television. She wore one of my bathrobes, her feet were tucked under her. She used the remote to turn down the sound when I said that I had played well but lost. I noticed a leather bound *Sonnets from the Portuguese* that I had purchased from a bookseller in Verona after my visit to Villa Santori was next to her. I had given her the slim volume our last night in Trieste, suitably inscribed, "If thou must love me...."

"Are you disappointed?"

"Not very," taking my eyes from the book. "Alec is a better player. Winning last year was a fluke."

"Well," she said, her face breaking into a smile. "I have news too. The 'suggestions' were withdrawn today! No idea why. Just an e-mail from the Chair saying that they were meant to be helpful and not an attempt to change my syllabus, and in any event, no need for further discussion." She threw her arms open to me. "Algy, I won!"

I went to the sofa and kissed her, and wondered if Charles Danby had dropped a discrete hint. She clung to me and I felt her body fold into mine. Then, she pushed me away. She took my hand, squeezed it tightly, her face lost its excitement and became gentle as her eyes brimmed with tears. Her breaths rose and fell. "Are you ready for something else?"

I wasn't, but I said, "What else?"

"Well, I've been thinking about us, that night in Trieste. Commitment has to have its symbols. I'm committed to you and I'd like to be married to you."

My mouth fell open. "Nadie, don't joke about this."

"No joke. It's time. *Carissimo*."

I said, without realizing I made little sense, "Together?"

She answered, "Together."

AUTHOR'S ACKNOWLEDGEMENTS AND STATEMENT

I want to extend my sincere appreciation to supportive readers of *Carom Shot* and friends who both challenged me and encouraged me to write *Straight Pool*. Particularly, I want to thank Donna Beals for putting up with the vagaries of drafts, cryptic handwriting, and revisions. Of course, my family was supportive and I appreciate their patience especially when I would disappear into my home office for writing, editing, and research. David Partridge especially deserves my thanks for his keen observations and grammatical skills.

As indicated in the publisher's note, this is a 'work of fiction.' That deserves further clarification. As the idea for *Straight Pool* was formulated, I became interested in two aspects of Rhode Island history, first, the plight of native people in Massachusetts and Rhode Island during colonial days, and secondly, the Great Hurricane of 1938.

For research, I want to thank the Rhode Island Historical Society for its many resources and library and suggest to all interested they read *Mayflower* by Nathaniel Philbrick, Viking (2006), William G. McLoughlin's *Rhode Island*, W.W. Norton (1986), *Sons of Providence* by Charles Rappleye, Simon & Schuster (2005) for an appreciation of Rhode Island's early history, its native people, King Philip's War, and the impact of slavery during colonial times through the American Revolution. For a contemporary colonist view of King Philip's War, John Foster, *The Present State of New-England. Being A Narrative of the Troubles With the*

Indians In New-England, from the First Planting Thereof in the Year 1607, to this Present Year of 1677. But Chiefly of the Late Troubles in the Two Last Years 1675 and 1676, available at the Rhode Island Historical Society.

Additional thanks to Dr. Francis Waabu O'Brien for his scholarship and his *American Indian Place Names in Rhode Island*, Newport (2003). On gaming issues, I appreciate the thoughts and scholarly research of many, including Dr. Taylor Adams.

As for Westerly and the Great Hurricane of 1938, among the very good recountings of that storm are *Sudden Sea: The Great Hurricane of 1938* by R.A. Scotti, Little, Brown and Company (2003) and *A Wind to Shake The World* by Everett S. Allen, Little, Brown and Company (1976). For photographs of the devastation, *Watch Hill* by Brigid M. Rooney, Arcadia (2004), provide some of the best. George H. Utter's *Old Pictures of Westerly*, Utter Publishing (1991) records the town at the height of its prosperity.

I suggest that a reader with any modicum of interest in Rhode Island's history take a moment to consider the historical saga of New England's native people. Their sovereignty should be taken seriously, openly, and honestly, howsoever it happened. It is time to take a deep breath and work out solutions that make sense without resorting to inappropriate and scurrilous stereotypes. Exceptionalism is always a problem in any democratic society but, occasionally, that is what the law requires.

Finally, don't forget to google 'Magua.'

Wunnohteaonk. May peace be in your heart.